Colorado
Melodies

Darlene Franklin

Colorado Melodies

Three Modern Couples Seek
Love That Will Endure Hardships

BARBOUR
PUBLISHING

Member of the
Evangelical Christian
Publishers Association

Dear Readers,

    Colorado Melodies contains stories near and dear to my heart for several reasons. For one thing, all three books take place in the home of my heart, Colorado.

    Romanian Rhapsody shines as my first-ever published novel. When an early mentor encouraged me to write about my passions, immigrants jumped to my mind. At the time I planned the first book, the plight of orphaned Romanians saddened my heart. So I decided to write about a college graduate who goes to Romania as a short-term missionary and a music teacher whose wife died in Romania.

My heroine, Carrie, is my most autobiographical character. Like her, I toured extensively with singing groups while in college. I also spent several summers in summer missions, although I never made it to Romania. I also had the same call as Carrie to work with children.

As I told Carrie's story, her best friend, Michelle, appeared.

Romantic Michelle meets her own knight (hero Joe Knight). He lives in a castle in a small town on Colorado's high plains. On a long road trip in my childhood, I caught a glimpse of a castle and wondered who lived there. Why, Joe Knight, who aspires to the ideals of knighthood. Only Michelle isn't a princess, and Joe doesn't live up to his ideal. I wrote Michelle and Joe's story in *Plainsong*.

At the end of *Plainsong*, a thief strips everything from Joe's art store. Sonia, an artist affected by the robbery, accepts the position as a six-month artist-in-residence. Joe's cousin Ty moves west to prove himself, and soon sparks fly between Ty and Sonya. But will Ty's secret destroy their chance at love? *Knight Music* completes the trilogy.

Although I now live in Oklahoma, I am thankful that I got to write these stories of mountain, music, and love for Colorado Melodies.

Darlene Franklin

ROMANIAN RHAPSODY

Chapter 1

"Rule number one: Pack light," Carrie recited, running fingers through her short brown hair. Despite her best efforts, her performance gowns, three pairs of jeans, five T-shirts (two of them emblazoned Victory Singers—Romania Tour), underwear, music, camera, and Bible barely fit into the one suitcase and one carry-on she was allowed on the plane.

Carrie glanced at the clock. 2:00 p.m. Time to kill until the first meeting and rehearsal at five o'clock. *When will my roommate get here?* She looked at the empty bed. Maybe from a part of the country as foreign to her as— Romania! She laughed at herself, the sound laced with excitement. *This is the beginning—the beginning of the adventure.*

A key turned in the door, and a maid wearing a loose-fitting maternity dress appeared in the doorway. But where was her cleaning cart?

The woman waited by the door, carrying on a conversation with someone hidden from view.

"You need to rest after that trip," a man spoke.

"Don't worry." Arms lifted as if in an embrace, the rustling of two bodies entwining, and then the woman entered the room, pulling two bags with her. Dark-haired, tall, and slender, she was heavily pregnant. She turned to Carrie with a wide smile.

"Hi! You must be my roommate." She plunked her bags down on the empty bed.

Carrie tried not to stare. She had expected a roomie like her best friend, Joan, another college junior, perhaps—not a mother-to-be. She found her voice. "Yes. Carrie Randolph from Penn State. Soprano."

"And I'm Lila Romero. Alto. Steve and I planned on one more trip with the Victory Singers after I graduated from CU last year. I never thought I'd be as big as a house by this summer!" She patted her belly and giggled. "God decided to bless us earlier than we planned." She reached out to shake Carrie's hand.

The *C* states paraded through Carrie's mind—Connecticut, Carolina, California. "Colorado?" she confirmed as Lila's hand gripped hers, long fingers squeezing into her palm.

"Uh-huh." Lila rummaged through her suitcase, arranging her belongings in the bureau.

"When is the baby due?" Carrie asked. By Lila's size, she looked like she would deliver while they were in Romania.

"In about ten weeks. I may go into labor on Labor Day." She laughed, a light sound that tinkled like a glockenspiel.

"I'm surprised you and—Steve? That's your husband?—aren't staying together." Carrie sat down on her bed and watched Lila unpack.

"Oh. Well. We're used to it, touring this way. It's our first trip with the Singers since our marriage. I think it's a lark. I get to pretend I'm just one of the girls again." She flashed a smile at Carrie. "I'm looking forward to it."

Some of Carrie's uneasiness lifted, and she found herself smiling back. "Yeah, it will be fun."

Lila slipped out of her dress and shrugged on a voluminous robe. "And Steve and I are planning on a second honeymoon after the tour, in Constanta on the Black Sea. Gloriously romantic." She stiffened for a second and then relaxed.

"Something the matter?"

"Just Braxton Hicks contractions."

Contractions?

She hastened to add, "Practice contractions. To make the actual labor easier, if that's possible." She yawned. "Steve was right. I am tired." Taking a tiny travel alarm, one of those the size of a mouse but that probably had a growl like an angry cat, she set the time. "If you don't mind, I'll rest for a little bit." She ducked under the sheets before Carrie could respond.

Carrie took out her music, turned on the pole lamp between two chairs, and started humming through her parts. One song called for a soprano solo. Maybe the director, Tim North, would ask her to sing it. She tried to shake away the thought. With thirty of the best singers from around the country, he could choose from plenty of talent. She practiced the solo anyway, then went back and hummed through the regular part.

The alarm sounded, as loud as an ambulance siren, and Carrie woke up, music still clutched to her chest. Lila sat on the floor, dressed in a loose-fitting sweat suit, doing some kind of stretching exercises. With an awkward push, she heaved herself up from the floor. "There's just about time to take a shower. Do you mind?"

Carrie shook her head, and soon water splashed in the bathroom like a distant waterfall. In her packet she found the blue-and-white name tag that read, "Hello! My name is. . . ," in English and Romanian. She slapped it on her Victory Singers shirt. Moths fluttered in her stomach. She didn't know anyone. She had met Tim only once, at the audition, and now Lila.

Someone knocked on the door. A young man, past college age, with crisp dark curls that sprang up on his head like grass after a rain, leaned on the doorpost. Pretty is as pretty does, but he certainly was handsome.

"Hi! You must be Steve. Lila's just taking a shower." She waved him inside.

"And you are"—he peered at her name tag—"Carrie Ran-dolph. *Incantat de cunostinta*—I'm glad to meet you, Carrie." He sat down on Lila's bed.

"Do you speak Romanian?" Carrie asked, fascinated.

"Just phrases from a Berlitz book that I've practiced."

Lila came out, already dressed, toweling her hair dry. "Hi, sweetheart." She kissed the top of Steve's head and rummaged through the nightstand drawer for a brush. "You've already met Carrie?"

Carrie nodded and ducked into the bathroom, brushed her teeth, and checked her watch. Quarter to five—was it too early to go downstairs? No.

Picking up her purse, she headed for the door. "See you folks later, then."

"In just a minute." With a few strokes, Lila had restored her hair to a lovely free-falling style.

About a dozen people wearing identical blue-and-white name tags congregated by the elevator. Even without the tags, the undercurrent of voices humming and feet tapping in time to piped-in music gave them away as musicians. *Maybe the name tags aren't so silly*. They had only three days to move from strangers to a cohesive choir.

The group steered toward a smallish room, the Franklin. Someone dropped a rehearsal folder, and the sound reverberated around the walls. A magnificent grand piano dominated one corner. *Where's Tim? There he is.*

At the opposite end of the room, a man with long graying hair who looked like he might have been a hippie back in the '60s directed the new arrivals. "Sopranos, altos, tenors, bass—left to right. Musicians, your instrument cases are by the piano." To Carrie's surprise, Steve moved toward the keyboard, pulled out the bench, and plunked out a few chords. The sweet harmonics carried into the air.

Carrie found a seat on the front row, where the short people would sit. *If for once I could stand on the back row!* A petite blond with long, curving hair that Carrie envied took a place next to her.

"Hi! I'm Amy. Is this your first year? It's mine and. . ." The girl continued speaking, clearly as nervous as Carrie felt. She relaxed and started the process of introducing herself.

◆

Steve flexed his fingers and ran through some arpeggios while he scanned the new group. A few familiar faces returned from last year, but he and Tim were the only people left from the original Victory Singers who went to Ireland five years ago. Lila had joined the next tour, after her freshman year at CU.

He glanced where his wife waited, leaning over the chair and chatting with one of last year's returnees. He smiled. Marrying Lila was the best thing that ever happened to him, that and the baby. He squashed a frown that tried to cross his lips. The doctor said he shouldn't worry; travel was fine until the last month.

"Hey, Steve, give me a C!" the trumpeter called. Trust Guy, another old-timer from the second year forward, to keep them on track.

"Sure." He pounded down on middle C five times while around him instrumentalists tuned up, creating the dreadful cacophony that preceded a musical event.

His eyes wandered to the right, and he picked out Lila's roommate in the soprano section. She reminded him a lot of Lila that first year—the same short brown hair, the way she perched on the edge of her seat, engaged in animated conversation with the girl next to her. Her finger jabbed at the paper in her hands, first a smile, then a frown crossing her face. What caused the consternation? He glanced at his own schedule to check. Bold print announced that Carrie Randolph would back up Amy's solo. His eyebrows rose. She must be good to beat out other talented, experienced singers. No need for her to frown.

"Hey, Uncle Steve, can I play?" A five-year-old body wiggled next to him on the piano bench.

"Just for a minute. Your Dad's about to get started." He scooted over so his nephew, the son of his sister Brenda and director Tim, could reach the keyboard more easily.

Maybe Lila and I will have a little boy like this, he mused, stopping his hands from rubbing the child's head so he wouldn't break his concentration. *A boy with dark curly hair and brilliant black eyes who loves music.*

A loud squawk interrupted his thoughts. "Testing, testing." Someone adjusted the volume, and Tim's voice rang out clear. "Welcome to the Victory Singers Romania Tour."

After five years, Steve could have given the speech himself. Get to rehearsals on time. When we get overseas, be careful what you drink. Sodas and bottled or boiled water are best; never ever drink from the tap. Instead of Montezuma, you'll have Ceausescu after you. At that, the group laughed like a programmed sound track. You'll be traveling as an American in a foreign country. You represent Jesus Christ, and the good old USA. Learn those Romanian phrases, and above all practice the art of patience.

Tim stopped speaking, and low-level noise rose as chairs pushed back and papers inside music folders rustled. Steve nervously played through a few bars of "Victory in Jesus," the group's theme song. The newest version of Victory Singers was under way.

◆

A local news anchor said good night when Lila entered the hotel room later that night. Carrie looked up from the desk where she was finishing a letter.

"Hi there! Where have you been?" *Silly question. With her husband, of course.*

"Seeing Steve's sister off at the airport. Little Sammy wouldn't say good-bye to Tim and turned his head away. It would have been funny if it wasn't so sad."

Tim? As in Tim North, the director?

Lila sat down on the edge of the bed, kicked off her shoes, and wiggled her toes with relief. "That feels good. You know, I should go to sleep. Long day tomorrow and all that."

"Me, too." They let out simultaneous long, dramatic sighs and grinned at each other. "I'm too excited," Carrie admitted. She signed the letter and stuck it in an envelope, then tucked pen and paper back into the luggage. She grabbed her camera.

"I'm not sleepy either, even though this is my fourth trip." Lila unearthed a ball of pastel ombré yarn and began crocheting a chain. "—thirteen, fourteen, fifteen. That should do it."

"What are you making?" Carrie asked, snapping a picture while Lila continued working.

"Oh, a sweater for the baby. The blanket was too bulky to carry on the plane, but I figured I could squeeze in a ball of yarn and a crochet hook. This will be a sleeve." The chain dangled in front of her. "Some day."

"My grandmother tried to teach me. But I wasn't interested, not enough to really learn."

"Me either. At least, not until the baby."

"Have you picked out any names?"

"Nothing definite." Lila shook her head, an expression of amusement mixed with exasperation crossing her face. "I want to use the name Steven somewhere in a boy's name—the ultrasound shows it's probably a boy, although we don't know for sure—but he says no way, one Steve is enough." She leaned back. The chain was now a couple of rows deep. "A girl's name was easy. Brandi Lynn, just because we like the sound of it. Steve is lobbying for Brandon for a boy's name. Keep it simple, he says."

Lila looked so maternal sitting there, crochet hook slipping through the yarn. Carrie felt a twinge of envy for the family Lila already had—Steve, Tim, his wife, young Sammy.

"I just love children!" The words blurted out. Hands still working, Lila glanced up as if waiting for Carrie to continue.

Encouraged, she went on. "I plan on working with children in some capacity. Maybe I'm trying to make up for being an only child."

"An only child?" Lila studied her roommate. "That must have been lonely. No brothers or sisters—"

"And now that I'm grown up, no nieces or nephews either. I'll have to marry someone with a large family, so I can claim his."

Somewhere nearby a clock bell tolled. "Midnight!" Lila rolled up the sleeve, now a couple of inches long. "Time for Cinderella to go to bed. Lights out?"

"In a minute." After the final evening toiletries, Carrie slipped into the bed. She turned out the lamp and whispered into the darkened room.

"Tonight, New York. This week, the world! Bucharest, anyway."

◆

A few days later, on the plane, Carrie punched the pillow with her fist, leaned back, and shut her eyes. Who could sleep with the never-ending panorama unfolding right outside the window? East, east the plane flew.

Someone passed down the aisle on the way to the restroom. She peeked at her watch. 3:00 p.m. in Bucharest. Early morning back home. They should arrive at their destination in three hours. She straightened her chair with a snap and stuffed the pillow overhead. Day blended into sleepless night, but she didn't want to miss a minute of the adventure.

Bucharest was only the first stop. They would sweep through the southeastern portion of Romania, angle through the Carpathian Mountains, follow the Danube River, which formed the border with Bulgaria, and end in Constanta on the Black Sea. She hummed a few bars of "The Beautiful Blue Danube" and tapped her cramped feet to the waltz rhythm.

Romania. She still couldn't believe it. Land of the Romans. Transylvania, birthplace of the vampire legends. Homeland of Olympic legend Nadia Comaneci. Victim of Nicolae Ceausescu's policies until Romania proclaimed its independence from Soviet domination.

A stewardess stopped by the seat. "Can I get you something?"

Carrie started to say no, then reconsidered. "Some orange juice."

She stretched out her legs and sighed. People packed in, nine across separated only by two thin aisles usually blocked by stewardesses or people headed for the bathrooms. After seven hours, she was uncomfortable, and her leg muscles cramped. She decided to take a walk and angled her legs over her sleeping seatmates. *Is anyone else awake?*

Two rows behind her Lila slept soundly, head nestled against Steve's shoulder as if he were an eiderdown pillow. He popped one eye open when she passed by. He nodded at her, smiling slightly. "Can't sleep, huh?"

She shook her head. "Too excited, I guess."

"Me, too. Even after all these years." He pressed his nose against the window. "Look at that sky! Some day I want to write a rhapsody to celebrate the vistas I've seen from airplanes around the world."

"Are you a composer then?" Carrie questioned, interested.

"Nah. Just a wannabe, a high school music teacher with dreams beyond his reach." Disappointment flitted across his face.

"I don't know about that. Working with teenagers—that's tough. If you can help them grow up, you should feel good about what you are doing." *That's me, all right. Trying to solve everyone else's problems.*

"Yeah." An awed smile crossed his face, and he shifted his embrace of Lila. "The baby just kicked. I want to help this kid, at least, grow up well."

"That's beautiful." Carrie sucked the last of her juice, and a wave of tiredness washed over her. "Maybe I am sleepy after all. I'll try to catch some shut-eye. See you in Romania!"

A few hours later, they landed in Bucharest. "This way, please." In a lightly accented voice, a pert young brunette directed Carrie to where the others were waiting. Momentarily isolated among people speaking a Babel of languages, not one of them English, she felt a moment's hesitation. Noticing the numerous flags in Romania's colors of red, yellow, and black, reality hit home. *I'm really in Romania!* She hurried to rejoin the group.

Tim checked his list. "Everyone's here. Our bus should be ready, so let's head for the exit."

Carrie's heart sank when she saw the bus, their home away from home for the next two weeks. It most resembled a yellow school bus, as old as the ones from her childhood and probably less comfortable to adult dimensions. She glanced at Lila. How would she manage?

Within minutes the bus was jolting down city streets. Eager to see as much as possible before the sun went down, Carrie cleaned off the window.

"It's all so new! I expected older buildings. After all, Romania has been around since Roman times."

Steve overheard her. "Another crime to lay at Ceausescu's door. He wasn't much into historic preservation—wanted to build a monument to himself instead."

"Look, there it is!" Lila pointed. "The Palace of the People on Victory of Socialism Boulevard. What a silly name." She paused. "But lovely, nonetheless." Her face tightened in pain. "Maybe a pillow will soften the bumps."

Soon they arrived at the hotel, and Tim gave room assignments.

"We're all on the second floor," Steve announced. He hoisted Lila's bag in his hand. "Of course there's no elevator." His mouth twitched in a grin. Accepting his arm for support, Lila had to stop midway to catch her breath.

A foot into the room, Carrie halted abruptly. A dingy washbasin stood in one corner, and a single bed dominated the tiny space.

Steve moved past her and dropped the suitcases in the corner. "Need anything else tonight?"

"No, I don't think so." Lila kissed him good night. "See you in the morning."

The two women were left alone in the room. "I was afraid of this," Lila admitted to Carrie. "We'll have to share a bed. I'll try not to snuggle up next to you!" Her laugh sounded forced.

◆

Carrie was swimming through a gulf-warm pool, almost drowning in the water.

"Wake up, Carrie, you've got to help me."

Lila's near-hysterical voice pierced through the fog of Carrie's dream.

She sat up. *It wasn't a dream.* The bed was sopping wet, warm, and sticky. "What—?"

"I thought you'd never wake up." Lila's alto voice rose to coloratura soprano. "You've got to get Steve for me."

The panic on Lila's face registered with Carrie, and her mind collated the facts—Lila's pregnancy, the wet bed—*Labor?*

"My water's broken. Those weren't false labor pains earlier. It's the real thing."

Fighting panic, Carrie asked, "Which room?"

"201—last door on the right." Lila's face clenched in pain as a renewed contraction hit. "Hurry!"

Carrie pulled on a pair of jeans and a T-shirt and ran out into the hall.

Chapter 2

Strong harsh knocks hammered the door. The knob rattled as someone tried to open it. Tim was already pulling on his jeans when Steve fought his way out of a deep sleep.

When he opened the door, still in a sleepy daze, for a second Steve thought he saw Lila outlined by the dim hotel light. Then his eyes focused, and he realized it was Carrie.

"Steve—Lila's in labor. You've got to come." She started back down the hall, then paused when he didn't immediately follow.

"Labor?" His sleep-drugged mind was trying to comprehend. "But that's impossible!"

"Her water's broken. Hurry!"

"I'll be there as soon as I throw some clothes on." *Oh, God, no! Help!*

"I'll get a taxi." Tim picked up the phone and dialed the operator. "No answer. The switchboard must be closed at night. I'll take care of it. You get Lila."

Steve nodded his head, not really hearing his words. *Lila.* Heart-pounding adrenaline speeded his every move, and he ran out the door and down the hall in less than a minute.

Carrie flung open the door at his first tap. The bed with its sopping wet sheets testified to Carrie's story. Where was Lila?

"Where is she?"

"Right here." Lila squatted in a chair, her suitcase on the floor in front of her. Carrie rummaged through the nightstand and pulled out deodorant, a hair brush, and a change of clothes.

By their front door in Denver, an overnight bag waited, packed in readiness for this moment since the fifth month. *It's not supposed to be like this! The baby's not supposed to be born until Labor Day!* Steve shoved the panicked thoughts aside.

"Everyone says this is the easy part." Tear-filled eyes looked to him for reassurance. "But the childbirth manual didn't come with instructions for premature labor. Uh oh, here comes another one." She clenched the sides of her chair. The material stretched across her abdomen crawled in an eerie imitation of a line dance as Steve watched, stunned.

She relaxed. "Eight minutes that time."

He hurried to her side and gripped her sweat-dampened hands between his. She smiled, as if she were trying to encourage him. "The baby will be all right.

He's got to be. "Of course. Babies are born early all the time." *Not this early.*

"But the doctor said I was fine for another month. I don't want my baby born in some foreign hospital!" Lila fought back tears. "I wonder if the hospital even has a neonatal unit." Her words echoed Steve's fears.

"We'll get you home as soon as possible," he promised. "Whatever it costs."

Their eyes locked, a mingled worry and excitement forging yet another link to the chain that bound them together.

The suitcase snapped shut. "That should do it," Carrie announced. "Where do we go?"

"You don't have to come." Steve wasn't sure if he wanted this girl—a total stranger less than a week ago—to encroach on this most intimate moment.

He could feel Carrie looking at them. "Well, take the bag with you," she said and handed the suitcase to Steve. When he grabbed it, her face crumpled like a used hankie, disappointment sketched on her mobile features.

"I would appreciate your company. Please come." Even in her pain, Lila's kindness won out. Pride in his wife and shame at himself chastened Steve. "You can be the honorary aunt," Lila offered.

The wrinkles on Carrie's face reversed direction as she grinned widely. "I'd like that." Currents Steve didn't understand underlined her voice, as if some unspoken communication had passed between the two women.

Another contraction hit as Lila descended the stairs. She flattened her back against the wall and gripped the handrail. Steve glanced at his watch—eight, eight and a half minutes? The second hand on the dial swept around slowly.

In the lobby Tim paced. "I finally raised the concierge. He's called a taxi. I contacted Radu, the pastor here, too. He'll meet us at the hospital." He looked straight at Lila. "How are you doing?"

"Okay, so far. It's the baby I'm worried about." She teetered over to the only chair in the lobby, a straight-backed, uncomfortable fixture with torn upholstery. Ten minutes and another contraction later, the taxi arrived.

The cab driver made up in speed what his car lacked in springs, racing over bumps that bounced them around in the backseat like loose basketballs. At one extra large pothole, Lila cried out. Another contraction? Yes. Steve checked his watch. *Lord, please help us!* Seven minutes that time. *How far away is the hospital?*

The taxi's headlights shone on a small rectangular hospital sign. Not one overhead lamp illuminated the tiny parking lot, and only one dim yellow bulb announced the entrance. Tim thrust a handful of *lei* at the driver as they scrambled out of the car.

A short, heavyset man with thick gray hair and Slavic features hurried out to them from the doorway and waved them inside. "Brother Tim. Come." He took Lila by the hand and led her toward the front desk. "You must be Mrs. Romero. This way please. They expect you."

Steve hadn't expected the Latin accent, rhythms familiar from working with Hispanic students in band. *I'm glad we have someone—anyone!—to translate.* The suitcase swung from his hand as he trotted along behind.

He pulled up short when he shouldered through the revolving door. He had been to emergency rooms a few times with band students, and he had somehow expected the same bustling efficiency. Instead, two groups huddled in shadowy corners, talking in quiet whispers amid low sobbing. Pastor Radu motioned for him to join Lila at the receptionist desk. *Paperwork and red tape are universal constants.*

Another contraction began—six and a half minutes this time. Steve swallowed hard, trying to control his irritation and fear. "Can't you take my wife to the maternity ward? Give her something?"

Pastor Radu relayed the request to the receptionist. She shook her head firmly. He translated her reply.

"The doctor is not here yet, she says. It is a first baby. There is time yet. Be patient."

Sweat beaded on Lila's forehead. She tried to smile, but pain lines flattened out her lips. "The breathing exercises—like we practiced—" Her words dwindled to a whimper of pain.

"I'll answer the questions," Tim volunteered. "You take care of Lila."

"Look at me." Steve knelt next to his wife and cradled her hands in his own. "Breathe deep and relax. You remember how." When he mirrored her breathing—one deep breath, three short puffs—he felt his own muscles relaxing. A grin built from the inside out. Maybe everything would turn out all right.

"I can't believe this is happening." She rubbed her hands over her abdomen. "Hello in there. I'll be seeing you soon." Her bright dark eyes stared into Steve's, calling his soul. "I'm sure the baby will be okay." The reassurance was meant for herself as much as for him, he guessed.

She turned to Pastor Radu. "They have contacted a pediatrician, haven't they?"

He exchanged more words with the nurse. "No pediatrician. Only the doctor on call."

"Wait a minute." *This is too much.* "The baby is premature. Ten weeks early. There—must—be—a—pediatrician on hand when he is born."

The expression on Radu's face registered his understanding of the emergency. He spoke again with the nurse and translated, his face concerned. "The staff pediatrician is out of the city for the weekend. There is no one to call."

Lila grabbed Steve's hand, panic written on her face, as if begging him to make the nightmare go away. It was pointless to try to control his own fear.

At that point, the nurse shuffled her papers into a pile, signaling the interview was over. She motioned for Lila to follow her. Steve fell in behind, but the nurse put up both hands in front of her chest in a gesture that clearly said stop.

"Fathers wait here," the pastor explained. "The doctor will see you soon." He pointed behind Steve. "She can come."

Carrie stirred. She squeezed his arm. "I'll do my best," she promised. She grabbed the suitcase and followed Lila.

Before the door slammed shut, Lila twisted her head for one final glance, her face filled with a mixture of fear, loneliness, hope, and excitement. When Steve tried to follow, the handle turned in a one-way lock.

◆

Carrie traipsed down the hallway after Lila and the nurse. Behind a glass wall she glimpsed a nursery, one nurse watching over a room full of bassinets that all looked occupied. Staring back over her shoulder, she nearly ran into their escort, who was pointing to the one empty bed in a ward full of women.

The sheets looked dingy gray, as if they were washed too infrequently or were old. An awful smell hung in the air, a mixture of disinfectant and sour milk. A gagging lump formed in Carrie's throat, which she forced down. Somehow she had to be strong for Lila.

The nurse handed Lila a hospital gown and indicated that she should change. She pulled a ringed curtain partway around the bed and disappeared.

Lila waited out the next contraction. "Seven minutes. I hope the doctor gets here soon. I hope he speaks English." Tears glistened in her eyes. "It's not supposed to be like this. Haven't they heard of Lamaze here? I want Steve." She sucked in her breath and patted Carrie's hand. "I'm sorry. I'm being rude. I'm very glad you're here." Strings dangled from the back of the yellow hospital gown when she drew it up her arms. "Tie it for me, please?"

"Sure." Carrie's hands trembled as she fumbled with the knots. A moan escaped Lila's lips, and Carrie looked into the face contorted with pain. Again she fought down a rising feeling of panic. Her only experience with hospitals came from having a tonsillectomy when she was five.

Somewhere a radio played rock songs in Romanian. Close by, a woman alternately cried and giggled. Metal clanged. Bed pans, maybe? *I haven't seen a doctor since we got here.* She wished she were back at the hotel—anywhere but here, in a maternity ward in a foreign hospital where only she and Lila spoke the same language. *Why did I offer to help?*

Lila's hand touched her arm. *Because of her.* Between sweat and tears, Lila's face gleamed. Carrie grabbed a towel and peeked around the edge of the curtain. In a far corner she spied a sink. "Be right back." The water ran lukewarm. Carrie soaked the towel, wrung it out, and hurried back to Lila's side. Another contraction had started. Carrie looked at her watch—six minutes, as far as she could tell. *The doctor better arrive soon.*

She sponged Lila's face. "How can I help?"

"Just having you here helps." Lila tried to smile but failed. "Do you happen to know Lamaze? Silly question. I'm supposed to relax and regain strength between contractions. Only they're much worse than I was prepared for. One ends, and I wonder how I can survive the next one—and the one after that—hours on end." Fat tears rolled down her face. "I suppose I sound like a crybaby."

"No." Carrie spoke softly. "I think you're incredibly brave." She sponged Lila's face again.

"At least we have the nursery all set up. Back home. Steve was so cute, ordering the crib as soon as the doctor confirmed my pregnancy. We even picked out the outfit to bring the baby home in." This time her smile held a little more real warmth. "I should look on the bright side. I get to shave two months off my pregnancy." She addressed her abdomen. "I don't care what you have to wear. I just want you to be healthy." She started to cry.

"I'm sure the baby will be fine." *I'm lying.* Carrie perched on the edge of the bed. *Change the subject.* "I hope someday I find someone as special as Steve. Handsome, talented, loves kids—" She broke off, a blush staining her cheeks with heat.

"You will." Lila spoke with calm assurance, pain free for the moment. "When God brings you together."

The calm shattered. "Aaah!" Lila's body jerked flat as another contraction hit. She grabbed Carrie's hand and squeezed hard enough to leave bruises, then let go. Seconds ticked by. Lila's abdomen stopped heaving with contractions. Lila remained motionless on the bed.

Watching Lila go through labor was enough to frighten a woman from ever having a baby. Carrie quieted her doubts. *She needs my reassurance, not an echo of her own fear.* Ready to pray, to listen, to do whatever she could to help, Carrie bent over the prostrate form, looking at the eyelids closed as if in sleep. *Something's wrong.* She felt Lila's wrist—no pulse! Wrong, a faint pulse throbbed deep down.

"Lila?" *Please wake up.*

"Lila?" Carrie spoke louder this time, loud enough to wake all the women on the ward. Lila didn't answer.

"Lila?" This time it came out a whisper. *Something's terribly wrong.* Panic built into a terrified scream as Carrie jerked back the curtain and yelled for help.

◆

When Steve heard Carrie scream, he jumped up and rammed the door, pounding with his fists as if the glass would break. The nurse stormed toward him, finger shaking with unmistakable authority. Then she, too, paused, listening to the sounds issuing from the ward.

Carrie's face pasted against the door, and Steve almost fell through the door when she succeeded in opening it. "Where's the doctor?" Her panicked voice echoed the fear in Steve's heart.

"Here I am." A voice spoke in British-toned English. Behind them appeared a young man. *He's no older than I am. Is he the doctor?* "Where is the patient?"

"In here." Carrie held the door open for Steve to squeeze through inches behind the doctor.

"How far apart are the contractions?"

"I don't know. Six minutes the last time I checked. But something's gone wrong."

"I will be the judge of that." They hurried down the corridor past the nursery.

At the door to the ward, Steve stood bewildered, searching for that one beloved form.

"This way."

There she is. Lila!

She lay without moving, hair tousled on the pillow, like a worn baby doll. No sounds, no smiles, nor even frowns hinted at what was happening inside. The sheet rose and fell slightly—once, twice, without a regular rhythm.

"Leave." The young doctor's pleasant expression darkened. "I must examine Mrs. Romero."

"I'm her husband. I want to stay." Steve's voice croaked in protest.

"Not now." Compassion lent an authority to the doctor's voice that Steve couldn't ignore. "Go back to the waiting room. I will talk with you when I have completed my examination." With a gentle push, he steered Steve toward the door and pulled the curtain around the silent bed.

"Let's go." Carrie slipped a cool hand into Steve's and led him away. "The doctor is here. He'll know what to do." Their shoes echoed on the linoleum floor, her sneakers squeaking against the tiles while his loafers tapped with a hesitant beat.

Tim met them at the door, eyes asking the questions he didn't voice. Steve shook his head and began pacing the floor.

Out of habit, he counted the steps like he did for band routines. *Thirty strides, turn right, thirty-five more steps, turn, complete the circuit. Two minutes.* He circled again, studying the pictures of dignitaries on the wall—ten of them, including one he recognized as President Iliescu. A dark rectangular space marked the place where a frame had been removed. Ceausescu, probably. Steve continued pacing a third then fourth round.

Carrie walked toward him, bearing a steaming mug. "I thought you might like some coffee. Probably strong enough to tar a ship, but it might help." She tucked her head to one side and held the cup in the palm of her hand as an offering, for the moment resembling a shy young band student.

"Thanks." The heat stung Steve's hand briefly when he grasped the cup. He stopped his pacing long enough to take a sip. She was right; it was strong. The sweet syrupy coffee soothed his throat, enabling him to voice the fears that tormented him.

"He said a few minutes." Flicking his wrist, a luminous dial shone against dark matted hair. "It's already been a quarter of an hour. What's going on in there?" *Stop shouting.*

His voice echoed around the nearly empty anteroom. A couple in the corner looked up at the noise then shrugged at the strange Americans.

Warily, like kittens sidling up to a bulldog, Tim and Pastor Radu joined Steve and Carrie. Tim hugged his brother-in-law, a brief, awkward gesture meant to encourage.

"It will be all right. Remember God is in control." Tim gently punched Steve's shoulder. "I've reached Brenda back in the States. She'll let the family know." He smiled as if to say, "That's that. Things will work out. You'll see."

They stood in a tight circle, Steve trembling from the effort it took to not start pacing again. He sank in a chair, hung his head low, and dangled his hands between his knees.

Lord. The uncertain cry issued straight from his heart. *I don't know how to pray. My feelings are too strong. But I trust You with the lives of my wife and our baby. I trust You to do what is best.*

Metal rattled as someone turned a door handle. Steve jumped to his feet. The doctor appeared in the doorway, blinking his eyes against the dark waiting room.

"Mr. Romero?"

He sprinted to the door, vaguely aware of the others at his heels. "How's Lila?"

"Let's find a place to sit down. Back here." The doctor pushed through a swinging door and settled at a desk behind the receptionist's spot. The shadowy light and black bags under his eyes added years to his face.

The doctor tapped a pencil on the desktop, as if stalling for time, then opened a drawer and rolled it in. Folding his hands together, he looked Steve straight in the eye.

"Mrs. Romero is in a coma. We're not sure what caused it."

Coma? "What can you do?"

The doctor continued as if he hadn't heard Steve. "Her heart is skipping beats. She is having trouble breathing—we are trying to locate a machine."

He spread his hands as if in apology. "You must make a choice. We can take extraordinary measures to try to bring Mrs. Romero out of the coma and hope she recovers quickly."

The words pounded in Steve's brain. *Choice? What choice? Save her!*

"What is the other option?" Tim asked for him.

"The longer you wait, the more danger there is to the baby. He is not receiving enough oxygen—he could die, or have unexpected disabilities. If we do a cesarean now, there is a good chance he will be born healthy."

"Then what would happen to my wife?"

"Mr. Romero, I will not lie to you. She will probably die if we perform an operation. She may die even if we don't."

Steve didn't need time to consider. "Save my wife." The words came out with a harsh, grating edge. Lila! Without her, a child, a family, meant nothing.

"Very well." The doctor stood up, ending the conference. Steve tried to follow him back into the ward. "No." The doctor warned him away in brisk tones. "You would only be a distraction. You might slow us down." Compassion softened the next words. "I will let you know as soon as anything changes." The door clanged shut behind him like a maximum-security prison.

One hour passed. Two. Three. Periodically a nurse slipped through the door and shook her head—no change. Steve resumed his pacing. Outside the glass doors, an angry red-and-orange sky announced the dawn of a new day.

Steve had lost all track of time when the doctor reappeared. The doctor's lab coat fell in dejected folds around his sagging body.

"She's dead." Steve spoke in a strangled voice.

The doctor nodded his head. "A blood clot went to the brain. Nothing we could do. We went ahead and took the baby."

"Is the baby alive? A boy? A girl?" Steve asked automatically. The news of Lila's death spread through his body, numbing nerve endings in its wake.

"You have a son, Mr. Romero. But there are problems."

The edge in the doctor's voice penetrated the fog clogging Steve's brain. "Problems?"

"He is premature, of course. Small and not fully developed. His lungs are not functioning properly. I believe there may be a problem with his heart valves as well. And only time will determine how much brain damage he suffered."

"Will he—live?"

The doctor's helpless shrug spoke volumes. "We are doing the best we can."

"Please—let me see them. I can't get in the way now." Steve's voice nearly broke.

"This way."

The doctor didn't object when Tim and Carrie followed Steve down the hallway. Empty stillness screamed in Steve's ears from where Lila's body lay on the bed, sheets drawn up past her shoulders. He stood at her side, smoothed her hair back from her face. *She's gone. All that's left is this shell.* "Absent from *the body, present with the Lord." No, God, not like this!* He started to cry, but the pervading numbness dried up his tear ducts.

"Where is my son?"

The doctor guided them to the nursery and pointed to a bassinet in a far corner. Half a dozen tubes hid the tiny body. A T-line from an oxygen tank, like Steve had seen hundreds of times in Denver, obscured the baby's facial features. In spite of the oxygen, his skin shone bluish-white, not healthy newborn red. Steve reached for the baby, but his arms ran into the glass. He hung there like a fly caught in a spider's web.

Tim tapped him on the elbow. Tears glistened in his eyes. "I'm sorry, man. We've got to go—fill the group in on what's happened, cancel tonight's concert. But I'll be back."

Next to him, Carrie pressed her face against the glass, tears leaving a salty streak on the pane. "What's his name?"

"Huh?" Steve tried to focus on her question.

"What's the baby's name? So that I can pray for him."

"Brandon. That's what we finally decided." Soundless sobs shook his shoulders. A featherlight hand touched his back then disappeared.

Steve continued staring into the nursery. His plans and hopes for the future lay struggling on a nursery bed, reduced to a single thin note.

Chapter 3

With sandpapered eyes, Carrie stared out the taxi window. Bucharest greeted a new day. Newspaper boys and milk vendors called cheerful greetings as they went about their business in the light morning sun. Life continued as usual—no cosmic pause commemorated the death of an unknown American or the child's life hanging in the balance. Unbidden sobs rose in her throat.

"Carrie." Tim's voice interrupted her thoughts. "Thanks for being there."

"I can't believe she's gone. We only met a week ago, but I really liked her."

"Not what you expected from Romania. A disaster for the tour. And Steve—if it was my *wife*, I'd go crazy."

They passed the Palace of the People. Beggars dotted the steps, visible symbols of communism's unfulfilled promises. "Only last night Lila was talking about this place." Carrie's heart contracted. *It just can't be. I wish I could wake up and find out it's all been a bad dream.* She closed her eyes, wanting to shut out the nightmare.

The taxi jolted to a stop. They had arrived at the hotel. Neon signs flashed as if it were still the dead of night. She began to cry.

"Go on up," Tim urged gently. "Try to get some sleep. We'll meet in the lobby at nine thirty." Shoulders hunched over in apparent exhaustion, he headed for the phones.

Of course. He has to let the families know, thought Carrie, as she shuffled off in the opposite direction.

Fatigue overtook Carrie at the staircase. To her tired mind, the steps had multiplied overnight to rival the climb she made the previous week at the Statue of Liberty. Wishing she could crawl or propel herself forward by her arms, she lifted one heavy leg after the other in slow progression. Each step became a resting place to stand while she checked her pockets for the room key and to catch her breath.

The room. Remembering the mess they had left, Carrie hesitated before opening the door. Nothing had changed. The middle of the bed sagged under the roll of wet bedspreads. She checked her watch. 7:00 a.m. *Too early for the maid.* Loud ticking emanated from Lila's travel alarm. Once again Carrie felt the sensation of waking up in a soaking-wet bed, the panic, and excitement, too, of Lila going into labor.

Sleep if you can. Tim said nine thirty. She reset the alarm. *But where do*

I sleep? Stifling a groan, Carrie turned the one cushiony chair toward the wall, curled herself up as small as she could in its depths, and tried to sleep. Sunlight leaked through the window shade, warming her back and relaxing tense muscles.

Lila's in trouble. I've got to help her! Aaah!

The alarm blared by Carrie's ear. She jerked awake, sliding out of the chair onto the floor. A musty, wet smell filled the air. *It's real. Lila is dead.* She checked the clock—nine twenty. *I'd better hurry.*

A few minutes later Carrie made her way to the lobby, where Pastor Radu greeted her. Daylight hours revealed a friendly, round face. An inner peace transformed his rather ordinary features. He took her hands between his own and patted them with thick, blunt fingers. "I am so sorry. It is sometimes difficult to understand God's workings."

Memories of stories about Radu's heroism surfaced. Tortured at the hands of communists, he refused to deny his faith. *And he still talks about God's love.* She hoped to get to know him better.

Maybe I can ask Tim about Steve. She saw the director conversing in low tones with one of the older tour members. Flipping through her memory banks, she placed him as Guy, the trumpeter who could make his instrument sing like the archangel Michael. *No, I shouldn't intrude.* She sagged against the wall to wait for an announcement.

Curious glances shot in her direction then looked away, unwilling to meet her eyes. Whispers circulated around her like strings of fog. Every now and then the words penetrated the wall of silence surrounding her.

"Lila. . .in labor."

"I heard she died."

"No, Steve died. . .car accident."

"Everyone's fine. . .Lila had a boy."

"Carrie went with them. . . ."

Heads swung in her direction like a pendulum swing.

"I'll ask." A determined Amy headed toward her, ready to voice their questions.

"Your attention, please." Tim's announcement saved her from having to answer. "Singers. Let's load the bus." In spite of his measured control, cracks showed in his razor-edge hold on reality.

No one moved. "Not everybody's here." Amy spoke for the group. "Steve and Lila are missing." The proverbial pin-drop silence descended.

"I know." Tim paused, looking at the bustle going on around them. "I'd rather not talk about it here. I'll explain what happened in a few minutes, at the church. Let's go."

Guy picked up his instrument case and headed out the door. One by one, others followed. An uneasy silence pervaded. Carrie groped her way to the back, unwilling to join in idle chitchat or to offer explanations. At the front Tim scrunched over his seat as if he were experiencing motion sickness. Radu took the seat next to him. No one dared to sit close to either one of them. Currents of muffled whispers eddied through the bus.

Eventually they arrived at the church, a cathedral with gothic spires worthy of a vampire movie. A banner hung across the front entrance. "Welcome to Romania." The unintended cruelty stung Carrie's eyes. *Some welcome we've had.*

Radu motioned them inside. Carrie paused for a moment to stare at a painting of a huge tree that dominated one wall. *Tree of Jesse.* Her mind dragged up the relevant description from the tourist information she had studied. Then she joined the others shuffling toward the front.

Tim grabbed a mic, flicked a switch, and waited for everyone to find a seat.

"Amy, you asked earlier about Steve and Lila." Each word resonated in a voice full of pathos. He surveyed the room, found Carrie, and looked at her as if seeking a way to put the night's tragedy into words. "The baby started coming last night. Early, as you know. We rushed Lila to the hospital, but she went into a coma, and a blood clot hit her brain and killed her. They're trying to save the baby now, and Steve is at the hospital with him." The words tumbled out quickly, as if rushing through the explanation could minimize their impact.

Shock held them silent for a moment; then the questions started. "Lila's dead?"

Tim nodded his head without uttering a word.

"And the baby—it's a boy?"

"Brandon." Carrie surprised herself by speaking. "His name is Brandon." The image of the tiny infant, tied to life by dozens of tubes, formed in her mind, choking further speech.

"How is Steve?"

"In shock, as you might imagine. He needs your prayers."

"Is the tour canceled?"

Half of Carrie's mind struggled to pay attention.

"We've canceled the concert scheduled for this evening, but the tour will go on with a modified schedule." He fielded a few more questions, expanding on the same information, letting it sink in. "Guy will lead today's rehearsal. Ask Radu for anything else you need." He started to bolt out the door when the Romanian stopped him.

"Let us pray." The pastor turned toward the altar and raised his arms in supplication. "Our loving heavenly Father, we pray for Your children Lila, Steve, and little Brandon. We do not ask for life but for peace and joy. We accept that Your will be done." *He prays as if he's talking to God over the breakfast table.*

When he finished, Tim took charge. "Join hands in a circle." Confidence and joy built in his voice as he prayed. "Lord Jesus, You have promised You are with us always. You called Lila home. We confess we don't understand, but we know You are with Steve and Brandon right now. We will go on, knowing You have given us the victory in Your Son Jesus Christ! Amen!"

The group waited in silence, continuing to hold hands when Tim concluded. Guy began praying. "Jesus. We need You today more than ever. . . ."

One by one they prayed, offering broken hearts to God with faith and love. Carrie added her unspoken thoughts to those of the others. *He is here,* she realized, feeling the presence of the Holy Spirit in an almost physical sense as if dove wings brushed her face. Peace erased part of the pain she had carried away from the hospital.

After what could have been minutes or hours, the sobs diminished and the circle broke. Tim had disappeared. Carrie guessed he'd headed back to the hospital.

In a few minutes the group assembled in the choir loft, everyone careful not to stare at the empty spot in the alto section and the unoccupied piano bench. Guy called for their attention.

"Can anyone fill in at the piano?" He gestured toward the empty seat. "Tim usually plays when Steve can't make it." He swallowed. "I know there must be at least one piano major out there."

"Kim plays for our college choir," one of the tenors offered.

"Just what we're looking for. Come on down, Kim. Don't be shy." Carrie twisted to watch a willowy redhead slip out of the back row.

The instrumentalists did their best—they all did—but heavy hearts and a different blend of voices and instruments took a toll. To Carrie's ears, their singing lacked balance. Lunch call came two hours later.

"All right, wrap it up for this morning." Guy sounded as relieved as Carrie felt.

Pastor Radu's wife, Anika, served a Romanian specialty in honor of their arrival, but Carrie ate it without appreciation. *Comfort food, that's what I want. A hot fudge brownie sundae. A supreme pizza. Has Steve eaten anything today?* She remembered Lila, who would never again enjoy a meal, and the food turned sour in her mouth.

◆

Brandon's tiny lips moved in a sucking motion. *He's hungry.* The bag delivering the life-sustaining fluids dangled, empty.

"Nurse!" Language barrier forgotten for the moment, Steve called for help. When no one responded, he raced down the hall to where the matron, a different lady from the previous evening, kept watch over the nursery.

"Nurse. My son's food bag is empty. . . ." She looked at him, puzzled. He tried to think of a way to pantomime the problem and gave up. "Come with me. Please."

Shrugging, she set aside the knitting that had occupied her attention and followed him through the maze of cribs. "Look. It's empty." He pointed to the collapsed bag.

On the way out, a couple of babies started whimpering. She checked her watch and lifted them from their beds. *Lucky kids. Strong enough to cry. Mothers here to feed them.* Angry, he listened as a feeble mewling noise issued from Brandon's mouth. *He belongs in a neonatal care unit.* Powerless fury at the inefficient, unfamiliar Romanian system washed over Steve.

Five minutes passed. The nurse returned empty-handed. She pointed to an empty spot in the cabinet. Moving with a minimum of effort, she retrieved an empty bottle from a sterilization unit and extracted formula from a refrigerator. She looked at Steve, asking a question with her eyes.

He nodded, and she poured about two ounces into the bottle before handing it to him. It felt cold in his hands. "Uh, is there any way to warm it? Microwave?" She stared at him blankly and gestured toward Brandon, inviting Steve to feed his son.

I can't give him cold formula. Steve's mind fished for a solution. Hot water, maybe? Worth a try. He turned the tap on at the sink. Thankfully the rusty water cleared and warmed to near boiling point. He stuck the bottle under the running water, frantic to get the formula ready before Brandon reached a critical point. At least the chill had disappeared. He scurried to Brandon's side.

The baby's mouth sucked frantically, searching instinctively for food. Weaving his hand carefully through the tubing, Steve offered the nipple to his son. Tiny gulping noises followed. *I hope this is all right. There must have been a reason for the IV.* Steve shoved the worries aside as Brandon's cries subsided, followed by small mewing sounds of contentment. Steve could almost see the nourishment filling out hollow cheeks.

Feeding wasn't supposed to be a problem. Inspired by the doctor's advice and Brenda's example, Lila had planned on nursing their child. *Lila! How can I raise our child without you? I don't have time to think about that now.* Pushing the grief into a locked corner of his heart, he gently extracted the nipple from Brandon's mouth. *Who's going to burp him?* Warming a bottle was a simple obstacle to overcome. Would his lungs ever inflate and function properly? Brandon's chest heaved in the effort to breath in air. *God, he has to make it. He just has to.*

◆

Carrie managed a few more bites of lunch by washing them down with a glass of lemon-lime soda. She turned her attention to the Tree of Jesse on the wall. The fresco fascinated her. Not quite symmetrical limbs branched out from a thick trunk. Portraits of biblical characters hung from the luxuriant leaves. David held a lamb. The boy Josiah wore a crown. Atop the tree, a radiant

Madonna cradled the baby Jesus in soft blankets.

Brandon. The IV lines that wrapped the tiny infant curled into Carrie's mind, and she wiped at her eyes. Grief washed over her afresh, and she stabbed a fork through a paper napkin and pushed away her plate. *This can't be real. Lord, be with Steve and Brandon.*

"I see you admire the Tree of Jesse." Pastor Radu addressed her. "So do I. I always notice some new thing. It reminds me that God became man, and He knows our weaknesses." He pointed to the infant Christ. "Even the Lord of heaven knew loss—Joseph. His good friend Lazarus." A peculiar light shone from his eyes. "But because He lives, we can face tomorrow. Isn't that what the song says?"

A newborn baby. Brandon. God does understand.

Radu smiled encouragement at her then tapped his glass for attention. "For those who wish to go, we have planned a sightseeing trip this afternoon. Or you may return to the hotel." He outlined some traditional tourist hot spots Carrie had included on her must-see list. *Does it matter now?* In light of Lila's death, everything diminished in importance.

"There may be other things you want to see." Radu was still speaking. "Let me know, and I will try to arrange something."

Surely they won't keep us in Bucharest indefinitely. Maybe she could escape the horror of the night and find a gentler Romania in the countryside. Her hunger sharpened for an excursion down the Danube River or up into the Carpathian Mountains.

But what about today? I'm exhausted. I feel like I could sleep all afternoon and night, too. She remembered the soiled sheets rolled in the middle of the bed. The maid must have cleaned up the mess, but Carrie was sure she couldn't rest with reminders of the previous evening surrounding her. Before bedtime she would try to change rooms. *Maybe sightseeing will take my mind off things.* Most of the group climbed on the bus with her.

Pastor Radu proved a relaxing tour guide. From time to time he passed on bits of history and culture, but as often as not he let the sights speak for themselves. Colorful clothing sparkled against gray buildings, differing styles separating Romanians from Hungarians from Gypsies. She had heard racial tensions rivaled those in the United States. *In Christ there is no Jew nor Greek.* Carrie studied Pastor Radu and his wife, the love of Christ radiating from their faces. *Language doesn't matter. We have the same Father.*

Catching sight of a mother surrounded by half a dozen youngsters, Carrie decided that large families must be the norm in Romania. Everywhere she saw children. Mothers stood in line with five or six pale-faced tots clinging to their skirts. The lucky ones bounced a ball in the street or ran laughing through a park. What had she heard about a government-dictated baby boom? Thousands of children crowded into space designed for hundreds.

Watching them, Carrie knew exactly where she wanted to go on the next day. She made her way forward on the wildly swinging bus and tapped Pastor Radu on the shoulder.

"*Buna dimineata,* Carrie. How are you doing?"

"Okay, I guess." She braced herself against the back of the seat and spoke. "I know what I want to do tomorrow, if you can arrange it." She hesitated. *What if he thinks I'm foolish? Pushy?*

"Yes?" he prompted.

"I want to visit an orphanage. You know, a home for children."

His face registered surprise. *At least he didn't say no.* "You see, I'm a social work major. I plan on working with children in some way."

"I see," he murmured. Anika looked on with surprised interest.

"And we've heard so much about the orphans in Romania. I'd like to see for myself." She almost didn't dare look at him, afraid of his response.

"You remind me of Solomon," he said in a seeming change of subject.

Me? Solomon? How?

"You ask for knowledge to help when you could ask for pleasure. You are a special person. A children's home—" He paused, as if flipping through mental files.

"Sister Pauline," his wife murmured.

"Of course!" Radu said. "We know someone who runs a home. We may be able to arrange something."

"Thank you!" Carrie shook his hand and raced back to her seat before he changed his mind. Her head settled against the hard red seat, and she dozed off and on through the remainder of the tour.

Back at the hotel, Carrie wasted no time eating, changing rooms, and settling in for a long night's sleep. Fighting yawns, she said a brief but heartfelt prayer for the father and son struggling at the hospital. She'd half expected visions of the previous evening to keep her awake, but three sleep-shortened nights took their toll. The instant her head hit the pillow, she fell into a drug-deep sleep.

During the next morning's breakfast, served American style with eggs, bacon, orange juice, and toast, Carrie wondered what the children in the orphanage were eating. *Probably not much,* she thought, guiltily laying down her fork on a not yet empty plate. *God bless all the hungry children everywhere. The ones in the orphanage. And Brandon, whatever is happening with him today.*

Pastor Radu's wife, Anika, walked into the dining room. She stood by the doorway, surveying the room until she spotted Carrie.

Anika joined Carrie at the table. "Can you leave immediately? Sister Pauline can see you this morning."

Yes! Then Carrie noticed Guy making his way around the tables. "I don't know yet. I hope so. I have to check with the leader." He headed in their direction.

"Good morning, Mrs. Babik," Guy greeted Anika. He looked a little bewildered, like an understudy called on as the curtain rises. "Carrie, I thought I'd let you know the schedule. Today's another free day. Tim is making arrangements to ship Lila's body home. Whatever happens with Steve and the baby, Tim will rejoin us tomorrow. Plan on a ten o'clock rehearsal in the morning." With a brief wave of his hand, he moved on to the next group.

Brandon must still be alive, Carrie realized, gratitude swelling her heart like lighter-than-air helium. *Thank You, Lord. Help Steve through this difficult time.* There was nothing more she could do for Lila. Children always cheered her up. Maybe visiting the orphanage would take her mind off the tragedy. She folded her napkin and laid it on top of her plate.

"I'm ready. Let's go!"

Chapter 4

Let's go." Tim steered Steve away from the crib and out of the nursery. "Man, you have to get some shut-eye. The hospital will call if anything changes."

Through the distorted glass, Brandon lay still, almost lifeless. Steve blinked hard, trying to flush moisture over exhaustion-dried eyes. He fought the urge to run back. Surely Tim understood his fear that the only phone call he would receive would be about a dead child.

"I know you're worried. I booked you a room in a hotel down the block. You can hole up there and be back in five minutes. I promise."

Steve couldn't tear himself away from the window.

"You're not doing the baby or yourself any good, carrying on like this."

Maybe a short nap. Steve's shoulders sagged, and he ran the back of his hand across his bristly chin. He hadn't changed clothes for almost twenty-four hours. A hotel room beckoned as a haven of rest to his weary mind. Turning his back on the nursery window, he followed Tim down the hall.

The planned nap lasted all night. When he woke, gentle pink light filtered around the edges of the window shades. Grabbing the phone, he dialed the front desk.

"This is Steve Romero in suite 116. Has the hospital called?"

"No, sir."

Thank goodness he speaks English.

"We would have called right away."

Maybe I have time for that shower after all. He stayed under the nozzle until it turned ice cold, the water stinging his back like needles. It was like a form of acupuncture, each jab removing a minuscule amount of the pain of the last two days. His mind cleared, and he realized he probably should contact the American embassy. They could advise him about what to do about a funeral and burial.

Wiping the mist off the bathroom mirror, he stared at his image, a gaunt-faced stranger looking back at him. Nothing to invite anyone to want to help him. *First impressions are important.* Tim's advice to the Singers echoed through his head with Lila's voice. Grimly he slapped shaving cream on his cheeks and starting scraping off two days' growth of beard.

He had just fastened his shirt cuffs, easily pushing the button through the loose hole, when someone knocked at the door. "Come in."

Tim appeared and looked him up and down. "You rested. That's good." Steve grunted.

"My next job is to get some food into you."

"No time for that. I want to contact the American embassy. When will the hospital release Lila's body?"

"I've already called." Tim polished his glasses then pushed them up onto his nose. "You'll have to sign some papers. It may take a few days. Breakfast now. No more excuses."

Steve allowed Tim to guide him to the hotel's dining room while he considered the problem of the interment. "The only funeral home I know anything about is Drinkwine Mortuary. It stuck in my mind because the name was kind of unusual, you know? We don't—didn't—have any burial plots." He swallowed, hard. "Or a will. We thought we had plenty of time."

In the restaurant, Steve was glad that the menu listed the selections in Romanian and English. Tim shoveled in the food in his usual impatient fashion, while Steve picked at the meal, not tasting the little he managed to swallow. He couldn't have told anyone if the eggs were reconstituted powder or fresh from the farm.

"Brenda is calling our church back home. The minister will arrange things on the Denver end." Tim settled back, coffee cup cradled between his hands, a pose Steve had seen hundreds of times. "Yeah, Brenda and I didn't get around to making a will until after Amanda was born. We even joked about it. How it made us feel like old married folks. Never imagined anyone our age needing it." He took a sip and glanced at Steve over the rim of the cup.

"Man, I feel so bad about what's happened. If Lila hadn't been on tour—"

"If, if, if." Anger crept into Steve's voice. "If we had been in Denver. If they had better facilities here. It wouldn't have made any difference. Lila might have died, even with the best of care. Nothing can change what's happened." The tears Steve had held in check tumbled out, cascading down his clean shirt, leaving streaks like the slats on a baby crib.

At his elbow Steve heard liquid being poured into a cup, and he forced himself to stop crying.

Tim handed him a wet napkin to clean his face and waited while Steve drank down his coffee. "Are you ready to go back to the hospital?"

"Yeah, I guess so."

"We can wait a few more minutes—"

Outside the window a passing cloud dimmed the morning sunshine. "No. I want to see my son."

◆

Carrie squeezed into the battered two-seater, making room between a pile of Bibles and a box of pamphlets. Anika handled the manual gears as smoothly as a race car, dodging the bumps Carrie thought unavoidable after her rides by taxi and bus. Bright sunlight created an illusion of prosperity in the passing residential districts.

"Radu tells me you were with Mrs. Romero at the hospital," Anika stated. "It must have been frightening." Her tone invited a response.

Carrie blinked. *How can I tell this stranger the way I felt when I don't know myself? I've never seen anyone die before. It was so sudden, like when someone pinches out the flame of a candle.* Although no breeze stirred the stale car air, she shivered.

"It was pretty frightening," she admitted.

"That took courage. Helping Mr. and Mrs. Romero even when you were scared." The admiration in Anika's voice shook Carrie.

I wasn't brave at all. I butted in, wanted to be the aunt. And I couldn't help Lila when she needed me most. Memories of Lila lying still on the bed filled her mind and choked further speech.

"Ah, here we are." The car turned onto a tree-lined lane.

Good. I need to hear children's laughter.

"The home is on the Dimbovita River. It used to be a pretty spot." She pulled into a parking space in front of an ancient building. At some point in the distant past it was a stately country home, since converted into an orphanage. Everywhere signs of neglect showed, from ivy climbing up crumbling brick walls to weatherworn slides and swings at the side in need of fresh paint.

Carrie stepped out of the car, breathed in the fresh air, and smiled. *What a wonderful place for kids.* Peering down the lane, she saw no sign of the children she expected.

To the right four more buildings, each more institutional in design than the last, crowded together. Small square windows occurred at regular intervals in the last two buildings, both three stories high. *It looks like a jail,* Carrie thought with a shock.

"This way." Anika lifted the door knocker with effort. *It* was old and gloomy enough that Carrie half expected Jacob Marley's face to appear. A minute passed. Two.

"Do you think they heard us?" Carrie asked, impatient, grasping the heavy ring in her fingers.

"Yes." Anika gently pushed away Carrie's hand. "Sister Pauline is old. It may take her a few minutes."

Patience, Carrie reminded herself. *Remember Tim's advice.*

The door opened by unseen hands. Carrie spied a skeleton-thin woman with fluttering hands and lively blue eyes.

Anika spoke briefly in Romanian, gesturing to Carrie.

"Buna dimineata." A dove soft voice transported Carrie back in time. Her kindergarten teacher had spoken with the same gentle nurturing tones.

I like this woman. A warm reassurance engulfed her.

Sister Pauline led them down the hall lined with sturdy furniture in need of polishing, past black-and-white photographs of rosy-cheeked children with bright smiles and old-fashioned clothes. Carrie stopped to study one picture. *Isn't that. . . ? It is!* A younger Sister Pauline, hair black, not gray, shoulders straight and not yet bent, peered at her with the same piercing eyes. *She's given her life to this place.*

"Sister Pauline speaks no English, so I will translate," Anika explained when they settled in the office.

Carrie watched the evident enthusiasm and joy on the director's face as she spoke of her early days with the home. There were always children, those orphaned by violence and circumstance, babies born to unwed mothers.

She's like me. A smile of camaraderie broke Carrie's face. *God called her to help "the least of these."*

The number of new workers diminished with the communist takeover, but they managed. Pauline became the director twenty-five years ago.

"For years, love and children filled our home." Happy memories eased some of the life lines of her face as she described life in the converted mansion.

One home? But there are five buildings.

"That changed with Ceausescu." Sadness etched furrows in the older woman's forehead. The government assessed a celibacy tax on women with fewer than five children and outlawed contraception. It quickly made a difference. The birth rate nearly doubled in only one year's time. At first, it wasn't bad. Families could absorb their increasing numbers. Only after exceeding normal resources did parents start turning to the orphanage in hopes that their children would receive better care.

"Soon we had to build a second home. Three more followed in quick succession, gradually replacing a homelike atmosphere with institutional efficiency. No new workers came to help with the ever-increasing number of children. We are growing old, you see, and there are not enough of us." Tears pooled in the corners of Sister Pauline's eyes. "One worker has to take care of forty babies. Forty!" She looked at a picture of Jesus blessing the children. "Lord, forgive us." She wiped away her tears. "At least with Ceausescu and the communists gone, now they can be baptized."

Before they die. The unspoken words hung in the air like clouds pregnant with rain.

I don't want to hear any more. And I haven't even seen the children yet. At her side, Anika stirred.

"Do you want to go on?" A gentle hand brushed her arm.

I don't want to. But I have to. Slowly Carrie nodded.

"God bless." Sister Pauline's peaceful smile conveyed her meaning before Anika translated. Rising from her chair to her full height that barely reached

Carrie's shoulder, she hugged her with surprising strength. "Cristina will show you around." She pulled a bell rope.

Minutes passed. *Another opportunity to exercise patience.* Carrie took the opportunity to study the office. Floor-to-ceiling bookcases lined two walls, and pictures filled the back wall like the bulletin board at her old pediatrician's office. On her right, worn toys overflowed from a box. To the left, a thick volume that could only be a Bible lay open on a prayer bench where the varnish had worn off.

In the hall, shuffling noises indicated the arrival of their guide. A middle-aged woman shambled toward them, and Carrie guessed at her Down's syndrome before she saw the telltale eyes. *Is this who takes care of the children?*

"Cristina has lived here all her life," Anika said as if sensing Carrie's question. "We're the only family she has. She helps in the kitchen and the laundry."

Sister Pauline talked briefly with the woman and moved from behind the desk to bid them good-bye. As they headed out the door, Carrie saw her kneeling by the prayer bench.

First Cristina led them to her domain, the laundry rooms and kitchens. Her face shone with pride as she demonstrated the assembly-line efficiency of preparing one hundred bottles at once. "For the babies." She cradled her arms and rocked to make sure Carrie understood.

"Yes, very nice." Carrie's mind boggled at the prospect. *What did Sister Pauline say? One worker to forty babies? And five were too many for me at the church nursery!*

Next she led through a long corridor.

"I think she wants to show you to the nurse's office." Anika explained their next destination. "They have a modern facility. A group of French doctors donated the equipment. Dr. Reynaud visits every two months or so."

Carrie checked her watch. Noon was approaching, and her stomach was rumbling. *Where are the children?* Turning to Anika, she asked, "Can we skip it for now? I'd like to see the wards. Please."

"Of course." Anika spoke with Cristina. Turning away from the lab with slow reluctance, she hoisted a full basket and walked with a shambling gait toward the farthest building. She opened the door on a dark, musty hallway.

Silence reigned. Not a toy nor a peep hinted at the presence of children nearby. Had Cristina misunderstood the request?

"Where are the children?"

"Right here." Anika opened another door. A woman, older than Sister Pauline, sat looking through a wall-length glass partition.

She can't possibly take care of the children by herself. A nagging doubt suggested she probably did. Carrie moved to where she could see through the window.

The room stretched as long as half a football field. Beds crowded together in clusters of four. Through the thin glass, Carrie heard the faint slapping of feet on the floor. Here and there she spotted a few brave adventurers, maybe half a dozen, walking and crawling along the linoleum. Some children poked noses through the crib railings, watching the movement with unblinking gazes.

"How old are they?" Despite their small size, they didn't seem to be infants. Anika translated, and Cristina held up three fingers.

Three years old? And still crawling?

"This is Marie." Anika introduced the elderly woman. "She will you take in."

Clamor like a dynamite blast broke the silence as soon as she opened the door. Children swarmed toward Marie and Carrie. Voices desperate for a second of attention cried, "Mama! Mama!" The sister bent over as far as her clearly arthritic back would allow, touching hair and fingers.

She paused for a second by each crib, calling the children by name and bestowing kisses or smiles on their drawn faces. Here and there a scrap of cloth, a well-worn doll, added a touch of color to the white-on-white cribs. Carrie thought of the riot of spring that adorned her home church's nursery—fitted crib sheets, rail bumpers, baby animals gamboling along the walls.

New sound pounded into her consciousness. Across the room, red streaked down the peeling paint where a boy banged his head against the wall. *Autostimulation.* She gulped.

Marie slowly crossed the room, lifted the child into her arms, and hugged him for a moment before she cleaned the blood from his forehead. Carrie turned her attention away, unwilling to watch.

A girl with pretty blond curls blinked at her with crossed eyes. Out of habit, Carrie initiated a game of peekaboo. She hid her face behind her hands then snatched them away. The child looked at her with the same fixed gaze, no giggle or glimmer of a smile suggesting she enjoyed the game.

Maybe she didn't see me. Carrie leaned over the crib and tried again. The child lifted a thin arm toward Carrie, dropped it, and resumed her cross-eyed study of the ceiling.

In the next crib, a boy quietly rocked himself, thumb in mouth. He also ignored Carrie's attempts at play. *I feel invisible.* The children reminded her of an experiment she had read about. Baby chimpanzees were divided into two groups. Both groups had every physical need provided. However, adults played only with one group. The second group, without that additional social nurturing, wasted away and failed to thrive.

As thin and pale as the children were, Carrie doubted if their basic living needs were adequate. Some of them looked as emaciated as famine victims from Africa. She jumped, startled, as twig-thin fingers wrapped themselves around hers.

"Hi, Miron." Anika kissed the top of his head. "I know him. An American couple almost adopted him last year."

"Almost? What happened?" Carrie stared at his black eyes and sunken cheeks.

"He has AIDS." Anika said it as casually as if she had announced he was left-handed.

Carrie pulled her hand away as if Anika had said sulfuric acid. "AIDS?" The words stumbled out in disbelief.

"Yes." Anika sighed. "For a time, babies were given blood transfusions when they were born. Doctors thought it would make them stronger. Unfortunately, some of the blood supply was tainted. And little ones like Miron are sick."

Carrie turned on her heels, suddenly angry—at Ceausescu, for causing hurt to so many parents, at parents who could not or would not care for their own, at an orphanage that barely provided for physical needs. *I'm even angry at You, God. Why do You let these innocent ones suffer?* Shutting her senses to the children, she bolted through the door.

◆

One black eye squinted at Steve, like every baby picture he had ever seen. *He looks perfect, a miniature human being.* His nose curled a bit to one side like Sammy's did when he was born. His ears hugged the side of his face, like Lila's had. A shock of dark hair stuck out at angles from his head.

Eyes, ears, nose—all accounted for. Ten toes and fingers. *Long, pianist's fingers—like mine. "It's not fair," Brenda used to complain. "I can barely reach an octave."*

He's perfect on the outside. My son—and Lila's. Steve's heart tightened in his chest. "He's beautiful, honey," he whispered. "But he wasn't ready yet."

The problems lurked inside. Brandon's lungs couldn't draw in enough air. His heart valves hadn't completely closed. Only God knew how much brain damage had occurred during childbirth.

My son. Steve looked at Brandon, gasping for air beneath the oxygen mask. Tears welled in his eyes. He brushed them away angrily. "If only I could hold you."

"Let him go, Steve," a voice inside him urged. "He still needs his mother. Let him join her."

Tears flowed down Steve's cheeks. "Just a few more days, Lord," he begged. "Even one more day." He collapsed, weeping, beside the crib.

◆

The last day, Carrie mused as sunshine beat down on her back. *Sand, sea, and sunshine today, concert tonight, flight home tomorrow. I'm ready to leave Romania behind.* Rays strong enough to blot out the ugly memories of the hospital and of the orphanage warmed her winter-white skin. She slapped sunscreen on her exposed arms and legs and turned over.

The original two days of rest in Constanta by the Black Sea had been cut in half because of a revised tour schedule. *One day is better than none.* It came as a welcome relief after ten days of constant travel and performance. *Good times follow bad as surely as sunshine follows rain.*

What will I remember most about Romania? Those frightful first forty-eight hours or the last ten days? Already she had forgotten details, like the color of the linoleum at the hospital.

One thing was certain, Steve would never forget. He waited in Bucharest, until Brandon was strong enough to travel. If he ever would be. *Bring them both home safe and sound. And if that doesn't happen—help Steve through this terrible time.*

Flicking sand off her feet, she glanced at her watch. Two o'clock— there was time for one last dip before dressing for the concert. Currents of memories crossed her mind as she floated weightless in the warm salt water. Tim directing from the piano. Singing solo one night. Her onetime jealousy of Amy. Daily bulletins on Brandon's progress. Plans for a memorial service for Lila. Half an hour later she emerged from the water, dried off, and slipped into her sandals.

"Carrie, wait up." Kim and Amy ran toward her. "Have you heard the news?" Their faces were serious.

"No. What's happened?" *Brandon?*

"Brandon died last night."

Oh, no. Although expected, the news rocked Carrie. Every day the child clung to life, she hoped he would make it, in spite of the odds. "How sad," she managed to say. The trio walked to the hotel in silence.

After taking a shower, Carrie rummaged through her suitcase for a hairbrush. A ball of yarn rolled out. In the confusion of leaving Bucharest, Carrie had packed the partially crocheted baby sweater with her things.

The sleeve dangled from her hand, and Carrie began to cry. The same anger and helplessness she'd felt that day in the orphanage returned. No child should have to die.

At least Brandon knew his father's love. Not like those poor abandoned children.

"You could love them." A voice sounded inside her head.

Yes, but how?

"When you love them, you love Me."

God?

In her mind she saw Miron, the toddler who had AIDS, pleading with her. "Come back to Romania and help us."

Chapter 5

F ather. Thank You for these men and women who have come to
Romania to help spread the good news of Your salvation. May we work
together for Your glory. Amen."

Once again Carrie sat in the warm quiet of St. Joseph's Church listening to
Pastor Radu pray. *I'm really here. Back in Romania.* One year and college graduation
later, she had returned. New faces with new names surrounded her. A smaller
group than the Victory Singers, about twenty adults of all ages had committed to
spending two years in Bucharest on short-term missions assignments.

"Mind if I sit here? I'm a little late." A vivacious blond close to her own
age took a seat next to Carrie. "Wow. My name's Michelle, by the way."

Mute, Carrie pointed to her name tag.

". . .will help Anika and me in starting new churches here in Bucharest.
Campus ministry, Bible studies, whatever is your special area of interest and
gifts. . ."

"Wonder what I'll be doing?"

If you listen, you might find out.

"A few of you have specialized interests, which we will discuss later. But
for the next month you all must concentrate on learning the language. If
you know any of the Romance languages, you will notice similarities."

Let's see. Good morning. Buna dimineata. *My few basic phrases won't get me
very far. I know, I'll learn with the children!*

◆

"Are you sure you want to do this?" Anika asked as she drove through the city
streets. "We would love to have you stay in Bucharest with us."

"Absolutely sure. God called me, and He'll get me through any rough
spots." *I sound naive, but I believe it.*

Anticipation and apprehension built in equal measures as they turned
onto a tree-lined drive and the stately old building came into view. Anika
pounded the ancient door knocker and smiled her reassurance. Minutes
passed, and the door swung open. At least a dozen elderly women crowded
around Sister Pauline, matching smiles obliterating facial differences.

"Buna dimineata." The director stepped forward. "We've been looking
forward to your arrival." Carrie rushed into her welcoming arms.

◆

"Congratulations, Coach. Great win. What do you think of the Broncos' chances this year?" A reporter was conducting a postgame interview.

Steve glanced up from the desk where he sat planning the marching band's next performance. *I missed the end of the game.* He smiled a rueful grin. Sports hadn't always marked the passage of time in his life. That had changed, like a lot of things, since—since Lila's death sixteen months ago.

Closing his eyes against the memories, he reviewed the band's marching patterns. *Get this one right, and we'll go to the state finals. What next?* The rake rested by the door, inviting him outside to tackle the golden aspen leaves that covered the lawn faster than he could take care of them.

Lila made a game of autumn leaves, jumping in tall piles like a child. Tears welled in his eyes. *Don't think about it.* He could imagine her standing by the door, rake in hand. *Not today,* she mouthed.

No, he had avoided the next task long enough. How often had Tim and Brenda offered to help him take down the nursery and find young families who could use the furniture and baby clothes? In his heart, Steve knew that the first time he turned the knob and opened the door to painful memories, he should go alone. He couldn't delay any longer. Today he was ready.

He flicked off the television set, turned his back on the inviting Indian summer afternoon, and walked toward the nursery. Lila had dubbed the hallway leading to the bedrooms the Romero Family Hall of Fame. How his fingers had trembled when he hung the picture of last year's Victory Singers, taken before they left New York. Lila's smile from the back row seemed meant for him alone, a shared joke, as if her fingers itched to make rabbit's ears. A snapshot of Lila crocheting something was stuck in one corner. Carrie had sent the picture along with a sympathy card. Nice kid. Kind to Lila at the end.

Dust obscured the glass now. Frowning, he located the paper towel and rubbed Lila's wedding portrait clear, restoring her white satin gown to shining brightness. The picture of his parents' twenty-fifth wedding anniversary anchored the other family pictures—Tim and Brenda, graduation, Sammy from infant to schoolboy, baby Amanda.

He dabbed at a few more spots and started straightening the frames. *I'm avoiding the nursery,* he realized. *It's got to be now.* Turning his back to the wall, he pushed the doorknob.

A musty smell tickled his nose, and he sneezed. He grabbed a tissue from a full box, where Lila had placed it so many months ago. Everything was the way he remembered it. Jungle animals danced around pale yellow walls. The crib, changing table, dresser, and rocking chair echoed empty loneliness.

On top of the dresser a stack of thank-you notes waited, ready to thank people for the gifts that lined the drawers. He tugged at the top handle. Dozens of sheets and baby blankets blinked at him with pastel colors. Sleepers in neutral shades of yellow and green filled the next drawer, with a few boyish suits and frilly dresses mixed in. The clothes were destined for a pregnancy center his church supported. He reached into the drawer then withdrew his hands. *How can I tear apart the nest we built? I need Tim and Brenda's help.*

He stumbled backwards into the rocking chair. A half-finished baby afghan draped across the wicker back, white, pink, and blue weaving in unpredictable patterns. A crochet hook protruded from a ball of yarn, waiting for Lila to return. He buried his face in the soft yarn. Tears came, gentle cries as if she joined him in mourning their son. Images of Lila and Brandon lived on his heart, undimmed by the passage of time.

The sky had turned dark when the sobs stopped, and he turned tear-stained eyes around the room. There was no reason to keep the nursery as a monument to love lost. His family stayed alive where they always would, in his memory. He crossed to the windows and opened them an inch. A draft of fresh autumn air flowed through the room, sweeping out the musty past with it.

◆

A week later, the front doorbell rang. A towel-covered casserole steamed in his sister Brenda's hands. Amanda, six months old at the time of the ill-fated trip to Romania, snuggled in Tim's arms.

"How you doing, Uncle Steve?" Sammy barged in, ran to the piano, and plunked out the first few notes of "Chopsticks."

"I'm fine, partner." Steve cocked his head, listening to his nephew play. "I think you're ready to start lessons."

"Really?" He hustled after his mother into the kitchen. "Can I, Mom?" Their soft voices carried whispers into the living room.

"Reporting for duty as promised." Tim glanced down the hall and pointed at the open door. "I see you've been in."

"Yeah." Steve took a deep breath, exhaled. "Last weekend."

When Steve didn't say anything else, Tim raised his eyebrows in silent questioning.

"I've put the casserole in the oven to keep warm." Brenda and Sammy reappeared from the kitchen. "Are you ready to get started?"

Something clicked inside Steve, as if a suit of iron armor meshed into place protecting his vulnerable inner self. He managed a half smile. "Sure. That's the plan." Before his resolve failed, he forged his way down the hall.

Sammy raced ahead of him then came to an abrupt standstill in the doorway, almost causing Steve to trip. "This was your baby's room," he said in a matter-of-fact voice. "The one who died."

Brenda halted beside Steve, eyes expressing distress over Sammy's thoughtless words.

"It's okay." Steve spoke to his sister over Sammy's head then tapped him on the shoulder. "Move out of the way, partner. You're blocking the entrance."

Amanda tottered into the room behind her brother and made a beeline for a soft brown teddy bear, the duplicate of one in her own nursery. Twisting a knob in the back, she laid her head against the chest that throbbed with the sound of a mother's heartbeat like a baby hears in the womb. The stuffed animal represented Steve and Lila's two-week search through baby stores and specialty catalogs.

"Wow! I love this!" The wall panel with its brightly colored jungle animals attracted Sammy. He hunched over and lumbered across the floor, clasping his hands where they dangled from his chest. "Guess what I am!"

"An elephant?" Tim answered from the doorway.

"Yes!" Sammy slid down on all fours and started growling. Steve couldn't drag his eyes away from the pretend lion. That could have been, should have been, Brandon.

Brenda gave him a side hug and looked into his eyes. They stood with arms intertwined for a brief moment.

"Thanks for coming, Sis."

"No problem. Where are the boxes?" She opened a drawer and began arranging sheets and blankets. "Sammy, give me a hand."

He tossed in a few toys before wandering out of the room. A minute later "Chopsticks" erupted in their ears.

Amanda looked into the rapidly filling container. Her arm dangled the teddy bear over the top. "Dark." She clutched the toy against her chest.

"Put the teddy bear in the box, Amanda."

"Later." Seeing the stuffed animal in Amanda's chubby arms connected the past to the present in Steve's mind. How could he give everything away? Pretend as if Brandon had never existed?

"Steve. Give me a hand here, will you?" Tim's voice floated through the air. Metal scraped against metal, and a bolt clanked to the floor. The crib tilted precariously as Tim unscrewed a second bolt with his right hand while holding another leg to the floor with his left. Glasses perched on the end of his long nose. The tool slipped and knocked his fingers. "Ouch."

Still all thumbs, except at the piano. A laugh rose to Steve's lips until he shushed it, ashamed at finding humor in Tim's awkward attempts to help. What would Lila think of this endeavor? During her pregnancy, exasperated, she had chased both men out and assembled the crib herself.

Once again Amanda tucked the teddy bear in the box and snatched it back. Music from the piano had switched to "Twinkle, Twinkle Little Star."

Steve looked around the room. Brenda had already emptied two drawers. A futon with plaid cushions waited in an opened box, ready to assemble and replace the partially dismantled crib. A sense of wrong washed over Steve. This room was perfect for a child. *I can't change it to a guest room. Not yet.*

"Ouch!" Tim exclaimed once more. "Help me, Steve."

Stop. "Stop!" Three pairs of eyes swung to stare at him, and Steve realized he must have shouted. "No more tonight."

The screwdriver slipped from Tim's hand, and Brenda folded the flaps of the box before standing up straight. "Well, I guess it is time to check on supper," she said uncertainly and walked out the door. Tim looked at him over the top of his glasses, shrugged, and left.

Mixed feelings whirled around Steve's heart as the room emptied. Amanda tugged at his hand. He looked down into her trusting eyes. *How can I explain to her parents?*

Over bubbly macaroni and cheese, he tried. "I'd like to use the room the way it is." He struggled to explain his sudden reluctance to follow through on dismantling the nursery. "Like when Sammy or Amanda comes to visit." He forked a mouthful of casserole into his mouth and chewed for a minute. "Or even having a child live here."

"A foster child," Brenda said, spooning out more macaroni. "I bet you'd make a good foster parent, with your experience with kids."

"Or even—adoption." The word slipped out but surprised Steve when it felt comfortable and familiar.

"Adoption?" Brenda's voice sliced sharp with incredulity. Steve could almost hear her thoughts. *He's on the rebound. Trying to find what he's lost.*

"Don't worry, Sis. I'm not rushing into anything." He gulped down some milk. "Only, taking apart the nursery kind of feels like Abraham sacrificing Isaac, if you know what I mean. It's like God stayed my hand and stopped me from doing anything with the baby's things." He swallowed past the lump in his throat. *Not just a baby—Brandon!* "And I need to wait and see how God will provide."

"Hear, hear!" Tim struck a note with his fork and raised his hands like he was conducting a choir. "Let's toast the future!" As their glasses clinked together, he added, "And when you figure out what you want to do, we'll be there to help."

Adoption grew in Steve's mind, blossoming as quickly as a dandelion in spring and threatening to die as fast. When he contacted a local law firm, the attorney counseled against trying.

"There are few infants available for adoption. As for older children—most agencies prefer placing children with parents of the same race. That eliminates many of them as well." The sad frown the lawyer assumed melted into an almost-greedy smile when he added, "Unless you know a birth mother who wants to give up her child. . . ?" When Steve shook his head in the negative, the lawyer handed him a schedule of expected costs for private adoption. Steve tried to hide his shock. *The fees shouldn't surprise me, but they do.*

He tried Social Services next. Some foster parents he knew had adopted children they had raised since birth. It was early November before a caseworker could arrange for a home evaluation.

Late one afternoon a middle-aged woman with straight, streaked-blond hair knocked on his door. "Hello, I'm Susan Stewart from Denver Social Services. I believe you're expecting me?"

He invited her in. Probing blue eyes swept over him, as if assessing his fitness for parenthood. Steve repressed a defensive reaction. *I want to get on her good side.*

She padded in soft-soled shoes through the house. In the living room she dived for the electrical outlets. "You will childproof, of course. Cover unused outlets." Steve nodded, thinking of the way Tim and Brenda had combed their house for danger points.

In the kitchen she turned on a burner. "Gas stove, I see."

I'll get electric if it's safer.

She turned on the faucets in the bathroom and poked her head in linen closets and Steve's bedroom before entering the nursery. For the first time a hint of a smile lightened her serious face. "What a lovely room for a baby."

A compliment. Steve's heartbeat began to accelerate before she continued. "But many children who need foster care are older, already in school. Most have a history of abuse and neglect and subsequent behavior problems."

"I know. Some of my band students live in foster homes." The words came out before Steve could bite back the defensive reaction.

"Ah, yes. I remember." The assessing tone of her voice unnerved Steve. "You're a high school music teacher." She flicked off the light switch. "I've seen all I need to. Let's go out to the living room. To talk."

"Can I get you something to drink?" Steve hunted for something to postpone the upcoming interview. "I can brew some coffee. Or would you prefer tea?"

"Nothing for me. Thank you." She sat down on the couch and snapped open a briefcase. "Mr. Romero. Relax. I promise I won't bite."

Her well-controlled voice might defuse tense situations, but it set Steve's teeth on edge. He poured himself a glass of tea, took a sip, and licked his lips. Settling in an easy chair, he motioned for the caseworker to begin. "Okay. Let's get started."

The questioning probed everything and overlooked nothing. The detailed financial worksheet made Steve wonder how he expected to support himself in retirement, let alone provide for someone else. Who would care for a child while he worked? How long had he been teaching? What about band trips?

Although expected, the questions regarding marriage disturbed Steve. *She knows my wife is dead.* Nowadays, the marital status box for "widowed" leaped off any application. *Why make me explain?*

"What about marriage? Family?" She repeated.

"My wife died while we were in Romania last year."

"And the nursery?" she persisted.

Steve borrowed her detached manner for a patient answer. "Lila was pregnant at the time. She died giving birth to our son, and he died ten days later."

She looked up from her notes. "I'm sorry." She wrote a few more words. "I must ask you. Are you involved in any serious relationships at present?"

He shook his head mutely.

The questions continued. What experience did he have with children? What methods of discipline did he advocate? What about religion?

She scribbled some final notes and locked her briefcase with a snap. "That's all for now. The department will be in touch."

"When?" Worry and longing filled his voice. Steve's efforts at mirroring her disinterested manner failed him in the end.

"In a few weeks." When they parted at the door, Steve couldn't read any indication either way.

Early in December, the phone rang. "Mr. Romero, this is Susan Stewart. The caseworker from Social Services."

"Yes?" Steve's mouth went dry.

"I wanted to tell you myself." Her voice held more warmth than she had demonstrated during the entire interview.

Steve steeled himself. *Either way, God is in control.*

"Your application was given serious consideration, but in the end it was turned down."

A coldness stole into Steve's heart. "What was the problem? Is there anything I can do?"

"I'm afraid not." After a brief silence, she continued. "I probably shouldn't be telling you this. You would be an excellent candidate if you were married. Or if you weren't so involved with your church."

Knowing he was fighting a rearguard action, Steve protested weakly. "But there are single foster parents."

"Yes."

"So the big problem is church?"

"Try to understand. The rights of birth parents come first, and the department has had problems when foster parents have a strong faith." Again her voice offered warmth. "Imagine if you can that a family of practicing Muslims was caring for your child."

Steve mumbled something, he wasn't sure what. What did one say when one's hopes were disappointed—again? Some of his friends would call this religious persecution.

"Mr. Romero. . ." He tuned out her attempt to end a difficult phone call until he heard ". . .foreign adoption?"

"What's that?" *I sound lame.* "I'm sorry. What did you say?"

"I asked if you have considered foreign adoption. The requirements may be less strict."

Foreign? As in Korean? Romanian? "No, I haven't. But I might be interested." *Are you crazy, Steve?*

"I'll send you a list of agencies that specialize in overseas adoption, if you like."

"Yes. Please."

"I'll put it in the mail tomorrow, then. God bless." The phone clicked in Steve's ear.

Not uncaring—just professional, Steve realized.

Romania? Maybe. Romania? Yes! God had opened the next door for him to explore.

◆

About a week before Christmas, Steve answered a ringing phone.

"You might want to sit down, Mr. Romero." Somehow the smile transmitted over telephone wires. Excitement built in Steve's heart and tingled to his fingertips, where the earphone trembled in his hand. He stood frozen in place, waiting for the announcement.

"Do you have a current passport?"

Passport? Romania! Sweat poured down his arms, and the phone slipped in his hand.

"Ah, yes. Does this mean—?"

"Congratulations! Your application has been approved! How soon can you fly to Bucharest?"

Chapter 6

So many women clustered around Carrie, introducing themselves, that she quickly gave up hope of remembering their names. One by one they returned to their duties, leaving her with the director and Cristina, the woman with Down's syndrome.

Carrie followed them inside. The door closed, shutting out sunshine and ties with America. The place loomed larger and gloomier than she remembered. *I thought it would be like my college dorm. But it's not.*

"I'm glad you're here." Sister Pauline added her welcome while she paused at the door to her office. "Cristina will take you to your room. After you've settled in, meet me here so that we can discuss your future."

Smiling widely, Cristina escorted Carrie to the end of the hall and opened the door. "Here is your room. I helped get it ready for you."

Sunshine slanted through transparent curtains, bouncing off a gleaming wooden floor. Simple cotton covers adorned the thin mattress. She was pleased to see a sink in the corner. Suddenly she felt grimy all over and hoped to freshen up before her visit with Sister Pauline.

"Thanks. It's lovely." Carrie spoke in what she hoped was a tone of dismissal to the lingering Cristina.

"Can I help you unpack?"

Carrie shook her head in the negative.

"I will wait and bring you back to Sister."

"No, really, I'm fine." Desperate for a moment alone in her new surroundings, Carrie spoke more sharply than she intended. Cristina's smile faltered.

Impatient already. "Thanks for all your help. Maybe I'll see you at supper?"

"*Jah,* that would be good." Smile restored, Cristina left the room, shutting the door gently behind her.

Carrie walked to the sink and turned on the tap. Cupping her hands under the lukewarm water, she splashed water on her hot neck. Unpacking took only a few minutes. It was time to brave the lion's den. After she said a brief prayer, she strode down the hallway and knocked on the office door.

"Please come in. Sit down."

Awkwardness as strong as her first day at freshman initiation came over Carrie. *What if she doesn't like me?* She sat down on the chair, slamming her knees together to keep them from knocking.

"Carrie Randolph from Pennsylvania. How wonderful that God has brought you here."

All of Carrie's doubts dropped away as she looked into Sister Pauline's peaceful, hopeful eyes. The director outlined the schedule for the next few days.

"We keep to a routine here, and we will expect you to do the same. We meet for prayer at 6:30 a.m. and 10:00 at night, except for the sisters on duty on the wards. Meals at 7:30, 12:00, and 7:00. Cristina does the staff laundry each Monday—leave your clothes in the hallway."

Carrie nodded her head impatiently. "Okay. Where will I be working?"

The sister smiled faintly. "I think it would be best for you to choose a small group of children—four, five at most—to work with."

"No." Carrie wasn't sure if she actually said the word. She rebelled at the thought. "I thought I might be spelling the ward sisters, you know, working with all the children."

Pauline bowed her head as if in prayer then dipped her chin in a gentle assent. "Very well. We will set up a rotation system for you to work this week. Next Monday we will see how things are going."

A few days later, Carrie didn't hear any alarm until the chapel bell pealed, calling her to morning prayers. Her muscles cramped in pain as she scrambled out of bed and into a short-sleeved shirt and jeans. The top went on the wrong way, and she wasted precious moments shifting it around. She flew down the stairs to the chapel and slipped into the back pew.

Upon her arrival, an almost audible sigh of relief rippled across the room. At times like this she felt a bit like Maria von Trapp, perpetually late, a likable troublemaker. The sisters welcomed her with open arms but didn't quite know what to do with her.

She wanted to fit in, to give aid, not require it. God knew she had tried. For five days she had run from ward to ward, ferrying bottles and laundry, changing diapers, walking with two or three howling babies, names unknown, in her arms. Every muscle ached with fatigue.

As she scurried about, she caught the director watching her at times. It made her uneasy, like when her music teachers coaxed and listened, waiting for something to happen. Finally the melody would sing out loud and clear, and they would smile in satisfaction. If only she knew what Sister Pauline was looking for!

On Monday she met with the director for a second time. They went back through each ward on every floor in all five buildings. Sister Pauline stopped periodically to prop up a milk bottle or to tug a blanket over a sleeping form. When they reached the end of the row, one child howled, starting a chain reaction in which all two dozen infants cried.

The sound caught Carrie as effectively as a trap, immobilizing her in place.

"Let's go. Leave the sister to take care of them." Pauline touched her arm and led her through the door. Outside the soundproof walls, away from the mesmerizing noise, Carrie broke out of her trance, and unbidden tears cascaded down her face.

"They're so demanding! And I feel so inadequate." Carrie wanted to storm back into the nursery and gather every crying child into her arms.

"Come with me to the chapel." Sister Pauline gently steered the weeping Carrie away from the wards.

They sat side by side in the pew. Clasping Carrie's trembling hands between her own gnarled fingers, Sister Pauline reminded her, "When our Lord was here on this earth, He chose to pour His life into twelve men only—and they were adults! You would be wise to follow His example." *That's what she meant—*

"Children require individual attention in order to thrive. You are only one person. Choose a small group of four or five. Ask God to show you which ones."

Carrie slowly nodded in understanding and agreement. "But how can I choose? They're all so needy!"

"Pray," Pauline reminded her. "Our Lord spent the night in prayer before He chose the twelve apostles. He will show you."

Prayer again. How about something practical?

"You seem impatient with the time we spend in prayer."

She knows me already. Carrie thought guiltily of all her late arrivals at the required chapel hours.

"We find that the busier we are, the more we need to pray. The chapel is always open, for any time you need to seek God's face." She gestured for Carrie to join her at the kneeling bench. "You will find your answers, and strength, here."

For the next week Carrie haunted the wards by day and knelt for hours at night. After seven days, she had decided. All five slept in the toddler ward in the building that she visited on her trip a year ago: sweet Jenica, cranky Octavia, active Adrian, puttering Ion. And first of all, dearest of all, Viktor, who sang himself to sleep in his crib.

◆

Her breath formed warm rings that floated through the frosty air as she walked to the toddler ward. It was time to begin the morning-long effort of going to market.

At the top of the stairs, Sister Marie waited, chin nodding against her chest. She willingly took the night shift, love enabling her to climb up and down the steep stairs.

Carrie pressed her foot against the top step. It squeaked as she expected, and Marie lifted up her head in greeting.

"Good morning!" Carrie started sorting the clothes that lay in a jumbled heap on the floor of the communal closet. Marie unbent her body with care and fumbled through the key ring with her bent fingers.

"How are the children?" Carrie located enough shirts, pants, and socks for everyone, and even an extra sweater for Ion. Shoes and coats were another matter.

"Ion's cough is a little worse, I'm afraid. Praise God, no fever."

Oh, Lord, please, make him well! She extracted the key from Marie's hand and, drawing a deep breath, unlocked the door.

Finding herself the mother of quintuplets at age twenty-two challenged Carrie to the limit. They were her constant companions. She fed, bathed, and dressed them, and somehow found time to play with them. Most of all they needed to be around people.

Dozens of voices cried, "Mama." Steeling her nerves, Carrie hustled through the room to where Jenica waited, silently watching. When Carrie neared her crib, the girl lifted her arms expectantly. Carrie's heart twisted. *This is why I'm here. So they can learn to love, to trust.* Moments like this made up for the long hours.

A few beds further on Adrian tugged furiously at his sock. *Always taking it on or off.* Not many of the children made an effort at dressing themselves.

A frowning Octavia waited in her usual spot in the middle of her crib, as if daring Carrie to reach her. Smothering a sigh, she called a cheerful greeting. "Good morning, Octavia." Stretching, Carrie latched on to the child with arms of steel. *Ion next.*

She could pick out Ion's cough from that of the other chronically sick children. *Marie is right; it's worse than last night.* It was discouraging. He needed medical care, but Dr. Reynaud wouldn't return for six more weeks. Hot compresses and tea with lemon and honey only did so much good. Why use the home's limited supplies when he wasn't getting better? A warm, dry room to sleep in would probably make a big difference. He spent most nights soaking wet. Carrie powdered his bare bottom and pinned a stiff new diaper in place. No disposable diapers here!

Carrie could always locate Viktor by his humming—snatches of Romanian folk songs, church music, tunes he made up himself. "Where is Viktor? Where is Viktor? Here he is!" She sang to the tune of "Frère Jacques" as she approached his crib. Soon he joined the others on the floor next to her.

After breakfast they were ready to go to market. The trip, easy by bicycle, involved an unpleasant trek over frozen mud by foot. Although Carrie used the bike in emergencies, most of the time she walked so that the children could go with her. She wanted them to have as much stimulation as possible—fresh air, new sounds, sights, colors. Besides, she enjoyed their company.

They padded silently alongside her, rarely speaking, even though child development charts said children their age should have a fairly extensive vocabulary. Not for the first time she wondered, *Do they even know how to speak?* Along the road she looked for things they might recognize and chattered the way she did with babies.

"Look! There's a sparrow! The tree has lost its leaves. It looks so sad. The squirrel must be looking for the nuts he hid away last fall."

"Cat," Jenica called out.

Yes! A scrawny tiger cat sat on a fence post watching their progress. "Here, kitty, kitty." The animal looked warily at the children then allowed Carrie to pick it up. Curling up in Carrie's hands, it licked her fingers and began purring with a loud, contented sound.

Carrie held Jenica's fingers to the kitten's throat so that she could feel the vibrating purr that shook the small body.

"Me next!" Not satisfied with fingers only, Viktor laid his ear next to the cat's neck and tried to mimic the sound. A small scuffle ensued as each child wanted a chance to pet the kitten. *Yes!* Carrie breathed a short prayer of thanksgiving. God had given them something that broke through their unnerving silence.

The sun began edging its way to the zenith of the sky, and reluctantly Carrie headed toward the market. *We'll be late for lunch if we don't get moving.*

First they stopped at the vegetable vendor's stand. "Feel this one. It's a good, firm one." Carrie picked through the potatoes, letting the children push and prod the spuds with her.

"Why don't you leave those stupid children at the orphanage? Then you and me, we could have some fun." The vendor, a heavy man she had heard was a widower with seven children, teased her.

"They aren't stupid!" Of all the customs that were different than ones in the States, calling children stupid because they had been abandoned bothered her the most.

"I know. They are the future!" He pointed at Viktor. "This one here you think will be a great musician!" Gesturing at Adrian, he said, "And this one, he will compete in the Olympic games! Pah!" He spat. "I still say they're stupid."

Forcing herself to ignore his gibes, she handed over the correct number of *lei*, the Romanian currency, and went to the next booth. With five children trailing behind her, she felt a bit like the Pied Piper, leading them with her songs and storytelling.

What I wouldn't give for a supermarket. Never again would she complain about lines. An hour passed, and each child carried a light bag as they trudged back to the orphanage for the noon meal.

After lunch—an hour and a half marathon that ended with folding clean sheets on Ion's bed and tucking each child in for a nap—Carrie headed to her room. During her afternoon free time, she hoped to finish one mitten, maybe a pair. Cold weather was a powerful motivator to practice crocheting! *I'm forgetting something.* She considered briefly but couldn't place the worry. Under her fingers, a bright yellow mitten cuff began to grow. Funny how Lila had sparked her interest in the craft. *I wonder how Steve is doing these days?*

"Carrie?" Sister Pauline called at her door.

"Come in." As Carrie stood up, a ball of yarn rolled out of her lap onto the floor. She stuffed it under her unmade bed covers.

The director ignored the bed and addressed Carrie. "I wondered if you wanted to come with me to say good-bye to Irina."

How could I forget? Irina was the blond toddler with crossed eyes that Carrie met on her first trip to the home.

"Of course." In short order Carrie shrugged on her downy ski jacket, hat, and mittens, and followed Sister Pauline down the hallway.

The sisters often asked Carrie to escort visiting Americans and Britons around the wards, a duty she usually enjoyed. Today was different, though. David and Donna Johnson were taking little Irina to their home in Cleveland, Ohio. The last papers had been signed and permission granted for them to take their new daughter home.

I won't see Irina anymore. The thought stabbed into Carrie, and she crossed her arms across her chest as if to keep out the impending loss.

"This day may come for one of your children, as well. I pray that it does." Sister Pauline, sensitive as always, somehow knew what Carrie was thinking.

"That would be wonderful for the children! Especially poor Ion." She meant it. Of course she did.

"I am praying for you that when that day comes, our Lord will give you grace to let them go." Sister Pauline laid a hand on Carrie's arm and halted their progress for a minute. "Loving comes with a price. It cost our Lord His life. But even though it will be painful to see your beloved children leave, He will see you through."

They exited the building. Donna held Irina in her arms. The couple's overabundant happiness more than made up for the child's bewildered silence. David kissed the top of her head. "Soon you'll be home with us. Your new grandparents can't wait to meet you." He spoke in English. *How will Irina manage? She barely speaks Romanian.*

Unexpected tears slid down Carrie's cheeks. "God bless you, Irina," she said in Romanian and kissed the girl's cool cheek. "Take good care of her, won't you?" she added in English.

David smiled his agreement, overjoyed and confident about what he was doing. Feeling her own heart wrench, Carrie better understood the parents who wouldn't agree to adoption, even though they knew it might be best for their child.

Soon Donna buckled Irina in a back car seat where she squirmed against the uncomfortable restraint. David dug through the bag with her few personal items, removed her security blanket, a worn scarf, and returned the rest to Sister Pauline.

"Keep them. Perhaps other children can use them."

They waved good-bye as the car spun out of the yard. The sisters returned to their tasks, and for the moment Carrie stood alone in the yard.

"Good-bye, Irina," The words seemed to hang in the air, frozen, and then float away with the departing car. She walked briskly back to the dorm. Thank goodness tomorrow was her free day. A good dose of big-city comforts and American companionship should cure her blues.

◆

"There's an American staying with Radu and Anika." From the tone of Michelle's voice, her romantic antennae were quivering.

"Oh? Tell me about him." Carrie stirred her coffee, basking in the deliciously warm American superstore in downtown Bucharest.

"He's so good-looking, with a touch of melancholy. Makes you want to cheer him up." Michelle's eyes blinked in surprise. "I didn't tell you their guest was a man!"

"I guessed right, though, didn't I?" Carrie grinned. During language study the previous summer, she and Michelle fell into an easy friendship. Immersed most of the time in a foreign culture, they welcomed the opportunity to meet together once a week and act like giddy American ingenues. Michelle was an incurable romantic, weaving fantasies about every man who caught her eye.

"What happened to that taxi driver? Anka, wasn't that his name?" Carrie asked.

"Oh, him." Michelle's cheeks dimpled. "It turns out he's engaged. He invited me to his wedding! How about you? Have you met anyone?" Michelle was a determined matchmaker.

"Well, there's Paul the potato vendor—"

"Oh?"

"He's single, and he has lovely wavy hair—"

"Why haven't you told me about him before?"

"—that's snow white. He must be at least sixty years old, with two dozen grandchildren!"

Michelle tossed a lettuce leaf on Carrie's plate.

"Seriously, how could I meet a single man at a Romanian orphanage?"

"It could happen. You do get visitors at the home, like that Dr. Reynaud you rave about. Is he single?"

A clock chimed in the distance before Carrie could voice her indignant reply. "Goodness, it's late. I suppose we should get started with the Christmas shopping." Michelle scraped her fork over the plate one more time, seeking out the last pastry crumb.

"I sent presents home a month ago," Carrie said as she perused her list. "Today I'm looking for gifts for my group. Dolls, soccer balls. Those should be easy. But where can I find a child's tool set? Or a recorder?"

"Tape recorder? Don't you think that's kind of extravagant?"

"No, a recorder. You know, the flute-thing children play in school as a first instrument. For—"

"Viktor. Your favorite." Before Carrie could deny the observation, Michelle swept on. "I know just the place to look."

Carrie folded the paper and tucked it back in her purse. "It's funny. I bought Romanian-made items for my family in Pennsylvania. Now all I can think of for the children are things I enjoyed as a child in America!" She drained her coffee cup. "Let's go."

It's such a very American store. Carrie sighed with pleasure. A fifteen-foot tall tree, adorned with red, blue, and yellow balls and metallic garlands, towered over the escalators. Miniature lights alternated with neon Santas on wires strung between every pillar and along every counter.

Rolls of colorful foil beckoned to Carrie. She pulled out three long packages, one each of blue, gold, and green.

"Red for me." Michelle made her selection.

"I can't wait to see the children rip their presents open." Carrie's forehead wrinkled. "Does this stuff tear easily? I don't remember." Glancing around furtively, she yanked at the edge of one roll. A piece came off in her hand. The friends smiled at each other with a hint of mischievous guilt.

Carrie shopped for the girls first. Even after excluding English-speaking dolls and ones that needed batteries, there were so many to choose from. She settled on a doll that changed facial expressions for Octavia and a simple baby with bottle for Jenica.

The store stocked a wide variety of soccer equipment, with a smattering of other sports. Carrie ignored the ads that announced, "The ball that won the World Cup!" and poked through the children's balls. Did a lower number mean it was bigger or smaller? She found one in the smallest size for Adrian.

"Why not a football?" Michelle suggested.

"It *is* a football. European football." Carrie stated the obvious. "Adrian is a Romanian, after all. Soccer gives him a way to connect with other kids." She paid for her purchases and stuffed them in a voluminous shopping bag. "Where did you think I could find a recorder?"

"A store about two blocks from here carries them." They walked down the street. "Why are you spending so much on toys?" Michelle asked abruptly. "With all their other needs—"

"Mom's missions society took on the entire ward as a Christmas project. You've never seen so many afghans and quilts and coats and sweaters. Knitting needles working overtime. So the practical presents were taken care of." Looking down at the packages in her hand, she said, "I guess I always go overboard for Christmas. Only I want the children to have some fun. I bet they've never had any toys."

"Poor kids!" Michelle's admiration was genuine. "I don't think I could stand working in the home."

"And I couldn't do what you do. Knocking on doors and waiting for people to show up at a Bible study." Carrie hugged her friend.

By the time they had purchased the remaining presents, a church clock was chiming four o'clock, time to catch the bus back to the home. A few minutes later, the vehicle jerked to a stop on the street, and Carrie climbed aboard. "See you next week!" she called through the closing doors.

◆

"You will like the director," Anika told Steve as they headed for the orphanage. "She is a sweet saint of God."

"But all is not sweetness at the children's home," Radu interjected. "I hear the American news has reported on our orphans?" The statement ended like a question.

Steve nodded his assent. "The situation sounded grim." He didn't elaborate.

"The situation is sad. But God is at work." A peaceful smile lit Radu's face. "He has used those reports to bring many foreigners to our country to adopt the children. Good from evil. Like your own tragedy." He never minced words.

The sting of the words couldn't penetrate Steve's excitement. "I can't wait. Ever since the idea of adoption occurred to me, I've been hungry for a child to call my own. After what happened here—" Momentarily his voice faltered. "Romania was one of the first places I thought of."

"And this afternoon you may find your answer. Here we are."

A few minutes later they were settled in the office. Introductions made, Steve shifted in his chair while an elderly woman studied his papers. "Your wife died?" Radu translated.

"Yes." Her eyes continued to question him, and he didn't mind elaborating. "She died giving birth to our son. He died a few days later." How could he explain his desire to adopt? "When the grief had passed, I realized I still wanted to be a father."

"You are a good man, Mr. Romero. Perhaps God has the child you seek here." Her smile radiated from the inside out.

Someone knocked at the door.

"Here is the person who will take you through the wards."

Crying baby in arms, Lila's image appeared, flickered, and reshaped into her look-alike.

"Carrie! What on earth are you doing here?"

Chapter 7

Steve?" Carrie's dumbfounded expression probably matched his own. "You're the American Michelle was telling me about!"

Why didn't Radu warn me?

Sister Pauline appeared to be asking for explanations. Radu spread his hands and gestured to the two young people. An expression full of understanding, then compassion, crossed the director's face.

"I'm on a short-term volunteer assignment," Carrie explained. "I've been here since I graduated from college in June." She shifted the child to her other arm. "And you? How have you been? Are you really thinking about adopting?"

Steve couldn't look at Carrie without remembering the night at the hospital. He swallowed back the tears that threatened and found his voice. "Yeah, I am. I understand you're going to show me around."

"Sure."

Any further dialogue was cut off by the arrival of one of the staff, a middle-aged woman with a placid face. Carrie handed over the now-sleeping child with apparent reluctance and motioned for Steve to follow her.

"Is he all right? The kid you were holding?" *Focus on the present. Don't talk about the past.*

"Ion? He has a terrible cold, can't sleep for coughing. They don't like me to walk with him, though. I guess I'm a softie." She folded her face in a self-deprecating grin. "Are you interested in any particular age group? The toddlers are taking their afternoon naps—"

"How about babies, then?"

Carrie nodded and led him to the second building. "Have you been to any other children's homes?"

Steve shook his head. "Radu and Anika brought me here first, since they know Sister Pauline."

"It's pretty grim." She paused at the door.

"I've heard." Suddenly the surroundings dropped away. His future lay in one of these buildings, and he was impatient with further delay. Hand on knob, he swung the door wide open.

The atmosphere of the room hit him like fog. The stench of urine, strong enough to bleach an army of uniforms, caused him to retch, a brief dry heave. Babies' cries born of discomfort, hunger, and loneliness streaked through the air, with no one seeming to hear or respond. His breath blew rings in the air, and he became aware of the coldness seeping up his coat sleeves. Carrie came in behind him and closed the door.

A thin woman walked toward them, exhaustion and disinterest showing in every step. Steam rose from a stinking bucket she held by one hand. Carrie called out a greeting. The woman waved thanks as she veered away toward the bathroom.

"Ready?" Carrie was already moving in the direction of the cribs, as if she didn't notice the assault on the senses.

C'mon, Steve, you're not going to let a little stink get you down! Okay, a big stink. Mentally pinching his nose, Steve followed along.

Carrie knew each child's name and often added a piece of personal information. "John—just arrived here a month ago." She tweaked a blanket over the sleeping form. "Ana's been here since she was born, but her mother won't give permission for adoption." Some of the babies were even tinier than he remembered Brandon to be. How did they survive? Did he want to adopt a child with obvious physical problems?

At his side, Carrie paused occasionally, as if waiting for him to express interest, ask questions. He noticed she was wearing only a thin sweater, and he shivered on her behalf. He started to offer her his coat then checked himself. The cold didn't seem to bother her. But what about the children? Coughing and sneezing punctuated the raucous cries.

The constant noise and oppressive odor combined the worst aspects of nursery duty at church. *Maybe I'm not cut out for this. At least not with a baby.* He found himself hurrying past the cribs, not really paying attention to Carrie. Doubts wrinkled his heart.

An hour later—or was it two?—they walked out into the sunshine. Steve gulped down the fresh air, not minding the cold burning his throat. *God, why did you bring me here?* He felt much like Samuel when he visited in Jesse's home. Is this the one? Not yet.

A strangely familiar, featherlight touch landed on his arm. It felt natural. "Are you all right?"

He breathed deeply. "I think so." *Exhale breath on a slow ten count.* "How do you stand it?"

"You get used to it." He noticed that she had pulled on a jacket. "You have to. What next? There's another nursery in the next building."

"No!" The word exploded out of his mouth. "Are the toddlers awake yet?"

"Sure." They walked past the stark high-rise.

"Back there, you were wondering how the children survive."

How did she know?

"A lot of them do die." Tears underlined her words. "But Sister Pauline says the question isn't why do so many die? Instead, we should ask, how do so many live? And thank God." Compassionate pain filled her grimace.

"I try to hold on to that."

The last building came into view, and her walk sped into a skip. "The toddlers. My favorites." A genuine, full-hearted grin lit her face this time. She flung open the door and scampered up a flight of stairs before he had taken the first step.

"*Buna dimineata!*" a quavery voice welcomed Carrie in a way that indicated a close friendship.

"Come on," Carrie urged him. "Most of them are awake." To judge by her enthusiasm, this room should be as cheerful as his home church's nursery. To him it looked just as dreary, if not quite as smelly, as the infants' room.

"Mama!" several voices called out, and Carrie darted around the room, lifting out first one child then another. Soon four children, two boys and two girls, crowded around her feet, and the same boy she had sent to bed earlier curled against her shoulder.

Carrie bounced back to Steve, children dragging at her heels. "Hope you don't mind the gang. They go wherever I go." She must have sensed his bewilderment.

"This is my group. Let me introduce you." She rattled off a string of Romanian words, of which he only recognized his name.

"You've already met Ion." The child stared dumbly at Steve, thumb stuck in his mouth. "And this is Jenica. Octavia. Adrian." She caressed each one on the head as she introduced them.

"And Viktor." Was it just his imagination, or did her voice have an extra lift?

The children clustered around Carrie, pushing each other for a chance to hold on to her jean leg. They reminded Steve of Amanda and Sammy vying for his attention, and he relaxed. They were only children, after all, and hopefully God would show him which one soon.

A low musical humming played with Steve's ears, a familiar Victory Singers number. It didn't sound like Carrie. "Who's singing?"

"Oh!" Her smile had all the pride of the parents of his band students. "That's Viktor. He loves music."

The singing stopped at Steve's glance, and something tugged at his heart. He crouched down and rocked on his heels so he could look the boy in the eye.

"That's one of my favorite songs, too." Steve hummed through the introduction, the intricate chords echoing in his head, and started singing the first verse. Viktor's eyes widened as if in surprise, and his body swayed to the strong beat. Steve grasped his hands and clapped them together in time to the music when he reached the chorus.

"Sing it, Viktor!" Carrie's voice intruded. Legs dancing a jaunty two-step, she whirled around the man and child, and her voice rose high above Steve's bass, a spontaneous descant.

Viktor laughed, delighted, and shouted what was probably the one recognizable word in the song—victory!—and pointed to himself. "Viktor."

This is the one. Months of longing and searching faded, replaced by certainty and joy.

The music died away, and once again the dingy, cold room forced itself into Steve's consciousness. A dozen children stared curiously at their outburst.

"That was fun!" Carrie's eyes danced with lively merriment.

Steve smiled in return, a smile he couldn't contain. *I've found my son!* As suddenly as thunder follows lightning, his decision was made.

Ahead of him, Carrie circled around the back of the room, singing nursery rhymes with the children. *She's like their mother. If I adopt Viktor, will she be pleased—or sad?* The room darkened, and outside the windows, dusk staked its claim over daylight. The thought of causing Carrie sadness pained his heart. *Don't be too hasty.* "It's time for me to go," Steve said, regret tingeing his voice.

"But you've only met half the children." Nosy excitement written on her face, she asked, "Or do you already have someone in mind? Who—?" She paused in midsentence. "I'm sorry. It's none of my business. But you could do worse than to choose one of these angels."

"I've seen enough for today." He hedged. "It's five o'clock. Radu and Anika will be waiting for me."

Carrie escorted Steve downstairs, children trailing behind. "Can you find your way back from here? If you don't mind waiting, I'll take you." She gestured at the children. "Putting on coats is a half-hour process."

"That's all right." They stared at each other for a long moment, Steve once again sensing the shadows of Lila's beloved face in Carrie's features. Spending two years in a Romanian orphanage was the sort of thing Lila might have done. A nearly buried pang of grief hit his heart. He needed to leave, but he couldn't tear himself away.

"I'm glad you're doing this." The words blurted out of Carrie's mouth. "Lila told me you'd make a terrific father."

Lila. Her image hung between them, Carrie but a pale imitation. Would he ever look at another woman without comparing her to his wife? "Thanks."

"I guess this is it, then." Octavia made a small cry, and Carrie patted her head. "It's their supper time."

"I'll be back." He needed a day or two to weigh his decision to adopt Viktor. "After Christmas, maybe."

"I'd like that." She smiled and turned in the direction of the smell of greasy food cooking.

The outside door swung open. "Carrie!" Anika's warm voice echoed in the entryway. "I'm glad I found you."

Carrie paused. Her shoulders sagged a quarter of an inch, and Steve realized how tired she must be.

"I want you and the children to join us for Christmas." Anika's oval face beamed, as if she were offering a priceless gift.

"But—it's not my day off. I'm needed here—"

"Sister Pauline agreed you could come."

"Well, then!" Carrie grinned. "I'd love to." Two of the children started to whimper. "I'm sorry, I must go. Bye for now!"

◆

Back at the small apartment, Steve and Anika shifted papers in an attempt to create a play space for the children. "I wish we could take them to the park. That would be perfect. But it's too cold," Anika fretted.

Steve shivered inside his thick sweater. The apartment wasn't warm, although compared to the children's home it felt like a desert.

Anika hummed to herself as she worked, cheerful songs that Steve guessed were Christmas carols. His suspicion was confirmed when he recognized the tune of "Silent Night," sung with unfamiliar words. He joined her, singing in English until the last note died away. What else might they both know? "O Come All Ye Faithful"? Soon they were singing an impromptu duet. Every tribe and tongue and nation—the words hit Steve afresh.

How could a baby born in a borrowed stable halfway around the globe be the Lord and Savior of the world? God's plans often didn't make sense. Like Lila's death?

Steve shook away the disquieting thought, only to have it followed by another idea. A red cord of love led from Lila and Brandon's death to the here and now—to Romania. To seeing Carrie again. To Viktor. The message of the incarnation—God came to the world to give beauty for ashes, the oil of gladness instead of mourning.

"Joy to the world!" Steve's voice rang out afresh, rejoicing in God's ultimate gift to the world—His only Son. Soon boxes were stacked and floor space cleared, awaiting their small guests on the following day.

That night Steve slept fitfully in the front sitting room. With the heat turned off for the night, cold permeated his bones and even the thick covers did not hold sufficient body warmth. What would Christmas in Romania be like? In all his previous trips overseas, he had always traveled in the summer. Back in Denver, it was still Christmas Eve. Tim and Brenda would be attending church with the children. *Next year,* he promised himself, *I'll go with them, my son or daughter by my side.*

He wrapped himself in blankets and sat by the front window, watching the day dawn. A light snow was falling, eiderdown soft and white with the promise of a new beginning.

Anika bustled into the room, lighting the fire. "Merry Christmas!" she called, kissing Steve on the cheek.

Radu blundered after her, caught her in a bear hug, and spoke, words muffled in her hair. "Christ is born!"

I don't belong here. Loneliness swamped Steve afresh. *I don't belong anywhere.* Half of a matching pair, he had lost part of his identity with Lila. *It's only the holidays. Things will seem brighter when they're over. It's not as bad as last year.* Maybe when Carrie and the children arrived, he wouldn't feel like the odd man out.

After breakfast—a feast of homemade sweet rolls, fresh fruit, and strong coffee—Anika drove to the home to pick up Carrie and the children. Steve walked with Radu to the church to turn on the heat for the service that would be held later that day. Anika's car chugged down the street when they returned to the apartment.

Steve nearly laughed. It looked so like a clown's car, every spare inch crammed. Four children perched on half the backseat, surrounded by gaily decorated boxes. Carrie sat in the front, one of the boys leaning against her. They stopped, and Anika stepped around to the passenger's side to let Carrie out.

Woman and child spilled out, with the rather awkward grace of a young colt. A Santa red coat wrapped around Carrie, a splash of cheer against the white snow. The children slowly climbing out of the car wore new coats that filled the street with warm yellows and greens and pinks.

Their matching expressionless faces stared at Steve. Only Viktor seemed to remember him, pointing his index finger and humming the chorus from "Victory in Jesus."

Yes! Steve's heart trembled with joy, and he sang the words, voice hoarse with emotion. "Merry Christmas," he whispered, as much to himself as to the boy. *Lord, please let this be the one.*

Around them Radu and Anika unpacked the car. "Come in where it's warm." Anika chased them inside.

"Can the children open their presents right away?" Carrie begged. "I can't wait another minute!" Excitement flooded her cheeks with a gentle pink. Anika nodded.

The stack of presents looked pitifully small. Steve thought of the hoard of gifts surrounding the tree at Tim and Brenda's house, enough to line an entire wall. No wonder the rest of the world thought Americans were rich. Watching Carrie's irrepressible anticipation, Steve realized these children were rich in the most important thing, their "mother's" love.

"Shall we do this one at a time or all at once?" Carrie's lips twisted in a thoughtful scowl. "All at once, I think. Keep them from fighting over each other's toys." She picked through the presents. "Adrian." She handed the boy a round-shaped package that could only be a ball. "Jenica. Octavia." Two rectangular-shaped boxes. "Ion." A long narrow package.

"Viktor." Her voice reflected the gleeful satisfaction of knowing the gift was just right.

Carrie sat down to wait and watch the fun. Jenica fingered the bright paper, but the other children didn't touch their gifts. Ion started coughing. Octavia stared around the crowded room and began crying.

"They don't know what to do." Carrie spoke in a surprised undertone. A flickering second of sadness passed over her face. Steve found himself missing her almost naive smile and hurried to help.

"Viktor. Come here." The boy looked up but didn't move. *Of course, he doesn't speak English.* Steve settled himself on the floor next to the child. "You do it like this." He hooked a finger under the edge of the wrapping paper and started to pull. Viktor watched then looked into Steve's eyes. "Your turn." Steve guided the child's hands into the opening, and together they tore away the paper to reveal a slender box. Steve pried open the end flaps and pulled out the present—a white plastic recorder. Viktor's eyes fixed on him, as if demanding an explanation.

"Listen!" Steve put the instrument to his mouth and blew a note. The boy drew back, startled. The adults laughed. "You try it." Steve handed the recorder to the child.

Viktor held the instrument in his hands, fingering the holes, chewing on the edge, and eventually put the mouthpiece to his lips. He puffed out his cheeks and blew. A squeaky note emerged.

"Bravo!" Carrie applauded. "That's the way!"

Another squeak followed. A series of them, all high pitched. Recorder clamped in his mouth, Viktor looked like he would play forever.

"May I?" Steve reached for the recorder. Viktor scowled at him and bit down on the mouthpiece.

"You do it like this." Steve knelt in front of the child and molded his fingers over the holes. Surprise flit across Viktor's face when the next note came out an octave lower. Soon he was blowing an experimental series of notes up and down the scale.

The rest of the morning flew by. The children clustered around Carrie, at least three of them occupying her lap at all times. She talked to them constantly, short sentences illustrated by gestures, certain words repeated often enough that Steve could guess their meanings—the color red, the number two. Fixing a bottle, changing a diaper, helping open a present—for two hours she never stopped moving.

Soon only a few presents remained. "For you, Carrie," Anika announced.

Steve hugged himself with delight at the surprised look on her face. *I hope she likes it!*

Almost reverently she pulled aside the tissue paper and opened the drawstrings of a soft cloth bag to reveal a bottle of hand lotion and a big bar of scented soap. Closing her eyes, she lifted the soap to her nose and sniffed deeply, sighing with pleasure. "Gardenias. Summer in the middle of winter." She looked at him with warm brown eyes.

"Brenda—my sister, you know—loves it. She complains about chafed hands—"

"It's wonderful. But I don't have anything for you!" Carrie pumped a minuscule amount of lotion onto Jenica and Octavia's outstretched hands before rubbing it into her own.

"That's okay." *But you already have given me something. Your warmth. Time with these children.*

Presents from their hosts followed, a cassette of folk songs for Steve and for Carrie, an intricately executed Tree of Jesse, the size of a sheet of notebook paper.

"How beautiful!" She traced the branches leading from Jesse to Jesus. "And there shall come forth a rod out of the stem of Jesse. . ." She clutched it to her chest. "Thank you, Lord." After a few moments she slid it back inside the envelope and set it aside, out of reach of the children.

"Good." Radu and Anika wore matching beaming smiles. They shared the closeness of a happily married couple. The love between Carrie and the children bonded them in a different kind of family. A pang of loneliness akin to jealousy crossed Steve's heart. *Be patient,* he tried to console himself. *God makes everything beautiful in His time.*

◆

"I'll take care of the children." Anika practically pushed Carrie out the door. "Go with Radu and Steve to church."

They'll be okay. Carrie steeled herself to withstand Octavia's wails and Ion's nose, going like a runaway train. Anika pulled Adrian back from where he clutched Carrie's pant leg.

"I'll be right back." She gave each child a quick hug and kiss. Thanking Anika, she walked out into the snowstorm.

On the sidewalk Steve and Radu stood waiting. Steve's ears burned red, begging for a covering. She adjusted the warm beret on her head. White snow blurred the outlines of buildings, creating a festive fairyland where anything could happen. Steve trudged next to her, immersed in his own world. He looked like he had lost weight, creating interesting angles in his facial bones that emphasized the loneliness lurking within.

What's he been doing for the last year? And why does he want to adopt? She had to admire a man who would spend a small fortune traveling halfway across the world to adopt a child. He was brave, all right. *But does he know what he's getting into?* Around the kids he acted slow and wooden. The old Steve, the one with a ready chuckle and a smile that could warm an entire room, stayed hidden most of the time. Now and then some of the old sparkle appeared, like when he showed Viktor how to play the recorder.

Inside she grinned. Who wouldn't warm up to Viktor? She loved him like he was her own.

Why not? The thought popped into Carrie's head like the scent of hot cocoa. *If they let single parents like Steve adopt, why not me?* The thought fit exactly, instantly taking hold.

She'd probably have to complete an adoption application. It couldn't be any worse than the mission society form. She could already imagine the future. Through a snowy looking glass, she dreamed of Christmases to come. Viktor gamboled in the ball pit at a McDonald's playland. Red backpack strapped to his back and Big Bird smiling on his shirt, Viktor walked with her to kindergarten. A shadowy figure marched in band, playing an instrument. Was it a clarinet? No, a trumpet.

Ahead of her the men had stopped, and she realized they had arrived at the church.

"Any luck with your search?" Radu asked Steve while he unlocked the door.

"Yes." Steve paused before saying more. Conflicting emotions flashed across his face.

"Really? Who?" Full of her own plans, Carrie longed to share his joy.

He glanced at Carrie then answered. "Viktor. I want to adopt Viktor."

Chapter 8

He's going to take Viktor!" Unable to believe it, Carrie spouted to Michelle at their next lunch meeting. "Thousands of children to choose from, and he wants Viktor!" She dabbed at the angry tears she knew she had no right to cry.

"Well, that's good, isn't it?" Michelle sounded bewildered. "That way you know Viktor has a good future. Why, you might even get to see him sometime." Her attempt at empathy failed.

"You don't understand." Tears flowed in earnest now. "I had just decided. I was hoping. I was going to try to adopt Viktor myself."

Surprised silence followed. "But could you?" Michelle had obviously never considered the possibility. "Adopt, I mean?"

"Why not?" Carrie threw her head back in defiance. "If they let a single man like Steve-stick-in-the-mud-Romero adopt, why not me?"

Michelle's expression suggested that she could think of several reasons, but she didn't mention any of them. Instead her eyes softened. "No wonder you're disappointed."

They sipped their coffee in silence. "He may still change his mind." Michelle attempted to console her friend.

"I don't think so." Carrie shook her head. "You should have seen them together on Christmas Day."

"I'll see what I can find out when we go to dinner." Michelle grinned at Carrie's surprise. "You know I'm a sucker for that hangdog look."

Carrie tried to ignore the feeling of jealousy that clogged her throat and increased the tension one more notch. She wanted, no, needed, to talk with Sister Pauline. A conversation with the wise old woman would clear up some of her confusion.

That evening Carrie walked around the wards with the director. The children, the atmosphere, the smells, all disappeared as she poured out her heart.

"And so I decided I would like to adopt. I thought about Viktor." Carrie swallowed past the lump in her throat. "But if that isn't possible, one of the others."

Sister Pauline didn't answer but continued her routine, making sure every child had a bottle or blanket or whatever else was needed. After finishing the evening round, she took Carrie with her to the chapel.

"Let us pray together about your desires." Her words reminded Carrie that she had not prayed before making her new plans.

Of course it's God's will. How can it not be? At the prayer rail, Carrie lifted her hands in silent supplication. *If it is Your will, let me adopt Viktor. Please. Or show me which of the others is the one You want for me.* Her mind raced ahead of her prayers, and she found it hard to focus.

Candles burned low before Pauline rose from her knees.

"Sit down." Her face was at peace as she settled next to Carrie on the pew. "My dear child."

I wish she wouldn't call me that. It usually signaled bad news.

◆

"Have you thought this through?" A thin hand gripped Carrie's arm. "The Lord has given you a great love for children and a tremendous gift for working with them. But are you prepared to take responsibility for one child's life from now until eternity? To provide for his physical needs and guide his spiritual growth?"

Why is she asking? Carrie frowned. "Of course!"

Sister Pauline sighed, as if disappointed in Carrie's answer. "I will help you complete the necessary paperwork, if that is what you wish." She stood, indicating the discussion had ended.

"Don't be weary in well doing," she said, quoting from Galatians. "Don't let your enthusiasm keep you from completing your work here." They parted ways at the door.

Carrie settled into bed for the night, somewhat puzzled and disappointed. Sister Pauline hadn't exactly encouraged her. *Am I doing the right thing? Isn't adopting a child just an extension of my calling to Romania?* She turned over and punched her pillow, chasing away the doubts. *Of course it is.*

◆

Steve paused at the door, questioning the wisdom of taking Michelle to dinner. At the time, the arrangement happened naturally. He needed a break from the inevitable letdown following the surge of discovery. She knew where to go for an American meal. Just like home, she promised. Later, he wondered if she was thinking "date." He shrugged. If so, that was her problem.

She arrived promptly—well, only fifteen minutes late. Dressed in typical college fashion, with makeup carefully applied, she gleamed with a purely American beauty. At the same time she soothed his loneliness in a foreign country and defined her expectations of the evening.

Maybe it's time, Steve decided. After all, his last date, before his engagement, had been four and a half years ago. Lila had been as comfortable as a worn glove. He didn't know how to begin with Michelle. Now if it were Carrie, it wouldn't be so hard.

Summoning a forgotten skill, he searched for an opening comment. Of course, a compliment. "You look lovely. That sweater—"

"Oh, this old thing. It must be out of date by now." She giggled nervously, but she was clearly pleased.

The restaurant proved to be everything she had promised. Large chandeliers illuminated tables covered with sparkling white linen; napkins were folded into tents on bread and butter plates. The menu, written in English, featured American favorites like T-bone steaks and fried chicken.

Michelle stared at him over the top of the menu.

"What do you recommend?"

She hesitated. *Price*, he realized. It was up to him to set the standard. "Uh, is the steak any good?"

"Yes, as long as you like it cooked somewhere between well done and burned tough!"

"Sounds—perfect!" He could eat decent American steak in Denver any time. Orders placed, an uncomfortable silence descended on the table. *I've forgotten how to make small talk, at least with someone besides band students and parents.* He looked at Michelle over the candles, and she smiled at him with orthodontist-straightened teeth. Her youthful idealism multiplied the five or so years' difference in their ages. The silence lengthened as the waiter brought salads to the table.

Michelle began telling him how she ended up in Bucharest. *Why did Carrie return?* Was it as complicated as Michelle's story sounded? Knowing Carrie, he suspected she jumped right in without much thought.

Michelle mentioned meeting with Carrie every Thursday and then started describing the ladies' Bible study she had organized.

"How is it going?" He tried to hold up his end of the conversation.

She beamed with pleasure, as if she had been waiting for some show of interest on his part. "Five women came last week. They're so hungry for God's Word! I guess I've taken it too much for granted." She was off and running again.

The one-sided monologue prompted by occasional questions from Steve lasted through the main course. Half an ear paying attention to Michelle, Steve found himself wondering if he could complete the adoption process before he had to return home after the new year.

They ordered dessert, a hot fudge sundae for Steve and apple pie à la mode for Michelle. "I've monopolized the conversation," she apologized. "Tell me about yourself. I hear you've decided to adopt Viktor. Carrie's just crazy about him. I suppose you know that."

"Yes." Tongue-tied, he didn't say any more. How could he explain the visions of the boy in his nursery in Denver, playing with Sammy and Amanda?

"How long will you be staying in Romania?" A pretty blush stained Michelle's cheeks, as if she were asking for herself.

"One more week. School starts again next Tuesday."

The waiter arrived, and the vanilla ice cream proved rich, buttery, and creamy. Steve let it slide down his throat.

"Only a week? Then when are you coming back?" Michelle returned to their conversation.

"Coming back?" Her words reminded him of the obstacles ahead, and the ice cream landed with a cold lump at the back of his throat. "I guess I've been hoping for the impossible, to cut through all the red tape."

"Someone at the agency must have told you. It takes months, years, even, to get a child out of Romania." She swallowed a juicy bite of pie. "Viktor may be old enough for school before you finish the process."

She pointed a finger at him. "First, have you got permission to adopt Viktor from his parents?"

Parents? He's at an orphanage.

A second finger jabbed. "Also, has he been tested for HIV yet?"

HIV? As in AIDS? He had forgotten about that part. It was too horrible to contemplate.

As if sensing his confusion, she explained. "A lot of babies were infected when they received a blood transfusion at birth, a routine practice in Romania. As many as forty percent in some places. And any child that tests positive isn't allowed into the United States."

Sighing, she lifted another finger. "Then of course there are all the papers to be prepared and translated."

Steve stirred in his chair. "I've contacted a lawyer here. He's already done most of that."

"And signed by the president. If he signs them at all."

"I guess I was dreaming." Steve slumped, leaving the last spoonful of fudge sauce untouched. She was right. He could not possibly finish everything in under a week. It had been foolish to think he could. Another dead end? Discouragement swamped him, and he slid a couple of inches in his chair.

Michelle resumed her monologue, now sharing humorous vignettes of an American abroad, kindly not seeming to notice as he withdrew further into himself. Finally he shook out of his funk. If it was possible to make the adoption happen faster, he would. He dug out the last spoonful of the now-melted ice cream, and the waiter reappeared with the coffeepot. "Not for me. It would keep me awake all night."

Michelle took her cue from him. "Me neither. I am a bit tired. Mind if we leave?"

"Of course."

She bustled them out of the restaurant and delivered him at Radu's apartment with surprising speed. Before he could get out of the car, she placed a warm hand on his arm. "I do hope you get to take Viktor home soon.

71

We're here to help—Radu, Anika, Carrie, me—if you need us."

Michelle's words echoed in Steve's mind. Phone dangling from his hands, he started to dial Carrie's number. *Don't call.* The phone slipped into the cradle. He was sure Radu would go with him. Perhaps he would be a better advocate than another American, even if she did know the boy and speak Romanian.

Call her. Hesitating, Steve picked up the receiver again and stared at it. Radu didn't love the boy like Carrie did. She would make an impassioned plea on his behalf.

Or would she? Would she let her attachment to Viktor stand in the way? There was only one way to find out.

Somewhere close by a clock chimed ten. *It's probably her bedtime.* He tapped the receiver against the table. It might be the best time to reach her.

Drawing a deep breath, he dialed the number given him by Radu. Ten, twenty rings later, a childish voice answered. "Hello?"

"I'd like to speak with Carrie Randolph, please. Car—rie Ran—dolph." Steve tried to slow down his natural speech and say the name clearly.

"Okay." A loud bump rang in his ear, and he heard footsteps slapping across a wooden floor. Had she understood? The second hand moved slowly on his watch dial, time Steve spent trying to curb his impatience. Eventually the clatter of nearing footsteps rewarded his wait.

"This is Carrie Randolph." She sounded breathless, as if she had been running.

"Carrie. This is Steve Romero."

"Steve!" Her voice conveyed genuine warmth. After a second's pause, she asked, "How is the adoption coming?" Only a slight quiver in her voice betrayed any ambivalence.

"Actually, that's why I'm calling. I understand I need to get permission from Viktor's parents before I can go further. Do you know if they're still alive? Or is he really orphaned?"

A brief silence followed. "They're alive. They live in a village north of Bucharest."

"Well." Steve cut off the word. Whenever he was nervous, his voice took on an impersonal business tone. The illusion of control worked well with high school students. *How will it go over with Carrie? Better be real.*

"I could use your help. I'm afraid I might do something to offend someone unintentionally. Could you come with me when I go to visit Viktor's parents?" Steve pictured Carrie, head pinning phone to her shoulder and chewing on her lower lip.

"I'll have to check with Sister Pauline. But I'd be glad to help if I can." She answered without hesitation.

"Tomorrow? Or the day after? I don't have much time—I have to return to Denver soon."

"Plan on the day after tomorrow. New Year's Eve."

Steve glanced at the calendar. That would be Thursday, Carrie's day off. His heart swelled with gratitude for her generosity.

"Thanks." They made plans and hung up the phone.

◆

"It's about ninety kilometers from here. A tad over fifty-five miles." Excitement laced with nervousness pounded through Carrie's veins as she drove to the village where Viktor's parents lived. The horizon gleamed white and cold, an unpromising backdrop to the day. Soon the city dropped out of sight, and paved roads gave way to frozen dirt, bouncing the vehicle around like a boat at sea. Empty brown fields sidelined the path, with occasional clusters of buildings indicating a village.

Carrie darted glances at Steve. Close-clipped curls hugged his face and drew attention to his sensitive mouth. It was the face of someone she would like to know better. He had changed since Lila's death. If only he didn't want to adopt Viktor! Her stomach tightened at the thought of the upcoming meeting. If Steve was nervous about the day's errand, he didn't show it.

She shifted her gaze to the undulating road. Hopefully her demeanor was as unrevealing. The bottom line was that she hoped Viktor's parents would agree to the adoption.

She checked the odometer as another village came into view. "This should be the place." A dozen buildings identified the center of town, and an assortment of farm animals roamed about. Brown earth enclosed by white fences outlined garden plots that would flourish with vegetables come spring. She stopped the car and rolled down the window.

"Where do the Grozas live?" she asked in Romanian of a woman passing by, carrying buckets of water.

"Over there." Only her eyes registered surprise at the arrival of Americans in her village.

Carrie thought she had grown immune to Romania's poverty, but the house still surprised her. The records indicated Viktor was the youngest of eleven children. The cottage couldn't be larger than seven hundred square feet. How could twelve people live in such a small place? She eased the car off the road, feeling ice crush and wheels sink into partially frozen mud.

"Just a minute." Steve's face was pale, his words shaky. He was nervous, after all. "Let's pray."

"Of course!" When would she learn? Always rushing ahead, she kept neglecting to talk with God about things.

"God, give me the words to say." As Steve bent over, head clasped between his hands, Carrie hurriedly closed her eyes. "Open the Grozas' hearts. Help me to accept whatever happens today." His voice quavered, and he didn't say anything more for a few seconds.

Words failed Carrie. She didn't know what to pray for. After a quick silent confession of her desire to keep Viktor for herself, she simply added, "We trust You to do what is best for Viktor."

"Amen." Steve concluded the prayer. "Let's go."

Dozens of eyes peered at Carrie when she looked up. A group of children stood at a respectful distance around the car, staring at them in curiosity. Viktor's bright black eyes and the bump at the end of his nose repeated themselves in the faces. Addressing the oldest, she asked in Romanian, "May we see Mr. and Mrs. Groza?"

The girl disappeared inside the cottage and reappeared a moment later with a thin, wiry woman, clearly every ounce a scrapper. She approached the car. "I am Mrs. Groza."

Carrie's mouth turned to cotton. They hadn't discussed an opening gambit. How could they explain their mission? At her side Steve stirred uneasily, clearing his throat. The woman made it easy. "Come inside."

Carrie gestured for Steve to follow her into the cramped cottage. Dishes, clothes, and furniture filled every inch, neatly squeezed into place.

"You are from the children's home." Mrs. Groza saved them from introducing themselves. "I recognize the car. Has something happened to my Viktor? Is he well?" Her anxious words and worry lines tightening her eyes hinted at a wealth of mother love Carrie could only approximate.

Steve stirred at the mention of Viktor, and Carrie translated for him.

"He is fine. In fact, we have some wonderful news." Carrie glanced at Steve, who nodded his encouragement. "This gentleman here, Steve Romero"—he smiled at the mention of his name—"is from the United States. He is interested in adopting Viktor and taking him to live in America."

The shocked mask that covered Mrs. Groza's face didn't need translation. "Wait a minute. I must call my husband."

A quarter of an hour later, the four of them faced each other across the crowded room. Once again Carrie explained their errand.

"No." Mr. Groza spoke without hesitation. "We believe things will get better soon. We will be able to bring our son home."

Carrie swallowed a protest. *Who does he think he's fooling?* She thought of the stick-thin children outside and the cramped conditions of the home.

"He says no," she said to Steve, trying to keep disappointment out of her voice.

"But Mr. Groza..." Without waiting for Carrie to translate, Steve pulled out a book of snapshots. Words and pleas spewed out as he hurried to convince them.

"This is my home. See, this is the nursery. Viktor will have it all to himself. Here is my piano. Viktor loves music, you know. I could teach him."

Carrie inserted an explanation here and there but mostly let the pictures speak for themselves. Steve continued urging the advantages of life in

America. Caught up in his plea, he appeared not to notice the way Mr. Groza drew back and sank into his chair.

"The answer is still no."

Shaking her head, Carrie communicated his refusal to Steve. Silence reigned. She hated to see him hurt like this.

◆

"Wait." Viktor's mother leafed through Steve's pictures and pointed to a view of him in front of a church. "You are a Christian?" She pointed to her only piece of jewelry, a simple cross necklace.

"Yes."

They had found common ground.

Mrs. Groza put a hand on her husband's knee. "That is good. The reason we took Viktor to Sister Pauline, instead of somewhere else, was so he could learn about our Lord."

Carrie explained to Steve. Mrs. Groza clutched her husband's hand, and he slowly nodded.

They looked at Steve with gazes full of a lifetime of pain that pierced Carrie's soul. "Now God has brought you here. You would teach our son about the Lord." She reached for the pen in Steve's hand. "We will sign the papers." Tears smeared the ink of their signatures.

Steve took pictures of Viktor's family and their home. "I will tell him about his parents, who loved him very much," he promised.

Mrs. Groza handed Steve a cloth-wrapped bundle. "Keep this for my son."

"May I?" Steve unfolded the material, revealing a well-worn Bible. "He will treasure this." His voice broke.

Carrie didn't speak much on the trip back to the home. The unselfish, painful sacrifice of Viktor's parents bore down on her, hammering her resistance to Steve's desire to adopt her favorite. *Do I love him that much? Enough to give him up?* The bleak winter landscape offered no easy answers.

Steve made up for her silence, talking nonstop like a toy that wouldn't wind down. How God had led him step by step to Viktor, and his conviction that everything else would work out. How he looked forward to having a son to cherish, to share life with.

Carrie concentrated on driving and let his words slide off without penetrating. Her thought followed a separate path. *If not Viktor, could I adopt one of the others? Adrian, perhaps?* Dark had fallen when they reached the home. Soon, she promised herself, soon she would be rejoicing the same way.

"Wait!" Steve stopped Carrie before she could get out of the car. Jumping out his side, he ran around and opened her door with a flourish. He leaned in and kissed her cheek. "Thanks for everything. I know how much Viktor means to you." Taking her arm by the elbow, he walked her to the door. "I know there's a lot left to do, more red tape. I want to spend as much time as possible with Viktor before I leave. Do you mind if I come tomorrow?"

Carrie automatically made arrangements. Glad to see him leave, she headed for the toddler ward. Perhaps a brief good night greeting would restore her sagging spirits.

Sister Marie dozed in her chair, and Carrie opened the door without disturbing her. She tiptoed past the cribs. At the far end, Ion's breathing rasped. Octavia twisted in her sleep as if she were having a vivid dream. Thumb in mouth, Jenica slept peacefully. Carrie tugged a blanket over her, stroking her soft hair and skin. Tears watered her cheeks. With or without Viktor, there were plenty of reasons to be in Romania. Adrian. She smiled and headed for his crib next.

From a few feet away, the mattress looked flat, no familiar lumpy figure visible. Her footsteps quickened, and she stopped worrying about making noise as she rushed to the bed—empty. Adrian was gone.

She ran out the door and shook Sister Marie awake. "Where is Adrian?"

The woman stirred and blinked eyes against the light. "Adrian? They took him away today."

"What? Who?" Panicked, Carrie realized Marie didn't know the answer. She raced down the stairs and to the main house, barreling down the hall to Sister Pauline's door. The director stood waiting, petite form outlined by the dim light.

"Come in, dear child."

"Where is Adrian?"

Sister Pauline did not answer until they sat down facing each other. Clasping Carrie's hand between her own, she said, "Adrian came to us because his mother was young and unmarried. She always hoped she could take care of him when her circumstances changed."

"So?"

"She came today. She has married now, and her husband has a good job in the city. He is willing to raise Adrian as his own. They left just before supper."

Nooo! I didn't even get to say good-bye! Carrie looked at the floor, away from the compassion shining in Sister Pauline's eyes.

"It is for the best, you know."

Without answering, Carrie rose from her chair and stumbled down the hall into her room and collapsed on her bed. In the privacy of her room, she allowed the tears to fall. *Who knew a happy ending could hurt so much?*

Chapter 9

With a whistle streaming between his teeth, Steve burst through the door and up the stairs to the toddler ward. He didn't want to waste a moment he could spend with Viktor. And Carrie—she had a way of making him relax. If only he could speed up the rest of the bureaucratic process. Oh, well, after six years of touring with the Singers, he knew how time consuming and inflexible government protocol could be.

Carrie was nowhere to be seen. Sister Marie smiled at him and pointed toward a door at the opposite end of the ward. Surprised that Carrie and the children weren't waiting for him, he knocked on the door.

"Come in."

A giggling Jenica stood before Carrie, wrapped in a thin towel that Carrie rubbed briskly against skin and hair. Three more heads bobbed in and out of the bath water, with a generous portion spreading across the floor.

"Rough morning, huh?" He chuckled. "How can I help?"

"Their baths are finished. Just need to get them dried off and dressed. The clothes are over there."

Steve looked for Viktor's head in the swishing water. There he was. He seemed to recognize Steve, a shy smile acknowledging his presence as he lifted the boy out of the tub.

"Hi there, Viktor." He held the towel-garbed boy close for a moment and took a second look at the tub. Someone was missing. "Where's Adrian this morning?"

"He's gone." Carrie pulled a shirt over Jenica's head and reached for Octavia. "His mother came to take him home yesterday while we were gone."

To someone who had so recently lost his own child, Carrie's grief was almost palpable. He stopped drying Viktor. "I'm sorry."

"No need to be sorry." Carrie brushed at the corners of her eyes and searched for matching socks. "It's what's best for him. Back with his family."

"Yes," Steve acknowledged. "But it must still hurt."

Tiny lines tightened around eyes brimming with tears. His heart went out to her, knowing the pain that came with losing a child. Without thinking, he extended his arms to embrace her, cradling her head against his shoulder, letting her tears soak into his shirt.

Ion sneezed, and Carrie instantly straightened. "What must you think of me. Look at your shirt. And the children."

"It's all right." Steve handed her a dry handkerchief. Comforting Carrie felt as natural as drying his sister's tears after her first boyfriend dropped her.

On the other hand, Carrie seemed embarrassed. Her actions sped into hyperdrive, whipping Jenica and Ion into clothes while Steve struggled to pin on a cloth diaper.

Viktor was still only half dressed when Carrie finished. "You need help with that?" Her amusement seemed to hold a trace of contempt at his ineptitude.

"Well." He flashed a sheepish grin in her direction. "Yes. I'm used to disposable diapers."

"Okay. You do it like this." She trifolded the cloth and pinned it snugly in place in a few seconds. Clothes followed in a matter of minutes. "There."

"Thanks." *How am I ever going to manage a child on my own? Practice, I suppose. All new parents have to learn sometime.* Remembering Tim's stories of 2:00 a.m. bottle feedings, he was glad Viktor was past the feed-me-every-two-hours stage.

Together they cleaned the bathroom, soaking up the water that splashed, taking the wet towels and discarded clothes to the laundry—the towels were so thin, Steve feared they might fall apart in the wash—and headed down the stairs.

Steve glanced over his shoulder from the bottom and grinned at the picture. The children carefully climbed the steps, maneuvering the stairs with about as much skill as a pull toy. At the back, Carrie held Octavia's hand, heavy diaper bag dragging down her shoulder.

"Let me carry that." How thoughtless he must seem, leaving everything for her to carry.

"I'm used to it."

I'm sure you are. Ignoring her comment, he climbed the steps two at a time and slid the bag down her arm into his hands.

"Where are we headed?" Carrie managed to raise a wan smile when they reached the car.

"My surprise." He tucked the children in back. Apparently no laws here governed safety belts and child seats. *What a ridiculous notion.* Danger to Romania's children came from more basic sources like starvation and lack of medical care.

"How about some songs to pass the time?" he suggested. "You lead. I haven't sung too many nursery rhymes lately." That wasn't entirely true—he read Mother Goose to Sammy and Amanda all the time—but he wanted to get Carrie's mind off Adrian. She started to sing in a lovely soprano voice.

"Hey Diddle Diddle" followed "Twinkle, Twinkle, Little Star." *It's working.* Laughter lines erased the grief in Carrie's face as she clapped along.

"I wish I knew Romanian rhymes," she confessed. "The only songs I know are in English."

"Try something universal, then. Like animal songs." He started "Old McDonald" and meowed.

"Cat." Jenica spoke up for the first time.

"Good for you!" Carrie grinned widely. Soon they were all singing along, a mixture of English and Romanian and animalese.

Country roads gave way to the busy city. Steve stopped singing and concentrated on following the directions Michelle had supplied. Soon familiar golden arches appeared.

"McDonald's!" Carrie exclaimed, delighted.

"Complete with a playland," Steve announced proudly. "Michelle told me about it."

Children's meals in hand, they took their lunches to the playroom. The children stared at the yellow and red ropes and slides. A couple of toddlers romped in the ball pit. Babies crawled, heads barely showing above the balls. Older children dove in, splashing orbs in every direction, some landing outside the net. A bright red ball rolled toward Octavia, a blue one to Viktor.

Solemn, Octavia carried the ball back to the net and pushed it through. A little girl in a Cinderella shirt waved to the group. "Come in." When they didn't climb in, she returned to her play.

Gradually the children drew in a tightening circle around the play equipment, still not quite daring to join in.

A couple settled in next to where Steve and Carrie apportioned the children's meals.

"Janie! Come eat!" The Cinderella girl reluctantly left the toys.

"Just visiting?" Carrie inquired.

"You're American!" The woman said with evident relief. "Yes, we're visiting family. But Janie has been dragging us back here every day since she discovered there was a McDonald's nearby."

For the next few minutes everyone concentrated on eating. Steve tore open a ketchup packet, squeezed it on Viktor's fries, and fed one into his mouth. His bright eyes widened in delight, and soon he was stuffing them in for himself.

Jenica slurped down her drink. Ion took apart his hamburger, trying pickles, bread, and meat separately. Within minutes it was impossible to tell any of them had taken a bath. Steve wondered if Carrie would resent the extra work.

"You can tell we don't do this very often." She looked at the mess they had made. "But what fun!"

"Birthday party? Or are they all yours?" The American mother asked in an unbelieving voice as she passed by their table on the way to the trash can.

"Neither." Carrie blushed. "They're all from a children's home, where I do volunteer work."

A solemn, oh-those-poor-children expression transformed the mother's face.

"And I'm hoping to adopt." Steve stated while he wiped Viktor's face and hands clean with a moist cloth.

"Congratulations!" A smile replaced the frown. "It's just that you looked so natural together."

The girl tugged on her mother's arm and whispered in her ear. "Of course," the mother responded.

"Come play with me," Janie invited, taking Viktor's hand. He followed as she tugged him toward the playground, looking over his shoulder at Carrie and Steve, uncertain what he should do.

Carrie fell in behind with Ion and Octavia. The children followed Janie's lead, climbing through the narrow opening into the ball pit. "Come on, Jenica," she invited. Soon five heads were bobbing up like buoys on the ocean.

"Thank you," Carrie told the mother. "Janie can show them how to play." A warm smile erased the grief Steve had seen earlier as they watched a giggling Jenica pitch a ball in Ion's direction.

Steve feasted his eyes on the sight of Viktor bouncing among the balls and falling against the ropes. How good to see him enjoying a few moments of carefree childhood, something Americans tended to forget was not the birthright of every child born in the world. There was so much he wanted to do and so little time to do it in. If Lila were here, she could stay when he had to return to his job, deal with the paperwork, and get Viktor home sooner.

If Lila were alive, I wouldn't be in Romania adopting Viktor. That was then; this is now. Viktor is my future.

Steve looked at Carrie, wondering if she was enjoying the day as much as he was. A worry arrow arched between her eyebrows, and tears glistened in her eyes.

"Adrian?" he asked softly.

She nodded. "He would have loved it here." She looked at her watch. "I hate to say it, but—"

"It's time to go."

The children slipped down the slide into their waiting arms, grins lighting their faces. Clean faces and hands and changed diapers later, they were on their way.

◆

Steve made a snap decision. "I want to make a stop," he told Carrie, steering the car toward Radu's apartment. He darted in and gathered together some of the supplies he had brought with him from Denver. Storing them out of sight in the trunk, he climbed behind the wheel and headed back to the home.

The motion of the car lulled the children to sleep, and Carrie leaned back against the headrest, eyes closed. "Thanks. What a wonderful day." Her head drooped against her chest.

In glances, Steve studied her profile, her face peaceful in repose, her body pleasantly curved. A nice girl. He hoped they could keep in touch, through Victory Singers reunions or something. He'd like to see how she turned out. He could envision her with a family of her own, three or four children. An unexpected pang of jealousy crossed his heart when he imagined her family—children and father and mother together.

Before long the car pulled up beside the toddler ward. Steve helped settle the children in their cribs.

"Thank you again."

"There's one more thing. Come with me to my car." Opening the trunk, he extracted half a dozen packages of disposable diapers and shoved them at a surprised Carrie.

"I brought them with me, just in case," he explained. "No point in lugging them back to Denver. They might make your life easier now and again."

"Oh, wow." She threaded her hands through the bag handles as if they were strings of pearls. "Thanks! See you tomorrow?"

"I wouldn't miss it!"

Two short days later, Carrie accompanied Steve and Radu to the airport with Viktor and the other children. Steve wasn't sure he wanted Viktor to be there. Saying good-bye the previous night had been tough. Today, in full view of an airport full of people, would be close to impossible.

The children behaved well, too well. Unlike Sammy and Amanda who fidgeted within minutes of arriving at the departure gate, they were too withdrawn to get restless and bored in the confined lounge area.

Steve held Viktor in his lap, savoring the fit of his body in his arms and the brush of his hair against his chin.

"So when do you think you'll be back?" Radu asked.

"Probably summer. Spring break lasts only a week, not enough time to finish everything."

The intercom crackled, and Carrie stood up. "That's your flight."

Steve stood up, holding on to Viktor. The boy nestled against Steve's chest, questions arising in his dark eyes. The thought of leaving him behind for six months sickened Steve. No matter how valid the reason, his departure betrayed the trust Viktor placed in him.

Now I understand. Pauline had counseled against informing Viktor about his plans. So many things could still go wrong, and six months was an eternity to a young child. Less disappointment for both him and Viktor if things didn't work out.

But of course they will. It's just a matter of time. Have patience. This summer. Trying to keep tears from spilling out and upsetting the children, Steve gently squeezed Viktor and kissed the top of his head before handing him over to Carrie.

"I guess this is good-bye, then." Steve shook Radu's hand.

"Not good-bye. Until next time."

"Don't worry. I'll take good care of him for you," Carrie promised.

"I'm sure of that." Unable to grasp her hand—she was holding Viktor—Steve patted her shoulder instead and walked away. If possible, he felt lonelier than he did on the first half of his trip. He had hoped to not return alone.

◆

Steve ran his fingers over the raised letters of the nameplate now hanging on the nursery door: V-I-K-T-O-R. God willing, he would be victorious in bringing his son home come summer.

Spring light bathed the room in a warm glow when he opened the door. Toddler toys filled the room, treasures found in his new passion for garage sales. He couldn't pass one without stopping for a look. Walking and riding toys dominated. His favorite find was a musical rocking horse, painted and polished to gleaming newness.

A snapshot of Viktor stood on the dresser, with a well-read letter from Carrie lying beside it. "He is doing well. He survived the winter without colds," she reported. "The pictures you send attract attention from all the other toddlers. In caring for Viktor, you are doing good for everyone here."

Should I go back during spring break? He argued with himself for the hundredth time. It didn't make any sense, but he would have a chance to see Viktor for a few more days. *And Carrie.* Missing both of them, he pressed the play button on his tape recorder and listened to Carrie speak about Viktor's progress with his instrument. Viktor's piping voice and fluting melody filled the empty silence. He kissed the picture frame.

"Oh, Lord, let it be soon," he entreated.

◆

A bird Carrie didn't recognize built a nest under the eaves. Tiny peeping voices greeted Carrie morning by morning and spring progressed. She studied the shadow of the intricately woven nest barely discernible against the dark walls.

Soon the nestlings would fly solo, abandoning their parents. Did birds feel as bereft as she did at the prospect of watching Viktor leave? His face hovered in her mind, and she allowed herself the luxury of a moment of regret.

Today marked another step in the process: HIV testing. Ion, Octavia, Jenica, and newcomer Angelica would be checked as well. Just in case, she wanted to pave the way for her own attempts to adopt.

I'm worried about Ion, she mused as she walked toward the ward. His cough persisted into the milder spring weather. Wasn't an inability to heal a sign of AIDS?

First stop—Adrian's old crib, now occupied by Angelica, a sweet girl with crippled legs. She was the physical opposite of her predecessor. Brought in by a mother who couldn't continue the level of care required by her disabled daughter, at least she knew how to smile and talk and yes, cry, in grief and anger.

Carrie didn't begrudge a minute of the extra time Angelica required. With her welcoming cry of "Carrie!" (not "Mama," like the other children called her), her spontaneous laugh when a soap bubble burst in her face, Angelica abounded in small moments of joy that gave Carrie the strength she needed to keep trying with the other four.

Next Carrie lifted Viktor down, careful not to disturb the snapshots of him with Steve and the colorful postcards that arrived on a regular basis. An older one was falling off. Carrie reread the familiar message before sticking it back on the crib. Viktor's thumbprints nearly obliterated the words. "This is Buffalo Bill, a famous American cowboy. I hope you can visit his house some day." A picture of the blond-haired, mustached entertainer stared at her. Apparently his gravesite was near Denver.

Carrie sighed. Although she would never admit it to anyone else, she looked forward to seeing Steve again. Viktor connected them in a tight bond. After all, Steve would soon officially be his father, and wasn't she like his mother?

Stop fantasizing. You can't have Viktor. Pick a different child.

No word had arrived yet on her application. *What's taking so long?* she wondered as she helped Octavia out of her crib. The child scampered across the floor toward the bath, bringing a smile to Carrie's face. She was definitely gaining strength, even if her legs stayed thin as string, too thin it seemed to support her ever-lengthening body.

After a hurried bath and rushed breakfast, it was time to meet with Dr. Reynaud at the clinic that Cristina had bragged about on Carrie's first visit.

The doctor visited at least once a quarter, helping the most desperately ill children and seeking to ease the way for American and French couples trying to adopt. An older, Gallic version of Brad Pitt, he flirted outright with Carrie.

"Hi, beautiful!" His usual greeting brought a blush to her cheeks.

"You always say that." He cheered her up and reassured her that she was still young and attractive.

Angelica saw the needle in his hand and wailed.

"*Non*, precious, it won't hurt." The doctor swabbed down Viktor's arm and drew a syringe full of blood. He blinked but didn't make a sound.

Next Octavia picked dubiously at the fluorescent pink adhesive bandage. When he came to Angelica, she decided to stick the proffered sucker in her mouth and turn her head away.

"Now it's your turn." Surprised, Carrie offered her arm as the doctor drew her blood.

"Thanks for taking time for all of them." Carrie watched as Reynaud examined Ion's ears. "When will we hear the results?"

"Hopefully before I leave next week." He pumped a syringe full of something into Ion's thigh. "His ears are still infected. Try to get him outside for fresh air, and keep him as dry as you can."

"I know." Carrie's shoulders sagged. "He just doesn't seem to get any better."

"Carrie." His accent caressed her name like a velvet glove. "He only made it through the winter because of your care. Stop being so hard on yourself." He smiled a crooked grin, and Carrie's mood lightened.

"You're a real shot in the arm," she teased, poking him above the elbow.

"I try." He shrugged elaborately with a mischievous wink. Turning serious, he said, "I'll call you with results next week. Let us pray for good news."

The days passed slowly. Carrie chose to take the call alone. Not that the children would understand, but she didn't want to be distracted. Both elbows planted on Sister Pauline's desk, Carrie held the receiver to her ear. "Carrie Randolph here."

"*Bon jour!* Congratulations! You may tell Mr. Romero that Viktor is fine. Undersized for his age, understandable in the circumstances, but in good health otherwise."

"The tests were negative?" She wanted to confirm.

"His test, yes."

Oh, no!

"Brace yourself, *mon petite*."

"It's Ion, isn't it?" Her worst fears were realized.

"Not Ion, although he is very sick."

"Who—?" Carrie couldn't bring herself to finish the question.

"Octavia. She tested positive for HIV."

Tears blinded Carrie. Poor Octavia, so often unhappy, now denied even the slim chance for adoption, and with a short, horrible future awaiting her. Carrie swallowed past the lump in her throat and spoke in a shaky voice. "Thanks for calling me, Doctor."

"I wish I had better news for you. Now a word about another patient—"

"Can anything be done for Angelica?"

"I believe so. I'm working on getting together a surgical team. But I'm talking about you. You have lost too much weight. You cannot care for the children if you don't take care of yourself first. We are concerned about you. Eat right, get plenty of rest—"

"And call the doctor in the morning?" Carrie tried to joke past her heaving throat. "Thanks for your concern. I will try."

They said good-bye, and Carrie continued staring at the phone in stunned silence. *How stupid.* She had hoped all of her children would be spared the killer virus. She wiped her hands on her jeans. How many times had she changed Octavia's diaper? Had she always washed her hands? She could have caught the virus herself!

Terror froze her for a few moments, visions of HIV racing through her veins like dye. Her hands rested on a book left by the phone. She glanced at the title: *Living with Children with AIDS*. Thumbing through the book, she noticed hundreds of practical suggestions. Trust Sister Pauline to find the right way to equip her to help. She must have known.

What a day! One more thread cut in the strings that bound Viktor to Romania. A new grief to bear, the news about Octavia. What had she been reading in the Psalms? "There be many that say, Who will shew us any good? Lord, lift thou up the light of thy countenance upon us." Faith, the evidence of things not seen, was all she could cling to on a day like this. It couldn't get much worse.

Sister Pauline quietly walked into the room. "I have been praying for you and Octavia in the chapel."

"Thank you." Carrie picked up the book. "May I take this to read?"

"Of course." The director settled her body in the hardback chair. "This may not be the best time to tell you, but I thought you would want to know as soon as possible."

Carrie only half paid attention.

"Your application to adopt one of our children has been denied by the board of directors."

Chapter 10

Your application has been denied. The words echoed around the room, mocking the snapshots of children taped to the walls. They pierced Carrie's heart, draining her of hope.

Why? Oh, Sister Pauline had offered an explanation. She was too young and inexperienced. She had no means of support. Try again in a few years when she had established a home for herself.

It's wrong! Unfair! Suddenly the heavy blankets smothered her, and she twisted in the bed.

I'm good with the children. They know that. I'll find a job. Haven't I proven myself? How can they say no?

She turned on her back and stared at the ceiling. *Maybe the sisters really don't like me. Maybe they think I'm doing a poor job with the children, and they'll be glad to see me go when my time is done.*

Unable to sleep, she flipped back over. *Octavia! Who's going to hold and comfort you when I'm gone?* She buried her face in the pillow, tears drenching the pillowcase.

"Take tomorrow off if you need to," Sister Pauline had advised. *"You've had several hard knocks in a row."* No need to set the alarm.

Viktor. Adrian. Octavia. Ion. No adoption. Broken images swirled through Carrie's brain until she fell into an exhausted sleep.

Brilliant sunshine burned through the windows by the time Carrie roused the following morning. She stretched, luxuriating in the well-rested feeling, until the momentary confusion of waking passed.

They rejected my application. She sat bolt upright in bed, propping her elbows on her knees and staring out the window. Tears welled, and she wiped them away angrily. Today she wanted to laugh, to plan, to think. Crying wasn't going to solve anything.

Underlying anger wouldn't dissipate so easily. *Immature? Irresponsible? I'll show them irresponsible*, Carrie thought crossly as she pulled on a worn pair of jeans. Unwanted guilt at deserting the children, even if only for one day, stole from the rest that washed through her muscles and bones.

Resolutely, she pushed it aside. Let the hoity-toity board take care of the children today if they didn't like the job she was doing.

Soon she boarded a bus headed for downtown Bucharest. She avoided the American section where she usually met with Michelle. The bus rolled through the city, reaching a park she had never noticed before.

Carrie disembarked, bought a sandwich from a street vendor, and headed toward the park. Ducks, returning north after winter, followed her, searching the dirt at her feet for bread crumbs. She sat down on a bench overlooking a pond and ate her meal, crumbling the last few bites for the birds. Crushing the waxed paper in her hands, she started to stuff it in her pocket to throw away later.

Why bother? Smashing it into a ball, she tossed it hard and high into the air, watching it come back to earth with a mild splash in the middle of the lake.

I used to be good at this. Carrie picked up a handful of stones and skipped one across the water. Rings spun out from the point of landing. Five stones, one for each child, plopped in the lake, the puddles of waves carrying her hopes until they flattened and disappeared. She watched the circles spread farther and farther, reaching to America in her imagination. Angrily, she threw a handful all at once.

Ducks took flight and flew to the relative safety of the middle of the pond. Behind her children's voices called to one another, feet pounding across the concrete in pursuit of the birds. A couple of preschoolers materialized at Carrie's side. Behind them she could see their mother slowly following, pushing a baby carriage, a toddler clinging to her skirts.

The young boy stood, bread crust in hand, staring after the ducks with longing.

"Don't worry, they'll be back," Carrie told him. She couldn't help herself. She was a sucker for kids.

The boy smiled shyly and held up the bread for her inspection. Squatting on her haunches, she took some crumbs and threw them on the water. His mother pulled alongside and reprimanded him. "Leave the lady alone."

Carrie stood up abruptly. Hadn't she come to the park to escape ever-present children? With a word of apology to the mother, Carrie sat down on the park bench and pulled out the romance novel Michelle had supplied her with at their last meeting.

The story focused on a young woman just out of college who made the mistake of falling in love with her employer, a man struggling to raise twin boys alone. Three chapters into the story, where the heroine made a fool of herself in front of the hero, she slammed the book shut. The fantasy hit too close to the truth of her feelings about Viktor and his father-to-be.

The mother had moved down the banks with the older children, leaving her baby in a stroller about five yards away from Carrie. Talk about irresponsible! The stroller was poised on an embankment, ready to roll into the water. *Maybe I should move it back.* She walked over to check.

Inside the carriage a newborn slept peacefully, wrinkled red face surrounded by soft pink blankets. Of its own will, Carrie's hand sneaked out and stroked the soft cheek. *If this were my child, I'd never let her out of my sight.*

Without thinking about what she was doing, Carrie found the baby in her arms. Tiny limbs stretched and a smile fled across the tulip mouth. Carrie pushed the blankets back, running her fingers over the thick pelt of dark hair. The baby opened one eye, a brilliant black that suggested her eyes would eventually be a lively brown.

"You're beautiful," Carrie cooed to the infant. "I wish I could take you home with me."

She held the baby in her arms and pushed the stroller to a safer spot further up the bank. *I could just walk away with the baby, and no one would know.* The baby scrunched her face, and Carrie adjusted the bundle in her arms. Forget about red tape and rejected applications. Baby in arms, Carrie sat on the bench.

Tiny fingers curled around Carrie's hand and dragged it in the direction of the pursed mouth. She laughed, and found herself talking in an absurd baby talk, part English, part Romanian, mostly gibberish that was so humorous in others.

"Get away from my baby!" a woman shrieked.

Startled, Carrie loosened her hold on the infant, and she clapped her knees together to prevent the baby from slipping through. The boy darted in front of her and planted his hands on his hips. "That's my sister," he accused.

"I know." Hurriedly Carrie tucked the baby back in the stroller. "She's beautiful."

The mother puffed to a stop in front of Carrie. In a voice as angry as her face was red, she launched a volley of speech so loud, so fast, and so obscene, that it exceeded Carrie's ability in Romanian. The meaning was unmistakable. *Get your dirty hands off my baby. Go back home where you belong before I call the police.*

Carrie stumbled blindly away from the park. What was she thinking? How had she sunk so low that—the word stuck in her throat—kidnapping would even occur to her? She climbed on the first bus that came by, not much caring where it was headed.

The bus passed recognizable landmarks. It was headed downtown by a route that would take them past Radu's church. The blocks rumbled by, barely registering on Carrie's consciousness. As if by instinct, she got out at the church and stumbled into the sanctuary.

She ran to the altar and flung herself down on her knees. Great, choking sobs shook her body. Words formed in her mind but couldn't push past the tears in her throat. *Help. Forgive me.*

Eventually the crying subsided, and Carrie sat back in a pew. The Madonna and child shining as the centerpiece of the Tree of Jesse mocked her. *All I want is to adopt a child. What is so wrong about that?* Tears filled her eyes again. Oh, she knew the answers. God's timing didn't have to match hers. It still might happen—some day. But she was twenty-three and lonely and far from home.

"*I am with you always.*" Jesus' words reassured her. "*You are not alone.*"
Even when I've made such a fool of myself?
"*Always. Nothing separates you from My love.*"

Carrie moved closer to the fresco, fingers tracing the branches that linked the heroes of faith. They rested on Sarah—ninety before she had her precious baby Isaac. Rachel watched her sister give birth to son after son while her arms ached to hold a child. But they believed and persevered and in due time they were rewarded.

So if not yet, what should I do now? The theme of waiting repeated itself along the branches of the tree. David caught her attention, crowned king more than a decade after Samuel first anointed him.

Ten years. In ten years, she would be thirty-three years old. She couldn't imagine being over thirty.

What did David do while he was waiting? Watch himself grow older year by year? Certainly not. She ticked off things he accomplished during that decade. He worked. He prayed. He made friends. He fell in love. He prepared himself.

In other words, he went about life as usual. For her, that meant going back to the home. Back to the children God had called her to help.

And after Romania? Home to look for a job? Fall in love? Unbidden, Steve's face formed in her mind. He exemplified so many things she admired in a man. Handsome, yes, but more than that, compassionate, great with kids, a talented musician to top it all off—and he was Viktor's father.

Viktor. When he left, she would miss him terribly. Again she cried, soft tears that washed away the frustration. God was at work. She would have to trust Him.

And maybe when Steve returned in a few weeks, she could show him a new Carrie—a woman, not just a glorified babysitter.

◆

"Two weeks?" Steve couldn't help it, a hysterical note of despair vibrated in his voice.

"Two weeks." The Romanian attorney Steve had engaged to help with the adoption, stated firmly.

"But—" Steve swallowed his disappointment. Lost revenue from summer teaching jobs, the Victory Singers tour he was missing, the overwhelming desire to claim Viktor as his son, now—none of his reasons for impatience could turn the wheels any faster. "I'll call you on the twenty-second, then."

The lawyer smiled as if he were doing Steve an enormous favor and pumped his hand with a powerful handshake. "Don't worry. Soon you and Viktor will be traveling to America together. Miss Randolph has done a lot of the groundwork."

A two-week delay would at least give him more time to spend with Carrie. The thought surprised him as it occurred on his way back to Radu's apartment. He meant he would have more time to spend with Viktor, didn't he? He remembered Carrie's warm smile and her patient care of the children, and he wasn't sure. She was growing up before his eyes.

Maybe he could convince her to leave the other children behind for a day. A day alone with Viktor and Carrie. He grinned. What a terrific idea!

◆

Five shirts, all chosen for simplicity of care and durability, draped across the bed. Steve had packed light, as usual. Why was he having such a hard time deciding what to wear? He needed something casual that he could run in comfortably; but to be honest with himself, he wanted to look his best. Blue? No, too predictable.

"I'd wear the yellow. It makes your eyes shine." Michelle's voice startled Steve. As usual, she had stopped by Radu and Anika's before starting work for the day.

Lila always said he looked good in yellow. "Yellow it is, then. Thanks." Steve refolded the other shirts and packed them away. He buttoned on the shirt, leaving the top buttonhole open, and reached with one hand for the cuffs.

"Let me help you." Michelle snapped the buttons in place in seconds. "There." Stepping back, she looked him over from head to toe. "You'll do. You're spending the day with Carrie." It was a statement, not a question.

"And Viktor." How did she know? "We thought it might be good for him to spend time with me without the other children around."

"Maybe I'll have better luck another time." Michelle grinned at him impishly. "Have fun."

She waved to someone in another room, signaling that she was almost ready. "And by the way, Carrie adores peanut butter cups if you can find them. The superstore is a good place to try." She left.

Shining eyes? Peanut butter cups? Did Michelle think he was interested in Carrie?

Further consideration of the question was postponed by the arrival of Carrie herself. She wore a bright red T-shirt adorned with smiling teddy bears, as cheerful in appearance as her sunshiny spirit.

At her side, no longer a babe in arms, a bigger, taller Viktor emerged, recorder clutched in his left hand. Steve fought the urge to crush the boy to his chest.

Viktor. Everyone else—Carrie, Pauline, Michelle—faded away as he saw the boy for the first time since Christmas.

The boy looked up at Carrie, who nodded her reassurance. He lifted the instrument to his lips, and notes streamed out, first "Frère Jacques" and then a remarkable rendition of "Victory in Jesus."

No one spoke into the silence. Dropping to his knees, Steve looked Viktor in the eye. "That was beautiful! Thank you for the music!"

Carrie repeated his words in Romanian, but before she finished translating, Steve leaned over and kissed the top of Viktor's head, tears of joy dampening his hair. He squeezed him briefly. "It's good to see you again."

Carrie stared at him, a look of sadness mixed with resignation clear on her face. "You two really connect. I'm glad you found each other." Her expression transformed into a let's-pretend-everything-is-okay-with-the-world look. "The picnic is packed. Let's go."

Steve resisted the urge to probe the obviously false tone of her statement. If she wanted to keep Viktor with her so much that she would deny him a chance for a better life in America—no, that couldn't be. The student who stayed by Lila's side at the hospital, the young woman who postponed her career to work long, lonely hours in an orphanage half a world away from friends and family, might be inclined to be immature, naive even, but she was basically kind and compassionate. Although she was sad about Viktor, something more troubled her.

They picnicked high above the Dimbovita River, where they could hear the dull roar of rushing water and raucous cries of seagulls. Steve suspected that closer to the river the stench of pollution would drive them away.

Carrie fluffed out a quilt and anchored two corners with the picnic basket and her purse. "Ready to play ball?"

"Sure, but I didn't bring anything."

"I did." She grinned. From the depths of her bag she extracted a bright red ball, the kind he'd seen on sale for ninety-nine cents in Denver supermarkets but as out of place here as a snowstorm in Tucson.

She tossed the ball at Steve, who caught it in his chest.

"I have to warn you. I'm not much good at this." He threw the ball on to Viktor.

It landed at his feet. He stared at it, then at Steve, as if uncertain what to do.

Steve gestured with his fingers, pointing at himself. "C'mon, kick it back to me."

With a tentative nudge of his foot, Viktor rolled the ball in Steve's direction. In turn, he angled it toward Carrie. She gave it a booming kick that bounced halfway down the hill.

"Sorry!" Long hair flapped against her back as she sprang down the hillside with the energy of a solar-powered battery. Viktor shifted to the edge of the hill where he could see her better.

"Don't worry, fella, she'll be right back. She's just gone after the ball." As if she heard him, she hoisted the ball over her head. "Got it!"

She chugged back up the incline, face flushed red, mud and grass stains smeared on her teddy bear shirt. Her earlier hesitation had disappeared, replaced by a vibrating *joie de vivre* and complete lack of self-consciousness.

"Let me take that." He reached for the ball.

"Come and get it." She ran an end zone pattern and evaded his hands.

"American football now, is it?" Giving chase, he caught up with her after ten yards, throwing his arms around her in a light tackle. They crashed to the ground and rolled, his arms offering protection to her limbs against the hard ground.

The ball stopped a few feet away as they stared at each other for a breathless moment. Something stirred in Steve that he thought long dead. Carrie's upper lip glistened, and he leaned in—

"Mama! Play ball?"

Viktor materialized at their side, red ball clutched in two hands.

Steve stood up, heat flushing through his face. Unscrewing a water bottle, he dribbled it over his hair and forehead before gulping down half the contents. Slowly the heat subsided.

What was I thinking? I almost kissed her. Steve looked where Carrie knocked the ball around in the grass with Viktor. Seeing her pink cheeks and infectious smile, a vibrant image of young womanhood, stirred him uneasily. *I wish I had.* Desire struck him with the force of a knockout punch.

Something hit his ankle.

"Got you!" Carrie laughed.

He steadied his breathing. If she could pretend nothing had happened, so could he. After all, he wanted to focus on Viktor, didn't he?

An hour passed before they called it quits. None of them had good aim, so Steve found himself chasing errant balls up and down a stretch of grass the length of a football field. An exhausted Viktor managed only a bite or two of sandwich before falling asleep, head resting on Steve's leg.

In contrast, Steve and Carrie ate hungrily, without conversation. While he was packing away the apple core, he noticed a pensive look had returned to her face. A haunting loneliness replaced the earlier ebullient enthusiasm. It reminded him of his own sense of inescapable loss in the months following Lila's death. Something must have happened to the children.

"Something's bothering you today."

She looked at him, startled, like a doe caught in a car's headlight.

"Does the possibility of losing Viktor hurt so much?" He had to ask.

"It's not that." Tears fell down a face scrunched up like a wet washcloth. "At least, not only Viktor. I'm worried about Octavia—I told you she's HIV positive, didn't I? Sister Pauline told me that now someone wants to adopt Jenica. And they turned down my application to adopt any of the children because I'm too young." Talking stopped as tears flowed freely.

Without thought, Steve circled her shuddering shoulders with his arms and pulled her close. If only there was some way to comfort her, to promise her that everything would work out. How well he remembered his own disappointment when his application for foster care was rejected. No wonder she was heartbroken.

The storm of tears subsided, but Carrie stayed snuggled against Steve's chest, hair obscuring all but sad brown eyes that looked at Viktor's sleeping form with a sense of resignation. "I thought it would be so simple."

The protective urge that catapulted Carrie into Steve's arms subsided, replaced by a growing sense of—what? Contentment? Desire? Startled by the thought, Steve separated from her. Dousing a pocket handkerchief with water, he handed it to Carrie.

"Thanks." The water didn't completely erase the streaks of tears that marked her cheeks, but she seemed more at peace.

"Life goes on, you know." Steve spoke into the silence. She looked at him, eyes still wet with tears.

"You're losing children who are special to you. Too many, all at one time. But just like Angelica took Adrian's place, other children will come. In helping them, you'll find your answers."

"I know." She gulped, almost swallowing the words. "But I was hoping for a family. A child. Someone I wouldn't have to leave behind. And they said no." A single tear traveled down the same path, and Steve raised a finger to wipe away the drop.

A longing to shield her from pain, to protect her, coursed through him. He covered her fingers with his own and raised them to his lips before tugging her toward him. His arms circled her slight body, his strength protecting her softness. Lips parted in a breathless smile, she invited his caress. Cheek to cheek, their lips met. Pleasure as keen as a soaring Chopin prelude flowed through him.

Chapter 11

Steve's kiss flamed against Carrie's lips, opening them up like a blast of warmth from a fireplace on a cold day. Of their own volition, her hands moved, pulling his head closer. His breath tasted sweet, like the apples they had eaten. A contented sigh escaped. It had been so long since she embraced a man.

Steve's lips grazed the corner of her mouth. *Correct that.* She had never kissed a man like this. Compared to Steve, her dates in college were children.

His lips moved over her hair, while his prickly chin brushed her forehead. Carrie relished the sense of belonging, of being cherished. Memories flashed across her mind, superimposing images of her and Viktor with Steve until they stood together like one happy family. *I'd like that.*

Steve's hands moved up and down her arms, sending shivers through her body. A soft murmur tickled her ear.

"Lila."

All the warm, cozy feelings vanished, replaced by a cold, hard ball in the pit of her stomach. Life drained out, leaving her stiff in Steve's embrace.

He opened his eyes, smoky brown irises boring into hers. "What's wrong?"

In answer, Carrie bolted out of Steve's arms and stood gawking at him. "You don't know?"

"Oh no." He looked up at her, eyes widening in realization. "I called you Lila, didn't I?"

Not trusting her voice, Carrie nodded.

"You must think I'm an insensitive idiot." He ran his fingers through his hair then stuck them in his pockets.

"If you want the truth—yes." Carrie stared in the direction of the surging river, trying to bring her anger under control. "I want to leave."

"Carrie, I'm sorry." Steve stumbled to his feet and reached out for her. She jerked away from his touch and started throwing things in the picnic basket. Silence lengthened between them like a stretched rubber band.

"You're a special person. With a lot to offer."

"Obviously not." She couldn't help it; she sniffed. "Not when you had Lila." Mad at herself for being so weak, she savagely rolled the quilt into a ball.

"Oh, Carrie." Steve drew a deep breath, like a whale coming up for air. "Some special man will want you." Taking the quilt away from her, he kissed her gently, briefly on the lips. "I envy that man."

In spite of her intentions, Carrie shuddered with delighted recognition. Maybe her fantasy wasn't so impossible after all.

◆

The phone jangled in Radu's apartment. Anika answered.

"For you." She handed the receiver to Steve. "It's Carrie."

Steve hesitated. Why was she calling? Since the picnic, she had seen him only long enough to say hello and good-bye when he picked up Viktor. Their meetings had the strained atmosphere of a divorced father taking his children for the weekend. He didn't know how to apologize, how to make it up to her. *Keep it casual.*

"Hi! What's up?"

"You brought some medical supplies with you?" She asked in a breathless voice, as if fear had erased her anger at him. "Electrolyte solution? Cough syrup?"

Viktor! "Yes. Who's sick?" Worry swamped him.

"They all are. The flu." A wail rose in the background. "That's Octavia. She's miserable."

"I'll be right out." Steve cut off further conversation.

"Thanks." The receiver clicked in his ear.

The baby supplies—diapers, medicine, bottles, formula—felt ominously light in his hands. There was barely enough for one child. But how could he say no to the others in need? Bottom line was, he couldn't. He'd have to trust God to provide.

He found Carrie in Sister Pauline's office talking on the phone. A fussy Jenica squirmed in her lap. The baby's skin looked flushed and dry, obviously fevered. Finishing the conversation, Carrie looked at Steve, concern evident in her eyes.

"That was Dr. Reynaud. He told me the equivalent of take two aspirin, go to bed, drink plenty of fluids, and call me in the morning." She laid a hand against Jenica's forehead and winced. "Their fevers are so high."

"I brought children's pain reliever." Surely they had such basic supplies?

"Great! Maybe that will bring down the fevers."

Hardly a breeze stirred the sultry summer air, and Steve could feel sweat beading on his forehead.

"Thanks for coming." Carrie spoke in a quiet voice. "After the way I've treated you this week, I was afraid you might take Viktor and run. I wouldn't have blamed you if you had."

"It's like I told you. You're important to me." Steve had to try to explain. "What matters to you, matters to me."

She flashed him a weary smile and opened the door to the toddler ward. The usual stench tripled in strength, reeking of vomit and soiled diapers.

Almost unable to breath in the sickening miasma, Steve slowly followed Carrie. *Steady,* he told himself, fighting the impulse to run.

"Take care of Jenica," he directed Carrie. "I'll check on the others."

When he passed Sister Marie, she smiled wearily from where she stood trying to change two diapers at the same time.

Viktor. His shirt bore evidence of vomit, and his face was flushed with fever. Still, he was breathing normally, and he summoned a smile for Steve.

Check on the others.

All the children showed signs of illness, but Ion's case was worst. Nearly every inch of his small body was soiled, and he lay motionless, sucking in air in great, rasping breaths. Smoothing back matted hair from his forehead, Steve cradled the boy to his chest and carried him to the bathroom.

Starting cool tap water, he stripped the soiled clothes from Ion and placed him in the tub. Sudsing a washcloth, he wiped away the grime that stuck to the boy's skin. Once the soiled water had washed down the drain, he left Ion under the running water and fished in his bag for the pain reliever.

Weight? Judging by Ion's light frame, he'd guess fifteen to twenty pounds. Somehow he got the medicine in the boy's mouth, but it stayed there, unchewed.

"Like this." Steve made exaggerated motions with his lips, and Ion seemed to understand.

Once again Steve started rubbing a cool washcloth over Ion's body. So little meat covered his bones—not like Sammy's plump fingers squirting water from a water gun. More like—Brandon.

Ion's chest heaved with the effort to breathe. Steve dug in his bag for the cough syrup. Not that it would do much good. This child needed a hospital.

But they didn't save Lila and Brandon. Steve remembered the poorly staffed, poorly equipped hospital in Bucharest. Maybe they wouldn't do Ion any good, either.

Sobs choked his throat. *Viktor. I can't lose you, too. Grieving hurts too much.*

Steve had done what he could for Ion. Now it was time to care for his son.

Somewhere Sister Pauline had resurrected two rocking chairs. Steve and Carrie lived in them for the next two days, rocking sick babies, sleeping, eating a few bites of whatever Cristina brought to them.

Only three bottles of the electrolyte solution remained. Still-damp diapers replaced soiled ones. Fevers continued to rage. They obtained some penicillin for Ion, but nothing slowed down the fluid building in his lungs.

A third night fell. Carrie slept with Ion propped up in her arms, trying to help ease his breathing. Sweat stamped dark curls against her forehead, trailing down her slender neck, a neck meant to be kissed. Not that she would welcome any more of his kisses. *Why did I ever call her Lila?*

Heat swamped him, sapping him of energy. Carrie seemed to handle the heat better than he did. Laying Viktor in his crib, Steve once again tried to open the head-high window. Grime glued the corner shut, and the catch was too high to turn effectively. He had to get some fresh air. A quick look around confirmed that everyone was asleep. Grabbing a bottle of water, he headed outside.

He drew in great gulps of air, the dampness cleansing away the sick stench that clogged his pores. It was no cooler outside; not much anyway. Romania didn't seem to have the same day-to-day variance that he was accustomed to, living in Denver where temperatures swung as much as forty degrees from morning to night. If only it would rain and break the oppressive heat.

Not much chance of that. No clouds marred the sky. Stars blinked in unfamiliar patterns.

The heavens are telling the glory of God. Familiar music pounded the Bible verse through his head. Nothing like a strange sky to remind him of God's infinite sovereignty and his own frailty.

"Oh, Lord! What more can we do?" At best, the children were maintaining, not improving. Ion's condition worsened regardless of their efforts.

Memories of standing by Brandon's bedside and watching him slip inch by inch back into the arms of Jesus surfaced, stronger than ever. *Thank God Viktor's not that sick.* The thought stampeded through Steve's mind, shame and gratitude trailing behind. No more than he could bear—losing one child was enough to last a lifetime.

Carrie appeared at the window, silhouetted by the pale light. Shamed again by his own callousness, he knew she would grieve the death of any one of the children. What if she caught the same bug? The thought squeezed his heart. *Oh, God, keep her well.* Drinking in one last long draft of clean air, one bowlful of twinkling stars, he headed upstairs for the next shift.

◆

A subtle awareness that something was wrong intruded into Carrie's consciousness, stirring her awake. Outside the sky gleamed light pink, dawn of the fourth day since the children had taken sick. A strange quiet reigned in the ward. Something was missing.

Ion lay against her chest like a leach, unmoving. The rattling, rasping sounds that marked his breathing had disappeared. Had the fever finally broken? Heat no longer sizzled through the blankets wrapped around his body. *Oh, no, he can't be—*

Fully awake, Carrie checked him in a panic. His skin was cool, no, cold, to the touch. No breath warmed her fingers. Refusing to believe that he was dead, Carrie unbuttoned his shirt and massaged his cold chest with her fingers. Not a flutter, not a hint of life remained.

Ion. Silent tears rolled down her cheeks. Death had turned his face pale and peaceful. She kissed his forehead and wept for the senseless loss. As an act of faith, a means of comfort, she started singing softly. "It Is Well with My Soul," "Jesus Is All the World to Me," "'Tis So Sweet to Trust in Jesus"—the familiar hymns came easily to mind, but they had never meant so much.

"O for grace to trust Him more." *Oh, Lord, I do trust You. I just don't understand sometimes.*

She ran her fingers over Ion's features, as if trying to memorize them. Other faces swam before her. Irina, long gone to Ohio. Adrian, thriving at home with his mother and stepfather. Dear, sweet Ion. Now in the arms of his heavenly Father.

Your work with Ion is done. The words slid into her mind. An image of the boy, running and playing in a grassy field, rose in her mind. He moved toward a group of children clustered around a white-robed figure.

"Let the children come to me. Ion has come home. I will take care of him."

Comforted at the thought of Ion at carefree ease, yet grieving for her loss, Carrie slipped back into a light sleep, holding Ion's body in her arms. When she next awoke, bright sunlight stabbed through the high window, and Steve was shaking her shoulder.

"Carrie." His voice nearly broke, clearly not knowing how to break the news to her. A single tear fell from his right eye.

"I know. He's dead." The words sounded harsh, grating against the silence. Unbidden, her eyes brimmed over, sending tears trickling down her face. Steve bent over and kissed the tear-stained spot before offering her his handkerchief. How she wanted the comfort of his arms around her.

"Mama?" Octavia pulled up in her crib, signaling the start of another day.

Carrie rubbed the tears away and looked again at Steve. "I'm not sure what to do with—"

He nodded, understanding her unspoken question. "I'll check with Sister Pauline." Tenderly rearranging the blanket around Ion's body, as though he could still sense the cold, Steve took him from Carrie and carried him out the door.

"Mama." Octavia called again. Her work with Ion was done, but four more children would need her full attention today. Giving Octavia a bottle, Carrie headed to her room for a complete change of clothes and real washing up.

Water splashed over her face and arms, purifying her spirits as well as her body. "When sorrows like sea billows roll—it is well with my soul," she hummed to herself. Pouring water in a lukewarm waterfall over her head, she scrubbed her hair once, then a second time. In the end, her body trembled with cold while her heart burned with grief. Half an hour later she joined Steve in Sister Pauline's office.

"Radu will conduct the funeral this afternoon, as a favor to us," Steve told Carrie.

She nodded. *How does he know what to do? Of course, he's been through this before. Knowledge gained at too great a price.*

Late that afternoon, a small group gathered in the home's cemetery. Carrie had hesitated before bringing the children. But they were the only family Ion had, and families grieved together, didn't they? It wasn't as though they had never seen death. They had, all too often, and they needed a chance to say good-bye.

Across the open grave, Steve held onto Viktor as if afraid he would fall in after Ion. Aside from that unnatural hold, his face was a blank mask. He had taken the burden from Carrie's shoulders for the day, doing what had to be done with robot-like efficiency. Like a turtle, he had rolled up his feelings inside a shell of taking care of business. She wished he would stop trying to be strong and cry with her.

Radu said a few words. "Ashes to ashes, dust to dust," sounded just as final in any language. But like Carrie's early morning vision of Ion at play in heaven, Radu reminded them of Jesus' love.

"Jesus loved children. He told us we had to become like a child to enter His kingdom. Even now He has restored Ion to perfect, eternal health. Even now He holds Ion on His lap, caring for him."

Around her, Carrie heard quiet sobbing. Tears traveled well-worn paths on Sister Pauline's cheeks. Anika's eyelashes glittered with the tears that watered the ground. Only Steve seemed unaffected.

"Does anyone else want to say something?"

Carrie stepped forward. Forcing her trembling limbs to quiet, she bent over and placed Ion's tool set, her Christmas gift to him, on top of the casket.

"Ion loved to take things apart," she said. "I promised him he could fix my car when he grew up." She stopped, sobs catching the words in her throat. Swallowing hard, she continued. "I'd like to sing a song." Hesitantly at first, her voice gained in strength as she started " 'Tis So Sweet to Trust in Jesus." Who else could she turn to?

"Lord, I commend Ion to You." She stepped back from the open grave.

No one spoke for a long minute. Then, with an amen, Radu concluded the service.

Carrie checked the children clustered around her. All of them needed a change. They were so sick. What more could she do? She was already exhausted. *God help us.*

Footsteps pounded the ground behind her. Steve appeared, eyes grim in a sweat-soaked face.

"Pack things for yourself and the children, enough for several days. I have an idea that might help." He strode toward the ward with Viktor.

"Why? What's going on?" She bristled at his commanding tone. *I don't want to move a muscle.*

"He wants to help." Anika joined her. She must have noticed Carrie's confusion. "Give him a chance."

Octavia chose that moment to cry. Carrie swayed, exhaustion catching up with her. "I just can't do it." She wasn't sure if she said the words, or if she only thought them.

Anika took Angelica from Carrie's arms. "Go get your things ready while I take care of the children. We'll meet you in half an hour."

After Sister Pauline gave her approval, Carrie agreed. A short time later, four adults and four children as well as a few pieces of luggage squeezed into Radu's car.

In Bucharest, they drove straight to the heart of the city, passing the hospital en route. The car stopped in front of a hotel where Carrie and Michelle had once ordered mocha lattes in a fit of indulgence. The opulent exterior reminded Carrie of how disheveled and grubby she must look.

Radu waved away the valet while Steve slipped around to her side of the car. "This is it," he announced. "I've reserved a suite."

Reservations?

Before she could frame her questions, a bellhop appeared and led them to their rooms. Cool, almost cold, air brushed her face, fanning her hair. He opened a door to a sitting room as large as many homes.

Carrie stared at Steve, silently demanding an explanation.

"The heat was getting to me." Already the air-conditioning was drying the sweat that slid down his face, leaving salty tracks. "And it wasn't doing the children any good either. I thought cooler temperatures might help us battle their fevers."

Oh. It just might work.

"And Tim is shipping extra supplies over, which should arrive today. So I'm hoping, with pain relievers and nutrition supplements and air-conditioning—" He stopped, looking to her for acceptance.

"It's worth a try," she agreed. "You didn't have to bring us all along. You could have just brought Viktor."

"No, I couldn't." A tired smile crossed his face. "You're his family." Brown eyes peered into hers, asking for understanding, as if he was trying to convey more than his words. "It's the least I could do. You shouldn't try to handle this all by yourself."

Yeah, we make a good team. If only we could be a family. Carrie gulped down the disappointment that rose in her throat and settled the children in their new surroundings.

Whether it was the additional supplies, the cool air, or simply the passage of time, all the children improved. Within three days, the flu-like symptoms passed.

"I think the crisis is over," Steve commented on the morning of the fourth day over room-service breakfast.

"Um-hum." Carrie nodded, mouth full of blueberry muffin. She swallowed. "It's time to go back to the home." She looked around at the luxuriant room. "Although it will be hard to leave fairyland."

Steve leaned back and rubbed his stomach. "It is nice, isn't it?" He paused, as if in the middle of a thought.

Carrie started packing their things into suitcases. The phone rang, and Steve answered it in the other room.

She was folding the last diapers into a bag when he returned.

"Who was it?"

"My lawyer." Steve spoke the words in clipped tones. She turned, startled to see his face turned pale, and sat down next to him on the couch.

"What's happened?"

Absentmindedly Steve pulled Viktor into his lap and ran his hand over the boy's springy curls. "The president has signed the adoption papers. We can leave at any time."

Carrie's mouth formed an O but no sound came out.

In the silence, she could hear the alarm clock ticking. "When?" she asked at last.

"Tomorrow. The lawyer counseled me to leave right away."

Carrie wondered if the loneliness that closed down over her heart showed as clearly in her eyes as it did in his.

He clasped her hands in his own. "It wouldn't have worked, you know. Us, I mean. Not now, anyway. Neither one of us is ready."

She refused to meet his eyes. He put a finger on her chin and forced her to look at him. "You're a wonderful, warm person, Carrie. You've been a wonderful mother to these children—to Viktor." His voice stretched thin. "And someday you'll have a family to call your own."

But not with you. How silly. But she could no more stop the thought than she could have prevented the children getting sick. She waited for his next words.

He looked at a spot over her shoulder. "Going through this thing with Ion—watching him die, wondering what would happen to Viktor—tore me apart. I'm ready to be a father, I think, although it will kill me if something happens to Viktor, too." He paused and took a deep breath, as if gathering his resolve.

"But I found myself worrying about you, too. Wondering what would happen if you got sick. Remembering how it felt when Lila died."

"So it *is* Lila." How could she compete with memories?

"Yes. No. Partly. I can't face losing someone else that I—love." So saying, he planted a sweet kiss on her forehead. "And you, your work here isn't done. I have to go back to Denver and you—"

"I have to stay here. I know."

For a long, rare moment, Carrie wished she could change her commitment and instead go home with Steve and Viktor. A tingling sensation ran up her arms from the spot where Steve clasped her hands, a reminder of what could be. Then Octavia tugged at her pant leg.

"Mama go?" she asked, bag in hand, ready to return to the orphanage.

Octavia. Jenica. Angelica. And others, not yet known. They were the reasons she must stay, to give them wings to fly to new homes.

Steve brushed her lips with a brief caress. "*Au revoir*, Carrie. I'll treasure these days always."

Chapter 12

The envelope felt warm in Carrie's hand, as if invisible hands reached across the miles and touched her own. Even before she noticed the Denver postmark, she knew it was from Steve. *He wrote to me!* Fighting the impulse to tear open the envelope, she tucked it in a pocket to savor during the children's afternoon naps. Almost as an afterthought, she wondered, *How is Viktor adjusting?* It was the first letter Steve had written since he had left Romania two months ago.

"Mama?" Mihail, her newest charge, called for her attention. Shaking herself out of her reverie, Carrie lifted him out of the crib—Ion's old bed. Next came Stefan, with cherubic blond curls and pale blue eyes, who had taken Viktor's place.

Gentle autumn light sneaked through the high windows, throwing a leafy pattern on the bare floor. Her spirit soared with thoughts of Steve and Viktor, and she started humming. "Rise and shine, and give God the glory, glory," she sang as she moved between the cribs. *I always know when I'm happy. I can't stop singing.*

A loud crash interrupted her thoughts. Octavia lay on the floor, one foot caught in the crib railings.

All set to scold the child for trying to climb out of the bed, Carrie raced across the floor.

"Mama," Octavia called, a smile shining out of her rheumy eyes.

A smile from cranky Octavia. Exasperation melted away in Carrie's heart, and gently she freed the offending foot. Cleaning the mucus from the girl's eyes, Carrie thought about Dr. Reynaud's upcoming visit. *Can he do anything to make her more comfortable?*

More important, what could she do? Somehow she had to prepare Octavia for their coming separation. While Carrie herded the children into the bathroom for their daily bath, a partial answer occurred to her: Teach Octavia some self-help skills. Running the bath, brushing her teeth, getting dressed—all things Octavia needed to learn to do for herself.

"Here, Octavia. I want you to help me run the bath. Can you lift the bucket?" The girl struggled with the heavy load; a generous puddle splashed on the floor, but in the end a thin layer of water lined the tub.

"Now another one. Fill it up this high." Pouring water until the tub was halfway full, Octavia added three more helpings of warm water.

"Now turn on the faucet." Carrie showed her how to mix a small amount of cold water with the hot water in the tub to make the water a comfortable temperature. Next she helped her find the laundry.

Proudly carrying in a stack of dry towels, Octavia announced, "I help."

It's a start. Pleased that she had figured out something specific to try with Octavia, Carrie started the day's routine. At lunch, each child seemed to take a minute longer to finish eating, an extra moment to fall asleep at naptime. *Will they never settle down?*

At last, she sat alone in her room and opened Steve's letter:

Dear Carrie,

    It doesn't seem possible that it's been two months since we left Romania. Everything considered, Viktor is adjusting well. He misses you terribly. The snapshot he has of you is getting worn around the edges.

    Does he miss me, too?

    I think of you often and say a little prayer. My time in Romania already seems like a dream. You and Viktor are the only realities that remain. . .

He does! Rubbing the page between her fingers, Carrie stretched out on her bed and read through the rest of the letter, reading and rereading special parts. Viktor's first trip to the doctor for immunizations—Sammy's delight at having a cousin close to his own age to play with—the high school band's adoption of Viktor as their mascot. She succumbed to the temptation to daydream. *What if Steve is still single when I leave Romania? What if Viktor still calls me "Mama"? What if. . .* The pages slipped from her fingers.

Viktor marched at the front of the band, dressed in a tiny blue-and-gold uniform. Beside him, walking backward, strode the drum major, a petite figure with Carrie's face. Her arms waved wildly in time to "Stars and Stripes Forever."

Steve walked alongside, smiling his encouragement and delight. *My two favorite people.* His lips moved. *When will you come to Denver?*

I can't. She tried to explain but couldn't get the words out of her mouth.

Late afternoon rays tickled her face when she returned to consciousness. It took a few minutes to reorient herself to the chilled room. *Steve's half a world away.* She splashed water on her face to chase away the loneliness that washed over her and pulled her midback-length hair into a ponytail. Time for the supper detail.

Dr. Reynaud arrived in the morning, bringing with him his usual breeze of enthusiasm and hope. "Good news! I have talked with doctors in Paris. We think Angelica can be helped. They would like to bring her to France for an operation."

"That's terrific! When does she go?" Inside she felt like dancing.

"As soon as it can be arranged. Funds shouldn't be a problem; a hospital board member will pay her airfare and other incidentals and provide lodging for her mother. The doctors are offering their services for free." Like two conspirators, they grinned at each other.

"My other news is not so good." He scowled at the results of the most recent lab tests. "Octavia's HIV has developed into full-blown AIDS."

Although she had always been aware of the possibility, Carrie's heart plummeted at the announcement. You could live with HIV; sooner or later, AIDS meant death. Tears blinded her eyes. "Oh, Octavia."

The doctor's hand squeezed her shoulder. "It is hard to understand why these little ones must suffer." She could hear the tears behind his voice.

"What can I do for her?"

"What you are already doing. Don't be afraid to hold her, love her. Help her live as normal a life as possible." He shuffled through some papers in his briefcase. "Here are precautions you must take. We've discussed them before, but they are doubly important now." Together they reviewed the safety tips.

Oh, Octavia. Who will leave the home first—you or me?

◆

The alarm jangled by Steve's ear. He groaned, turned over, then sat up in bed. Time for early morning marching band practice.

He stumbled to the kitchen and plugged in the coffeepot before heading for the shower. Stinging jets of hot water shook him out of sleepiness. He hadn't expected taking care of a child to require so much energy. All the little tasks added minutes, hours to each day. Still, he wouldn't change a minute of happy exhaustion for the lonely existence of the last few years. While the water needled him awake, he hummed—snatches of band music, melodies he had learned from Viktor. One folk song kept running through his head, reminding him of Carrie and the grave poverty of Romania. *How much I take for granted. Carrie didn't have a hot shower when she got up this morning.*

When he finished dressing, he headed for Viktor's room. The boy was already awake, holding a diaper in his hand as if ashamed that he had soiled himself overnight.

Steve hugged his son good morning and started with the diaper change. *I'll be glad when he is toilet trained. Patience. No one warned me that American pasteurized milk would make Viktor sick.*

"Which one do you want?" Steve held up two choices, a T-shirt with cartoon characters and a western-style button-down shirt. Shyly, Viktor pointed to the T-shirt. "Cat."

"Good choice. I like Sylvester myself." Funny, the thing he had thought would be hardest—the language barrier—was proving to be the easiest. Of course they said children learned languages much easier than adults.

Steve pulled the shirt over Viktor's uplifted arms and handed him a pair of jeans. Precious minutes crawled by while the child sorted out which foot went in which pant leg. As for the button at the waist, his pudgy fingers struggled to push it through the hole.

"Let me help you with that." Steve reached for the waistband.

The boy twisted away. "Viktor do it."

Suppressing a sigh, Steve sneaked a glance at his watch. If Viktor didn't finish soon, they might not have time for breakfast. Again. How did Carrie manage with five children? He could use some tips. Looking at the dial again, he grimaced. Ten minutes passed before they made it to the car, heading for the empty field where the band practiced marching routines.

"Where shall we eat this morning? McDonald's? The donut shop?"

"McDonald's." Viktor always asked for McDonald's.

Carrie would be ashamed of us, eating out every morning. Maybe it isn't so bad after all. A breakfast sandwich with cheese and orange juice provided a meal-in-one—bread, protein, dairy, fruit. *Nah, I'm just kidding myself.*

Except for the early hour, band rehearsal was the highlight of most days. Viktor picked out the melodies on his recorder and happily marched alongside the band, leading with the wrong foot half the time but always in time with the music.

A small group had already congregated at the end of the field. Two girls swooped down on Viktor. He stared at them beneath dark eyelashes.

While the girls entertained Viktor, Steve called aside his drum major. "We finally got the music for 'Rock-n-Roll Part 2.'" The band had begged for the song ever since pro sports had adopted the theme. "And this is what I'm thinking about for our uniforms during the Parade of Lights at Christmas—"

When practice ended, Steve ran Viktor over to day care, the same one Tim and Brenda's children attended. His heart twisted with a sinking sense of dread. *A lot of kids stay with babysitters. Why is it so hard for Viktor?* Oh, he knew the answers—fear of abandonment, fear of the other children. None of them helped when the boy started holding back at the door, burrowing his head into Steve's chest. How much better it would be if he could stay home with a mother.

Steve pulled into the parking lot and steeled himself for the battle ahead. Viktor slumped in his seat, not moving. Circling to the passenger's side of the car, Steve bent through the door and unbuckled the seat belt. In a cheerful voice, he said, "Let's go. Sammy's waiting for you." *They say it's best if he walks in on his own.*

Viktor didn't move. Steve grabbed the diaper bag and again gestured for Viktor to climb down. *Patience.*

"Viktor! You're here!" Sammy's voice rang out in welcome. "C'mon in. There's something I want to show you."

One leg slowly descended to the ground, and Viktor slid out of the car, allowing Sammy to grab his hand and run toward the door. Tempted as always to leave while Viktor was distracted, Steve forced himself to do the right thing—say good-bye. *They say if you disappear, he'll be more worried next time.* "See you tonight, Viktor."

Like an insect's antennae, Viktor's head swiveled, and he barreled in Steve's direction, clutching one leg. "Daddy go." He cried.

"Yes. I have to go teach. But I'll be back later." After hugging the boy, he gently pulled his arms away from his leg and left, shutting the door behind him.

A busy day lay ahead at the high school—orchestra rehearsal, jazz band, music classes for the general student body, some individual instruction. Today he had lunch duty. As he sat in the deafening noise of the cafeteria, one of the other teachers asked, "How is Viktor doing these days?"

Raising his voice to decibels high enough to be heard over the din, Steve answered. "Better. It only took fifteen minutes at the day care this morning."

The teacher, mother of an eighteen-month-old herself, groaned sympathetically. "Don't I know what you mean. Has the soybean milk helped the diarrhea problem?"

Steve nodded. "Much better. Although I'm sure McDonald's doesn't help."

"Naughty boy." She shook a finger at him. "I've got some quick-fixing recipes if you'd like them."

Everyone wants to offer advice when what I really need is a wife. "My sister has already given me a bunch of cookbooks. I just have to get organized."

"Yeah, it takes practice." She frowned at something across the room. "Looks like trouble's brewing."

Two upperclassmen looked ready to pounce on an undersized freshman boy. "I'll take care of it."

After lunch, Steve had a free period. Shutting the door against distractions, he pulled out sheets of music manuscript paper with several pages already penciled in. He wanted to capture the morning's melodies before they disappeared.

At last his rhapsody was taking form. In one burst of inspiration earlier in the fall, he had composed the opening. Like he had once described to Carrie, he tried to catch the glory of sunrise as seen from an airplane. Quiet strings and woodwinds suggested the gentle lightening of the night sky until trumpets blared to announce the arrival of the bright morning sun.

Now he wanted to incorporate some of the Romanian folk songs he had heard Carrie and Viktor sing. His hand poised over the paper, mentally striving to break down the unusual tones and rhythm into the standard musical alphabet of sharps, flats, and quarter notes. Intent on his work, he missed the ringing of the bell until loud conversation outside his door announced the arrival of the afternoon jazz band. He stared at the page with satisfaction. Snatches of melody covered it from top to bottom, a good start.

The day flew by, and soon he was at home. A letter from Carrie waited in the mailbox. "Hey, look, Viktor, Carrie has written us a letter!"

"Viktor see." His pudgy fingers traced the familiar letters of his name. "For me?"

"For both of us." Steve slit open the envelope, and two sheets of paper slipped out. He tucked the one addressed to him in his shirt pocket, where it warmed his heart as if it were on fire. "This one is for you." Settling in the big easy chair, he started to read, "Dear Viktor: I am glad you like your new home.... Angelica will have an operation to help her walk.... Jenica has gone to America with her new family...." Steve let Viktor study the paper while he read his own letter.

"Dear Steve: I am so glad things are going well with you and Viktor.... You were right. Right now, my place is in Romania. There is so much I want to do before I have to leave.... Octavia has full-blown AIDS. We knew it was coming, but I ache when I see her suffer so.... I am thinking about graduate school, getting a master's degree in counseling children...."

Does she miss me? Carrie's letter seemed restrained, as though she was afraid to express what was on her heart. Carrie, holding back? That didn't seem possible.

Absentmindedly browning a pound of ground beef, Steve read through the letter again. Master's degree? Didn't Denver Seminary offer a counseling program? Maybe he could send Carrie a catalog. The thought of having Carrie close by gave his heart a jump start.

A little later, dinner eaten, a sleepy Viktor snuggled in his arms. "What do you want to read tonight?" Steve asked.

Viktor handed Steve *Millions of Cats*, the story of the one special cat out of millions chosen by an old couple. A favorite from his own childhood, Steve wondered if its appeal lay as much as being the one cat adopted as in the repeating rhymes. Viktor joined him each time the refrain appeared: "Hundreds of cats, thousands of cats, millions and billions and trillions of cats."

One more thing needed to be done before Viktor would go to bed: sing at the piano. As usual, Viktor asked for "Victory in Jesus."

Some evenings Steve could hardly sing for the memories of Singers' trips that clogged his throat. Tonight, however, the familiar words stirred images of his first meeting with Viktor at the orphanage, Carrie dancing as they sang together.

Carrie. Two reasons to write: send a catalog and ask for more folk songs. His mouth twisted in a wry smile. *I'm ignoring the real reason. I miss her.*

As did Viktor. Every night he kissed Carrie's snapshot that was tucked into the corner of a picture frame.

After tucking his son into bed, Steve stared at the photo for a long moment. His fingertip traced the broad smile that lit Carrie's face. It was one of the things he missed most about her. Her lips turned up, inviting his kiss. *Stop wanting the impossible.* He stuffed his hands into his pockets and walked out of the room, shutting the door behind him.

◆

Carrie paced up and down the baggage claim area, waiting for the passengers from the Paris flight.

How much time had she spent at the airport, saying good-bye? Most recently Jenica had flown to the United States with her adoptive parents. And of course she had been there with Steve and Viktor.

Steve and Viktor. Viktor and Steve. Their names echoed through her head like the hooves of an approaching horse that caused the ground to vibrate. With their departure in the summer, a part of her had metamorphosed, growing past the need to cling jealously to each child, yet at the same time aching more than ever for a family of her own—with Steve. It was as if someone had changed the prescription of her glasses and she saw the world with sharper vision.

A group of passengers arrived at the baggage claim.

Shifting her gaze from the shadows of the past, Carrie called the children around her and surged forward with the crowd. All smiles, Mrs. Sorbul was one of the first down the ramp. Angelica rode proudly in her arms, arms clutching a gigantic teddy bear, legs swinging straight in brand-new braces. She broke into a broad grin when she spotted Carrie and the children.

"Carrie!" The childish voice pierced through the noise.

Carrie hurried to her side, hugging her. "Welcome home!" Hospital pale, Angelica still managed to glow with new health and hope. For the next few weeks, the children's home would serve as a rehabilitation center, Carrie providing primary care and exercising the reformed limbs. Dr. Reynaud had sent detailed instructions.

The crowd swept them. "How was Paris?"

"It is beautiful! And the doctors were kind."

"Thank God."

Angelica made remarkable progress in therapy. Triumph came at last on a snowy winter afternoon. *She's on the verge; I just know it.* "Come on, you can do it," she pleaded with the girl.

Angelica stared at her, unmoving, as stubborn as only a toddler could be. *Make me*, her stance declared. She sat down and started crawling away.

"Oh, no, you don't," Carrie muttered to herself. Rummaging through the few toys available, she pulled out the old red ball, a little tarnished by hours of play.

"Tell you what—let's play ball."

Eagerly Angelica crawled toward it.

"But you have to try to walk to get it."

Scowling, Angelica settled back into a sitting position.

What else can I try?

Carrie stirred through the toys again, seeking inspiration. When she turned, Angelica had risen to her feet.

"Mama!" With that joyous cry, as if drawn by a powerful magnet, Angelica moved one foot tentatively, then another.

"You're walking!" Mrs. Sorbul ran across the room. "Oh, my little angel, you're walking. Thank you, God." Mother and daughter embraced, tears and laughter mixing in equal measure.

She wanted her mother, Carrie realized with a start. A surge of resentment flared through her. Watching the absolute joy and pride lighting Angelica's face, the hurt ball inside her heart melted. *This is perfect.*

Angelica moved a few steps in Carrie's direction, showing off. "I can walk!"

"Yes, oh, yes!" Carrie hugged the girl to her. "You were waiting for your mother, that's all."

"I don't know what to say." Mrs. Sorbul could hardly speak for the joy trembling through her voice. "You're an angel, the way you work with the children here. I can never thank you enough for all you've done with my little girl."

"That's what I'm here for." *And I mean it.* Joy coursed like adrenaline through Carrie's veins, leaving her giddy with excitement. *This is what I'm meant to do. Give children wings.* She wanted to howl like a hyena at the inner confirmation.

Hours later, she reopened Steve's letter that contained the Denver Seminary catalog. ". . . thought you might be interested in the counseling program." *Yes!* Pen in hand, she filled in the lines. As she folded the papers to insert them in the envelope, she paused. *Why Denver? Reopen an old wound?* She blinked against the longing to hold Viktor in her arms, to feel Steve's kiss against her lips. *Well, why not Denver? Maybe God knows something I don't.*

Chapter 13

Carrie tore a page off her calendar. June 1st—only six weeks remained until she left Romania for good.

But where will I go? No answer yet from Denver Seminary.

She cinched a belt around her waist, two notches tighter than when she arrived almost two years ago, and ran a brush through her hair. *Item number one on the agenda when I get home: Get my hair cut.* She peered in the mirror, mentally trying on different hairstyles.

Item number two: Catch up with old friends. So many families had invited her to dinner while she spent two weeks with her parents in Philadelphia, she doubted that she could see them all.

Thinking of friends. *Will Steve and Viktor come to the Victory Singers reunion?* In his last letter, Steve wasn't sure if they would make the trip. Her heart tugged in opposite directions. How she longed to see them both again. For Viktor's sake, maybe it was best if she didn't see him for a while. The sooner he forgot about her and Romania, the easier his adjustment to his new life would be. *But I'll never forget him. Or his father. And what will happen if I go to Denver?*

Carrie checked the mailbox on her way to the toddler ward. Nothing yet.

"Good morning," Sister Marie called, cheerful as ever, as Carrie topped the stairs. "They are all awake, I think."

"Terrific." Bittersweet feelings, an eagerness to squeeze in every possible minute mixed with a distancing to deaden the pain of separation, filled these last days with her charges. In fact, one of her final challenges was how to prepare the precious children, who had come to depend on her, for her departure.

How can I even think about leaving? But I must! Sealing the pain away in a corner of her heart, she pushed the door open.

"Mama!" Even though Zizi had only been at the home since Angelica's departure two months earlier, she already clung to Carrie. Her parents had died in a car accident. Carrie hoped she would be adopted soon.

Unlike Octavia, for whom adoption was impossible. Each day her cry seemed weaker, her limbs thinner, as AIDS took hold. Her diseased body couldn't fight off illness anymore. Another winter cold might kill her. The only remaining child from her original group, she was more precious to Carrie than ever.

Setting the girls on the floor, Carrie collected Stefan and Mihail. "Bath time!" she called, heading for the doors.

111

She sneaked a look at the clock. Nine o'clock. At least four more hours remained until she could check on the mail again. Octavia confidently mixed hot water with the cold tap water. *Mission accomplished.* In addition to the bath, Carrie had shown her how to brush her hair and teeth and other basic skills appropriate for an almost five-year-old. *But who will take care of you when you are too weak to get out of bed?*

"*Trust Me.*"

I know they're Your children, Lord. Thank You for reminding me. She turned her attention back to the daily routine.

When Carrie returned to her room after lunch, Sister Pauline was waiting. "You received a letter. I believe it's the one you are waiting for."

Carrie grabbed the envelope and stared at it a long moment. Denver Seminary's logo glistened in the upper left-hand corner.

What does it say? She almost feared to open it, in case they said no.

"Remember God is in control," the director encouraged her. "Go ahead and open it."

As usual, she seems to know what I'm thinking. Slipping a thumbnail under the flap of the envelope, Carrie tore it open.

"Congratulations! You have been accepted to begin work in the counseling program...invaluable insight from your work in Romania...."

"Hooray!" Carrie hopped and leaped from sheer joy and relief.

"Praise God," Sister Pauline said quietly. "You have taken another step on the way to the work God created you to do."

Carrie hugged the older woman, mentor, friend, and spiritual counselor all in one. "Thank you." Feeling the brittle shoulder bones beneath her fingers, she could hardly imagine that the elderly woman was ever young or insecure. "I suspect that whenever I wonder what to do, I will ask myself, 'What would Sister Pauline do?'"

The tiny saint chuckled. "Keep your eyes fixed on the Lord," she gently chided. "Now I must return to my work." She closed the door behind her.

She means she must return to prayer. That's her work.

Carrie's feet skipped. *Thank You, Lord!* Nestled against the backdrop of the Rocky Mountains she had never seen, Denver Seminary had emerged her first choice for graduate school. She could continue her grounding in the Bible, in ministry, and in counseling, all at the same time.

And it's close to Steve and Viktor, she reminded herself, not for the first time. She shut the thought out. There were a lot of good reasons for going to Denver. Not many seminaries offered a degree in counseling. The Romeros, father and son, were only an added bonus.

◆

Steve laid down his pencil and slumped in his chair. Fighting for the right melodies and instruments to carry the overwhelming loss of wife and son had proved a difficult catharsis of spirit. *I loved you, Lila. I will always miss you. But I don't think about you all the time anymore.*

Checking the clock, he decided he had time to assemble Viktor's new swing set before the boy woke up from his nap. He dragged the heavy box outside. While he twisted the pipes together, squinting against the sun, he tried to figure out the instructions. It looked so easy when the salesman did it in the store. He had long ago resigned himself to being quick with his fingers but not with his hands. Grinding his teeth, he tried one more time. There! Half the frame was complete.

The patio door slid open, and Viktor ran across the grass. Strong brown legs pumped beneath red shorts, shorter than when they were purchased in the spring. *My son. Thank You, Lord.*

Only a week before, the courts finalized the adoption. Tim and Brenda would join them for a celebration dinner in the evening.

"Daddy play ball with Viktor?" The boy clutched a foam football in his hands. He reached down and touched the aluminum tubing. "What is it?"

"It will be a swing." Steve looked at the half-assembled materials. *There's always next weekend.* "Come on, let's play some football." Tucking boy and ball under his arm like a football running back, he ran to the fence at the back of the yard. "Touchdown!" Steve shouted, thrusting a giggling Viktor high into the air. He let him down, and they rolled together in the grass, Viktor still clutching the ball. Grass filled Steve's nostrils as Viktor plunked down on his back before jumping off. Memories of another football game intruded, a time when his arms cradled Carrie's slender body. A tremor of remembered desire jolted through him.

Breathless, Steve struggled into a sitting position. Drawing in one gulp of air, he said, "Let's toss the ball for a few minutes."

Rough and tumble play continued for another hour. The sun slanted west when they stopped for the afternoon. Heading inside to prepare for the evening's celebration, Steve flicked on the television for the five o'clock news.

The local sports reporter was giving the teaser. "And how was the first week of training camp for the Broncos? Stay tuned and find out."

The Broncos' season is starting already? Thinking of the many empty hours he had whiled away in front of the television set during football season, Steve was thankful once again he had Viktor to fill his days with joy.

He checked the clock. 5:15 p.m. Uh oh. Tim and Brenda were due in about an hour. Time to get the barbecue grill going.

An hour later, father and son surveyed the results of their efforts. Viktor had carefully torn lettuce into tiny pieces for the salad while Steve had started up the grill, laid out the steaks, and set the table. The front doorbell rang.

"Uncle Tim!" Steve's heart warmed at the way Viktor reached out to his family.

Sammy and Amanda raced into the room ahead of their parents. Brenda proffered a bouquet of roses. "Congratulations, Daddy! It's finally official," she said, kissing her brother on the cheek.

"Thanks. I have a vase here somewhere." He dug a cut glass vase out of the china cabinet.

"And this is for you." Brenda handed Viktor a package, winking at Steve when Viktor started to open it. Wrapped inside were a faded Broncos hat and a child-sized Victory Singers T-shirt.

"That hat."

"Broncos." Viktor recognized the logo immediately.

"You shouldn't have." Steve said to Brenda. Pulling the cap over Viktor's head, he explained, "Not just any hat. This was your Grandfather Romero's favorite, lucky hat, the one he wore during every game of the Broncos' first Super Bowl season."

"And he wanted his grandson to have it," Brenda said firmly.

Tim leafed through the packet of pictures taken of Steve and Viktor about a month earlier. "They turned out well."

Steve studied the portraits again. How tall, how tanned and healthy Viktor appeared.

"You both look so happy," Brenda said. "Viktor is actually smiling. How did they coax a smile out of him?" She glanced over to where he sat, watching the proceeding as solemn as usual.

"The usual gimmicks." Steve grinned at the memory. "The photographer said Viktor looked a lot like me. When I explained that he was adopted, she couldn't believe it."

Head cocked to one side, Brenda studied their faces. "Viktor does have the same dark curly hair and onyx eyes as the Romeros." She ran a hand over her own head. "But it's more than that. You both have the same shy smile that sneaks up on you like sunrise behind the mountains." She picked up the 11 x 14 print, already in an ornate frame. "Where are you going to hang this one?"

"On the wall of fame, of course." They headed for the hallway. Steve looked down the row of pictures, from high school graduation to wedding to his last tour with the Victory Singers. Carrie's face stared at him from the front row, teeth gleaming in a face framed by short, bouncy hair. *She's here with us in spirit.*

Turning his back on pictures of the past, he tried the frame against the opposite wall. "Over here, I think. New life, new wall." Spoken half in jest, the words sent joy pulsing through him. *This is it. Viktor is my son.* He tugged another frame out of a plain white envelope. "This belongs next to the picture." It was the adoption certificate.

"Viktor Timothy Romero. I'm honored." Tim's voice cracked as he read the name emblazoned in bold print.

"My victorious son in the faith. That's my Viktor." Steve hammered nails into the wall and hung the frames side by side. Gathering Viktor in his arms, they stood staring for a moment longer.

"Viktor." The boy pointed to the letters of his name.

"Viktor Romero." Steve emphasized the surname.

"Daddy." Viktor tucked his head against Steve's chest.

Into the emotionally charged silence that threatened to make all the adults cry, Sammy's voice intruded. "When are we going to eat? I'm hungry!"

Steve blinked away tears and looked at his watch. "The potatoes should be about ready. Time to put the steaks on. Well done for you, Tim, and rare for Brenda. What about the kids?"

Over the meal, conversation turned to the upcoming Victory Singers reunion. "Do you think you'll go this year?" Brenda inquired gently. "A lot of people are anxious to see you again. And they're curious about Viktor."

"And Carrie Randolph has sent her registration," Tim added.

Viktor's head popped up at hearing the name Carrie.

Blood raced through Steve's veins at the mention of her name. Almost a year had passed since he last saw her. Did she want to see him as much as he wanted to see her, or had she changed? *If not me, she'll at least want to see Viktor.*

"That's right, her two-year stint must be just about over," Brenda said. "I wonder what she plans on doing next."

"She's going to graduate school. Maybe Denver Seminary," Steve answered automatically.

"Really? I hadn't heard that." Tim blinked in surprise.

"About the reunion—I haven't decided yet. Viktor doesn't deal well with large groups of strangers."

When Steve tucked Viktor into bed that night, the boy asked, "Mama coming?" He pointed to Carrie's picture that he still kept by his bedside.

"Not here. She's going to the reunion in Texas. Do you want to see her?"

"Yes." No hesitation slowed his answer.

"Then maybe we'll go."

Tossing in bed, Steve turned the questions over and over in his mind. *Would it be too much for Viktor? Do I want to see Carrie again when we're surrounded by other people? Do I want to drag up Viktor's past?* He started to drift off to sleep before he realized he hadn't thought of Lila all evening. Only Carrie. *Maybe I'll go after all.*

◆

The jet sped down the runway, exhilarating Carrie. *I'm going home!* For a few weeks anyway, before heading to the reunion and points west. "Pennsylvania, here I come!" she sang out.

"Right back where you started from." At her side, Michelle responded. "I've never been to Philadelphia. This should be fun. Birthplace of our country, and all that."

"I suppose you'll want to do all the tourist things." Carrie groaned. "The Liberty Bell and Independence Hall."

"Of course! And I want to check out the Philly fanatic—"

"You and baseball. Don't forget we've been asked to speak at my church," Carrie reminded her friend. "They're anxious to hear about Romania firsthand."

"Yeah." The friends fell silent as they thought about the country they had left behind. Carrie wasn't sure that she could show pictures of the children without crying. *Maybe I should stick to a prepackaged program.*

"Have you heard if Steve Romero is planning on going to the reunion?"

Always the matchmaker. Carrie didn't want to admit that she had been wondering the same thing. "I don't know." She shrugged, trying to act like it didn't matter. "The registration packet should be waiting for me at home. Tim promised a list of people who were attending."

"I hope he does." Michelle dug in her purse for a book. "You two need to see each other again. You belong together, although you don't seem to realize it yet." She started reading.

Remembering the intimacy of their last week together in Romania—the picnic, *the kiss*, the hectic days spent caring for the sick children—brought an unexpected yearning. *But we've both moved past that,* she rationalized. Steve had spent a busy year raising Viktor while she had stayed in Romania. An equally important time lay ahead, earning her master's degree. *But school and romance don't have to be mutually exclusive.* She couldn't keep the thought out.

Ouch! One ear popped. She yawned to lessen the impact of the decreased air pressure in the cabin, and her mouth swung open in sleepiness. As she drifted off to sleep, Steve's and Viktor's voices sang a lullaby in her mind, and their faces danced and merged together. *Maybe he's had time to forget about Lila by now. Fat chance.* Turning her head against the cushion, she fell into a light sleep.

It was only midday in Philadelphia when the plane touched down at the airport. Carrie and Michelle walked slowly through the tunnel, letting families and children rush past them. *How strange to hear English everywhere.*

Trailing behind the other passengers, they halted at the spectacle that greeted them.

Signs proclaiming WELCOME HOME, CARRIE! and HELLO, MICHELLE crammed the baggage claim area. Carrie stopped counting after she saw her parents, grandparents, two aunts, an uncle, and her pastor and his wife waiting with the crowd.

"Carrie!" Her mother was the first to spot them. She ran toward her daughter. In Carrie's mind it took on the slow motion aspect of a commercial then sped up like fast-forward. Her mother reached both arms around her, crushing her close, and kissed her on both cheeks.

They looked into each other's eyes, tears blurring Carrie's vision. "It's good to be home, Mom."

Mrs. Randolph looked Carrie over from head to toe, as if committing the changes that had taken place to memory. Then she turned to welcome Michelle.

The spectators surged forward, engulfing Carrie in the tide and sweeping them to the baggage carousel.

"You look great."

"How was the trip?"

"Joanie couldn't make it to the airport. She's coming over later." Joanie was Carrie's best friend in high school.

After awhile, Carrie gave up trying to follow all the conversation thrown at her. *It would be easier if everyone spoke Romanian!*

Somewhere close by a phone jingled, and her dad pulled a phone out of his pocket. "Yes, she's right here." He handed the contraption to his daughter. "It's Joanie."

Carrie stared at the instrument and held it gingerly to her ear. "Carrie! Welcome home!" They spoke briefly, making plans for the next day, and said good-bye.

Carrie tried several buttons, but nothing seemed to break the connection. "How do I turn this thing off?"

"Like this." Her dad laughed and showed her how. "I used to scoff at cell phones, but now I wouldn't know how to function without it."

Cell phones? Carrie thought of the one phone in Sister Pauline's office that serviced all four buildings of the orphanage. She shook her head in disbelief.

Soon Carrie and Michelle were ensconced in the familiar family brownstone on Maple Street. By evening, tiredness swamped Carrie—after all, in Romania it was the middle of the night—but she couldn't go to sleep. *Maybe a cup of hot cocoa will do the trick. Like it used to.*

She wandered down to the kitchen, where her mother was putting finishing touches on a cake.

"Mmm, German chocolate, my favorite." Carrie dipped a finger into the coconut pecan frosting.

"Stop that." Her mother batted away her fingers. "Did you have a good nap?"

"Not really." Carrie rummaged through the shelves, not finding what she was looking for. "Where's the cocoa mix?"

"We ran out. You want some?"

"Yeah." Carrie grinned sheepishly. "I thought it might help me sleep.

Maybe I'll take a shower instead." *Make that a long, hot shower.*

"Wait a minute." Spreading the frosting to the edges of the cake, Mrs. Randolph handed the bowl and spatula to Carrie. "That's it. Let's run to the convenience store. I need some butter, too."

The convenience store? That's right, they were open twenty-four hours. No need to wait until the market opened in the morning.

Keys dangling from her hand, her mother had slipped her purse strap over her arm. "Ready to go?"

Even at this late hour, cars filled the roads and streetlights brightened every corner, transforming night into day. Walking into the air-conditioned store, Carrie shivered. While her mother picked up a few groceries, she leafed through recent magazines and studied the styles.

Shopping. I have to buy clothes. Planning a wardrobe fit for a princess— the reunion, anyway—occupied her attention until her mother reached the checkout line.

A couple of days passed before Carrie and Michelle made it to the mall. "Everything's so expensive," Carrie complained, holding up a pink dress against her face.

"Uh-huh." Michelle agreed. She pulled out a yellow dress identical in style to the pink one Carrie held. "Try this one. Yellow is Steve's favorite color."

Steve again. "Who cares?"

"Try it on anyhow." Michelle grinned, thrusting it into Carrie's hands as she headed for the dressing rooms.

"Very well." She pulled the dress over her head. *Michelle is right!* The soft color made her dark hair shine, and lacy edges added just the right touch.

"Ta da!" She waltzed out in front of her friend. "I love it!"

"Told you so."

This is fun! Next Carrie searched for a suit. She found one in navy blue with yellow accents and a white blouse with yellow stripes. It made her feel grown-up and pretty at the same time. After a couple of pairs of jeans, a full two sizes smaller than when she left for Romania, and new dress shoes, she had blown most of her shopping budget.

All too soon Carrie and Michelle returned to the airport, a day before Carrie would leave for the reunion. It was time for Michelle to return home.

"You have my address," Michelle said for the hundredth time. "I'll let you know if I decide to move. I get restless if I stay with my parents too long."

"And I'll send you my address as soon as I get settled in Denver."

Michelle reached the ticket agent and received her boarding pass.

"Well, this is it." They hugged tightly in a reluctant farewell; then Michelle quickly walked toward the security checkpoint.

Tears flowed into Carrie's eyes as she said good-bye to her last direct link with Romania. *But soon I'll see Viktor again. And Steve.* In spite of herself, a thrill raced down her spine at the thought.

Two days later, she walked confidently down the hallway to the room where the Singers would practice. Lemon chiffon material swished against her legs, emphasizing her transformation from collegian to young woman. *If only Steve is here to see it.* Through open doors she heard a quiet glissando across piano keys.

Rubbing her sweaty palms on a dry handkerchief, she paused at the doorway. She quickly located the piano. It looked like—

"Mama!" Viktor's voice rang out, and he ran across the floor to hug his beloved Carrie.

Chapter 14

Steve watched as Viktor hurled himself at Carrie's knees. "Viktor!" Carrie's voice rang out cheerfully. "How are you?"

"I am good!" He answered in English proudly.

"Terrific!" She bent over and hugged him close to her. "It's so good to see you!" Leaning back, she studied him from head to toe. "You've grown." Laughing at herself, she added, "I bet people tell you that all the time."

"Two inches." Viktor confirmed, thrusting two fingers into the air.

About the time Steve wondered if she had noticed him at all, Viktor tugged her in his direction. "See Daddy."

As she walked slowly toward him, lemon folds swishing around graceful legs, he took in the details of her appearance. A new haircut emphasized her high cheekbones; makeup-enhanced eyelashes highlighted velvet brown eyes. She seemed not so much older or taller as more self-assured and mature. Why had he ever thought she looked like Lila?

A broad smile created tiny dimples in her cheeks. "Steve! I wasn't sure if I would see you. Your name wasn't on the registration sheet."

"I know; it was a last-minute decision. Viktor insisted when he heard you were coming." He could feel a wide grin splitting his own face. Impulsively he reached out and hugged her, the way alumni all around them were greeting each other.

"I was glad I got back in time." She clasped his hands between her own and studied him much as she had studied Viktor. Tension built during her silent inspection.

"You're looking well. Being a father must agree with you."

He relaxed. "Couldn't be better."

Silence fell between them. Steve wanted to say, *I've missed you; have you missed me?* but the words stuck in his throat.

"How are you doing, Carrie? Steve, introduce us to your son." Guy came up beside them. Reluctantly Steve dropped her hands and turned his attention to the trumpeter. A skirt swirled against his leg, and Carrie was gone, taking her place in the choir loft.

Returning alumni arrived in waves, everyone eager to meet Viktor. In the first row of the choir, Carrie held court, passing around snapshots and gesturing excitedly. Steve heard occasional snatches. "Viktor...Octavia..." He tried to catch her eye, but she was too involved in her stories to notice. Vaguely unhappy, he took his place at the piano and helped the instrumentalists warm up. Viktor stood at his side.

"Come play with me," Sammy invited, leaving Steve alone on the piano bench. *How can I feel so alone in a room full of people?* He found himself answering questions automatically.

Tim signaled for Steve to run through their signature number, "Victory in Jesus." After a short warm-up to review songs for the reunion concert, the group dismissed for supper.

When Steve hurried to the dining hall after retrieving Viktor from the nursery, he found Carrie seated at a table, surrounded by several other sopranos, including Lisa and Amy and their families. *Is she avoiding me? Don't be ridiculous.* He sat down next to Tim and Brenda. A hurt feeling gnawed away at his stomach, diminishing his appetite.

Over salads Viktor waved a greeting. Steve searched the room for Carrie. Her eyes fixed on his for a brief second before she abruptly turned away. After that he noticed her studying the two of them throughout the meal. Irritation replaced worry as he became uncomfortable under her scrutiny.

He made sure he went to the dessert table at the same time as Carrie. Catching her by the elbow, he asked, "Is something wrong?" He could have sworn he saw hunger in her eyes, a loneliness akin to the feeling he experienced at the piano.

"No."

"Then why are you avoiding us? I was hoping you would join us for supper—"

"Let's find a place where we can talk privately for a minute." She grabbed a cup of coffee and headed for a corner.

"Viktor called me Mama. Even after all this time." Her voice sounded bleak. "And as much as I wish I was his mother—I'm not. I never will be. And I don't want to confuse him about who is his real parent."

As simple, as generous as that. In spite of the hunger evident in her eyes, the lurking pain that she returned from Romania without a child, she thought of Viktor first. How much she had changed from the young woman who held on to the children as if she would never let them go. He looked at her with new respect.

"I appreciate what you're trying to do." *But I'm selfish; I want time with you myself.* "But Viktor will be heartbroken if you don't spend time with him. Can we talk about it later? After he's gone to bed?"

"I'd like that." She opened her mouth in a smile as dazzling as her dress.

"Daddy?" Viktor stood on his chair, searching the room for Steve. His heart warmed at the wholehearted trust his son placed in him. The awesome responsibility scared him at times.

Tim tapped on his glass.

"It must be time for the slide show. Until later, then," Carrie said gently.

Steve admired her departing back, almost regal in its straightness. When she sat down with a feminine flounce and flash of hair, he shook himself out of his reverie and chose a brownie for Viktor before sitting back down.

◆

Carrie watched Steve make his way back to the dinner table. Viktor hugged him like a drowning man clinging to a life preserver. He fed Steve bits of brownies, laughing at the mess they made.

Joy and envy fought as she studied the family they had formed. Her remaining regrets about Romania centered around Viktor. Losing him felt like losing a part of herself. And she could only have Viktor if she also had—Steve. Double or nothing. Sister Pauline's words stayed with her: "Jesus promised that anyone who gave up father and mother, brother and sister, son or daughter for His sake would be blessed a hundredfold." She was reminded of an old maxim: You can't outgive God.

Casting one last look at the father and son, she turned to greet yet another Singer headed for the dessert table. "Leslie? Is that you?"

They hugged, and Leslie introduced her family—her husband of two years and their three-month-old baby. All around her alumni had multiplied; their original group of forty had grown to close to a hundred. Carrie was one of maybe a dozen still unmarried.

"Find your places, please," Tim directed as he dimmed the lights. "It's time for the slide show."

Eagerly Carrie slipped back into her seat. In addition to pictures from their trip to Romania, everyone had submitted pictures and information about the intervening years.

Slides flew by, chronicling early rehearsals, the airplane trip, Radu and Anika, scenery and concerts. Suddenly, Lila's smiling face filled the screen. The room fell silent.

Steve rose to speak. In a quiet voice that managed to reach into every corner of the room, he began. "You all know that Lila and our baby son, Brandon, died while we were in Romania."

An uncomfortable murmur stirred around the room.

"I wanted to thank all of you for your prayers and your help. I never would have made it through those dark days alone. To honor Lila's memory—we would like to dedicate this year's concert to her."

Tentatively at first, then gaining in strength, spontaneous applause broke out around the room. The tears that flowed down Carrie's cheeks joined a surging tide shed by the group. While she approved of the idea of a memorial concert, she couldn't help wondering, *Is he still in love with her?*

Gradually the applause died down. A new picture appeared on the screen—Steve and Viktor in front of the children's home. "I decided to return to Romania to adopt a child. Many of you have met my son Viktor."

Laughter and applause rippled across the room.

"I don't want to steal anyone's thunder, but I want to thank Carrie Randolph for her part in bringing us together."

Carrie felt her cheeks burning red as people looked in her direction. Although her return to Romania was no secret, she was still embarrassed. Her attention wandered as Steve continued speaking of the joys of fatherhood. How handsome he was, how natural he was in front of an audience. Of course, he dealt with his band class every day. She was more comfortable one-on-one.

He spoke about his students next. "Next to being Viktor's father, teaching is the most important thing I do. I try to make band a place where the students can succeed and learn to work together and feel good about themselves." He ended with a picture of Viktor dressed in a miniature uniform, recorder proudly in hand, posing at the front of the band. Steve looked almost military in his bandleader's uniform, seemingly oblivious to the rabbit ears some students had stuck up behind his head.

Steve had rarely spoken with Carrie about his work. The adoption had filled their conversations. Now she realized that they had more in common than Viktor. They both burned with a desire to help children and young people through difficult times. She resolved to discuss it with him in more depth.

Steve sat down, and Carrie was startled to hear her own voice. "Speaking to me out of a dream just like Paul's Macedonian call, God told me to return to Romania." She had opted for a taped presentation. Besides discomfort with public speaking, she feared she would break down in tears when she talked about the children. There they appeared in front of her: Sister Pauline, Cristina, Sister Marie, Dr. Reynaud, Michelle—the children, all of them. Viktor and Adrian's parents. Ion's empty crib.

"Viktor!" The boy's voice rang out when he recognized his own picture. A couple of people laughed out loud.

I won't cry. But she couldn't help it. The tears came. A chair behind her squeaked as it was dragged across the floor, and Steve leaned forward, offering her a tissue. His own eyes glistened with tears.

"I miss them, too," he said softly. "Every day I thank God for Viktor and pray for the ones left behind." A montage of pictures appeared on the screen. Carrie's voice concluded, "I left Romania with a renewed sense of purpose: God wants me to work with troubled children here in America. To that end, I will start in the counseling program at Denver Seminary in the fall."

"Denver?" Steve's eyes lit up like a Christmas tree. "You didn't tell me—"

"I didn't want to say anything until I was sure. The acceptance letter arrived just before I came home."

Please tell me you're glad I'm coming to Denver. Carrie's unspoken request went unanswered. Viktor climbed into her lap, long legs dangling almost to the floor, and she breathed deeply of his squeaky clean hair. How she had missed him.

Congratulations and well wishes flowed Carrie's way as the program continued. Graduations, weddings, and babies were punctuated by a few serious notes.

"My father died last year—"

"I sang with the Metropolitan Opera Company last season!"

"We moved to Chicago—"

Soon Viktor fell asleep in Carrie's arms. About nine thirty, Brenda joined them at the table, Amanda asleep in her arms and a yawning Sammy at her side. "You two stay and enjoy yourselves. I'll put Viktor to sleep with the others."

Steve smiled his thanks and roused Viktor. "It's time for bed. Go ahead with Aunt Brenda."

The child blinked, rubbed his eyes, and hugged Carrie tight before he climbed out of her lap. Kissing Steve on the cheek, he said, " 'Night."

About half an hour later, the meeting broke up. Carrie remained in her seat, unwilling for the evening to end.

Several empty coffee cups stood on the table. *No wonder I'm not sleepy, after all that caffeine.* Stacking the cups, she started to get up from her seat.

"Please don't leave."

Surprised, Carrie looked at Steve and remained in the chair. Her heart hammered beneath her ribs.

"Would you like to join me for a late-night stroll? They say there's a beautiful path where the San Antonio River flows through downtown." He gazed directly at her, his eyes begging her to say yes.

He smiled, and she was lost. "I'd love to."

Slipping an arm around her shoulder, Steve said, "C'mon, let's go."

Minutes later they descended stone steps outside the hotel to the waiting river. Gentle light glowed from old-fashioned lanterns, and cobblestones lined the walkway. They leaned over the embankment and stared into the river pulsating downstream. Water slapped against the walls in a syncopated rhythm. A flatboat powered past them in the darkness, crowded with shadowy figures and voices laughing in the night.

Another river, another time flowed into Carrie's mind. The Dimbovita. An impromptu game of soccer with three unskilled players. A kiss that brought to the forefront the feelings simmering between Steve and herself.

That was then; this is now. Shaking her head to clear the unwanted memories, Carrie focused on the present, Steve at her side. *We've never been alone before without Viktor.* Giddy with the thought, she couldn't suppress a wide grin.

Steve didn't say much, seemingly content to soak in the atmosphere. Mariachis strolled by. Spotting the couple, they paused and began playing. Trumpets wailed a sad song of love won and lost. Steve tossed coins in the wide sombrero. The musicians smiled their thanks and continued on their way.

◆

"Music. It's the language of the soul." Carrie twirled, her skirts flying in an imitation of a Mexican folk dance. "Have you finished the rhapsody yet?"

"Almost." Steve bit off the words. "I can't seem to end it. Nothing works."

"Mmm. Must be frustrating. But I'm sure you'll figure it out."

They stopped to buy a drink of papaya juice. "It's so different from Romania," Carrie commented.

"Denver, too." Steve sipped his drink. "Have you ever been there?"

"No. I've never been west of the Mississippi before this trip. But I've wanted to visit the Rockies for years." She couldn't say that the main attraction of Denver was the man opposite her and a beloved child.

"Carrie." Steve leaned in toward her and started to speak.

As he neared, Carrie's cheeks warmed. Wanting to cool the rising heat, she gulped the juice. The pulpy liquid choked her, rendering speech impossible. Or was it the energy sizzling between them? Would he kiss her?

Steve pulled back and looked at his watch. "It's late. We should get back." Taking her arm, he steered her toward the hotel, leaving her with the feeling of something left unsaid.

◆

Steve collected Viktor from his sister and made his way to his room next door. He adjusted the child's ever-lengthening body in his arms, and young eyelids fluttered open for a moment. He hugged his father's neck.

Steve tucked blankets around Viktor and bent over to kiss him good night. *Thank you, God, for this child. For my new life.* He thanked God for the miracle that brought them together.

Viktor opened a sleepy eye. "See Mama again?"

Mama. "Yes, we'll see Carrie again in the morning."

"Good." He slipped back into sleep.

Mama. Steve stared down at the sleeping form for a few more minutes. Carrie was, maybe always would be, mother to his precious son; and she was moving to Denver. Their lives continued to intertwine like vines on the same branch, past, present, and future.

Thinking of the future, he wanted to rework the rhapsody's finale. The band had practiced it, ready to premiere the composition at the reunion concert. He wasn't satisfied with the ending; he hadn't found the right note to end the music. *Until now.*

In a flash, he knew what would complete the rhapsody, what was missing in the song that was his experience of Romania. He sank into the chair and stared out the window at the San Antonio landscape. *Is it true?* Looking over at his sleeping son, he reviewed the emotions surging through him. *Yes!* Furiously he began to jot notes on manuscript paper.

Day dawned before he wrote the final notes, and, with a final flourish, he jotted a few words on the first page of the composition. *That's it. Now to get the band to perform it.*

◆

Tim's voice trailed after the choir as they left the stage. "While the Singers prepare for the next part of the program, our band will premiere a new work by our pianist, Mr. Steve Romero. It is entitled, appropriately for this reunion concert, 'Romanian Rhapsody.'"

Carrie stood, rooted to the spot. He had finished it! She had to hear it. Somehow, as French horns and drums rumbled, she could see Lila, and brass proclaimed the grandeur of St. Joseph's. Children played through a lively Romanian folk melody that sang across violin strings. Woodwinds took over, and her eyes flew open. She was right! A simple child's recorder carried the melody briefly, and once again she saw the first meeting between Steve and Viktor.

"Carrie, you have to change." Amy tugged at her elbow. Reluctantly, she moved away from the music that evoked Romania and all that she loved about it.

A haunting oboe melody, full of love and longing, followed her into the dressing room. Passion tingled along her nerve endings. *Oh, Steve.* She shut her eyes against the unwanted pain. Mechanically she exchanged her choir robe for the evening gown and took her place at the end of the line. *I'll have to congratulate him. It's beautiful.*

The concert ended. She couldn't find Steve alone to congratulate him on the premiere. Audience and Singers alike crowded him in an attempt to be the first to praise his work.

Ready to give up until a later time, Carrie started for the dressing room to change into street clothes.

"Carrie! Wait!"

She turned at the sound of the familiar voice, a certain panic emphasizing the words. A smile bubbled to her lips and burst forth as he pushed his way through the crowd. "It was wonderful. It took me back."

"Well, thank you." A look she couldn't interpret passed over his face. "Can we meet later? When things die down?"

"Of course." She squeezed in the words before another group of admirers swept between them.

In the dressing room, Carrie took her time, toning down her makeup since she wouldn't be on stage, slipping into her new navy suit. Checking in the mirror, she nodded her satisfaction. It did look good on her.

Snatches from the rhapsody rang through her head. He had found the elusive musical answer. It evoked mental images of the Romania she had left behind—Lila, Radu and Anika, Sister Pauline, St. Joseph's, the home. The children.

Viktor—and Steve. Playing the recorder. Taking care of sick children. The dreams and kisses they had shared. A pang stabbed her heart. She still dreamed that somehow they could get together and become a family, the three of them. How could she settle for friendship when she wanted a family?

Someone knocked at the door. "Come in."

Tim poked his head into the dressing room. "Steve asked me to tell you that the coast is clear, if you're ready." She could have sworn that he winked at her.

Carrie felt her cheeks flame red, negating the need for the blush she had so carefully applied. "I'll be right out," she called to the closing door. *What's going on?*

With one last glance in the mirror and check of her hair, she left the room and headed for the stage. With auditorium lights dimmed, a gentle glow played across the platform. What looked like a candle cast flickering shadows across the music stand on the piano.

"Carrie." Steve's voice caressed her name, husky tones vibrating from his throat. "Thank you for waiting. I thought they'd never clear out."

"They all wanted to congratulate you." She moved closer, ascending the stairs to the platform. Clearing her throat, she tried to put into words how the music made her feel. "It was moving. Beautiful and sad and happy. Beyond description." She started to cry.

As if from a distance, Steve handed her a handkerchief and started speaking. "I just finished it last night. No matter how hard I tried, I couldn't get it to tie together. For the longest time something was missing, and nothing I put in worked. Not Viktor's songs, not Radu's unshakable faith, nothing."

He took her by the hand and led her toward the piano. Flickering candlelight obscured the sheets of music sitting on the stand.

"Then I found the answer." He scooped the pages in his hand and displayed them to Carrie.

"Romanian Rhapsody." She stared at the page for a moment. What did he want her to see? By Steven Romero. *For Carrie.* A warm tide washed over her, head buzzing from excitement. *Could he mean—?*

"I realized what was missing was you. For my music—my life!—to be complete, I need you."

Removing the music from her and grasping her hands in his own, he leaned forward and kissed the lips that Carrie offered. *I can't believe this is happening.* Delight and puzzlement raced through her mind, dazzling nerve endings in their wake.

"Carrie." Steve's arms had found their way around her shoulders. "I never thought I would love again after Lila died. But you became part of my life—part of Viktor's life—and I couldn't get you out of my mind. Or my heart."

She leaned into his chest, rejoicing in the moment.

He tilted her chin so that he could look into her eyes. "Carrie Randolph. Do you love me? Will you marry me?"

She found her voice. "With all my heart. Yes."

As one their hearts beat in time to the rhapsody that echoed in her ears. His embrace tightened, and his lips claimed hers for another kiss.

PLAINSONG

Dedication

A special thanks to Kathy Brasby for helping me with the layout of Coors Field and to Regina Jennings, Erin Young, and Sharon Srock for helping me bring this "child" to birth.

Chapter 1

Do you want to know the way to heaven?" A young man dressed in a suit coat and tie, unexpected on the hot July night, asked people as they surged past him to Coors Field for a night of Colorado Rockies baseball. Before walking on, Joe Knight glanced at the tract with a bright red cross on it.

"You're not interested in heaven then?" The man's voice trailed after him.

Joe stopped to explain that he already knew the way to heaven and to wish the evangelist Godspeed, but the man had already turned his attention elsewhere. Joe shook his head as he watched the man approach an attractive young woman. She flicked sweeping blond hair over her shoulder as she accepted the tract and stopped for a minute to talk. Joe took in her long, shapely legs and well-tailored slacks.

Coins jangled nearby, and one of the street bums who cluttered every corner stopped Joe. His sign read HOMELESS VET. PLEASE HELP. How much money had he stashed away during the course of the day? Joe had heard news reports about the scams some of the street people pulled. The woman he had seen before approached, dug in her purse, and tossed in a handful of change.

Joe hesitated then followed her. "Ma'am, I wouldn't do that again if I were you."

She turned deep green eyes in his direction. "Excuse me?"

For a moment he forgot what he was saying, and then he found his voice. "That man. He'll probably just use the money for alcohol or drugs."

"Or maybe he'll buy a meal. He could use one. There's no reason people should go hungry in a rich country like America." Her eyes clouded.

She turned away, and Joe noticed a couple behind her who looked vaguely familiar.

"Joe Knight, what brings you all the way to Denver tonight?" the husband asked.

His brain made the connection. "Steve and Carrie—Romero, isn't it? I'm in town on business but had tickets to the game tonight. What a surprise to run into you here. But I don't believe I've had the privilege of meeting your friend."

Carrie turned to the stunning blond. "Michelle, this is Joe Knight. Joe is on the mission committee of one of the churches that supports the work in Romania. And Joe, this is my friend, Michelle Morris."

Green eyes fastened on his face. "That's wonderful." She extended a manicured hand. "I was in Romania at the same time Carrie was. That's where we met."

Was Michelle a missionary as well? I'd like to learn more about her. He felt for the baseball tickets stashed in his pocket, given to him when one of his clients couldn't go to the game. *Why not?* "Ma'am?"

She glanced at him again, her smile questioning. "Yes?"

"Do you like baseball?"

"I love it. I'm afraid I'm the one who dragged Carrie and Steve here tonight." She glanced at the brunette.

"Although we're headed for the rock pile," Carrie said. "Not the best seats."

"Well." Joe paused. *What would she think of a total stranger inviting her out? I'll never know unless I ask.* "I have an extra ticket along the right field line to tonight's game. It's the Mets." He waved the tickets as if the Yankees were in town. "Would you like to join me?"

◆

Michelle took stock of the handsome man in front of her. He was tall—taller than her own five-ten in stocking feet—good-looking in a cowboy kind of way, well-spoken.

Her friend Carrie nudged her elbow. "Go ahead. You'll have a better view of the game. We can catch up with you later."

When Michelle still hesitated, Carrie pulled her aside and whispered, "He's single and he's Christian, and he loves baseball. Go for it." They smiled at each other. Ever since Carrie's marriage to the widowed Steve Romero, she'd been bent on making a match for her friend.

Michelle faced the stranger. *At least he can look me in the eye.* She hated being taller than the man she was dating. "I accept." She waved good-bye to Carrie and turned to face the mysterious Mr. Knight.

"Have fun," Carrie called over her shoulder as they headed for the turnstiles.

"We'll meet you by the front gate after the game," Steve added.

"Are you visiting Steve and Carrie?" Joe asked.

"I'm thinking about moving here, but I'm just visiting at the moment, from Chicago. You? You don't live in Denver?"

"I lived here for a while. Now I make my home in the great metropolis of Ulysses, out on the eastern plains." He guided her through the sea of Rockies purple, silver, and black that swam toward the gates.

Hundreds of people strolled down the sidewalks, fathers and sons, mothers with babies dressed in miniature uniforms, old men in faded caps. Michelle watched the crowd, fascinated. "It's like a parade. Or a town fair—or something."

"Yeah, it's a lot of fun. One of the few things I miss about Denver."

A lone clarinet sang above the noise of the crowd, serenading them with "Take Me Out to the Ball Game." Joe tossed a couple of bills into the collection hat. "How about 'God Bless America' for the lady?"

"Anything you say." The old performer slid into the patriotic hit, swaying in time to the music.

Michelle clapped, delighted. "That was wonderful. Thanks." She added some change to the hat.

"Do you mind if we buy some snacks out here? More choices than inside. Cheaper, too." Joe grinned.

"Lead the way."

Joe led her to a table piled high with every conceivable snack they might want at the game. He grabbed a bottle of cold water and a box of Cracker Jacks.

Michelle did her own exploring. Peanuts? No. "Pistachios. And Gummi Bears. And Circus Peanuts. How can I choose?"

"Take them all." Joe grabbed everything Michelle had mentioned.

The vendor, a black man with a grin inviting them to join the Rockies' party, made change for Joe. A few seconds later, they rejoined the thousands streaming toward the main gate.

"Get your programs here."

"Caps, only five dollars each. Ten dollars inside."

It's like the whole city is having a party. What a wonderful place to visit. Another reason I'm glad I'm moving to Denver. Michelle stopped, savoring the atmosphere, but Joe took her by the hand and pulled her toward the turnstiles.

Pounding music poured from the loudspeakers as they made their way to their seats along the right outfield line. A jumbo screen over center field featured spectacular plays by Rockies players. They crawled over a dozen people to the center of the row.

"Good. We made it in time," Joe said, taking a swig from his water bottle. "I hate it when I miss the first inning. Sometimes by the time I get settled, the opposing team has already scored three runs." Almost as an afterthought, he offered, "Can I get you something to drink?"

Michelle chuckled inwardly. At least he asked. "I have my bottle of water here. Maybe later. They're about to start."

True to Joe's experience, the Mets' lead-off hitter blasted a home run into right field. Beside her, Joe sighed. "Looks like we're in for one of those games. If you like home runs, it's great."

"Oh yes, much more exciting than a pitchers' duel anytime—don't you think?" She poked him with her elbow.

Eyes dancing in merry disagreement, he said, "Maybe. Especially if I can catch one of the balls."

Surveying the packed stadium, Michelle laughed. "Do you really think you have a chance? Are they going to send one to you special delivery?"

"I can always hope." He reached into his gym bag and pulled out a catcher's mitt.

A beer vendor hawked his wares, but Joe ignored him. Instead he purchased a couple of iced lemonades. They didn't talk much until the top of the inning was over. The Mets had scored two runs.

"Have you been in Denver long?" Joe asked.

Michelle shook her head. "Only a few days. I love it so far. I'm staying with the Romeros while I look for a job." *If I get a job. Lord, help!*

"I hope I didn't disrupt their plans for the evening."

"Oh, they won't mind." Michelle smiled, thinking of the dates she had talked over with Carrie while they were missionaries together in Romania. What would she say about the man next to her tonight? So far, so good. "What about you? You said you used to live in Denver. Why did you leave?"

"A family emergency." Joe's lips flattened momentarily. "An opportunity came up to open a business in Ulysses. I took the chance, and it's starting to pay off. Ah, the Rockies are up to bat now. This is a new guy. Haven't seen him before."

Minutes later, with two batters on base, the cleanup hitter came to the plate.

"Here's my chance." Joe slipped his glove onto his left hand.

Michelle stared curiously.

"He's almost as good as the old Blake Street Bombers. Hits a lot of home runs. He's the best there is at hitting with men on base. This may be my chance to snag one."

Around her Michelle felt anticipation growing. The jumbo screen flashed the hitter's name, with the crowd screaming in time to the syllables. He stepped into the batter's box, and a hush fell on the stadium.

The first pitch was a ball, the second a called strike. On the third, Michelle heard the crack of the bat. The ball hurtled in their direction, and the batter raced down the first-base line.

An older woman next to them squealed and ducked. "I'll protect you, ma'am." Joe waved his arm in front of him. Around them other men were doing the same thing. Michelle couldn't pick out his arm from the sea awaiting the ball. Joe leaped in the air.

"Got it!" Triumphantly he twisted his glove around to show Michelle the prized ball. All three Rockies players trotted home, putting the team ahead 3–2. Joe's image appeared on the jumbo screen, and he grinned like he'd won the World Series. Waving his arms in the air like a conquering hero, he pulled a laughing Michelle to her feet beside him. Around him men were high-fiving him.

"Good catch."

"Maybe I can get it autographed." Joe wiggled back into the seat. "You must be my good-luck charm. I've never managed to catch one before." He bounced the ball in his hand and looked at Michelle, warmth flooding his eyes. "I want you to have it." Taking Michelle's hands between his own, he gently rolled the ball into her palm.

"But. I can't take it. You just said—"

"No arguing. Maybe I'll catch another one. I want you to enjoy it."

"Thanks." Michelle closed her fingers around it, savoring the weight of the tiny packed ball, imagining it on her shelf next to the pennant autographed by Chicago Cubs all-stars, a memento of one of her favorite childhood memories. "That was quite a performance."

Joe grinned a bit sheepishly and opened his game program. "Three-run homer. That should be easy to mark."

Michelle peered over his shoulder at the bewildering chart of lines, x's, and numbers he held, much more complicated than a bowling score sheet. "You know, I've been to lots of games, but I've never tried keeping track of the plays like that."

"It's pretty easy. Let me show you."

The innings slipped by, Joe arguing calls by the umpire, mentioning tidbits of Rockies lore, showing Michelle how to keep score. By the seventh-inning stretch, her voice was hoarse from cheering awesome catches and groaning over foul balls. The game organ struck familiar opening chords. Joe dragged her to her feet.

"You have to sing."

Words flashed on the jumbo screen. All the fun of the evening raced through Michelle's veins and burst out in a wide smile. Buoyant high spirits cracked Joe's face into a matching grin.

Catching her hands, he swung her arms in time to the music. "Take me out to the ball game," they sang at the top of their lungs. Michelle couldn't hold a tune, but she didn't care if anyone heard her or not. "For it's one, two, three strikes. . ." They punched fingers emphatically in the air. The jumbo screen showed fans all over the stadium dancing to the music. They held out the last note as long as they could and collapsed in their seats, laughing.

The Rockies hadn't scored since the home run in the first inning, while the Mets piled up a 7-3 lead.

"It doesn't look good," Michelle said as the first Rockies hitter struck out in the bottom of the seventh inning.

"I've seen 'em come from six—even nine—runs down late in the game. Four runs, that's nothing," Joe said comfortably. "Hey, you want to walk around a bit? It's a beautiful place."

Michelle nodded, and they made their way out of the stands. Souvenirs like plastic bats, autographed balls, caps, and pennants from teams across the league filled booths as far as she could see.

"Who's your favorite team? The Cubs or the White Sox?"

"The Cubs. My Dad took me to opening day every year when I was growing up. He said that was the only game worth watching, since the Cubs' two seasons are spring training and next year."

Joe laughed.

"Did you grow up a Rockies fan? Or did you grow up somewhere else?"

"Well, I'm not from Denver, but I remember the excitement when we got the baseball team. I am a native Coloradoan, though. One of the few, I think. Ah, I smell hot dogs up ahead."

The delicious aroma convinced Michelle to try one with Joe, although she didn't think they tasted quite as good as ones she'd had in Chicago. They never did. They meandered down the concourse, stopping at each booth. Michelle wondered at the warm winter jackets that looked so out of place on the hot summer night. Ahead of them a commotion broke out.

"Hey. Stop. Thief!" A vendor with heavy jowls burst from behind his stall. "Security!"

A blue-garbed officer rushed to his aid. "What's up?"

"Catch him! A white guy, a kid, about five-ten, five-eleven. Braves hat."

Michelle stared in the direction the man pointed but saw no sign of the thief in the crowds. The guard ran after him anyway.

The vendor shook his head. "Vandals. Here at the ballpark. I mean, once in a while a kid walks off with a ball, but this was. . .this was. . ." He couldn't finish the sentence.

"I'm sorry." Michelle was tempted to buy something, as if she could make up for the loss. She looked around for Joe, but he had left her side.

He'd sprinted after the security guard.

Chapter 2

"So he took off running after the thief?" Carrie shook her head in disbelief as Michelle related the story.

"Sure did." Michelle stared straight ahead, eyes unfocused, slowly sipping the cup of Good Night Tea Carrie had fixed for her. "They caught him, too."

"Really?" Carrie leaned forward, elbows sticking out of her housecoat and resting on the table.

"Yeah. A few minutes later they brought this scruffy-looking teenager back in handcuffs and escorted him to the gate. Joe looked pleased as punch with himself." She stirred a third teaspoon of sugar into the tea and sipped it. Her nose wrinkled at the overly sweet taste, and she pushed the cup away.

"I wonder if he's always that impulsive."

"I'd say so." Michelle extracted the ball from her purse. "Did you see when he caught that home-run ball in the first inning?"

"Oh yeah! What a catch."

"He gave me the ball."

"Impulsive. Generous." Carrie ticked off the qualities as if she were making a shopping list. "That boyish quality that can make men so sweet."

"Yes." The two women sighed in tandem.

"So when are you seeing him again?" Carrie grinned.

"The day after tomorrow. He's taking me to the Cherry Creek Arts Festival. I told him I had to work on my résumé after church tomorrow."

◆

Michelle ran her finger down the list of Denver's hundred largest employers again. Where should she start?

"Why don't you try a placement agency?" Carrie snapped green beans.

"Maybe later," Michelle said. "But human resources is supposed to be my area of expertise. If I can't find a job for myself, how can I expect a company to trust me with their personnel decisions?" Studying the list again, she crossed out a few more lines. No beer companies, medicine-related, or sports. Legal? Maybe. Computers? Not enough people contact. Communications. "I'd like that." She marked her top five choices with bold red stars. "I'll start with these."

"Now for my résumé." She looked at the large amount of white space surrounding the few lines of type and sighed. "It would help if I had more experience. Part-time jobs in college, two years in Romania, that last job in Chicago. Nothing related to my supposed career, except for that last one that I lost when they downsized."

"You can't get down on yourself since that job didn't work out. People are people, whether in Romania or Denver." Carrie had emptied one sack of green beans and reached for another. "And you have cross-cultural experience. You have a lot to offer."

"But is it what they're looking for?" Michelle studied the résumé without inspiration. "I reviewed tons of these in school, learning what to watch for. I want to look professional. I know I can do better than this." She tapped her pen against her teeth. "I know—I'll mention working at my father's store."

"That's a good idea. I'm sure you learned a lot about customer relations and dealing with the public." Carrie examined a green bean and threw it away.

"The customers were the best part." Michelle smiled at the memory. "Like old Mrs. Westlake. She'd stop by every day for a pint of milk. Dad said she liked my company. She didn't really need anything." She added a few lines to the résumé and read it again. "I need to make the sentences active. Show them what I actually did." She rewrote several lines. "There. I'm done."

"Let me see." Carrie read the revisions. "That ought to wow 'em. They'll be knocking down the door."

"That's the idea." Michelle decided she had done as much as she could and printed out several copies. "I don't know what's happened to me since I got back from Romania. I had the courage of a she-wolf when we were there. But after losing my job in Chicago, I'm scared I can't get the kind of job I need. Not with everybody downsizing."

A green bean snapped in the silence. "It's okay," Carrie said. "You're allowed to ask questions. Just keep trusting the Lord."

The door opened, and Steve burst in with their boy, Viktor. He dumped a couple of bags on the table. "How's my favorite wife?" Steve hugged Carrie as if he hadn't seen her in days, not hours. *Oh God, will I ever find someone like that?*

Joe. Michelle pushed the thought away. She had no business thinking like that about a man she met only last night—and certainly not with her other obligations. But when she remembered his infectious grin, ready laugh, and gentle touch, the idea thrilled her. *Stop it*, she scolded herself. Her heart didn't want to listen.

◆

Joe woke up early, even though he had tossed and turned all night. Hotel rooms always did that to him. Or was it the prospect of seeing Michelle again? Yesterday had dragged by, but he had filled in some of the time by calling home to make sure his mother didn't need anything.

Michelle. Her name rolled off his tongue and lingered in his mind, a beautiful name for a beautiful woman. Their date at the game had confirmed his first impressions of her.

Why had he invited Michelle to go to the arts festival with him? The last thing he needed while he conducted business was a date with a city girl—even one as pretty as Michelle.

Even with a long shower and careful grooming, he slipped behind the wheel of his truck before eight—forty-five minutes before he would pick up Michelle. He ran his finger over the tooled-leather wheel cover while he decided what to do. He drove around the city, catching up on changes, until his watch read 8:30. Time to head south to the place Michelle was staying.

He recognized the house from Michelle's description: a modest ranch house with a nearly new play set visible in the backyard. A small boy sat on the swing, kicking the ground with his feet. Joe waved to him.

Grabbing his cowboy hat with one hand and opening the door with the other, he jumped out into the oppressive sunshine of another midsummer day. He tucked a stray patch of shirt back into his pants and headed to the front door.

◆

"Where did he get that hat? He'll think I'm too dressed up." Michelle frowned nervously at her aqua knit shell and navy blue linen slacks.

"He does look like he stepped off the set of *Gunsmoke*." Carrie shrugged. Her husband, Steve, wasn't the cowboy-hat-and-boots type. As if sensing Michelle's unease, she added, "You look great. He'll think you're beautiful."

"I'll change into one of my patriotic tees. It *is* almost the Fourth of July after all. Tell him I'll be right back."

When she came back a few minutes later, she hesitated when she saw him chatting with Carrie. He must have sensed her presence, for he turned sapphire blue eyes in her direction. An electric jolt coursed through her, tingling down to her toes. "Good morning, Joe." Breathless, she sounded like a high-school girl.

Joe's eyes slid up and down her body, smiling at what he saw, until he frowned at her feet. "You might want walking shoes. We'll be on our feet all day."

"I'm used to it." She didn't have to defend wearing heels. She couldn't explain the sense of style, of feeling attractive and feminine, that the navy pumps gave her. Tossing a chain purse over her shoulder, she said, "I'm ready. Bye, Carrie. See you tonight."

A dusty blue truck waited in the driveway, and her heart quailed a bit. Trucks seemed more common than cars in Denver. The things she was learning about the West.

"Let me help you." Joe swung the door open and offered his arm for support. Accepting it, she lifted her left heel onto the floor of the cab and slid onto the seat. He circled the vehicle and swung onto the driver's seat with one easy movement.

When he turned the key in the ignition, a wailing love song blasted for a moment before he turned the radio off.

Country music?

Returning to the main street by a route Michelle had never taken before, Joe headed down Federal Boulevard. "You seem to know Denver pretty well."

"I should. Lived here for three years."

"You've been to this festival before, then? Tell me about it."

"Somebody came up with the idea a long time ago. You may know that Cherry Creek is kind of a yuppie mall. Someone wanted to add to the highbrow tone, and they decided to sponsor an arts festival around the Fourth of July to showcase local talent, both artists and musicians. It's grown to the point where people come from across the country to attend."

"You must like art to travel to Denver for the festival."

Joe made a noncommittal grunt. They turned into a residential neighborhood then turned by a church. Soon they reached barriers festooned with yellow flags. "Here we are. The edge of Cherry Creek North."

A young woman dressed in crisp blue slacks and a white blouse with a red and blue bowtie approached. "Do you want me to park your car, sir?"

"Please." Joe handed her a twenty-dollar bill.

Michelle stared down the ordinary city street transformed into an art market. Red and white tents crowded both sides, stretching ahead for as many blocks as she could see. Artisans called greetings to each other while they opened their tents and arranged their wares for maximum effect. The sight reminded her a bit of the early-morning bustle of the street markets in Bucharest. Warm memories engulfed her.

"—breakfast?"

Michelle brought her attention back to Joe. "I'm sorry. What did you say?"

"Things won't get started for a half hour yet. Would you like some breakfast?"

"Oh, sure." She was a little surprised when he guided her to a bagel and coffee shop. Somehow pancakes with bacon and eggs seemed more Joe's style.

Michelle ordered a tall latte, iced, with skim milk, and a whole-grain bagel, light on the cream cheese. They found an empty spot at a corner table, and Joe crunched into the toasted onion bagel with a thick layer of cream cheese.

Michelle opened her bagel and took a small bite. At home she often used ricotta as a spread, but at restaurants she allowed the indulgence.

"There's nothing like an onion bagel with cream cheese." A dollop of the filling fell onto the plate, and Joe scooped it into his mouth. "Yummy."

It really was. Michelle took a bigger bite the next time. A piece fell off.

"Let me." Joe brushed the renegade crumb away from Michelle's cheek. His fingers were surprisingly soft and supple, a gentle caress of a touch. Her skin heated to his touch, and she hastened to change the topic.

"This bunch doesn't look anything like the crowd at Coors Field." Not with Gucci shirts and Italian shoes. "I began to think everyone in Denver dressed casually—or in gear from their favorite sports star."

Joe leaned back and laughed, a warm, comfortable chuckle. "Not true." He leaned close. "You have to come to Ulysses for that." He winked at her, and she giggled.

They finished their bagels and ventured back onto the street. Already a couple of hundred people milled around the stalls. The artist in the tent across from the café caught sight of Joe and waved in greeting before rearranging her glassware on the front table a fraction of an inch.

"Ready?" At Michelle's nod, he headed across the street.

"Good morning, Annie. What have you got today?" Joe greeted the middle-aged artist, who sported soft brown hair pulled back in a braid.

"You might be interested in this." She pulled out a thin bud vase made of pale gold-blown glass.

Joe bent down and looked at his luminous reflection in the glass before showing it to Michelle. "It's different from your usual work."

"Yes, I'm using different materials. . . ." Annie relaxed as she described how she created the new effect.

Michelle admired the pieces in the booth. Exquisite, delicate work, they would complement a lot of the renovated turn-of-the-century homes dotted around Denver. Joe's voice interrupted her perusal.

"Annie, I'd like you to meet my friend, Michelle Morris. Michelle, Annie is an old business associate of mine." Introductions completed, he made arrangements to come back later and pick up a couple of pieces.

"Are you a collector?" Michelle was curious.

"You mean Annie?" Joe seemed bemused. "No, not a collector. It's my business."

"You mean. . ." The light dawned for Michelle. "Your business in Ulysses. You own an art gallery? Or a museum?"

"Gallery. Buy direct from the artists, resell at my store. Ah, here's Jonah's shop. He makes interesting things out of wood."

The morning continued in much the same vein. Joe stopped at every tent. Michelle would have skipped a few, like the Georgia O'Keeffe–type flowers and the sculptures of twisted metal. But Joe examined every piece with an appraiser's eye.

Pictures of tall mountains and meadows teeming with wildflowers filled one tent. Michelle studied them, absorbed in the play of light in the paintings.

"I wish I could buy this one." The price tag of $1,000 was far more than she could afford.

"Really?" Joe studied the painting with her. "It's kind of derivative."

"Maybe that's what I like about it. It reminds me of paintings by Charles Russell." When he lifted an eyebrow at her, she said, "What? I've heard of Russell, even in Chicago."

Joe cocked his head and looked over the painting, his finger tracing the brushstrokes in the air. "You may be right. And it's a popular site in Colorado, the Maroon Bells. I'll think about it."

A few tents later, Joe surprised Michelle by asking her about an abstract painting vibrant with angry reds and yellows. "What do you think?"

"It would give me headaches hanging on my wall." The words blurted out of Michelle's mouth before she thought of the artist standing within hearing distance. His mouth thinned to a tense line.

Joe turned to study the painting from a different angle. "It's powerful, though. It's hard to look away." Nothing else in the tent interested him, and they left, Joe promising to think about the painting.

Michelle wouldn't admit that her heeled feet hurt, but she wanted a break from the serious pursuit of art. She should be glad her escort took his time; so many men avoided art museums altogether or rushed through at hiking speed without bothering to look at anything. But shopping with Joe was a bit like watching meat marinate. Nothing happened for a long time.

A few feet away she heard the sweet notes of a soprano saxophone. She tapped Joe's elbow. "I'll be over there." She found a spot at the back of the staged area. A thin black man, noticing her rub her heels, offered her a seat. Gratefully she sank down and let the music carry her away. Eyes closed, she could imagine she was sitting on the shores of Lake Michigan on a perfect day, sun dancing on the waves and wind rippling lightly through the air and curling her hair around her face. The music felt as cool as that breeze.

"Michelle?" Joe's voice intruded, jolting her back to the hot sticky July day. "It looks like you're ready for a break. How about fresh-squeezed lemonade and some real music?" His voice had music in it, too—music that drew her to her feet like she was hypnotized.

Michelle stayed rooted to the spot for a moment, and he gently tugged her arm. The saxophonist launched into the rendition of one of her favorites, and Michelle said, "Can we come back later?"

A surprised look darted across Joe's face. "Sure. Why don't you grab one of those schedules and decide. But they're starting karaoke down at the country-western stage. That's always fun to watch."

Karaoke. Oh no.

Grabbing her hand like a toddler on a field trip, he bounced through the crowded streets to the spot where a guitar twanged and voices wailed.

A tall, tanned man dressed in the cowboy uniform of boots, blue jeans, and a ten-gallon hat, with silver points decorating the collar of his denim shirt, announced, "Our next contestant will sing the Hank Williams' classic, 'Your Cheatin' Heart.'"

Michelle resigned herself to enduring the set. Country music had never appealed to her. Southern twang and clanging chords drowned out everything else as far as she was concerned. Joe obviously felt differently.

Beside her, Joe swayed in time to the music. "You can't go wrong with Hank Williams." His voice joined the performer's along with many others in the crowd.

Unable to resist the infectious enthusiasm of the crowd, Michelle found herself clapping her hands and tapping her feet. *I can understand the words.* A change from most popular music she heard on the radio. The next performer sang a couple of songs that brought tears to her eyes.

"This doesn't sound like any country I've heard before." She dabbed at her eyes.

"Still the great living, loving, and leaving songs they've always been. Real-life stuff."

A cowgirl took the mike and announced, "We have time for a couple more numbers. Any volunteers?"

Joe pirouetted in his seat, bouncing with fun. "You want to give it a try?"

"I don't know any country songs." Her insides trembled at the thought of performing in front of all those people.

"Bet you know your American history, though." Joe had her on her feet, sauntering down the center aisle in time to the clapping crowd. "It *is* almost the Fourth of July after all." He winked at her.

He told the sound technicians, "We're going to try 'The Battle of New Orleans.'" A couple of chords blasted over the loudspeakers, and Michelle found herself on stage with a microphone stuck in her hand, words rolling down a screen to her right. The *rat-a-tat* of a drum set her foot tapping.

"In 1814 we took a little trip. . . ." Joe started singing a melody that sounded vaguely familiar, his voice a pleasant baritone. The microphone dangled from Michelle's hand. When he got to the chorus, he motioned for Michelle to join in. Nothing for it but to go ahead.

"We fired our guns, and the British kept a-comin'. . . ." Joe pumped his arms, urging the audience to sing along. He skipped around her, grinning as widely as the brim of his hat. She returned the favor as he sang the second verse, clapping her hands over her head in time to the music. Minutes later the song ended, and she came back down to earth, face red-hot, breathless. The audience clapped wildly as they exited the stage.

◆

She's a lot of fun when she lets her hair down. Joe loved hamming it up—he had considered pursuing a career as a musician but decided he just wasn't good enough. Every now and then he allowed himself to step back into the limelight, like today. He appreciated the break from the serious business negotiations that had dominated the morning. Michelle was a good sport, playing right along with him. They laughed together as they joined the crowds walking among the booths.

"Joe?"

The voice pierced, pinning him to the ground where he stood.

"It *is* you. I thought I heard your voice, Sir Cameron."

Joe winced. His past had caught up with him.

Chapter 3

Joe deliberately relaxed his facial muscles before he turned around to greet his old girlfriend. "Sonia. I didn't see your name on the list."

She came up and kissed him on the cheek. "I don't have a booth, if that's what you mean." She tightened the knot of the brightly colored scarf draped around her hips. "But I wouldn't miss the festival. An artist has to keep an eye on the competition, you know." She flashed bright teeth in Michelle's direction. "And who is your charming friend?"

"I'm Michelle Morris." She held out her hand in greeting. "I'm new in Denver, and Joe was kind enough to offer to show me around today." She paused. "But who is Sir Cameron?"

Joe shuffled his feet, but Sonia laughed. "Why, Joe, of course. He hasn't told you about the castle yet?" When Michelle shook her head, Sonia said, "Don't worry. He will." She flashed white teeth in his direction. "And I'm Sonia Oliveira. Joe and I, uh, used to date."

Joe didn't know how to respond. Explain that Joseph was his middle name? Escape from Sonia before the situation became even more complicated?

But Michelle seemed at ease in the awkward situation. He watched the two women, noting the contrasts between his former girlfriend and his current interest. Both were tall, independent, articulate, fun—but there the similarities ended. Michelle was a gentle summer rain where Sonia was a thunderstorm, tasteful style versus artistic flamboyance. Sonia never needed encouragement to let her hair down.

"Can you come by my studio while you're in town? You promised the next time you came to Denver. . ."

Joe scrambled to remember his last conversation with Sonia. He did remember some kind of vague promise to that effect. "I'm pretty busy."

"I'll be in this evening, say, after seven? I've got some pieces I think you will want to handle." Sonia beamed a beguiling smile his way.

Joe heard himself agreeing to the time. With a sinking heart, he realized how much he'd hoped that he and Michelle could go somewhere to relax after the festival shut down—a quiet restaurant, maybe, where they could make small talk and learn more about each other. He sneaked a glance at Michelle, her face unreadable. No clue if she had any regrets about Sonia's suggestion.

Sonia made polite excuses and took off. Not a moment too soon, as far as Joe was concerned.

The scent of hot dogs on the grill tickled Joe's nose, and he realized he was hungry. He didn't want frankfurters again, though, not after the ball game last night. Michelle had wandered into a leather-goods booth, examining the stitches on some purses.

"Sorry about the interruption." Why did he feel he had to apologize? Sonia was an old flame, that was why.

"It's fine. I understand." The edge to her voice suggested perhaps she had had enough of taking care of business. Joe resolved to let go of the rest of the day's planned itinerary and to enjoy himself with this beautiful woman. First order of business: lunch.

◆

Michelle slipped her feet back into her heels and pushed away from the table. Her feet had rested while her taste buds savored the delicate blend of Chinese cuisine they had ordered.

"Ready?" Joe tossed an after-dinner mint in her direction. "I have a great idea. . . ."

"More country karaoke?" Michelle smiled. "Or maybe jazz this time?"

"Neither. Come on, you'll see."

As soon as they exited the air-conditioned restaurant, oven-hot air blasted her face, melting whatever makeup remained from the morning. Temperatures must have been close to a hundred degrees. She was glad she had put on sunscreen that morning, or else she'd be lobster-red by late afternoon. If she had some with her, she might even add a fresh coat.

Twice as many people crowded the streets as in the morning, but Joe wove his way through the foot traffic as if heading for a specific destination. They approached a booth with a long line of waiting children. "Here is one of my favorite artists. Gil is famous for his body art, but he volunteers his services at the festival."

Body art was an understatement. Michelle could hardly keep from staring at the vines, flowers, and animals that crawled up the artist's massive arms to a pirate's ring dangling from his left ear. An incongruous assortment of water, colors, and sponges lay on a table before him, and the sign over the booth announced FACE PAINTING. Face painting? Surely children would run the other way when they saw this rough giant. But a couple of young girls perched on high stools, giggling as he put finishing touches on matching unicorns.

Joe crouched, studying the featured designs hanging from the front of the booth. "What do you think, Michelle? Maybe a cowboy hat for me and—"

"You can't be serious. This is for children."

"No it's not." He pointed to a mother walking away with her daughter, both of them with matching roses on their cheeks. Joe grinned and took a place in line.

When Michelle glanced around, she saw a handful of adults waiting their turn and relaxed. The young boy ahead of them chose a dinosaur.

"My son loves dinosaurs, too." The deep voice surprised Michelle with its soft gentleness. Gil held a purple paint stick crayon with the delicate touch of an artist, deftly creating a T-rex as the child squirmed under tickling fingers.

"What do you think?" Gil showed the boy his reflection in a mirror.

"I love it." The boy flung his arms around Gil's neck, reminding Michelle of her pastor-mentor in Romania, a man who loved children. She swallowed the lump in her throat.

"Joe, my friend." The two men embraced. "What can I do for you today?" Michelle could almost hear Gil mentally rubbing his hands together. He leaned back in his chair, studying both of them in turn. "No, don't tell me. I know what you need. Who's first?"

Michelle shook her head, and with a shrug Joe perched atop a high stool, one toe dragging the ground. What kind of face did Gil have in mind for Joe?

Joe wiggled his eyebrows as Gil applied a base of white paint. White everywhere—forehead, cheeks, chin, only skipping the nose, until Joe resembled a street mime. An orange triangle on his chin pointed to his lips, bright yellow circles spotted his cheeks, and blue ringed his eyes. Joe started to grin but stopped when the paint smudged around his mouth. Add a green wig and big red nose, and he'd be set to join the circus. His eyes followed Gil's movements, causing the rings to seem to twirl. Michelle covered her mouth and turned her head to keep from laughing out loud.

Gil finished the nose in bright red. Michelle couldn't meet Joe's eyes. In spite of her best efforts, a giggle bubbled up through her throat, exiting in a tiny snicker.

"What have you done?" Joe grabbed the mirror and studied his face. He didn't bother holding back, letting out a loud belly laugh. "You know me too well." When he wiped the tears of laughter from his eyes, blue circles contracted in the effort, and he smeared paint on his knuckles.

Michelle reached into her purse for a tissue and wiped the offending paint away, giggles escaping in spite of her best efforts.

"Okay, your turn next." Joe guided her onto the seat, her heel catching on a rung of the stool.

"Oh no." Michelle tried to get off.

Gil and Joe stared at her, waiting, as children behind them stirred.

"You can't get out of it now. Turnabout's fair play."

I guess I have to go through with it. "Just no clown for me, please?" she said in a small voice. She hadn't done anything like this since she was a child herself.

"Never a clown for the lady." Gil selected an assortment of paint sticks in soft pastels. "You will like what I have in mind—I promise."

"Let's see if he knows you as well as he knows me," Joe said. "He has a way of seeing into people."

Unlikely—we just met. Instead of applying an overall base, Gil dabbed a small sponge in brown and black paint and made a long streak down her right cheek. The cool water in the sponge made Michelle's pores close up, and she forced herself to stay still under Gil's fingers. Greens, blues, pinks, and lavenders followed in quick succession. She tried to picture the patterns he was making, but she couldn't guess. When Gil brushed her hair behind her ear, she twisted in her seat.

"Don't worry. I'm almost done." A few strokes later, he put down the sponge and held up the mirror.

Whatever Michelle had expected, her imagination hadn't come close to the garden blooming on her face. Trees and flowers à la Monet adorned her cheek, leaves and branches circling her ear. The colors glowed on her skin like a makeup artist's palette, highlighting her coloring and complementing her outfit. She almost wished she wouldn't have to wash it away that evening.

Joe appeared in front of her, producing a pink rose with a magician's sleight of hand. "To the prettiest flower in the garden." He bowed.

Gil stood back, a wide grin indicating his pleasure with the result.

"Thanks. I don't know what I expected, but nothing like this. You've made me feel beautiful."

Joe's grin said "I told you so" as loudly as if he spoke out loud.

"You *are* beautiful, on the inside as well." Gil waved away payment. "Just tell people who did the work. You're walking advertising."

Michelle slid off the stool, cupping her cheek with her hand, almost expecting a flower to drop into her palm, and followed Joe into the crowd.

◆

Joe watched Michelle's transformation. The elaborate design might have looked out of place on someone else, but on her it only emphasized what was already there. Even better, she seemed to realize it, her back a fraction straighter, her head a smidgen higher, an extra bounce in her step. She carried herself like a queen. *That's what we'll do next.*

"Where to now?" Michelle's voice shimmered with excitement for whatever adventure awaited her.

He shook his head. "Can't tell. It's a secret."

"Oooh, I like secrets." And she seemed to mean it.

They didn't reach his destination as soon as he had hoped. As they strolled toward the opposite end of the festival, they passed importuning artists who made Joe promise to return another day to look at their work. Michelle directed people interested in face painting to Gil's stall. They stopped for more lemon ice to ward off the heat. At last brightly colored awnings came into view, and Joe steered her toward the CHILDREN'S ART ZONE sign.

"Children's art?" Doubt crept into her voice. "But we're not—"

"Children? They don't care. Anyone who wants to can experience art hands-on. Last year I helped paint one of the local buses, a paint-by-numbers kind of thing. It's fun."

Several different tables held materials from plain paper to wood and nails to wire. Joe found an empty corner at the wire table. He selected strands of purple, yellow, red, and blue, but as he twisted the wire, he felt Michelle's warm breath on his neck, her hands resting on his shoulder.

"You're making me nervous," he said good-naturedly. "Sit down." The child next to him had finished his piece, a circular contraption that looked remotely like an igloo, leaving a chair empty for the moment.

"No thanks." Michelle dropped her hands from his shoulder. "Wire's not for me. I have a hard time knotting thread with a needle. I think I'll stick with construction paper, over there."

"Tell you what. I'll make something for you, and you make something for me."

Michelle studied the bundle of wires in front of Joe, wrinkling her nose as if imagining what he might create. "Let's do it."

Joe studied Michelle's departing back, admiring its straight lines and mentally measuring the circumference of her head at the same time. The wires he had so carefully gathered had disappeared, the rare purple one finding its way into a preschooler's pile. He started over again with four yellow bands, twisting and tying them together. Looking up from his work, he saw Michelle absorbed over her work, coaxing glue out of a bottle.

"How's it going?" he called.

She looked up as if startled at the intrusion of his voice. "Great. I'm having fun."

They finished their projects at the same time. Someone took Joe's chair before he lifted his masterpiece off the table. He met Michelle midway. Her right hand was tucked behind her back, her picture out of view.

"This is for you." Sunlight glinted off the blue, red, and green wires nesting interlaced with the yellow base. "A tiara for a beautiful princess." *Now I sound like Sir Cameron.* He smiled to himself.

"Is that how you see me? As a beautiful princess?"

To answer, he set the tiara on her head. He kissed her cheek and bowed at the waist. "Sir Cameron has vowed his fealty to her royal highness, Princess Michelle of the Cherry Creek Arts Festival."

"You have to explain about Sir Cameron."

"Blame my mother for that. She named me after a long-ago ancestor, Sir Cameron Innis."

"So your name is. . . ?"

"Cameron Joseph Knight." He rolled his shoulders. "But she soon figured out I was more of an ordinary Joe than a knight of the round table."

"Sonia doesn't think so. She called you Sir Cameron. You can't tell me she's only a business associate."

"It's. . .complicated."

"And it's really none of my business. Sorry I asked."

"No harm done." Joe shook his head. "Come on. Yours next."

"Now mine seems so ordinary."

"Let me be the judge of that."

Brightly colored shapes created a park scene. A yellow sun cheered the sky, and small pink flowers sat atop triangular green stems. Music notes danced over the head of a small boy.

"It's—interesting." He tapped his chin with his forefinger. "Is that supposed to be me?"

Michelle blushed. "You have such a playful spirit."

"Like a little boy who hasn't grown up yet?" Joe grinned.

Michelle's face turned pink in embarrassment. "Well, yes. And you love to surround yourself with beautiful things."

"I'd better watch out—you know me about as well as Gil does." The idea pleased him.

"Anyone who can be a knight and a clown at the same time is bound to be interesting." She giggled as she reached out and touched the end of his red nose.

"Are you saying I'm schizophrenic?" He made a funny face.

She laughed. "Multifaceted. It's a good thing."

A couple walked by, matching handmade stovepipe hats atop their heads. "Want to try that next?"

Michelle threw a startled glance in his direction but agreed. One by one she was shedding concealing layers, each new "skin" more attractive than the last. Joe anticipated discovering the core.

◆

I can't believe I'm doing this. Michelle stared at the paper grocery bag in front of her. She had folded and stapled the open edges, adjusting the opening to fit her head. Gold foil stars and red, blue, and white ribbons lay scattered on the table around her. She had chosen a patriotic theme in keeping with the Fourth of July.

Sounds of a high school band floated through the air from a nearby stage. From what she could hear, the musicians were playing a painful adaptation of The Beatles' classic "Strawberry Fields Forever." Better than some of what passed for music nowadays, she supposed. How well she remembered the arguments with her high school band director. He had wanted them to play Sousa classics like "Stars and Stripes Forever." As drum major, she argued for more contemporary music. He suggested a democratic process—one representative from each section of the band would help him choose music for the marching band. How seriously the committee had taken their work, and what an odd assortment of music they had chosen. They wound up marching to everything from Beethoven to Bacharach with a heavy dose of rock and roll.

The music set her feet to tapping, and her knee banged the table in time. She glanced at Joe and noticed he was waving a wire in time to the rhythm. "I used to play the bass drum." He matched his words with acting out banging either side of an invisible drum in front of him. She giggled.

"And I was the drum major." She lifted her hands in the air, directing a couple of measures in four-four time. She squirted more glue on the last gold star and let the hat dry for a few moments.

"May I use the glue?" a little girl with Chinese features asked. Michelle handed her the bottle, studying her dark hair and serious eyes, which reminded her of many children she had seen in Romania. The thought dampened a little of her enthusiasm. The children at the orphanage didn't have the opportunity to make funny hats. *Oh Lord, open the doors.*

She and Joe finished their hats at about the same time. His creation belonged in a circus. He had curled paper like confetti, and ribbon streamers floated down the sides like a circus tent. With a bow and a pretend honk of his red nose, he took off his cowboy hat and put it on. The bag covered half his forehead, coming to rest just above his eyebrows.

"Let me try something." Michelle placed the Stetson on the table and tugged the clown hat over the crown. "I think this will hold it in place. I could staple it to secure it."

He shook his head. "No staples on that leather, please."

Michelle held her hat out for inspection.

Joe studied her creation. "I like it. But it could use one last thing." He unearthed a tall white feather and stapled it to the front of the hat. "There." He eased it over her head and frowned. "But now you're missing your tiara." He took the hat off and gently put the tiara into place around the bottom of the bag. When he put it back on, he made sure it rested snugly behind her ears. "Now we're dressed to go out on the town. You ready for some jazz?"

They glided away from the table, high-stepping as if they were Ginger Rogers and Fred Astaire. She joined in the impromptu dance. Smiling people watched their progress.

Sweating under the heavy hat, Michelle felt her hair sticking to her scalp and longed for another cold drink. Up ahead she spotted a coffee shop. They must serve iced drinks in the heat. "Let's stop for a minute."

Joe opened the door for her. She reached for her hat, but Joe stopped her, pointing to other customers in the store. Several of them were wearing similar stovepipe hats, some handmade, some purchased. Among the customers she spotted the same little girl who had borrowed the glue. Her hat was decorated with a 3-D flower made out of a cupcake liner and green construction paper. Cute. Her mother's hair was blond, and Michelle realized the child must be adopted.

Chapter 4

What am I doing here at this festival, as if nothing mattered more than having a good time? The girl looked at Michelle and giggled, pointing at her hat. Michelle touched her hat and made a face. The child giggled some more. They communicated without language, and once again Michelle thought of Romania. Then their drinks were ready, and she and Joe found seats. She removed the hat, keeping it out of the way of their glasses and the shortbread cookies Joe had purchased. Taking a bite of the cookie, she looked at the passing crowds, wondering how she was going to meet her commitments.

"What's wrong?" Joe's tone shifted from lighthearted humor to compassion. He stretched his muscled arms across the table, light from the nearby window glinting off the blondish-brown hairs.

She shrugged, embarrassed. "Nothing." *Not with you.* "I'm thinking about the résumés I sent out and wondering if I'll ever get a job in this economy."

Concern flickered in his cobalt blue eyes. "God will open the right doors."

"I know. Sometimes it gets to me, but I'll be okay." She looked at the plate, almost surprised she had finished the cookie. "Do you mind terribly if we call it a day?"

◆

Joe swallowed his disappointment. To get back to the truck, they had to walk the length of the blocks cordoned off for the festival. Michelle hummed quietly to herself, and Joe took heart. As they passed the jazz stage, she asked, "I'd like to stop for a minute. Is that okay?"

Joe would have agreed to almost anything to prolong his visit with Michelle. They took a couple of seats toward the back, and when Joe reached for her hand, Michelle let him. As the bass picked out the rhythm and a saxophone carried the melody, her fingers lost their stiffness, and he found himself rubbing his thumb along her palm. A glance at her feet revealed she had kicked off her high heels. Joe still didn't enjoy the music very much, but he did enjoy watching the woman by his side.

When the set ended and the band struck the stage to prepare for the next act, Michelle turned to him. "Thank you." She turned the hat she had made in her hands. With a small smile, she returned it to her head. "I might as well get back in the spirit of the holiday."

They continued making their way through the booths, and Michelle stopped long enough to buy the purse she had perused earlier. All too soon they arrived back at Joe's truck. He unlocked the door on the passenger side, but Michelle climbed in before he could offer his assistance. He shut the door for her and returned to the driver's seat. "Where do you wish to go, princess? Your wish is my command."

"The Romeros', please."

The truck started with a loud growl and idled through the stop-and-go traffic around Cherry Creek Mall. Michelle stared at the crowds through the side window. Her hat slid sideways, and she took it off. She fingered the tiara. "I wish I were a fairy-tale princess who could call on all the creatures of the forest to make everything right with the world." She glanced sideways at him. "Or that I had a knight in shining armor to do it for me."

They arrived at the Romeros' house. Michelle's hand was already on the door handle.

"Wait." Joe jumped out and ran to her side.

"I'm not used to such chivalrous treatment."

"Camelot is alive and well." He grinned. "I'd like to have dinner with you tomorrow night." *Please say yes.*

Michelle's eyes probed his. "Are you sure you want to?" For a second, her defenses dropped.

"Absolutely."

"Very well." A hint of a smile lifted the corners of her mouth, and she disappeared inside the door.

❖

An hour later, Joe waited while Sonia undid several locks on her studio door. "I see you added extra protection."

"Several studios have been broken into lately. And with what happened... you know...it seemed like a good idea. Come in; look around."

Sonia had changed things since his last visit. Angels and cherubs stared at him from all four walls.

"Not quite your usual work." He bent forward to study a cherub watching over a sleeping child.

"No, but it sells. Even starving artists have to eat." She tucked her arms around her waist for dramatic effect.

"Huh." He stopped to study her pose.

She waved him away. "Keep looking."

Sonia specialized in her use of bold primary colors, marrying the simplicity of a children's picture book with themes that resonated into adulthood. In her newest pictures, he sensed someone watching over the angels as they watched over their charges. God, of course. His heart quieted as he contemplated the involvement of the Heavenly Father in every aspect of life. He shook his head.

"You don't like them?" Sonia frowned. "I thought you would see what

I was trying to do."

"It's not that." He mentally shook off the cobwebs of the afternoon and concentrated on the business at hand. "You don't need me to tell you they're good."

"Compliments are always welcome."

"They're a powerful testimony to God's intimate involvement in His creation. I can't take them all, but—"

"Great. We'll settle the details later." Tension flooded out of Sonia, almost drowning Joe in its release. "Since I've been painting angels, I baked an angel food cake. Care to have a slice? With strawberries, to celebrate our continuing association?"

Joe waited while Sonia fixed fresh-ground coffee and served a thick slice of cake dripping with fresh strawberries. One bite, and he closed his eyes as the flavor sensations flooded his mouth. As perfect as he remembered. The cake slid down his throat, and he quickly emptied the plate.

Sonia laughed. "There's plenty more where that came from." Without asking, she slid another slice onto his plate.

He smiled his thanks, sopping the cake in the strawberry juice. Sonia left a bit of her tiny piece. *Women, always worried about their weight.* Dabbing at the corner of his mouth with a napkin, he pushed away from the table. "Thanks."

"My pleasure, Sir Cameron." Sonia liked to tease him about his knightly dreams. She nodded her head as if pleased with what she had accomplished. "There's something else I want to show you. Something I'm working on."

Joe followed her into her inner room. A sturdy easel supported a large canvas. Jagged mountains, tall and unassailable, divided the picture in two halves. Black shadows cast a pall over a band of travelers seeking a way to the other side. A garden of paradise's delights awaited them there, surely the goal of the explorers.

Sonia's hand reached for the light in the painting, her fingers stopping millimeters away from touching the surface. "I know you blame yourself for what happened that night. I blamed myself, too."

"It wasn't your fault—"

"Stop it." She put her fingers to his mouth. "I went to a counselor at my church. She suggested I paint how I felt about what happened. So I started this. Every time when I felt scared about going back to that part of town, or whenever guilt attacked me for my part in putting us in danger, I would paint the shadows a little darker, the mountains a little taller. I couldn't figure out how to get to the other side until recently. Then I found the way. Do you see it?"

Joe cocked his head and scanned the painting inch by inch. Sonia's brush had blocked all passes over the mountains. Tucked away in a deep crevice between the two tallest mountains was a fissure of light, a light so pure that the source must be God Himself.

Sonia saw he had found it. "God showed me He would guide me through my deepest fears instead of removing them from my path."

Joe only shook his head. He had never reconciled what had happened with the powerful God of scripture.

Sonia didn't press her point. "I want you to handle this for me when it's finished. I'm in no hurry to sell it. Hold on to it long enough to absorb the sense of peace God has given me." She laughed lightly, as if embarrassed at her suggestion that the painting could help him.

"We'll see." Joe didn't relish a visible reminder of an episode he was trying to put behind him.

Sonia nodded and turned off the lights as they exited the room. "More coffee?"

"No thanks."

"I have something for you before you go." Sonia disappeared into her studio and reappeared with one of her angel paintings, a cherub watching over a child watering a flower. "I want your mother to have this one."

Joe thought about the gardens at his mother's house. "She'll like it. Thanks." He chose a handful of angel pictures for his gallery and left.

All the way to the hotel, Sonia's and Michelle's voices argued in his head. They both needed someone strong, a man of faith, a knight, indeed, and he was little more than a bungling squire.

◆

"The sun must have been strong today." Carrie rubbed aloe vera lotion onto Michelle's sunburned skin. "Maybe you need a higher SPF at this altitude."

Michelle knew Carrie was curious about the day, but somehow she didn't want to share the special memories. Not yet. Carrie didn't push. "Should I plan on your being here for dinner and fireworks tomorrow, or have you made plans with Joe?"

Dinner. Michelle had forgotten tomorrow was the holiday when she promised to go out with Joe. Maybe she should beg off. "I'm not sure. Can I let you know later?"

"Of course." Carrie paused at the door. "I'm looking forward to hearing all about it, when you're ready."

Michelle stretched out on the bed, reviewing the day. She had a lot of fun with Joe, but was it fair to go into a relationship when her future was so uncertain? "Oh Lord, You're going to have to help me. Not that I was ever in control. You are."

Chapter 5

Joe combed his hair, a tuneless whistle streaming through his teeth. Excitement bubbled out in song for him. He couldn't wait to see Michelle again. In spite of the way yesterday had ended, she intrigued him more than any woman he had met for a long time. No woman in his hometown came close. Between the excitement of the holiday and the anticipation of seeing Michelle again, he had struggled to keep his mind on business all day.

His hand hovered over his suit, and he debated whether to dress up or stay casual. Casual, he decided. Somehow barbecue and fireworks clashed with the attire of a debonair businessman. He wanted to set the right tone tonight, to avoid the crowd-crushing scenes of the baseball game and the arts festival and find a place where he could learn more about this vulnerable woman who fascinated him so much. Dinner at a quiet restaurant, maybe followed by fireworks—that was the ticket for the evening.

When Carrie answered the door, a questioning look on her face, his spirits plummeted. "Michelle will be ready in a few minutes. Why don't you take a seat in the living room?" She disappeared up the stairs.

Joe shrugged and walked past a grand piano to the couch.

"Hi there. Joe Knight, isn't it?" A dark-haired man extended a hand in welcome.

"Mr. Romero, good to see you again." Joe shook his hand then sat on the couch to wait.

"It's Steve. And this is Viktor." The father ruffled his son's dark curls. "We're playing a close game of Candyland. He won last time, but I hope to even the score this time."

Joe watched the matching dark curly heads bent over the board. Steve groaned when he hit Molasses Swamp. "Just when I was ahead." Then Viktor landed on a shortcut and sped to the finish.

With a start Joe remembered the child was adopted from the orphanage his church helped support. He certainly looked like he was born to the Romeros. A child. Someday, maybe. When he found the right woman.

"Do you want to play?" Viktor asked.

"Please, join us. Maybe I can beat you." Steve flashed a smile at him.

Beyond the door he heard the murmur of women's voices, interspersed with giggles. Apparently Michelle wasn't ready yet.

Joe had made it halfway around the board and slid back behind the others when at last Michelle came in. No makeup today, her hair pulled back in a ponytail, and wearing jeans, she looked as beautiful as ever to him. He stood and bussed her cheek. "It's good to see you again." Somehow he knew tonight was important.

"I'm sorry I took so long." She looked away for a moment. "I couldn't decide whether to cancel tonight or not." Her cheeks reddened, and he felt an answering heat flare in his face.

"The thing is, I had made plans with the Romeros for tonight."

"Then I convinced her we could survive without her for the night." Carrie grinned. "Go ahead." She steered Michelle in Joe's direction.

Steve's gaze flickered between Michelle and Joe. "I guess we'll be seeing you later. Have a good time."

"So I'm ready if you are." Michelle's lips turned up in a smile.

"But Auntie Michelle, I thought you were going to the fireworks with us." Only Viktor seemed surprised at the change of plans.

"Not tonight, sweetheart." She bent down to kiss his dark head. "I'll see you tomorrow."

They walked to the truck without speaking, and she swung easily onto the passenger's seat. Joe turned the key in the ignition but didn't drive. "We could do this another time if you'd rather." Although he didn't know when. He needed to get back to Ulysses soon.

"No." Michelle's laugh sounded a little self-conscious. "I'm looking forward to tonight. Really."

Joe tapped the steering wheel. "What appeals to you? Dinner at a restaurant or a picnic on a mountaintop?"

"No contest. The picnic on the mountain."

When they got on the road, Joe flipped the air conditioner switch, but no air flowed out. "Looks like the air conditioner's on the blink."

Michelle had already rolled down her window and nestled her head in the crevice by the seat, the wind whipping her ponytail like confetti streamers. The truck shot onto the interstate.

"Where are we going?" Michelle projected her voice over the roar of air blowing through the cab.

Joe looked where the fast-approaching foothills paradoxically shut out the view of the highest peaks. One thing he did miss about Denver was the constant view of the mountains. Ulysses sat in the middle of the prairie, not quite a hundred miles from the first glimpse of the Rockies. "Have you been to Lookout Mountain yet?"

She shook her head. "Haven't been in the mountains at all."

Good. He relished the opportunity to be first to share one of Denver's greatest attractions with her. They approached the ascent up the mountain, past familiar landmarks: the Mother Mary Cabrini Shrine and the rich town of Genesee that for some reason always made him think of the book of

Genesis in the Bible. Soon they reached their exit.

"Buffalo Bill Cody is buried up here," Joe told Michelle. Away from the speed and noise of the highway, they could hear each other. He had driven the road often enough that he almost knew the twists by heart. Mountain splendor alternated with panoramic views of the plains.

"He was that guy with the enormous yellow mustache, right? The original stage cowboy?"

"Before that, he was the real thing. Rode scout with the army, hunted buffalo, the whole bit. He started his Wild West show to keep the tradition alive."

For the next hour they poked through the Buffalo Bill Museum. Michelle read every word of the plaques. Dusk was darkening the sky as they sat at a table near the gravesite, enjoying the view and munching on their food.

"I wonder what it looked like down there back then," Michelle said.

"I expect it was a lot like where I live. Flat land dotted with trees and animals. Although Denver was a city, even then." He jumped off the rock where he was sitting. "Come on, I want us to watch the sunset over the mountains. And this should be a good place to watch the Denver fireworks, too. High enough to see them across the city."

Joe led Michelle to his favorite westward-lookout point. Row upon row of mountains stretched back into a purple haze. The fireball of the sun burned away the last remnants of day in a turquoise blue sky. He drew in a deep breath of the crisp, clear air. Silence reigned in the mountains, wind rustling through the trees, birds calling, but none of the noises of the city. He prayed the scene would work its magic with Michelle.

She sprawled beside him on a broad rock, long legs dangling over the edge, bare toes tipping in the sand and grass underfoot. A gentle rain sprinkled a few drops, and she lifted her arms as if welcoming the moisture. " 'I lift up my eyes to the mountains—where does my help come from? My help comes from the Lord, the Maker of heaven and earth.' That verse takes on a whole new meaning up here."

"Whenever I need a refresher course about how small I am and how big God is, I head for the hills." In fact, he had spent a weekend backpacking through the mountains before he'd decided to return to Ulysses.

"I know what you mean."

Joe lifted an eyebrow. "Didn't know there were mountains in Illinois."

"You'd be surprised. Actually, I was thinking of Romania. We had a couple of retreats in the Carpathian Mountains. It helped to get away from the pressure of our work for a few days."

"Did you enjoy your time in Romania?" Joe prompted when she stopped speaking.

"Oh yes. The need was so great. I felt like I was making a real difference."

"What did you do?"

"Outreach and evangelism—I led a Bible study for women, and we saw every one of them come to Christ."

"Praise God."

The sun disappeared from view, leaving them in darkness.

"Do you ever think about going back?" Joe held his breath. Someone committed to missions overseas would have no interest in an art dealer.

She shrugged and sighed. "No. That part of my life is over. But. . ."

"Yes?"

"I've promised to support the work. If I'm going to live in the lap of luxury—sorry, that's how I see the United States sometimes after being in Romania—it seems like the least I can do. And I'm paying on college loans. My parents paid on my loans while I was in Romania—they said it was their part of supporting my work—but then Dad lost his job, and it's been hard for them. I want to give them that money back."

He whistled. "That's a lot to manage all at once."

"I was doing okay, as long as I had a job."

"What happened?"

"The company downsized." She frowned. "And I've had trouble landing another position that pays enough for my commitments."

He reached for her hand in the dark and covered her fingers with his, offering his support. "I'll pray God provides just the right job for you. Soon." They sat for a few moments, absorbed by the scene in front of them. Joe hummed a few measures then started to sing. "Let all mortal flesh keep silence, and with fear and trembling stand; ponder nothing earthly minded, for with blessing in His hand, Christ our God to earth descendeth, our full homage to demand."

He stopped singing, and silence reigned absolute. He worshipped in the open air and beauty of God's creation.

Beside him, Michelle trembled. "That's beautiful. I've never heard it before."

"It's an ancient song that made its way into one of my mother's hymnbooks. She thinks it may be a plainsong—you know, like one of those Gregorian chants monks used to sing."

"Christ descended to earth with blessing in His hand. I like that thought."

They turned east again, looking over the city lights before them. Joe drew Michelle against his shoulder. He wanted to help her, protect her, fight her battles, love her—

The thought hit him hard.

God, I love her.

I can't love Michelle. I've only known her a couple of days. Joe's mind reasoned with his heart without success. Joy sang through his body. His breath quickened, and he slipped his arms around her shoulders, wanting to protect her from all harm.

Michelle's breathing settled into the same rhythm with his heartbeat. In the distance, color burst into the velvet darkness.

Chapter 6

Michelle relaxed, relishing the comfort of Joe's arms and letting go of her worries about the future and enjoying the moment. She shifted in his arms, catching a glimpse of the mountains stretching south of her. The mountains were still visible, black silhouettes against a dark sky. In this idyllic setting, she found it easy not to ponder earthly minded things.

A breeze caressed her, whispering peace to her heart. Joe's breath warmed her inside and out. For the moment she relaxed, resting in the awareness of God's presence, thanks to Joe. He knew how to bring out the best in her. She felt like she had known him for years, not a matter of days. *But he'll be leaving soon. He's only in Denver on business. He has to go home sometime.*

The thought panicked her, and she sat upright, leaving the safety of his arms. "How long will you be in Denver?" She bent over and put her socks and shoes back on.

"I'm not sure." Joe stood up slowly, as if stretching kinks out of his legs. His voice sounded ragged, torn by some strong emotion. "I had planned on going home tomorrow, but. . ."

Will I see you again?

"I have some unfinished business. Maybe I'll stay another week."

Michelle's heart soared. She stood beside him, tingling from the buzz that sped from her head to her sleeping legs.

He glanced at his watch. "Wow. It's after ten."

"I'd better get back. Now that the holiday is over, I'm going job hunting in the morning."

Joe kissed her fingers then cradled her hand in his as they walked to the truck. The gentle pressure sent a message of strength and support. He opened the door for her and leaned against the frame. "When can I see you again?" His voice was light, but it throbbed with an unspoken deeper emotion.

Michelle warmed to the sound. "I really need to do some job hunting tomorrow. Thursday maybe?"

"Thursday it is, then." His face scrunched in a happy smile as if he were calculating the number of hours until then.

The Romero household had gone to bed when Michelle returned. Carrie had left a note. "Hope you had a good time. See you in the a.m."

A pang of guilt jabbed Michelle. Carrie was taking off the summer between finishing her Master's degree in May and sending her son to school for the first time in the fall. The two friends had looked forward to spending time together—at least until Michelle met Joe. Bless Carrie, she didn't seem to mind. If anything, she was delighted, but Michelle hoped to make up for the neglect. She went through her bedtime routine, pushing thoughts of the evening with Joe into the background, focusing instead on the tasks that lay ahead.

◆

Keep your mind on business, Joe reminded himself for about the hundredth time. He had tarried too long at the wood-carver's booth, entranced by the many figurines of couples. Old couples, young couples, expectant couples, even young children. *Everything reminds me of Michelle,* he admitted to himself. He had to make a decision if he wanted to visit all the booths before the festival ended later today. "So, Roger, have you had a successful time this year?"

The artist, a gray-bearded man of fifty-something, shrugged. Sometimes the entry fee exceeded the profits for the artisans, the major benefit coming from the exposure they received. Joe thought a few of Roger's pieces had sold, but he didn't trust his memory about anything that happened Monday—the day Michelle stood at his elbow, distracting every thought.

Joe quickly chose a fiftieth anniversary piece, a bride and groom, and the expectant pair. Roger shrugged, perhaps a little disappointed at not making a bigger sale. Flushed with full-blown romantic feelings, Joe relented. "If these sell quickly, I'd like some more. Are you willing to lower the price at all?" Although the figurines were lovely, he knew most buyers would balk at the high price tag.

Roger caressed a carving with his hands, probably remembering the countless hours required to bring it to life. "If you think it's necessary. What do you suggest?" They arranged a more attractive price. "Minus your commission, I suppose?"

Joe simply smiled. They shook hands on the deal and made arrangements for shipment. After that he moved swiftly from booth to booth, conducting business. Shortly after noon, the strains of karaoke grew stronger as he approached the country-western stage. He stopped for a second to watch.

A young couple in their early twenties pranced around the stage, singing an old Garth Brooks song. "We're two of a kind, workin' on a full house."

He smiled at the memory of the good time he and Michelle had shared performing on that stage. Not that either one of them could sing well enough to win a contest, but it hadn't mattered. Her natural warmth and enthusiasm drew people in.

Michelle. He could sink in the depths of her sea-green eyes, glimmers of a beautiful soul within. Tomorrow couldn't come soon enough for him. Resolutely he pushed the thoughts aside to concentrate on the business at hand.

◆

On Wednesday, Michelle stayed too busy with job hunting to think much about Joe, but as the afternoon drew to an end, she kept glancing at the clock, as if she could make morning come more quickly. She was studying her wardrobe, contemplating what to wear on her next date with Joe, when she heard the phone ring in the other room.

Carrie rushed to her door. "It's for you—Mercury Communications."

Mercury? Michelle didn't think she stood a chance with Denver's third largest communications company. Her head spun as she took the receiver.

"This is Michelle Morris." Good, she kept a clear, professional tone.

"This is Chavonne Walker from Mercury Communications. I've reviewed your résumé. I'd like to schedule an interview with you on Friday, if possible."

"I'd love to." Michelle struggled to keep her voice even. "When do you want me to come in?"

They set the time for 10 a.m.

"You have an interview?" Carrie inquired eagerly.

Michelle nodded.

"Praise God."

Michelle grinned and skipped a short step. " 'My God will meet all your needs.' Oh Carrie, it's starting. I just know it is."

The phone rang again. Carrie answered then grinned. "She's right here." She handed the phone to Michelle. "It's Joe."

"Hello." She sounded as breathless as a person accepting an award.

"Hey, you don't have to get all excited. It's only me," Joe teased.

"Mercury Communications just called."

"That's cause for us to celebrate."

He said us. The implied closeness warmed Michelle's already-giddy spirits. "It's just a job interview." She downplayed it, striving for a casual tone.

"It's a foot in the door." He sounded hesitant.

"What is it?"

"Some people I know that worked there loved it. But others. . .well, they left before long."

"I need this job, Joe."

"I'm sure you'll be fine. Everything is better with Michelle Morris in it." He made it fit the jingle for Blue Bonnet margarine.

She giggled. "So, what's up?"

"I wanted to hear your voice."

She smiled. "Well, now you have."

"I wanted to make sure we're still on for tomorrow."

"Absolutely." Michelle might have promised to go to the moon if he suggested it, as excited as she felt.

"Ask Steve and Carrie if they mind if we hang out there for a few hours."

"What—?"

162

"You said you liked secrets."

"I'll wait if I must." She covered the receiver with her hand. "He wants to know if we can spend a few hours here tomorrow."

"Of course," Carrie said.

"See you tomorrow, then." The morning seemed very far away.

Michelle woke early on Thursday, wondering what Joe had in mind for the day. When he arrived midmorning, he held a large bundle under his arm and carried a bag with his other hand. She opened the door for him. "Come on in."

Joe set down the parcels and returned to his truck for another bag.

"Would you like some coffee?" Carrie asked when he came back in.

"Sure. That sounds good. Do you have a table where we can work for a while? And can we borrow your son?"

"Sure. Would the coffee table in the den work?" Joe nodded, and Carrie poured coffee for all of them then led the way to the den. "Viktor, come here, please."

Joe was already pulling packages of various sizes out of his bag. "We're doing some product testing today. Hope you don't mind."

Michelle stared at the assortment of paper and paints and other art supplies spread across the tabletop, reminiscent of the festival. "What's up?" She pasted on her best smile. "Why do you have all this stuff? More children's art?"

"Didn't I tell you? My store is part art gallery, part art supplies. I want to interest people in art any way I can. My kids' classes are always full; that's why I thought Viktor might like to help."

Viktor dashed into the room and skidded to a stop. "Here I am."

"Mr. Knight would like your help, Viktor." Carrie pushed him toward Joe.

"I need a strong boy."

"I'm strong." Viktor pounded his chest.

"Then you're just the one I'm looking for. I want you to help me test these supplies. What color do you like?" Joe opened a box of chalk, and Viktor chose the red stick. "Draw me a picture."

"Of what?"

"Whatever you like."

Viktor stuck his tongue out and pressed down on the chalk, drawing a house. The chalk broke in half, and his mouth turned down. "I'm sorry. I broke it."

"That's okay." Joe leaned close to Viktor and said in a stage whisper, "It happens to me all the time. It's the chalk's fault."

"Why don't you try these next?" Michelle sharpened a few colored pencils. Viktor chose red, blue, and yellow. Midway through coloring a blue roof the pencil lead broke.

"It's the pencil's fault," Viktor told Michelle.

"We can fix that." She handed him the pencil sharpener. He finished a picture of a red house with a blue roof and a yellow door. "I want to hang this on the refrigerator."

"Good idea." Carrie walked with him into the kitchen. She stuck her head back in. "Anybody want more coffee?"

"No," Michelle said.

"I'm going to start on cookies to bring to church on Sunday."

When Viktor came back out to the den, Joe handed him modeling clay. The boy rubbed it between his hands, working it into a long green snake.

"They say this project is quite popular." Joe pulled a photo album the size of a three-ring binder out of the bag then dropped a bunch of fabric and whatnots on top of it. "I don't see what the attraction of scrapbooks is. Why would somebody pay that much money when they can buy an ordinary photo album for a third of the price?"

Michelle hardly listened. Fingering the leather binding, she eyed the bright paisley print against the soft brown cover. "It's beautiful."

Joe cocked an eyebrow at her. "So you like it?"

"Oh yes. It would make a perfect gift. . .or a special family project. . . doesn't take any special talent. Just scissors and time and tape."

"But why package it? Wouldn't people rather make their own? It would be cheaper."

"Some people do." Joe obviously didn't understand the appeal. "But I'd love something like this. It's easier than trying to pick up all the odds and ends I'd need. I want to do something with the hundreds of pictures stored on my camera cards—from Romania and from Carrie and Steve's wedding. This would get me organized."

"Take this one then. It's yours."

Michelle wanted to refuse, thinking of the expensive price tag, but something in Joe's face stopped her. Her fingers rubbed the leather as if it already belonged to her.

"There's a catch." His smile grew wider.

"Of course there is."

"I'd like to display a sample at my store. Can I borrow it for a month or two after you're finished?"

Put my life on display? Before Michelle could put her refusal into words, Joe tucked the materials back into the bag. "Do it. Convince me it will sell."

"Very well." Michelle smiled weakly.

Viktor's snake had fallen apart in the middle, and now he was putting together an animal of some kind. Michelle looked at the stacks of materials. "What else?"

"Who wants fresh cookies?" Carrie appeared in the doorway.

"I do!" Viktor dropped the clay on the table and ran to his mother.

"That's pretty much it, except for the finger paints."

"If you want to go on, I can supervise him while he tries those," Carrie said.

"Sure, if you think he'd like it."

"Are you kidding?" Carrie laughed. "He still gets a kick out of soap bubbles."

"Well, then. Maybe he'd like to assemble this model car."

Carrie wrinkled her nose when she saw the small box. "I'll let Steve help Viktor with that one. But thanks—they'll both love it."

After that Joe whisked Michelle away into a summer wonderland. For lunch they dined at a restaurant that had a wall-sized screen that took them through a day in the African jungle. They punted down Cherry Creek in a boat while their guide regaled them with stories of Denver's beginnings as a mining town. Last of all they toured the Tivoli Student Union, a converted brewery that looked like a castle out of a fairy tale against Colorado's trademark blue sky.

Much later Joe drove slowly back to Carrie's house, Michelle's head resting on his shoulder. Joe had a way of looking at her that made her feel as beautiful as Miss America and as fascinating as the latest pop star. What a special man. He seemed to like her from the inside out.

Feelings of contentment and peace swirled through her. The gentle humming of the truck's engine lured her to sleep. Her last conscious thought was, *I could love a man like that.*

Chapter 7

"Well, what do you think?" Carrie stepped back so that Michelle could look at herself in the mirror.

Not bad, Michelle decided, turning her face from side to side. The faint sunburn she had received on the Fourth had turned into a healthy tan. She'd hardly needed makeup. "It's good."

Carrie fixed a strand of hair here, a fold of the skirt there, but Michelle's mind was elsewhere. Somehow she had known she would look her best today—and she suspected the extra self-confidence came from her time with Joe. "If they don't want to hire you, it's their loss," he had said. Platitudes, perhaps, but he made her feel special.

"Want to tell me about it?" Carrie straightened the hem of Michelle's skirt. "You've been mooning around all morning, sighing like you're love struck."

Carrie had been Michelle's best friend too long to put her off. "I think I am. Love struck, I mean."

"Ahh." Carrie drew in a breath. "I thought so. Good."

"What do you mean, good? I'm here to find a job, not—"

"And we both were in Romania to spread the Gospel, but that didn't keep you from dating while you were there."

"And you're the one who fell in love." Although Michelle meant it as a lighthearted comment, even she could hear the slight edge.

"Yeah, I did. I still can't believe how God brought Steve and Viktor and me together." Carrie smiled at the memory. "Whatever the reason, you're happy, and that should help you at the interview."

"As long as I can keep my mind on the questions." Adrenaline surged through Michelle's veins, boosting her self-confidence to almost ridiculous levels. She could do it, with God's help.

"Keep that confident smile, and you'll do fine." Carrie pointed to Michelle's reflection in the mirror. "I see a capable young woman. You're good with people. You're an experienced leader. You have the right training."

Michelle's chin rose a notch as Carrie rattled off her skills.

"And don't forget you're multilingual."

"I doubt if there is much need for Romanian in Denver." Michelle giggled.

"Don't forget your French. And you're picking up Spanish fast. You already know as much as I do."

Carrie was right. Michelle had an ear for languages, and learning another romance language presented almost no challenge at all. She had learned a lot of Spanish in only one month's time, bombarded as she was by the media and people around her.

"*Buena suerte*," Carrie said. "Good luck. Although with your skills, you won't need it." They smiled together as if on cue, leaving Michelle ready to conquer the world.

"And one last thought about Joe," Carrie added as if unable to stop herself. "Jobs come and go, and careers change, but the right man is 'till death do us part.' What's more important in the long run?"

That's true, Michelle realized with a start. *But I can't think about him now.* She put the finishing touches on her toilette and left.

She followed traditional job-hunting advice: leave nothing to chance. Reconnoiter ahead of time. Thanks to the scouting trip she'd made, she knew how to maneuver through downtown Denver's confusing one-way streets and where to park.

Leave early. Bring an extra pair of hose. She had heard horror stories of getting a run down the back of the leg or breaking a heel right before an interview. *Which is why I wear a simple pump, with a spare pair in the trunk of my car, of course.*

She arrived at the Mercury Communications building with half an hour to spare. The receptionist, a wispy-looking young woman whose name tag read Susie, greeted her warmly and handed her a lengthy application form.

Michelle had come prepared with names, addresses, and phone numbers for her job history and references, even though they already had her résumé. Had someone actually called Pastor Radu in Romania? She doubted it, but it looked impressive.

"Would you like some coffee?" Susie gestured toward a half-full pot.

Visions of coffee stains on the all-important application flickered in Michelle's mind. "No thanks." Instead, to ease the dryness of her throat, she sucked on a breath mint. After she completed the form, she studied the company portfolio left as the only reading material in the reception area. With the burgeoning Internet industry, Mercury had grown exponentially, gobbling up half a dozen competitors along the way. No stats were available for the current fiscal year, but the president promised continued growth.

With still five minutes to go, Michelle walked around the reception area, wanting to give the appearance of studying the artwork and not of nervous pacing.

"Miss Morris?" a friendly voice inquired.

She turned and swallowed her surprise at the speaker's appearance. With her slicked-back hair and black horn-rimmed glasses, she looked like she had escaped from the classroom. Only no schoolteacher had ever dressed so stylishly.

Michelle found her voice. "Yes, I'm Michelle Morris. And you must be—"

"Chavonne Walker." The woman extended a manicured hand and beamed a thousand-watt smile, the kind designed to put anyone instantly at ease. All vestiges of the schoolmarm vanished, and Michelle recognized Chavonne as a warmhearted professional.

"This way, please."

Michelle followed her hostess through a maze of corridors.

"This is all confusing at first, I know." Chavonne named each department in passing.

What's the difference between Information Technology, Web Technology, and Computer Technology, anyway?

Many of the employees looked like they were straight out of college. Chavonne herself couldn't be older than thirty. Michelle's résumé sparkled with experiences these young kids wouldn't have yet. *Maybe my lack of experience doesn't matter as much as I thought it did,* she realized with a lift of her heart.

The tour ended close to where they had started, and they went into Chavonne's office. Michelle registered details of the room's—and the owner's—personality as she refused another offer of coffee. Paper neatly stacked, a potted plant in the corner, family snapshots on the wall—the personal details confirmed what Michelle had already observed about Chavonne. She was personable, approachable, competent, and professional.

"Are those your girls?" Michelle remarked as an opening gambit.

"Yes. Annie is six, and Nettie is two." Chavonne pulled a folder out of the top drawer of her desk.

"My best friend's son just turned six." Michelle smiled at the memory of Viktor blowing out the birthday candles. A pang struck her heart. She had no pictures of children to hang on her wall. *No husband either.* Another, deeper, pang.

Chavonne did not inquire about Michelle's family. Children fell into the "don't ask, don't tell" category for potential employers.

Both women seated themselves, and the interview began in earnest. They dwelt at some length on Michelle's time in Romania. "You were with a mission board?"

Michelle couldn't read anything into her neutral tone, but she refused to apologize for her faith. "Yes, sponsored by my denomination."

Chavonne flicked away an imaginary dust ball. "I dreamed of doing that back in high school. Before my girls were born."

Was she a Christian, then? "You still can someday, if you want to. Several of the volunteers were older people. Sometimes an entire family goes to the field to help out for a week or two."

"Maybe." With a smile Chavonne turned the discussion back to Michelle.

"So do you speak Romanian?"

"Oh yes. French, too. And here in Denver I'm working on Spanish."

Chavonne leaned back in her chair. "Excellent. What do you consider to be your strengths?"

This was Michelle's favorite part of any job interview—a legitimate reason to brag about herself. She mentioned her computer skills, foreign languages, leadership traits, her experience working with people in a variety of situations. "I've worked with the public since I was a little girl, helping in my dad's store."

Chavonne smiled. "And your weaknesses?"

Bingo. "I can get too caught up in details and forget about the bigger picture." She hurried to turn it into a strength. After all, weaknesses were only strengths turned around. "I'm very good at organization and prioritizing my work."

Chavonne patted down a stray hair and rose from her chair. "I'd like you to meet Mr. Spencer, who handles employee training."

Meeting another supervisor—a good sign. Michelle matched Chavonne's quick pace down the hall.

"While you two talk, I'll go ahead to Bible study. A group of us meets once a week, during our lunch break. Oh, here's Jim."

Bible study? Michelle was thrilled to learn about an organized group of Christians in the company.

Mr. Spencer was a tall man with wire-framed glasses and a neon yellow bright shirt with a conservative black tie. He sat scowling at his computer screen, but a smile broke out when he saw Chavonne.

"Jim, I'd like you to meet Michelle Morris. She is here about our human resources position."

"Glad to meet you."

Chavonne slipped away. Jim covered much of the same ground Chavonne had, describing the responsibilities for the position she had applied for. "I'm in charge of training, but frankly, the way we've been growing, we need more help. I'm glad you're here." He grinned.

The hour had reached noon, and Michelle's stomach churned. She regretted the breakfast she had skimped on due to nerves.

"—would you like to join us for lunch?"

Had Jim read her mind? She looked guilty, she knew she did, with the warmth flooding her cheeks.

"I'd like for you to meet some of the others in our department." He steered her to the cafeteria.

Two hours later she had shaken hands with at least two dozen people and completed the required I-9 form. She took out her cell phone and punched in Carrie's number.

"Guess what? They want me to start on Monday."

Chapter 8

Joe packaged up the last of the paintings and handed them to the UPS clerk. He had ended up buying so many pieces he couldn't carry them all in his truck. *And where will I put them in my store?* He needed to get home and start making money again, not spending it. But not yet. He wanted to let Michelle know how he felt about her, but he was as shy as a schoolboy on his first date.

A ragged poster fluttered against the wall, and a robust King Henry VIII winked at him while he chowed down on a gigantic turkey leg. Joe recognized the advertising for the Renaissance Festival held in Larkspur, a town south of Denver, every summer weekend.

A picture flashed into his mind—Michelle with a circle of flowers on her head, her long gown sweeping the ground, himself in breeches and a doublet, down on one knee kissing her gloved hand.

That's where he would take Michelle next: the Renaissance Festival. She'd love it.

◆

"Unhand the lady, you yellow cur," a raucous voice called from high ramparts overhead.

Joe looked up and saw several men dressed in velvet doublets. He waved his arms as if to say, "You mean me?"

One of the men leaned farther over the edge of the rampart. "Sir, if you dare enter through the gate, I challenge you for the fair lady."

Another face appeared beside his.

"Prospero, you couldn't beat a turtle in a three-legged race. Fair lady, sir knight, enter the kingdom of Larkspur under the protection of his majesty, King Henry."

Joe glanced at Michelle, and she smiled. The medieval mood commenced outside the gates to the Renaissance Festival. Street performers vied for a few coins. A fake knight rocked back and forth on a two-legged horse, and jugglers added one colored ball at a time to their display. Bow and arrow tied to his back, a man introduced himself as Robin of Locksley and offered his protection from unwanted attention. Michelle tucked her hand around Joe's arm and prepared to enter the make-believe kingdom.

A dozen things competed for his attention at the same time—charming British accents, the ringing of a blacksmith's hammer, the scent of food sizzling over an open fire, the sight of clothing in color and texture not seen in contemporary life. As always, he felt he had stepped over a threshold into another world.

"My chariot caught fire—"

Joe caught the end of a conversation between two of the actors. *His chariot? Does he mean his car?*

He hurried, tugging Michelle in the direction of a dress shop that displayed finery of every kind, from dresses in brocade and silk to lace shawls to tall, black lace-up boots. A sign hanging over the door said BELLE'S SHOPPE.

"Milord, milady. Thank you for gracing my shop." The owner, presumably Belle, a tall woman in a plain cotton gown, greeted them warmly.

Joe gestured to Michelle. "What do you have that would be worthy of my lady Michelle?"

Michelle's mouth dropped open while Belle rustled through the gowns hanging in her shop.

Joe whispered a few words in the clerk's ear. "I'll be back." He disappeared out the door.

◆

He left me here?

Before Michelle could follow, the shopkeeper blocked the entrance, holding up a pale blue silk gown with a dropped waist for Michelle's inspection. "What do you think?"

"I'm sorry, I'm not interested." Michelle tried to move.

"Your knight was most insistent. A complete outfit for his lady. Now if you don't like the blue, perhaps you would like a wine brocade?"

Sensing she wouldn't escape easily, Michelle gave herself over to enjoying the variety of fabrics and styles offered in the shop. *They must cost a small fortune, even as a rental.*

At length the shopkeeper produced a dress that caused Michelle to catch her breath. A pale green bodice dipped into a forest green velvet skirt—perfect.

"There is a change room, if you would like to see how it fits."

Michelle caught sight of the price tag. She couldn't, wouldn't, let Joe spend that kind of money. . . .

"Any luck?" a familiar voice called from the door. Familiar until she saw him. That tall man with brown leather breeches hugging his legs and a midnight blue doublet emphasizing his well-muscled chest couldn't be Joe. Then his deep blue eyes peered out from under a feathered cap, and Michelle smiled from deep down inside.

"Oh Joe, you look fantastic."

"Milady Michelle was about to try on this gown." Belle gestured meaningfully with the garment in her arms.

Michelle heard Joe suck in his breath, as if imagining her in the garment.

She wanted—needed—to wear the gown, if only to be worthy of his finery.

"I'll try it." She slipped into the side room, where Belle assisted her with the multitude of fastenings down her back. The gown fit the lines of her body perfectly, emphasizing her good points and hiding her flaws.

"You are beautiful." Belle sighed in appreciation. "But perhaps one more thing?" The clerk disappeared through the curtains.

She returned with a snood in her hands, made with fine white lace, and fit it over the back of Michelle's head. Without the weight of her hair down her back, Michelle felt surprisingly cool.

"As for shoes. . ."

Michelle studied her feet, glad she had chosen sandals instead of gym shoes. "I'll be fine." Somewhat shyly, she stepped outside the curtain where Joe waited.

For a long moment, they looked at each other without speaking. Then slowly, almost reverently, Joe removed his hat and bowed to his knee.

"My lady." He reached for her hand, and his lips grazed the tips of her fingers. Slowly he rose, not once removing his gaze from her. His expression said she was the most precious thing in the world.

Michelle wanted to say, "It's just me; I'm not worthy." What came out instead was, "I can't let you rent this." To her ears, her objection sounded only halfhearted.

"I think the lady protests too much." Clasping Michelle's hand in his, Joe raised it to his chin and pulled her closer to him. Staring into her eyes, he declared, "You must do me this honor. If only for today, let me play at being the brave knight Sir Cameron." He looked at her with such a mixture of boyish excitement and manly pride that her heart melted.

Slowly, she nodded.

He raised her hand to his lips and blew softly across her knuckles. The gentle warmth of his breath tickled unknown nerve endings, thrilling her to the soles of her feet until she almost swooned in his arms. When they stepped outside the tent, they left the twenty-first century behind with their clothes at a check stand located conveniently outside the shop.

Michelle wanted to hug him. "If you are Sir Cameron, I must be—"

"Lady Michelle. A beautiful name for a beautiful lady."

Heat swept across Michelle's face.

They wandered a few steps without noticing where they were headed when a tall man in a helmet and brandishing a spike barred their path. "Hold there. What is your business before the king's court?"

Directly in front of them a semicircle of twenty or so men and women in period dress held court. At the center sat a man with full beard and rounded chest, with a dark-haired beauty at his side. King Henry, as promised, with Anne Boleyn.

"Begging your pardon, sir, we meant no disrespect," Joe said. They stepped aside to enjoy the spectacle.

While they watched, horns sounded and the monarchs rose to their feet, starting a stately procession downhill.

"It must be time for the first joust." Joe checked his watch then offered his arm to Michelle, and they fell in behind the royal court.

A sudden thought struck her. "I thought Robin Hood lived during King Richard's time." Michelle reflected back to the encounter at the gate.

"Time has no meaning here." Joe waved aside the discrepancy. "They mix centuries of the Middle Ages and the Renaissance in equal measure."

They paused long enough to buy water bottles, a necessity in the heat. Then they joined the crowd gathering at the rectangular tourney field. King Henry and Queen Anne had already settled in a shaded pavilion on the far side.

A couple of jesters worked the crowd, preparing them for the upcoming joust. "Sir Roland is a lout. His colors are silver and black. When he makes a pass, boo him."

The second jester, merry in scarlet and orange, added, "Sir Jerome is a heroic knight. He will be wearing gold and blue. Cheer for him."

They practiced. "Sir Roland." Loud catcalls and hisses rose from the crowd.

"Sir Jerome." Enthusiastic cheers and an occasional yee-haw erupted in increasing waves.

Trumpets announced the arrival of the contestants to a satisfactory chorus of cheers and boos. The first jester explained the rules of the joust. "Points may be earned on each pass the contestant makes at the target. Each target demonstrates a necessary battle skill."

The contestants faced their horses to the king and queen. Anne leaned over the parapet. "For you, Sir Jerome." She tossed him a white handkerchief.

The crowd cheered as loudly as they might a winning home run. For this day, this game, Sir Jerome was their hero.

Sir Roland scowled. "Lady's favors never won in combat." His voice was magnified loud enough for the spectators to hear.

"No, but with such an inspiration, how can I fail?" Sir Jerome said.

The crowd cheered once again and then fell silent as the squires set two hoops chest-high for the target.

Both knights easily lanced the two rings, as well as the four set for the next pass.

The second challenge appeared much more difficult. They had to hit a round ball suspended on a rotating pole hard enough to swing it around, or it would knock them to the ground.

Sir Jerome raced around the field on his horse, a magnificent white stallion, but pulled up short. Gaining speed on the second lap, he lunged at the target, a perfect hit with sufficient strength. The ball swung harmlessly out of the way, and his horse galloped to safety.

Sir Roland didn't fare so well. The ball didn't complete the circle and instead struck him between his shoulders, throwing him from his horse. The crowd roared with laughter. Sir Roland stood, wiping dirt from a surprisingly handsome face. Silently Michelle rooted for him to get back on his horse, to try again. His eyes scanned the crowd, as if searching for someone.

"I think I need the favor of a lady myself." He held out his hands in a plea. "Who will honor this poor knight?" He walked around the field.

Michelle felt her smile widen at the spectacle. Whom would he pick? He stopped in front of her.

"You, my lady. May I have a token of your esteem?"

Michelle looked into his eyes, black as coal. "Me, Sir Roland?"

He nodded.

She searched her purse for something appropriate. Beside her, Joe stirred.

"She will not." His growl deepened into a roar. "The lady is with me."

◆

The crowd came to life at Joe's challenge, cheering for one side or the other. Joe couldn't believe the jealousy that surged through him, shaking his voice. The knight stared at him strangely.

Michelle came to his rescue. "Sir Roland, I cannot. Sir Cameron forbids it."

A laughing light brightened Sir Roland's eyes. "Sir Cameron, I desist. Perhaps we shall meet again?" He said it with convincing menace.

"Oh Sir Roland?" A few yards away, another spectator leaned over the fence, waving a lacy handkerchief. "You may defend my honor." The crowd laughed with her.

Joe relaxed when the attention turned away from him and Michelle. The joust concluded with Sir Jerome soundly beating Sir Roland.

Michelle's cheeks burned bright as they strolled down the lane. "That was rather sweet, the way you defended my honor back there."

"So I didn't embarrass you?"

"Perhaps, for a second." She flashed a grin at him. "But then I thought of all the times I wished I had a Sir Cameron to defend me. There's a lot to be said for chivalry."

If only protecting someone in the real world was as easy as standing up to Sir Roland today. Were things really so much simpler in the Middle Ages? More direct, at least, face-to-face with your enemy; and all knights, regardless of their allegiance, adhered to the same code of honor.

Michelle was studying a daily schedule. "The next joust isn't until two o'clock. There's storytelling and puppets and bagpipe music—"

He heard it then, a low voice singing. "Let all mortal flesh keep silence."

Joe caught the edge of a shadow with his peripheral vision and whirled around.

"Pardon me, sir." Less than a yard away a tonsured figure in a monk's robe crouched close to the ground, humming to himself. He twisted the rope tied around his waist between nervous hands. "Would you care to give an offering to the poor?"

"It would be my pleasure." Michelle's laugh rippled through the air, and she dropped a coin into the man's outstretched palm. "That song, it sounded familiar. What was it?"

"A snatch of plainsong, milady, such as we sing at the monastery." He smiled, a gap showing between two broken front teeth—probably a prosthetic device.

Joe remembered the street person she had aided the night they met. She was compassionate and generous, even at play, but this actor's behavior filled Joe with the same uneasy disgust as the shameless beggars on the 16th Street Mall. "You have your money. Begone then."

The beggar scuttled away as silently as he had approached. Joe let out a deep breath.

Michelle glanced at him sideways. "I saw the side of his bucket. There was a discreet web address for a rescue mission noted. I think it's legit."

Joe shrugged off his uneasiness. "There's a first for everything, I suppose. What next?"

"I can't decide. You've been here before. What would you suggest?"

"You might like the puppets—a variation on Punch and Judy—but if it's the same storyteller who's been here before, he's excellent at fractured fairy tales."

Michelle studied the schedule. "There's just about time for both, before the next joust."

A couple of men passed by, biting down on gigantic turkey legs. Joe's mouth watered.

"Yuck." Michelle's brow wrinkled as if in disgust.

No turkey legs today. A brave knight could endure long combat without sustenance. His stomach growled in protest.

"But it is lunchtime. What are our choices?" Michelle gazed around, searching for booths selling food.

In the end they settled for beef on a stick en route to the storyteller's tent. By the time they arrived, they found standing room only.

A thin man with a lively face underneath a tasseled hat began speaking. "Once upon a time there was a feautibul lirg maned Rindercella who dilved with her neam metstother...."

Joe had heard it before, but once again wondered how the man managed a half-hour monologue in butchered language. At his side, Michelle first trembled with glee then reared back in laughter, the snood slipping off, letting her blond tresses fall in silken locks over her shoulders. Joe enjoyed watching her more than listening and soon lost track of the story.

How do I tell her how I feel? He couldn't ask for a more romantic setting than the Renaissance Festival, but Michelle seemed determined to wring every minute of pleasure out of it. So far they had run from one activity to another. He'd have to make an opportunity.

Soon the performer passed his hat, seeking donations. The businessman in Joe applauded the enterprising spirit, but the spectator resented being expected to pay even more money than the hefty entrance fee.

The afternoon passed swiftly. Joe thought he had his chance to speak from his heart when they sat alone in Da Vinci's Flying Machines, a man-powered ride. But Michelle craned her neck to see all the inventor's ideas and to exclaim over the strongly muscled men slowly pushing the cars around.

Toward dusk Joe led Michelle to a bench underneath a leafy tree. She plopped down, dropping her purse on the ground beside her. They sipped lemonade while Joe searched for the right opening. Her golden hair, once again tucked in the snood, gleamed silver in the setting sun. She took her sandals off and wriggled her toes in welcome freedom. She was so precious, everything he'd ever dreamed of and more.

"What a wonderful day. Thank you, Sir Cameron." She took a long drink of her lemonade and sighed contentedly.

Joe found himself sinking down on one knee. "My lady. My lady—"

A low humming buzzed in his ears. Before thoughts could form in Joe's mind, a hand slashed between them. Michelle's purse disappeared.

Chapter 9

Before Joe could rise to his feet, the monk blended into the crowd, shedding robe and wig as he sped away.

"Stop him!" Joe roared in a voice loud enough that several people stopped to see what caused the commotion. He sprinted after the thief down a thin path cleared by curious onlookers but saw no trace of the man he sought. Nearby he heard low singing, louder than before. He traced the source. A group of "monks" sang in unison on stage, but none of them looked familiar. The thief had gotten away.

"There you are," Michelle called from behind him. She sounded breathless. "I lost him."

"I looked for his robe and wig but didn't find any trace of them. He must have taken them with him." Michelle sounded grim. "I doubt that money is ever going to make it to a rescue mission."

"No." Joe stood with his hands on his hips, turning in a slow circle, hoping to find some sign of the disappearing monk.

"We'd better tell someone what happened."

"I suppose." Joe put his arm around her shoulder, holding her close as they made their way back to the entrance where they found a burly man who looked like he could be King Henry's chief guard.

The chief of security scowled as they described what had happened.

"I'm ashamed to admit I gave him a few pennies earlier in the day. He pretended he was a beggar, you see." Michelle gave a description of the thief. "But I doubt I would recognize him, not without the costume." Her shoulders sagged.

"Is this the man?" The chief drew out pencil sketches of a man who captured the thief's look, toothy smile and all.

"Yes," Joe and Michelle answered together.

He grunted. "The singing monk strikes again. Our guards at the front gate have been alerted, of course, but our best guess is that he arrives in everyday clothes then changes after he arrives. He looks like anybody else the rest of the time."

"So you know who it is?" Joe asked. *Why haven't you caught him?*

"Unfortunately, no. But his MO is always the same. He stalks his victim sometime during the day. She hears a bit of humming, and then her purse is stolen. Otherwise, he is as stealthy as a shadow. The beggar is a new twist."

"I knew something about him didn't feel right. But Michelle said the sign indicated it was for the rescue mission. Sounded like it could be legit."

The chief frowned again. "We wouldn't allow something like that. Besides," he added with a trace of a smile, "I doubt there were rescue missions in King Henry's England."

Joe thanked the chief for his assistance. Michelle filled out the necessary paperwork and called her credit cards to cancel them. People were beginning to stream toward the exits. "Do you mind if we leave?"

"Of course not."

Joe hesitated for a moment outside of the clothing shop. "I wish I could get a picture of you in that dress."

She blushed. "Photography is a very *modern* invention."

He lifted her hand to his lips for one final kiss. "Then let me engrave the sight upon my eyelids." He held her eyes for a long moment before he slapped his forehead. "Of course. My phone." He dug it out of his pocket and snapped a picture before she could protest.

"Now it's my turn." She grabbed the phone and took his picture. "Perhaps Belle will take a picture of us together?" Belle was agreeable, and she snapped several shots before they exchanged their finery for their street clothes and headed for Joe's truck.

A few minutes later they were back on the road to Denver. Tension radiated from Joe's neck down his spine.

"Sir Cameron—"

"It's Joe. I'm no knight, not in the real world."

"Sir Cameron," Michelle repeated firmly. "Is there an inn nearby that will take two weary travelers such as ourselves?"

"There's a restaurant up ahead."

"Thanks." Michelle removed the snood and brushed her hair. "And Joe? You will always be my knight. Always."

Joe glanced at Michelle's pale face, dirt smudged on one cheek. What a horrible end to what he had hoped would be a very special day. At the restaurant's parking lot, he jumped out and rushed to get the door for Michelle. Weary as she was, she was beautiful in every way, a true lady. He held her hand as they walked into the restaurant.

"Did you folks come from the Festival?" The waitress's friendly banter burned like a brand on his spirits, and his stomach tightened. He had enjoyed the day until. . .

Michelle made some polite response and escaped for the lady's room as soon as they ordered their beverages. "What do you want?" Joe called after her.

She paused long enough to answer. "I'll get whatever you're having."

Neither one of them said much until midway through the juicy half-pound burgers the restaurant specialized in. The food sent messages along

Joe's nerve endings like a drug, loosening the anxious knot in the pit of his stomach and relaxing his muscles. He finished his Dr Pepper in one big gulp. The waitress reappeared immediately with a refill.

Michelle squeezed lemon into her iced tea. "I can't believe what happened."

"Yeah." Joe bit off another chunk of his hamburger and chewed. After he swallowed, he said, "I want to be a knight, and instead I keep ending up like the court jester. Fooled by that stupid singing monk. I feel like I ought to be beheaded for incompetence."

"You heard what the chief said. It's happened before. This guy works the fair, and so far they haven't been able to catch him."

"Yeah, but sometimes it feels like trouble seeks me out." Drawing on his remaining dregs of courage, he dragged out the words. "It's happened before. One time I was out on a date—"

"With Sonia?"

He nodded. "And we were robbed—at gunpoint."

She reached out with her hand, silently encouraging him to continue.

"There were two robbers. One held a gun on us while the other one took our wallets, purses, jewelry—everything."

He jammed a few french fries in his mouth as if he could chase away the memories with food. "What's worse is that my parents were with us that night."

"What happened?"

"Dad already suffered from a weak heart, and the stress brought on a heart attack. He died not long after that."

"Oh wow. And you—"

"—went home to take care of Mom. Since I felt like it was my fault. My brother has his own family to take care of, and Mom needs help keeping up with everything." He sighed. "Sometimes I feel like God's fall guy."

"But God doesn't work that way."

"I know that. But—"

"But it doesn't always make much sense. Let me tell you a story. You know I met Carrie in Romania."

Joe nodded.

"And that Viktor came from an orphanage near Bucharest."

Again Joe nodded, wondering where she was headed with her story. "Our church supports the orphanage."

"Well, what you may not know is that it was a return trip for both Carrie and Steve. They went there the first time as part of a singing group."

"Oh?" *So what?*

"Steve was married at the time. To someone else."

Huh?

"And his wife was pregnant. She went into premature labor. She died, and the baby with her."

Joe's mind reeled. The cheerful man with the perfect family—Joe had envied him, he admitted it.

"I won't pretend to explain why God took Steve's first wife and child home so early, but I do know God gave him a beautiful new family. God never takes away something without giving us something even better." She laid down the last of her hamburger and looked him straight in the eye. "And neither you nor God sent the thief after us. The thief chose to do that all on his own."

"You're probably right." Joe twirled the straw through his Dr Pepper. "But after what happened today—again—I wonder if it's ever safe to open your heart to someone. People close to me end up getting hurt. And if there's anything I want right now, it's you, close to me." He took a deep breath and studied the glass. "You're the most wonderful thing that's happened to me in a long time, and I think I love you." There, he had said it. Blurted it out, in fact—nothing like the poetic phrases he had planned.

Michelle sank back against her seat as if stunned.

"But after what happened today—again—I wonder if that's a mistake. I can't afford to love somebody. Not if it means both of us getting hurt." Bitterness colored his words.

The waitress reappeared at their table. "Would you folks like dessert?"

◆

Michelle was grateful for the interruption. She gathered her thoughts while they ordered dessert before continuing the conversation. *I think I love you.* "Oh Joe."

"I know. I shouldn't have said anything, especially not after today."

"But Joe, I think I'm falling in love with you, too." She closed her hands over his, and for a moment the world stood still.

A warm flame flickered in Joe's eyes and then disappeared. "I refuse to be your bad luck charm." He withdrew his hand from hers and picked up the check.

"Don't be foolish. It could have happened to anyone."

"But it didn't. Not today." He clenched his jaw.

We're going over the same ground. Maybe we'll see things more clearly later. "When do you plan on going back to Ulysses?"

Joe blinked at the abrupt change of subject. "Tomorrow after church."

"Do you have any idea when you'll be back in Denver?"

"I usually wait several months between trips." He raised an eyebrow and grinned as if he couldn't help himself. "But I suspect I'll be back sooner this time."

The seriousness beneath their banter breathed life into Michelle's heart. *Is Joe the one for me, Lord?*

◆

Early Monday morning found Joe at his store, arranging his stock to show the new pieces to their best advantage. He ran his fingers over the carving

180

of the bride and groom. The bride was tall and willowy with long flowing hair—like Michelle. If only. He set the piece down with a sigh.

Should he have stayed and helped Michelle with all that was involved with replacing the contents of her purse? Not that he could do much except hold her hand. Business called him back to Ulysses, but his heart stayed behind in Denver.

Their parting words returned to him. "Will I see you when you come back to Denver?"

"Definitely." He couldn't stop the words.

"Make it soon." She had kissed him on the cheek before she darted inside Carrie's front door.

Already he was counting the days.

Chapter 10

Hardly any wind stirred. Joe lifted the Rockies baseball cap and wiped the sweat off his forehead. The weather was hot, as hot and dry as only July in Colorado could be. He grabbed a hot dog and took a swig from his water bottle. His niece waited her turn at bat during her Tuesday night softball game.

"Hey, batter, batter, batter," an overanxious mother called from the bleachers behind home plate. The girl tapped her bat on the ground, sending dust swirling into the air. Moments later she struck out and headed for the bench, head hung low. The mother leaned over the bench and whispered to her.

Pepper, his niece, came up to the plate.

"Choose a good one," his sister-in-law Judy called from beside him on the bleachers. They both cheered loudly when Pepper, a gangly seven-year-old redhead, managed a base hit.

Joe looped his legs over the seats in front of him and leaned back on his elbows. He breathed in the clean, fresh air, so much cleaner than Denver, and let out a contented sigh. "It's good to be back."

"It's good to have you back. Pepper's convinced they lost last week because you weren't here."

The next batter made contact with the ball, and Pepper slid into third base. The next two batters struck out, though, so she didn't score a run. Joe flashed Pepper a thumbs-up when she glanced at him from the bench.

"Did I miss anything?" Joe's older brother Brian slid onto the bleachers beside them.

"Pepper got a base hit. They weren't able to get her home."

Brian shook his head in apparent disappointment. "I'm sorry I'm late. But Mrs. Feldkirk kept me talking for twenty minutes."

"That's okay. It's one of the things that makes you a good country doctor." Judy kissed him on the cheek. "I hope you don't mind that I locked up and came ahead."

"Of course not."

"At least your clinic is only five minutes away." Joe thought of the endless hours he spent driving from one end of Denver to the other, chasing down artists in their studios.

Conversation paused while Pepper scooped a ball out of the dirt and tagged the runner out at second base. Her team headed for the bench.

"I think I'll go say hello to my daughter." Brian stepped off the bleachers with one easy stride. Judy dug a bag of chocolate chip cookies out of her purse.

"Want one?" She passed Joe a handful, the chocolate melting and smearing all over his hands. "Sorry." She dug in her purse for a tissue.

Joe remembered the time Sir Roland had requested a token from Michelle. He missed her already. In fact, he had hardly stopped thinking about her.

Brian reappeared and grabbed a cookie. "So what kept you in Denver so long? We expected you back before the weekend."

Joe didn't want to talk about Michelle, not yet. His practical physician brother would scoff at the idea of falling in love with a woman he had known for only a week.

"Uh, some business came up that I had to attend to."

"Business with Sonia?" Judy grinned.

Uncomfortably close.

"Some, yes. She's working on a powerful new painting that she wants me to handle for her."

"And?" Judy prompted.

"And what?"

"And did you two get back together? You look like a cat who's feasted on cream."

"No." Joe shook his head emphatically. "That's all over with."

"Something happened."

"No, honestly, it didn't." *Not with Sonia at least.*

"Okay. You can have your secret for now." Judy turned her piercing eyes back to the game. Joe breathed a sigh of relief.

◆

Michelle read through her new employee handbook a second time. She had spent Monday in an orientation class for new employees, and Tuesday she was in training for her department, so today was her first day to work. She hoped someone gave her something to do soon. While she waited, she rearranged her workstation to her liking, stocked supplies, and sharpened pencils.

She stretched in her seat, stood up, and walked around. Notebooks that appeared to be training manuals stood on a low-lying bookshelf. She grabbed a couple and headed back to her desk. The first one, for Customer Service, outlined the rules of phone etiquette—smile in your voice, no one left on hold for longer than thirty seconds—familiar ground. Then it gave flowcharts for answering customers' most common complaints. She had worked with that kind of material before and found it easy to use.

Material in the second notebook failed to impress her. Michelle returned both books to the shelf and glanced through the other volumes. Checking against the list of departments within the company, she found no material at all for a third of them. No wonder the turnover was high, a problem Chavonne had mentioned at her interview.

"Michelle. Glad I found you." Jim, the man she had met at her interview, paused in front of her desk.

She shook his hand. "Good to meet you again."

"Welcome aboard. We're having our departmental meeting in five minutes. I'll show you the way."

Minutes later they took the two remaining seats around a large oval table, surrounded by several faces Michelle remembered from her tour of the department. Their team consisted of an interesting mixture of races and gender, predominantly young. Chavonne sat at the head.

In the far corner a couple laughed. Michelle looked forward to developing the same camaraderie with her coworkers. That was the best part of any job. Their laughter grew louder. Michelle's heart lurched a bit. What would it feel like to be half of a couple sharing secret jokes that only the two of them knew about?

Chavonne called the meeting to order. She reeled off a list of things Michelle didn't yet understand, acronyms every company seemed to develop for their own way of doing business.

"—a warm welcome to our newest employee, Michelle Morris."

A few people applauded, and they went around the room introducing themselves. Michelle worked at associating something unique about each individual with his or her name, a skill she had honed to perfection with strange Romanian names. Remembering the women came easily, the men, less so. Rick had steel blue eyes, but none of the laughing merriment that shot warmth into Joe's sky blue irises. Gary wore an obvious toupee, nothing like Joe's glorious thatch of thick brown curls that made her fingers itch to run through it.

Why am I comparing every man to Joe? Michelle focused on what Chavonne was saying.

"Today we have the honor of being addressed by Glenda Harris, our senior vice president." From the covert grimaces exchanged around the room, Michelle guessed the VP wasn't well liked.

The door opened, and in strode a woman who emanated such authority that it took a minute for her petite size to register. From her carefully coiffured hair to her power suit, she demanded respect. Ms. Harris spoke about specific goals for employee training, with the aim of improving performance and reducing turnover throughout the company. She left little doubt that jobs were on the line—including Michelle's. She had to make an impact—fast.

◆

Joe turned the key in the lock, a simple dead bolt affair. Up and down Ulysses's main street, shopkeepers shut down for the night, turning off lights, rolling down blinds. Most stores now opened on Saturdays, but the mom-and-pop operations shut their doors at six on weeknights so that they could spend the evenings at home with their families. Even the chain grocery store closed at ten. At times Joe missed the twenty-four-hour convenience Denver offered.

Since his house was only a mile away, Joe often walked back and forth to work. Tonight he relished every step, reacquainting himself with the minute changes a week had brought to his town. The mechanic had repainted his truck a bright red. Pictures of the candidates for Queen Penelope for the upcoming Odyssey Days had replaced wedding pictures in the portrait studio window.

He turned the corner. As so often happened, a pride of ownership surged through him. He had taken a ramshackle house and worked on it until it shone inside and out. He took special pleasure in the way he had Xeriscaped the yard to allow for Colorado's semiarid weather.

Best of all, I don't even have to lock my house, Joe thought as he opened the front door. A black Labrador retriever skidded across the front hall and slid to a stop in front of Joe, his whole body wiggling with delight. Joe knelt down and cuffed his ears, offering his hands for a slobbery greeting. The dog's tail thumped the ground like a steam engine.

"Yeah, I see you, too, Gawain. Want some food?" The dog raced for the kitchen door at the words.

A package from Sonia had arrived in the mail. He set it to one side.

A quarter of an hour later, he plopped down in his easy chair with his microwaved pizza, Gawain lying beside him with his head between his paws. Joe flicked on the TV and took in the nightly news. The reporter told of a drive-by shooting in one of Denver's more well-to-do neighborhoods. More crime. He switched it off. If only they had a closer TV station than Denver. He activated the radio to discover the Rockies had played an afternoon game. The talk show held no interest for him, so he turned it back off.

He considered playing Frisbee with Gawain. One look out the front door nixed that idea. The fickle weather had turned into an early evening rain. He stood behind the screen door for a minute, enjoying the rush of moist, cool air. When the raindrops began filtering through the screen and beading the floor, he closed the door. The package from Sonia caught his attention. He carried it to his chair, slitting open the accompanying letter.

"Thought you might like this. . . . Don't forget me. I'm almost finished with my painting, and I hope you can handle it for me. . . . And isn't it time for a commission check?" She kept the tone businesslike and casual. Sonia had proven to be a true friend, even after they stopped dating. *I wonder what book she sent this time.* He carefully slit the wrapping with a knife.

On the shiny cover, flags fluttered in the breeze atop turrets over a medieval castle, a column of knights riding across an open drawbridge. The title piqued his interest, as Sonia had known it would: *Beyond Camelot: Other Legendary Knights.*

He flipped to the table of contents and found what he expected—a chapter about Sir Cameron. Flipping through the pages, he read the material. The author carefully defined what was known for certain and what was speculated about the little-known knight.

Sir Cameron had earned his fame by felling a hundred—a thousand in the more embellished versions—enemies, single-handedly protecting his lady's castle. A full-color illustration accompanied the story. Sword flashing, Sir Cameron stood in front of the castle gates. High atop the tallest turret, a tiny figure peered down on the battle.

How times had changed. Nowadays the lady would battle the villains by his side, and even together they might not succeed. He slammed the book shut. He could no more live up to Sir Cameron's chivalrous standard than he could walk on the moon. And people he cared for suffered for it. He still wondered if Dad would be alive today if he hadn't made the ill-fated trip to Denver.

◆

Michelle dug out the scrapbook kit Joe had left with her. *I promised.* And when she finished arranging the pictures, she would have a perfect excuse to contact him.

She slipped the first disk with pictures into the computer and scanned for her favorites. *Where do I start?* At the beginning, and the beginning in this case was language school in Romania. The only two volunteers fresh out of college, Carrie and Michelle had formed a friendship that grew even stronger when they returned home two years later. When they left Romania, Michelle didn't expect to move to Denver on the strength of Carrie's recommendation.

After Joe displayed the album in his store, Michelle planned to give it to Carrie as a present, a testimony to a special friendship and a fairy-tale romance. The file of "must include" pictures quickly grew. She was glad she had caught Steve and Carrie on camera several times while they were still in Romania.

From there she selected shots of the bridal shower, rehearsal dinner, the ceremony, and reception. Michelle slowed down as she looked at each picture, her mind deceiving her by superimposing Joe's face over Steve's in each shot. *Focus*, Michelle scolded herself. *Stop fantasizing.*

She stumbled on a snapshot she had forgotten. A light snow fell all day on the day of the wedding. Steve and Carrie left the church, with him tucking Carrie protectively under his arm to shield her. Compassion and commitment and love were stamped on his face as clearly as a redhead's freckles.

Tears sprang to Michelle's eyes. She wanted that for herself, for Joe, but for some reason he didn't seem to think he was worthy. Maybe she imagined that more existed between them than was truly there. They needed time and distance to sort things out.

Chapter 11

I can't believe I'm doing this, in spite of the promises I made myself to create some distance from Joe. Less than two weeks had passed since Joe had left Denver. Michelle checked her odometer. The exit leading to Ulysses should be coming up in a mile.

"Blink, and you'll miss it," Joe had explained when he invited her to come to Ulysses for the annual Odyssey Days. He paused a second before he added, "Once you're off the highway, you'd have to blink twice to miss Ulysses." She could still hear his chuckle down the line.

A few silos rose above the prairie, but she saw no other signs of settlement except for cultivated fields as far as the eye could see. For the first time Michelle realized how isolated Ulysses was and marveled at how Joe had grown a successful business.

South of the highway, one building's outline changed as she neared it. Michelle squinted, not believing what her eyes saw. A castle rose like a sentinel above the prairie, as out of place as a snowstorm in July. She'd have to ask Joe about it.

At the exit, a small sign announced ULYSSES 3 MILES. Michelle turned onto the narrow road. The distant cluster of buildings grew larger. She was meeting Joe at his store. He promised to stay late until she arrived after work on Friday night. "Just park anywhere along Main Street," he advised. "Then look for my store, the Trojan Horse."

The posted speed limit dropped to forty before the town began and then twenty-five as she rounded a bend in the road, and she saw the city limit sign. A truck roared past, country music blasting from the stereo. Trucks outnumbered cars three to one at the hamburger stand. Kids ran up and down the sidewalks. *Friday night in a small town.*

Over Main Street, a banner hung suspended between two tall columns announcing 35TH ANNUAL ODYSSEY DAYS, JULY 21–22. Lamps fashioned to look like torches sat atop ivy-entwined light poles.

She slowed down and spotted a wooden horse painted on a shop window. Like the fabled horse, its side pivoted open to reveal beautiful treasures inside. A small sign announced PARKING AVAILABLE IN BACK. She slipped her car in front.

Joe hustled out the door and enfolded Michelle in a bear hug. "You made it."

187

He looked so happy, sunshine itself radiating from his eyes, a face as carefree as if life had not yet made him wary of disappointment. He had shed ten years in two weeks. "Welcome to Ulysses." He relaxed his hold. "Come inside."

Michelle hadn't quite known what to expect, perhaps something like an art museum, but nothing prepared her for what greeted her eyes when she entered the store. The late-day sun filtered through the window, casting a golden glow over white plaster walls. Paintings hung on the walls, and other pieces—wood carvings, pottery, steel sculptures—sat displayed atop Grecian columns of different heights. The atmosphere most resembled an ancient grotto. Like at the gates to the Renaissance Festival, she felt like she had entered another world.

"This is fantastic. And it looks like you've found buyers for several things already," she added, noting the SOLD signs on some of the paintings.

"Yeah, I've done pretty well this week. C'mon. There's more."

The back room created an entirely different world—a play haven for children, with a pottery wheel, painting easel, building blocks, and tables ranging in size from preschool to adult. A model car Viktor had assembled was on display, as well as artwork by people of various ages. Shelves held art magazines, how-to books, and coffee table tomes with full-color photographs.

"We offer different art classes during the year. Right now we're doing pottery—always a favorite."

"Children, too?"

"Of course." He grinned at her. "Wait 'til you see it tomorrow. Sometimes it feels like all one thousand residents of Ulysses plus most of their friends throughout the county traipse through here on weekends. The rest of the week I keep busy handling sales online."

"The store is open tomorrow?"

"Busiest day of the week."

What about our day together?

"Don't worry. I'll be here in the morning, but we'll close shop for Odyssey Days in the afternoon."

Michelle hoped the relief didn't show too clearly on her face.

Joe checked his watch. "Speaking of my mother, she's expecting us for supper. She'll never forgive me if I'm late for her pot roast." He walked Michelle out to her car, holding her hand as if it was the most natural thing in the world. Goose bumps of pleasure pimpled Michelle's skin from her shoulder to her wrist.

Joe sketched a map to his mother's house.

"Why don't I just follow you?" Michelle asked, staring at the crossing lines and directions like "red barn—two more miles."

"In case we get separated. Besides, don't worry. You can't miss it. My mother added her own unique twist to the old family homestead." He spread his hands as if words failed him. "You'll see."

Michelle wondered briefly what that meant, but Joe's mother must be as nice as he was. They headed south and west out of town, parallel to the highway, driving up a slight incline. Acres of green corn and wheat waved in the dusk sky, with occasional fields with cows grazing on tall grass. She saw nothing out of the ordinary until they crested the hill.

It can't be. But it is. Michelle gulped in surprise. Straight ahead of them stood the castle she had seen from the interstate, now a black silhouette against a fiery sky. Guard towers rose from three corners of a flat roof, and a tall circular turret rose into the sky at the entrance. A proliferation of flowers like an English garden surrounded the walls. It looked more like a baronial estate than a farmhouse in Colorado.

Sir Cameron. Now it makes sense. And no wonder his mother needs help. If Joe's mother lives like this, what is the rest of his family like? And how big is his family? Two cars and three trucks, including Joe's, were already parked in the yard.

Joe barely made it to her door before two slight figures raced around the edge of the house and hid behind his back, weighing down his arms like two millstones.

"Let me go. You'll have your chance. I want to help Michelle out of the car."

"That's not necessary." She unfolded herself from the low-lying seat with a minimum of fuss.

"Be nice now, girls," Joe whispered to the figures still hidden behind his back.

"We will, we promise." Different-sized versions of the same red-haired, freckled-faced girl pressed in front of Joe, thrusting a nosegay of flowers at Michelle.

"These are for you," the taller girl said.

"We picked them all by ourselves," the younger girl added proudly.

Michelle fussed over the wilting flowers, touched by the gesture.

"An' Grannie let us pick a rose for you to wear in your hair." The littlest girl handed Michelle an open rose with dark red petals as soft as velvet. "We chose red 'cause it's the color of love." She drawled out the word.

"That's enough now, girls." Joe's cheeks turned as red as the rose. Michelle pretended not to notice and tucked the rose behind her ear.

"May I present my nieces? Pepper"—he indicated the taller girl—"and Poppy." He pointed to a girl who couldn't be older than three.

Pepper? Poppy?

"Nicknames," Joe confirmed in answer to her unspoken question. "We're big into nicknames around here."

Like Joe. With hair as fiery as cayenne pepper and as brilliant as the poppy flower, Michelle could guess how the girls had come by their nicknames.

"Our real names are Teresa and Christina. But only Grannie ever calls us that," Pepper said.

"Cameron?" a cultured voice called. The chatelaine of the castle waited, ready to receive her guest. With her stood a couple, the man with a strong family resemblance to Joe and a woman with hair as red as the girls'.

"Grannie, she's here," Pepper announced.

Michelle hadn't known what to expect from the woman who called the castle home. Aside from her formal attire, compared to everyone else's casual jeans, she looked ordinary. "Aren't you going to introduce us, son?" The lady strolled over the lawn as if it were red carpet. "You must be Michelle." She extended a manicured hand in greeting. "Welcome to my home, my dear." Her smile was as warm and welcoming as Joe's, and Michelle felt at ease.

❖

"Good night." Joe waved good-bye to his brother's family as they drove away in their truck. He breathed a sigh of relief. *Phew, that went better than I expected.*

"They're nice," Michelle said. "That's something that gets lost in the city, a sense of roots. Your brother's the town doctor, right?"

"And my father was, too, until he died." Joe cleared his throat. "And my grandfather before that. I'm the odd one out, opting to tilt after windmills instead."

"I don't know that I'd call running a business tilting after windmills."

Bless you for that. "So you don't find it too strange?"

"I don't know about that." Michelle chuckled. "I've never been entertained in a castle before."

"Yes, well, it was my father's wedding present to my mother. So she wouldn't miss England too much."

"How charming." Hand in hand, they walked across the lawn—the grass had grown a little high, he needed to mow it soon—surrounding his mother's home. Michelle's hair fell over her shoulders, a slight wind lifting the ends. She looked like she belonged, a princess at ease on a baronial estate.

"So your mother is from England?" Michelle followed her own train of thought.

"My grandmother was. Mother spent most of her summers there when she was growing up."

"Oh," was Michelle's only comment.

Oh, as in, isn't that interesting? Oh, as in, no wonder she's so strange? Forget about Mother. Joe led Michelle to a canopied double swing inside the rose arbor. "Shh. Relax. Listen." Joe nudged the ground with his toe and rocked the seat. Fireflies flickered in the velvet night sky. Moisture from an earlier shower gathered the scent of roses, filling Joe's nostrils with their sweet fragrance. The hoot of an owl, the gentle neighing of horses, cows bawling—

the noise of a country evening throbbed through the air.

Late evening twilight darkened to deepest night, lit by a thousand stars. They sat long minutes without speaking. The peace of the evening permeated Joe's body, conquering all of the day's accumulated tension. Crickets sang in rhythm with the swing, the sound soothing enough to lull an insomniac to sleep. *Let all mortal flesh keep silence.* Out here man was silent, and all nature sang the praise of their Creator. "Do you hear it, Michelle? Do you hear the song of the plains?" Joe held his breath. Her answer mattered—a lot.

"Yes." She snuggled closer to his chest. "But only because I'm here with you."

Joe looked down, gazing at her upturned face, features transformed into precious alabaster by the moonlight. He saw a reflection of the desires of his own heart.

At last Sir Cameron claimed his kiss from Lady Michelle.

Chapter 12

How long they kissed, arms entwined about each other, Michelle couldn't guess. She only knew that her pulse roared in her ears loud enough to drown out the crickets, and the light in Joe's eyes outshone the constellations of the sky. She felt his chin with her hand, fingers touching the slight imperfection where he had nicked himself shaving, the bristles reappearing. This was her Joe, bumps, bristles, and all.

He loosened his embrace and kissed her chastely on the forehead, as a knight should. His breath came out ragged. "I've dreamed of doing that for a long time."

"Me, too. It was"—Michelle groped for a word—"nice." *Fool. You say "nice" about a person's appearance or personality.* Not about a kiss that she felt down to her toes, that sealed the sense of rightness of loving Joe.

"And now I'd better see you inside." Joe stopped the swing. "Before my mother catches me kissing you again."

In the dark, Michelle could sense more than see his grin. Walking over the graveled pathway to the castle gate, she danced down a lane sprinkled with fairy dust. If she pinched herself, would she wake up from the dream? More importantly, could her feelings for Joe stand up to the light of day and the pressures of the real world?

She shook the questions away. She refused to let practical questions ruin the magic of the evening. *But that's what you came to Ulysses for—to see if there is more to your love for Joe than some fairy-tale romance.* Her conscience refused to quit.

In the courtyard, Joe kissed her once more, briefly, on the lips. They stood holding hands. "Are you ready to come in?" Mrs. Knight stood silhouetted against light glowing from inside the castle.

"I'm just leaving, Mother." Bending forward, he whispered in Michelle's ear. "Go with God." He let go of her hands and climbed in his truck.

Michelle wrenched her gaze from the road where the taillights disappeared. She joined her hostess inside the fortress—as if stone and mortar could protect her from the emotions thundering through her body.

"Thanks for dinner, Mrs. Knight. It was delicious."

"Call me Nel." The words were more command than invitation. "You must be tired after your trip from Denver. I'll show you to your room." Grabbing Michelle's overnight bag in one hand, she headed for the staircase at the opposite end of the entrance hall.

Large tapestries hung on the walls, and Michelle stopped long enough to study them. "That must be your family's coat of arms." She identified a unicorn and a bear facing off against each other, intertwined by cords of heavy rope.

"Yes. My ancestors on my mother's side came to England with William the Conqueror." A definite note of pride vibrated through Mrs. Knight's voice.

What was it like to know centuries of your family's history? As far as Michelle knew, her ancestry was a typical American melting pot, British by name, Scandinavian by complexion, with a dash of eastern European mixed in. Beyond American shores, she didn't know her history at all.

Opposite the tapestry with the coat of arms hung a beautifully embroidered gigantic letter *I*. Michelle approached it. Vines trailed from the *I*, forming a border around the verse quoted on the hanging, appearing much like a monk's illumination of a page of the Bible.

The letter *I* began a quote from the Bible. She read the words aloud. "It is better to trust in the Lord than to put confidence in man. It is better to trust in the Lord than to put confidence in princes. Psalm 118:8–9."

"I see you've discovered our family motto." Mrs. Knight didn't give the picture a second glance.

"Did you make it yourself?" Michelle asked, admiring the intricate needlework utilized in the pattern, although a patina of age gave sheen to the material.

"Me? Oh no. It was done by my great-grandmother when she waited for news of her husband and son during the Great War. A reminder that only God is our true refuge. A lesson that my knight-errant son still needs to learn."

"I've noticed." Memories of Joe challenging Sir Roland flooded her mind. "He seems to think it's his sworn duty to protect me from all harm."

"I know." They climbed wide stone steps, covered by a thin carpet to help ward off the chill. "I talked about the chivalrous ideal a lot when the boys were small. Better than the violence on the nightly news."

"It's rather sweet," Michelle said in defense of Joe. "But—"

"But my younger son carries things a bit too far. Confronting bullies more than twice his size in grade school. Inviting two girls to the prom because he was afraid neither one would be asked."

Michelle smiled at the image of a young Joe, handsome in a tuxedo à la James Bond, fighting off bad guys with one hand while two lovely girls clung to his other arm.

Further discussion ended when they arrived at the guest room, named the Rosebriar. Michelle stepped over the threshold into a fantasy of pink. Someone had fluffed the king-sized bed high enough to make her wonder if she were being tested like the princess and the pea. A canopy fluttered in the breeze from the open window.

"I hope you like it." Mrs. Knight—*Nel*—hung Michelle's few clothes in the closet. "With two boys demanding variations of knights on chargers, I indulged myself in this room. Your privy is through this door."

Michelle peeked in after her hostess and was relieved to see the usual modern conveniences.

"Find it a bit much, do you?" Mrs. Knight's pink-silvered lips curled in a smile. "Most people do."

"It's charming, Mrs.—I mean, Nel."

Nel patted Michelle on the arm. "I'm in the opposite tower, if you need anything." With a quiet rustle of silk, she left Michelle alone in her room.

Michelle sponged her face, enjoying the cool water against her hot skin. She slipped on a white organza nightgown, relishing the feel of the smooth fabric, and perused the other items on the stand. She peeked into a handheld mirror—too small for anything besides fixing her hair. She was glad for the full-length mirror in the washroom. An immaculate silver brush and comb set with a rose etched into their handles shone, inviting use.

She tested the weight of the brush in her hand and slowly lifted it to her head. She brushed her hair with long, firm strokes in rhythm with the song of the crickets outside the window.

Lady Michelle brushes her hair to a pale gold. She wants to please her knight when he returns. She pinches her cheeks for a bit of color.

Ouch. The painful pinch brought Michelle back to reality. She shook her head. Enough of playacting for the night. No wonder Joe had trouble separating reality from make-believe, growing up in a house like this one. It seduced the susceptible into a simpler time. What did he need more? Someone with her feet planted firmly on the ground—or someone to dream with?

Oh Joe. Warm memories of their kiss flooded over her, infusing her with fresh confidence. *We're right for each other. I know it.*

◆

Joe awakened as the midsummer sunrise streamed into his room. By his bedside Gawain stretched his long body forward and back and stuck a cold nose against Joe's cheek.

"Ready for a morning run, huh?" Gawain would settle down if Joe turned over, but he felt as eager as the dog for the day to begin. He shrugged into a faded T-shirt and running shorts and headed out the door, the Lab at his heels.

No need today for headphones to drown out the she-loves-me-she-loves-me-not litany of the past week. Instead his feet pounded in time with his heart, singing—no, shouting—a love song to the skies. Michelle's kiss had branded his soul. He couldn't wait to show her around Ulysses. He hoped she loved it as much as he did. She had accepted his eccentric mother without as much as blinking her eyes. Appreciating his hometown should come easily after that.

The day had already started to warm up when he drove to his mother's home a short time later. Gawain sat beside him in the truck, as proud as the griffins standing guard at the entrance to the castle.

"Stay." He jumped out of the cab. Gawain ignored his command and followed him through the front doors.

Joe found his mother and Michelle in the kitchen, a long narrow room. They huddled together at one corner of the table, Michelle wrist-deep in flour. One tray of triangular-shaped pieces of dough rested beside her, and his mother was pulling a second one out of the oven. He watched the two women sharing a laugh. *Better and better.*

"Joe." Michelle beamed with such obvious joy that he took a step in her direction, drawn by a magnet beyond his control.

"Your mother is showing me how to make real scones. Here, try one." She lifted the rich, buttery bread to his mouth, so close that when he took a bite, his mouth brushed her fingers. The intimacy of the touch sent a shiver to his toes. Michelle jerked her hand away as if burned.

"Mmm, good."

Gawain growled and planted himself at Joe's feet, forcing space between them. Joe's chest tightened. He had never seen Michelle around animals. Did she even like them?

He didn't need to worry. Michelle reached out to pet him and then stared at her flour-covered hands. Instead she bent over and went nose-to-nose with the dog. "You're a sweet boy—yes, you are." The Lab's tail wagged, indicating he was her slave for life. *Just like me.* "He's beautiful. What's his name?"

"Gawain." Joe looked sheepish when he mentioned the unlikely name. "King Arthur's nephew. He was one of the Knights of the Round Table."

"Of course." Michelle laughed. "Pleased to make your acquaintance, Sir Gawain." She rubbed noses with the dog one more time and straightened up. "Someday I'll have a place where I can have a dog again."

How well Joe remembered the struggle in the city to find a place to rent for someone with a dog, especially a big dog like a Labrador. Sonia had grudgingly kept him a few times when Joe went out of town. *Love me, love my dog.* And Michelle liked dogs.

After a very American meal of bacon and eggs and coffee, the only English touches being the fresh-baked scones and tea for his mother, Joe and Michelle headed to town. He pulled up in front of his store, which waited as always for someone to flip the switch and bring it to life. His palms slipped on the wheel. Would Michelle like his work enough to want to be a part of it?

This morning he might find part of the answer.

Up and down Main Street people were raising shades and opening doors. His first customers should arrive within fifteen minutes. Michelle would love the mixture of clientele that came through the store on a festival weekend like Odyssey Days. He just knew it.

◆

"Miss?" A white-haired waif tugged at Michelle's arm. "Did I do this right?"

Michelle turned from the twins she was helping to the girl holding a misshapen lump. Beyond a body and a head, she couldn't decipher what kind of animal it was supposed to be. "I like it. Tell me about it."

Joe peeked over her shoulder. "That's an interesting spider you have there."

"It's not a spider." The child held it up for closer inspection. "It's a cat."

"That's funny." Joe frowned. "I could have sworn I saw eight legs, ready to crawl up your arm." He ran his fingers across the table like a bug, and she giggled.

Michelle enjoyed watching Joe with the children. He had a knack for communicating with little ones. *He'll be a good father*. She smiled at the thought.

In any case, the children's workshops worked well for Joe. One or two small bodies crammed onto every seat in the back room of Joe's shop. He said the Saturday morning classes brought in a lot of money. Judging from the number of children at this Creating with Clay session, he hadn't exaggerated.

Michelle labeled all the works in progress and set them on the shelf. A fire engine siren blared in the distance, and the room emptied.

Joe tugged her arm. "C'mon. The parade's starting. We can watch from the front."

She pushed chairs under the table, rushing to leave.

"We'll miss the grand marshal. It's the high school principal this year."

Michelle hung back, staring about the now-empty store. "But what about the shop?"

"It's closed this afternoon for the festival." Joe pulled her outside, where the hot summer air pinned her blouse to her back like a dry cleaner's bag even as it seared her throat. They could see the lead motorcycle cops, lights flashing, horns beeping. She couldn't believe she saw an actual Dalmatian riding next to the ladder on the fire engine, surveying the scene as if he were the king.

"I wonder how they'll handle this year's theme—Quest for Success," Joe said. "Ah, there's the bank float."

Letters reading BANK WITH US—WE'LL GUIDE YOUR QUEST adorned the sides of the flatbed. Two seekers in Grecian costumes worked their way through a maze to a treasure of homes, cars, and cash.

Joe studied the float. "So that's why they needed the purple paint."

"Do you help plan any of the floats?" After all, he was in essence the resident art expert.

"Me? No. I tried it once. It's too much work for me by myself. But I always donate some of the supplies. Tit for tat. It brings in business."

Children danced by in semiragged rows. Michelle spotted a head of red hair and waved and then returned to fanning her face with a newspaper. "That was Pepper, right?"

Joe grinned, waving wildly.

Men in clown suits rode by on oversized tricycles, tossing candy to the crowd. Soon the strains of horns and drums announced the arrival of the high school band. Girls whirled by in Grecian robes, tossing column-like batons in the air. Togas in blue and gold—the school colors, Michelle assumed—covered white uniforms. The drum major marched by, a girl in a golden helmet instead of the more traditional plumed hat. She lifted her arms to initiate a drum roll, and the gold button on her tunic slipped down her shoulder.

Michelle sponged away the sweat from her forehead. Heat clamped its hand on her throat, making it difficult for her to breathe. *If it gets any hotter, I'm going to faint.* Black dots floated behind her eyelids as she crumpled to the ground.

Chapter 13

Someone pressed a cool cloth against Michelle's forehead, and large fingers checked her pulse.

"Is she gonna be okay?" a small voice piped somewhere behind her head.

"I'm fine, really." Michelle's words came out somewhere between a whimper and a groan. When she tried to sit up, she couldn't lift her head.

"She's coming around," a deep voice said. "Give her room. She needs air." Feet shuffled as people moved away.

This time Michelle succeeded in opening her eyes. Someone had moved her inside Joe's store. Two men knelt beside her, resembling one another enough so that for a moment she thought she was seeing double—Joe and his brother Brian. Her head rested on Joe's lap. His sister-in-law Judy clasped her legs. Poppy held the washcloth to her head. With the Knights, family medicine took on a new meaning. Perhaps they played games of Operation with pretend patients. A giggle burbled from her throat.

"Here. Drink this." Joe's strong arms lifted her to a sitting position, cradling her head against his rock-solid chest. She sipped the water and the light-headedness that had sent her plunging to the ground receded.

"I put on sunblock this morning, I don't know what happened." She stood on her own, a chair providing sturdy support.

Nel appeared in the doorway, flourishing a wide-brimmed straw hat that would fit in at Wimbledon. "Wear this," she instructed Michelle in her best "mom" voice. "It will keep the sun off your face." Given the imperious note in Nel's voice, Michelle felt compelled to don it.

Joe smiled at Michelle, whether from relief or in appreciation of her appearance, she couldn't tell. "I'll be back in a minute." He left the room.

Police sirens sounded, and Poppy ran to the window. Judy turned to Michelle. "Glad you're feeling better. I have to find Pepper." She took her daughter outside.

Brian hung around a minute longer. "I don't think it's serious. Keep drinking water. The hat's a good idea, Mother." He paused, as if uncertain whether he was the doctor or the concerned brother at this point. "You know where to find me."

Michelle wished everyone would depart and leave her alone. Passing out was embarrassing enough without all this fuss.

"Are you sure you want to stay? I could take you home." Nel patted Michelle's hand, and she thought about accepting.

"Michelle?" Joe reappeared, holding a glass jar filled with ice cubes and water. "Are you ready to rejoin the festivities?"

Nel opened her mouth but waited for Michelle's response.

What should she do? A day in the quiet coolness of the castle gardens held great appeal, like a chance to go to Disney World instead of the county fair. But she had come to Ulysses to spend the day with Joe. She smiled at him. "Yeah. I'm fine."

"You two go on. I'll lock up here." Nel waved them out the door. "Should I expect you for dinner?"

"I thought about heading over to the steak place." Joe bounced on his heels like a boy waiting for his turn at bat, displaying the same boyish quality that alternately charmed and infuriated Michelle.

More time with Joe. "That sounds good." She placed her hand in Joe's, and when he grinned at her, the world spun to the right position. She didn't want for anything more than Joe by her side.

◆

"We missed the end of the parade." A wistful note crept into Joe's voice. He hoped Michelle didn't think he blamed her.

"I'm glad I got to see Pepper dance. She's so cute. What's next?"

"If we hurry, we can still make it for the presentation of Queen Penelope's court."

"Who was Penelope anyway?" Michelle plopped his mother's hat on her head, and it transformed her into an English lady. "Or Ulysses for that matter? I've forgotten a lot of my mythology since high school."

"Ulysses, or Odysseus if you use his Greek name, went off to fight the Trojan War—Homer immortalized the story in *The Odyssey*. Penelope was his wife. She waited for Ulysses to return for twenty years. Convinced he was dead, suitors vied for her hand. She promised to choose between them as soon as she finished her weaving—only every night she tore apart what she had sewn during the day."

Michelle giggled. They approached the park in the center of town. A raised platform sat along one side. Dozens of booths crowded the small area with a large tent standing in the middle, perhaps the center for food and drink.

Joe made his way through the crowd, finding Brian and his family by the platform. Pepper and Poppy stared at the candidates in open admiration.

"I hope I'm Queen Penelope someday." Pepper gazed with adoring eyes as a floral garland was placed on the head of a fair-headed farm girl with a winsome smile.

"That would be nice," her mother agreed. "Or you might win the state spelling bee—"

"Or the state science fair," her father added.

"Or even your softball tournament," Joe said.

"Whatever you do, we'll always be proud of you," Judy concluded.

Joe's attention drifted during the presentation speeches, rendered unintelligible by the excessive amplification. He noticed people casting quick, curious glances at Michelle, and pride surged through him at the beautiful woman at his side. How lucky he was.

Before long, curiosity overcame shyness. Hugh Classen, the high school art teacher, ambled over, his two young boys at his heels. "Hey, Joe, want to introduce us?"

Joe made introductions and admired the way Michelle responded to his friend. She grasped Hugh's hand firmly, not the wilted-cabbage handshake some women affected. A warm smile accompanied a look straight in the eye. "Pleased to meet you, Mr. Classen."

"Hugh, please."

"Pleased to meet you, Hugh. And who are these handsome young men?"

Even after the tenth such introduction, Michelle continued to exude genuine interest in each person. They meandered around the park, stopping at every stall. Joe tried his hand at a few of the show-off booths. That was what he called the places that challenged guys to shoot a duck or toss a ring over a bottle and win a prize for the lady. He failed, more or less on purpose, until they reached the darts booth. "Here's another one."

She groaned. She looked right at home, one hand clutching a plastic bag full of freebies and the other lifting the remains of a wand of purple cotton candy to her mouth. "You don't have to throw any more money away on carnies for me." She wiped a smidgen of purple dye from the edge of her mouth.

Joe resisted the urge to kiss it away. "I'll have you know I'm supporting the"—he squinted at a small sign at the back of the booth—"the local Ducks Unlimited. My favorite charity. Three chances, please." He handed a dollar bill to the carny.

The object of the game was to puncture balloons of various sizes with darts. The smaller the balloon, the bigger the prize.

Joe took aim.

Pop. "Yellow for hope."

Pop. "And green for renewal."

Pop. "And finally, red for love."

He had shattered three of the smallest balloons. "I'll take the large black dog, please." He turned to Michelle with the Gawain look-alike. "You said you wanted a dog. Even the fussiest landlord can't object to this fellow."

She hugged the dog so tightly that he would have stopped breathing if he were alive. "It's great. Wherever did you learn to throw darts like that?"

"It was as easy as taking candy from a baby." They moved away from the booth, Michelle's face dwarfed by the gigantic toy. "Don't you know that throwing darts is an English obsession?"

"And your mother—"

"My mother challenges me every chance she gets." He tossed a pebble into the air. "I actually beat her every now and then."

When Michelle stubbed her toe on a power cable she couldn't see because of the stuffed animal, Joe insisted that he carry it. His free hand reached for Michelle's. "Too bad that dog doesn't have a recorder inside. He could whisper sweet nothings in your ear when we're apart."

"What would he say?"

"That you make me feel all three, you know—hope, renewal, love."

Michelle turned away shyly, her cheeks turning a delicate pink.

"At the least he can be your guardian angel dog."

Michelle giggled, some of the embarrassment receding.

A moment later they ran into Brian's family. Poppy's eyes grew as big as pennies at the sight of the stuffed animal. "Where did you get that?"

"Playing darts." Joe imitated the throw.

"He's beautiful." Before Joe could warn Michelle about Poppy's propensity to beg, the girl said, "I wish I had one like him."

Michelle laughed and glanced at Joe. "Then he's yours."

"Really?"

"Really." Michelle took the animal out of Joe's arms and set it on the ground next to Poppy. "He's a very special dog. Joe gave him to me to watch over me, and now I'll tell him to watch over you."

"Thanks." Poppy threw her arms around Michelle. The dog was taller than the child, and Brian had to take it. "We'll take this out to the car. See you later, Joe, Michelle."

Joe watched the departing toy with regret. "I got that for you. But that was sweet of you."

"Oh Joe. I don't need a stuffed dog. . .and I'll always remember what you said."

As if in slow motion Joe's fingers caressed her face. He leaned close, wanting to seal the moment with a kiss, to capture the new closeness between them.

"There you are." His mother swung around the corner, scattering the two lovers like pigeons at the approach of a car. "I was hoping Michelle would judge the pie contest for me."

◆

Michelle couldn't decide whether Nel's interruption relieved or disappointed her more. What would Nel think of her face, heated as it was? She glanced at Joe. Warmth shone from his eyes, comforting her with a sense of love and security.

His mouth twisted as if disappointed at the unexpected interruption.

Nel swept on. "This is the first time they asked me to judge the contest, but two of my best friends have entered. I can't possibly judge between them. Please, do help me out." Her regal smile was more command than invitation.

"Good idea, Mother." Joe whispered in Michelle's ear, "Please say yes. It's too much for Mum." Turning back to his mother, he said, "Michelle will find something kind to say about every entry, even if it tastes like it was made with apples from last year's crop cooked between cardboard crusts."

Heartened by Joe's affirmation, Michelle let Nel lead her in the direction of the contest arena. No sweet smells indicated the trail. Like Hansel's bread crumbs, they had been devoured, not by birds, but by the mixture of diesel fumes, animal odors, and the press of humanity common to every fair.

Half a dozen anxious women hovered around a table, ranging from a young mother with a baby in her arms to a senior citizen too experienced to let her nervousness show. A middle-aged woman as thin and angular as a tree in November marched in their direction.

"Nel. Now that you're here, we can get started." She spoke with the confidence of someone who expected to win.

"To tell the truth, Esther, I've abdicated. This lovely young woman with me is Michelle Morris. She helped me bake this morning, and from what I observed, she's well qualified to judge." She graced Esther with the same regal smile and maneuvered Michelle into a corner where she could whisper instructions. "Here are the tally sheets. Appearance is always a good place to award extra points even if the pie tastes terrible."

Nel's nose wrinkled ever so slightly. "Esther has won for the last three years, but young Molly is hoping she'll win the contest and use it as a springboard to start her own bakery. In case you're wondering, the pies are unmarked, so cut a small piece of each. You don't have to eat more than a bite or two." Speaking loudly enough so the crowd could hear, she added, "Thanks to all of you for participating. And good luck."

Michelle sidled up to the table and tried to look like she knew what she was doing. A wide assortment of pies greeted her—meringue, lattice-top, graham cracker crust, crumb topping. How could she compare them? The meringue was high and fluffy, perfectly sealed to the edge. She bent down to check the graham cracker crust through the glass pie pan—perfect. The strips of the lattice top were even, glistening with sprinkled sugar. In fact, the only thing she could fault in appearance of any of the candidates was a small overly brown section of the two-crust pie. So far, so good. She made notes on the clipboard Nel had handed her.

Silence reigned over their corner of the festivities. Grasping the knife, Michelle cut a tiny wedge of what appeared to be apple pie. The piece slid easily out of the pan, a smidgen of flaky crust dropping to the side. The pastry was excellent, but nutmeg and allspice overwhelmed the flavor of the filling. Not a winner. She set down her fork and wiped her mouth.

No one moved as Michelle wrote on the score sheet, "Wonderful crust—perhaps rethink the spices."

The other pies were perfect examples of their kinds—fluffy meringue that melted in her mouth over a decadent chocolate filling, a lattice pie chock-full of blueberries with just the right amount of sugar. She left the graham cracker crust to last because it resembled nothing so much as a no-bake cheesecake, yellow custard in appearance that could taste like lemon or banana or even vanilla.

The last pie was in fact a flan-like banana custard, chunks of fruit in the mix, rich caramel on the bottom, dots of whipped cream across the surface, and a trace of cinnamon in the crust. Michelle knew she had found the winner.

She made appropriate comments on the tally sheets. "I love blueberries," and "Just the right spices for the crumb topping." Ribbons in hand, she looked at Nel, wondering how to proceed.

"Speech. Speech." Joe grinned at her from the sidelines.

She changed her look of concentration to the most welcoming smile she could muster. "First of all, let me say all your pies are delicious. I couldn't bake pies like these if my life depended on it."

The tension level increased although no one said anything.

"Because the pie was perfectly done, third place goes to"—Michelle turned over the name card—"Mary Robbins, for her lemon meringue pie."

A bubbly, round lady who looked like she spent a lot of time in the kitchen beamed her happiness as she accepted the ribbon.

"Because it was as beautiful as it was delicious, second place goes to"—a quick glance at the card—"Laura Simmons, for her blueberry pie."

An elderly lady slipped forward, hands fluttering. "Oh my, I never expected."

Michelle wondered which participant had baked the award-winning pie, but resisted the urge to peek at the name card she held in her hand. "One of the pies stood above the rest—exotic, unique in its flavor. First place goes to"—now she checked—"Molly Perkins, for her banana flan pie."

Even as the delighted young woman stepped forward to receive the award, Esther flew at Nel.

"How could you pawn this woman off on us as an expert? She obviously doesn't know what she's talking about."

Chapter 14

Nel silenced Esther with a look, a regal glare that would silence all but the most obnoxious reporters at a press conference. "Congratulations to the winners. And a special thanks to Michelle Morris for her assistance in judging." She clapped her hands together once, and a smattering of applause broke out. She spoke a word or two to each winner before she swept Michelle away from the furious Esther.

Nel walked at a deliberate pace in the direction of the midway with Joe trailing behind, but a small laughing hiccup drew attention to the merriment in her eyes. "That was priceless." The wide grin that captured her face testified to her effort to restrain laughter. "Someone finally was able to let Esther know how awful her apple pie is."

"She made that apple pie? I didn't say anything about it."

"You didn't have to, child. The fact that she didn't win said it all. Molly's shop is off to a good start, and two of my friends were runners-up. How nice."

"Esther was so full of herself, I was rather pleased when she didn't win," Michelle admitted. "Not that I did it on purpose. I didn't know—"

"Of course not," Joe chortled. "I wouldn't have missed it for the world."

All thousand residents of Ulysses probably connected in a myriad of ways. Best friends, bitter enemies, new rivals, third and fourth cousins. The Chicago neighborhood where she grew up had some of the same qualities, but it felt stronger here. Today she was the outsider looking in and wished she could share in Nel and Joe's glee.

◆

"After all that pie, do you still have room for supper?" Joe asked.

"Maybe something light. Does Ulysses have any salad bars?"

Joe's stomach tightened in protest. Watching Michelle sample half a dozen mouth-watering pies had accelerated his appetite, not dampened it. "The steak place I mentioned earlier has a salad bar." Hand in hand, they headed for the parking lot. Half the people they met greeted Michelle warmly, news of her pie-judging exploits already spreading through the crowd.

Michelle responded in kind, remembering everyone's names, a smile springing to her face whenever someone stopped to say hello. Joe's stomach growled low, complaining about the delay in mealtime.

Hugh Classen approached, his shirt the worse for wear with a few ketchup stains. "What do you think of Odyssey Days?"

"It's been great. And have you boys had fun?" She winked at them, and in return they displayed their temporary tattoos proudly.

She did it again. Joe wondered how many more people would stop them on the way out. He began to feel like he had crashed his own party. His grip on her arm tightened, and Michelle slid a sideways glance in his direction.

"Is there a more direct way out of here?" She must have sensed his feelings.

"Not really." He shrugged.

"I guess I don't want the day to end. I've had such fun." But the next time someone called a greeting, she waved and continued walking at a brisk pace. Soon they reached the car.

"Do you want to freshen up first?" Joe felt the layers of sweaty grime and a five o'clock shadow on his own face. He had something important to say to Michelle tonight, and he knew he didn't look his best.

"I can't." Michelle giggled. "The only other clothing I brought is my dress for tomorrow." She brushed a stray pie crumb from her blouse and frowned. "The steak place isn't fancy, is it?" She rubbed at a stain on her blouse.

Concern over his own appearance melted away. "You're perfect." He pulled her in close and kissed her briefly to let her know she was beautiful and desirable.

She pillowed her head on his shoulder and played with the top button of his shirt. "Thanks."

A few people threw curious glances in their direction, but Joe ignored them, rejoicing in the feeling of Michelle in his arms. After a few moments Michelle separated from him and straightened her back, a confident grin in place. He wished he could help keep it there all the time. "Shall we go then?"

About a quarter of an hour later they stood in line at the restaurant, waiting to place their orders. Signed autographs from rodeo stars and country singers lined the walls, with the obligatory rack of elk antlers at the door.

"What fun," Michelle said. "I haven't been in a place like this for years. My goodness, there's a picture of Bill Pickett."

"You know about Pickett?" That surprised Joe.

"Of course. He was my brother's hero when he was a kid. He dreamed of being a rodeo rider until he grew up and went to dental school instead." Internal mirth curved her lips.

"Yeah, maybe he'll strike up a business replacing teeth knocked out in the ring." They laughed lightly.

They had arrived at the cashier. Joe ordered a sixteen-ounce T-bone and wondered if it would be enough to satisfy his hunger. Michelle stuck with the salad bar. They both went to the large table in the middle of the room. Joe took a little of the green stuff but also added a generous helping of potato salad and carrot-raisin salad and two of the perfectly browned yeast rolls with a generous slather of butter. Michelle chose a high pile of lettuce leaves, tomatoes, and bean sprouts, topped with a light dressing and a couple of bread sticks, then added a grilled chicken breast from the buffet. No wonder she stayed so slender.

Joe led them to a secluded corner of the restaurant, away from the salad-bar traffic, not that they had any privacy. Crowds from the fair filled every table, and Joe almost had to shout to make himself heard.

During dinner, several well-wishers and curiosity seekers stopped by the table. Under the strain of constant interruptions, Michelle's friendliness eroded a little. They sure annoyed Joe. Conversation between them lagged.

Lord, You know I have something important to say to Michelle. But I guess this isn't the time or place. He knew of the perfect place to take her after dinner and addressed himself to his steak. Michelle surprised him by partaking in the dessert bar, making a small sundae with soft-serve ice cream and chocolate sprinkles. Less than an hour later, they headed out the door.

They drove down Main Street, which was still humming with the fair in full swing. Michelle stared out the window, hunkered down as if she might slide off the seat if not strapped in, a picture of relaxed contentment. "I thought you said things closed down here on Saturday nights."

"Except during Odyssey Days. They'll have fireworks after dark and then close down." He glanced at Michelle. "Do you want to watch the fireworks?"

She shook her head and sank back against the seat, her eyes closed.

"Are you all right? Do you need to go to the castle?" He hoped she would say no. He had pinned so many dreams on talking with her tonight.

"I'll be all right." She popped her eyes open and straightened in her seat. "Where are we headed?"

"We're almost there." The spot he was headed to had a reputation as the local Lover's Lane, not that he would tell Michelle. He chose it for its natural beauty, a place he often retreated to when thinking things through.

A small park—two cement tables with a small play set—nestled under towering ponderosa pines, a creek swollen with recent summer rains rushing by. He fished an old quilt from the back of his truck and led them to the creek bank.

Michelle sat on the quilt with him, leaning her back against his chest. He resisted the temptation to kiss her, knowing it would distract from the importance of what he had to say. He settled for skimming his hands over Michelle's hair. It shimmered like gold, soft as silk. Against his will, he lifted a strand to his lips and kissed it. Michelle shivered, and his hands dropped to her shoulders. "Your muscles are bunched up." He massaged her back. As he continued to work his hands, she relaxed, some of the exhaustion he noticed in her earlier draining away.

Ever-present doves hopped closer, hoping for the food crumbs humans often scattered about them. A few ducks paddled downriver, green-banded males accompanied by sedate brown females. High in the trees lark buntings called to each other, a song of joy unlike any other. In the west the sun sank low in the sky, melding turquoise blue and brilliant gold.

"All nature sings of God," Michelle said. "It's beautiful here."

Not as beautiful as you. But Joe didn't voice his thought, afraid it might sound blasphemous, although Michelle was a work of God as much as their beautiful surroundings. "This is where I come when I want to make decisions. I sense God's presence here. Mortal flesh keeps silence while nature testifies to God."

"I can see why."

It was time. "At the fair today everyone was curious about you. Who you were, why you were with me."

Michelle giggled. "I noticed. I wouldn't be surprised to find my face plastered on the front page of the newspaper with a headline, 'Outsider Defies Tradition in Pie Contest.'"

"They wouldn't go that far," Joe said. "But I was wondering the same thing. Why were you with me?"

Michelle shifted in his arms so that she could look at his face. Cupping his face in her hands, she said, "Because I love you."

Her simple words took Joe's breath away. He longed to lean forward to take the kiss that she offered, but not yet. He had another question to ask.

"Then would you marry me? Build a life with me in Ulysses?"

Chapter 15

Michelle froze in Joe's arms, her mouth moving but no words coming out. She didn't know what to say. Long seconds passed.

"Did I offend you?"

"Of course not." But she shifted away from him by half an inch. Standing, he moved to the creek bank and tossed stones in the water.

Michelle joined Joe beneath a tall blue spruce. He gazed into the sky as if the stars held the answer to the mysteries of life. What must he think of her? He had offered her his most precious gift—his heart—and she had set it aside as unimportant.

"I guess I have your answer." He spoke without turning around.

The bleak note in his voice brought tears to Michelle's eyes, but she blinked them away. She had to explain, somehow. "Sit down, please." She sat on the blanket, and after a moment he joined her. "I do love you, Joe." Her voice was so quiet that she wondered if he could hear her.

"You have a funny way of showing it." He shifted to create more space between them.

"It's not you. It's, well, complicated."

He twisted around and stared her in the face. "What does that have to do with it?"

"You asked me if I wanted to build a life with you in Ulysses. But I just started the job in Denver, and. . .I need to succeed. I spread my wings and went to Romania. It was the right thing to do at the time, but now it's time for me to take care of my responsibilities. And God led me to the perfect job. I can't just up and leave it."

"So, what, you refuse to consider moving?"

"As much as I like you, Joe—I need more time. To get settled." She drew in a shaky breath. "We've known each other for less than a month. There's no need to rush."

"You seemed to enjoy yourself today. Like you belong here already." He spread his hands apart.

"I did. It was marvelous, the way a vacation is wonderful fun. Maybe I'm wrong, but I just feel like I'm supposed to stay at Mercury." Could they find a compromise, somewhere in the middle? "Do you ever think about moving back to Denver? Better opportunities for your wonderful store."

"No." Joe shook his head. "You went to Romania to spread your wings.

I went to Denver. It was—okay—while it lasted, but the time came when I had to take care of my responsibilities to my family. Mum needs me."

Michelle's heart lurched. "I understand." She reached for his hand, and this time he didn't pull away. "What are we going to do?"

"Wait things out? Ask God? If we're meant for each other, we'll find the answers." He drew a deep breath that sounded like it hurt him. "I just don't like having to wait."

They both ran out of words to say and left the creek by common consent. Once in the truck, Michelle leaned out the window, feeling like Juliet waiting for Romeo to appear. Only her Romeo wouldn't come. Shaken by the turn the evening had taken, she parted from Joe with a peck on the cheek.

Later, high in her tower, Michelle longed to accept Joe's proposal with all of her heart. High above it all, she could believe true love conquered all obstacles. But down there—in the real world where she had to balance checkbooks and pay bills—it was difficult. She closed the shutters and curled up on the bed, half wishing she had her favorite teddy bear for company.

"God, if You're going to put Joe and me together, You'll have to make the way. Show me if I'm supposed to move. Or if he is."

Be still, and know that I am God. The familiar verse from Psalms came to her. She relaxed, peaceful in the arms of God's love, and fell into a restful sleep.

◆

Joe paced the floor of his living room, hands clenched into tight fists curled at his side. Gawain followed his every footfall. He whined, as if wondering what had upset his master so.

The familiar household objects didn't bring their usual pleasure without someone to share them with. Michelle was the one for him—Joe knew it. God wouldn't bring two people together that way, meeting in downtown Denver of all places, only to have them go their separate ways. She could find work here, if she was willing to look.

Gawain whined again, and the two of them went out for a brief run in the dark. Joe needed to find something to take his mind off the impasse with Michelle, and he stopped by the store. Lately he'd seen brisk sales, including two of the pricey wood-carver's figurines. Buyers had snatched up all the paintings. *Sonia.* He punched in the number from memory.

"Hello?" a groggy voice answered.

"Sonia, it's me, Joe. How soon can you get that painting to me?"

"Joe?" He heard muffled sounds through the receiver. "Do you have any idea what time it is?"

A glance at the clock showed midnight. "I'm sorry. Look, I'll call back later."

"No. That's okay. What's wrong?"

"Nothing."

"I don't believe you."

"I don't want to talk about it." She deserved a modicum of honesty. "It's personal."

"Girl trouble, huh?"

Did all women have the ability to read minds? "Kind of."

"Uh-huh."

The need to confide in someone overrode his misgivings. "I asked Michelle to marry me tonight."

"But you've only known her—" Sonia's voice sharpened.

"Three weeks. You don't have to worry. She said she wasn't sure."

Sonia didn't speak. He felt her hurt leaping across the invisible wires, and he wondered if he had made a mistake. "I guess you'll look for someone else to handle your painting now."

"Nonsense." Sonia used a brisk, business tone. "We'll always be friends." They made arrangements to ship the painting and disconnected.

I've got both the women in my life upset with me. Great going, Joe. In the back of his mind, he had always counted on Sonia, even after they broke up. On the heels of Michelle's rejection, he wondered why he ever let Sonia go. The truth was, plain and simple, he loved Michelle like he had never loved Sonia.

Joe struggled to stay awake during the pastor's sermon in church the next morning. It lacked its usual punch, at least it seemed to after the night of sleepless heartache Joe had spent. Three cups of strong coffee helped, but even so the hen scratches he used to take sermon notes looked worse than a doctor's handwriting. He rubbed his eyes again, as if that could eliminate the sandpapered, red-eye feeling.

Michelle sat beside him, their sides touching in a pew crowded with his family. She was infinitely desirable in a pink floral sundress with wide straps and a flared skirt. She seemed at ease. Did last night mean so little to her? He hoped to talk with her in private before she left, if he could find a time during Sunday dinner at the castle.

Joe wrenched his attention back to the pastor's sermon. After an agonizing twenty minutes that felt more like three hours, the organist played the chords of the closing hymn. He headed for the back door, but his hopes for a quick escape faded as everyone who hadn't met Michelle at Odyssey Days crowded in. No one seemed to notice the tension simmering between him and Michelle. She threw herself into the swarm, pumping hands, calling greetings to people she had met on the previous day. By the time they made it past the preacher at the front door, his mother and Brian's family had left.

As soon as they stepped outside, heat triggered a torrent of sweat down his back, but Michelle still looked cool. She moved with such grace, a figure skater on dry ground. She even made climbing into the cab of his truck a work of art. A lift of a leg, a swoosh of skirt, and she sat enthroned on the passenger side.

She seemed so at ease that when he climbed in beside her, he was surprised to see the flush on her face. Concern swallowed up the uncertainty of the night. "Are you feeling all right?"

◆

Michelle didn't answer. She couldn't. If she opened her mouth, she might throw up. Somehow she had survived the morning service. How she would get through an afternoon's chitchat and the drive back to Denver, she didn't know.

"Michelle?" Joe's hand felt cool against her arm.

"I'm feeling sick." She threw open the door and heaved half her breakfast on the ground.

Chapter 16

The heaving stopped, but the truck's low rumble set waves tossing in Michelle's stomach.

Joe was on his cell phone. "—meet you at the clinic." He folded up the instrument. "I called Brian. His clinic is about five minutes away."

"Don't suppose you have a bucket in here."

He glanced at her, and she forced a smile. She threw up twice more before they reached the clinic.

Judy waited for them at the door. Nel's presence surprised Michelle. She settled with the two girls in the waiting room.

"You didn't have to come." Michelle Morris, a three-ring circus all by herself. Bile rose in her throat, and she swayed.

"Come on back." Judy ushered Michelle to an examining room. She checked her temperature and blood pressure, making notes on a standard medical form.

"Do I have a fever?" Michelle asked.

"It's slightly elevated." Judy frowned at the thermometer.

Brian walked in. "What seems to be the problem?" Concern flooded his eyes, so like Joe's. A doctor seeing her on a Sunday—how kind they all were.

"I've been nauseated all morning. And I have this pain in my abdomen."

"Where?"

"Down here." She pointed to the right, below her navel.

"Throw up anything?"

"Three times since church ended. Oh, and a tiny bit last night." She had blamed the nausea on the unsettling conversation with Joe.

"Okay. Here's what we're going to do. We'll run a CBC and a urinalysis, but we won't get the results back until tomorrow. So for now we'll start an IV, give you some fluids. . . . You'll feel better, and we'll be set up if you need more aggressive treatment later." He flashed a smile at her reaction. "I confess, I'm being overly cautious. I want to take good care of you."

Fear jumped down Michelle's tender throat. Judy had already set up the lab tray. The assortment of needles scared her more than a gun to her head at that point.

"I want to rule out infection. Based on your pain and symptoms, you could have appendicitis, so I want to monitor you closely. Although I suspect you may just have the flu. We'll give you something for the nausea with the

IV." He looked over his notes at her. "If your symptoms don't improve, you'd better plan on spending another night."

"Spend the night?" Michelle gulped. "But I have to be at work in the morning. In—" Before she could get out "Denver," she had bent over, heaving again.

"You're not going anywhere like that." He looked ready to lock her in if necessary.

Michelle had something else on her mind. "I need the bathroom." She sat on the stool in misery. She hadn't felt this sick since, well, since the last time she'd had the flu. Of all the bad timing.

A knock sounded on the door. "Do you need help?" Judy's voice asked.

"Just a minute." Michelle heaved again but didn't produce much. She struggled to her feet and opened the door.

"Do you feel up to walking? We have one hospital bed here for times like this, and you'd be more comfortable."

"I'll try."

Judy led her down the hall and helped her into a hospital gown. "Nel will wash your clothes." She nodded at the spot where Michelle had soiled her garment. After she lay down, Judy reached for her hand and wrapped a tourniquet around her elbow. Michelle looked away. She didn't mind getting stuck nearly so much if she didn't watch.

After a discreet knock, Brian reentered the room. "If your fever spikes or the pain worsens, I'll run further tests. But for now I suspect you just need to wait it out."

"All right." *Be still, and know.* God reminded her of His promise the previous evening. She closed her eyes as the needle pierced the vein in her hand. *This isn't what I expected when I came to Ulysses. Not at all.* The IV made shifting positions impossible. The cool saline solution dripped into her body, soothing her and relieving some of the dryness in her throat, but not all. "May I have some water?"

"Sorry, no. NPO. That's medical jargon for nothing by mouth. Give it a few minutes, and the IV should take care of it."

Michelle told herself she wasn't hungry, and the IV did take care of most of her thirst. Even the thought of mashed potatoes made her nauseous. "Where's a basin?"

Judy rushed to her side. "Steady, steady." She grabbed a basin, and Michelle spilled brown bile. With a needle, Judy drew medicine from a bottle and squirted it into the IV. "That's for the nausea. You should feel better soon."

She laid back, too weak to argue.

"Joe and Nel are anxious to see you. Feel up to company?"

"Yes." She blurted the word. She didn't want to be left alone in this unfamiliar, uncomfortable room.

"I'll send them in, then."

In the waiting room, Brian, Joe, and Nel made plans. Doctor's calls had interrupted other Sunday dinners, but rarely did the entire family get involved with the patient's care.

"I'd like to keep her here. Easier than transporting all the equipment to the castle," Brian said. "I suspect this won't last much longer."

"I'll take the girls with me, then, and come back later with supper for you. Joe, do you need anything else?"

Joe shook his head. Worry for Michelle occupied his mind. An idea jumped out. "Yeah, see if you can find some flowers."

"That will be nice. I'll be back later." Nel slipped out the door.

Judy came in. "She's resting more comfortably now and asking for company."

"I'll go in." Unlike his physician brother, Joe felt uneasy in hospital-like settings. They reminded him too forcefully of his father's final days. He opened the door to the examining room and fought the urge to flee the scene of sickness. Michelle looked so fragile, her slight figure covered with a light blanket, the IV tube trailing from her hand like an oversized earthworm. He couldn't let Michelle sense his fear. With a purposeful swagger to his walk, he crossed the room, grabbed a chair, and sat next to Michelle. "You gave me a fright there."

"Me, too. I'm so sorry. I didn't mean for our weekend to end like this."

"You know what they say, in sickness and in health." When he realized what he had said, he colored. He hadn't meant to bring up marriage. "If anyone's sorry, it's me. You're stuck here with strangers." He took her free hand with his. "Except for me, of course."

"You're all I need." A renewal of a warm current sparked between them, erasing some of the pain of the previous night's impasse. Joe didn't know the answer to their dilemma, but they would find it, somehow.

Judy knocked and came in. She took Michelle's temperature and blood pressure. "No change. Brian and I will check on you regularly."

"How long?" Michelle asked faintly.

"Brian wants to keep you all night."

"Can I help?" Joe asked.

"Check her temperature, maybe. Let me ask Brian." Judy checked Michelle's pulse. "Are you feeling better?"

"The nausea has subsided a little."

Joe stayed by Michelle's side until Nel returned later, insisting that he take time to eat. She handed him a bouquet of flowers—brilliant yellow and pink daisies. "Thank you." Judy found him a drinking glass to use as a vase, and he set it down on the cabinet next to Michelle.

"Oh, they're beautiful. Thank you." She found the strength to sit up and smell them before sinking back.

The afternoon passed slowly, Michelle drifting in and out of sleep with an occasional attempt to empty her stomach. Not much came out.

Late in the day, Brian checked on her while Michelle slept. "You should go home and get some sleep yourself. She's not in any immediate danger."

"I want to stay with Michelle." Even with her silken hair matted and tangled from a day on her back, blue veins throbbing beneath her paler-than-usual skin, lips cracked and dry, she was beautiful, at least to him. He wanted to offer her any comfort he could.

"You love her, don't you." Brian made it a statement, not a question.

"Yeah, I do." The blanket slipped from Michelle's shoulders, and Joe pulled it up. He stared at her, drinking in her loveliness, wishing their unresolved differences would go away.

"But something's wrong?" Brian probed.

"Yeah. She's got financial problems."

"Don't we all," Brian said.

"And she thinks that job in Denver is God's answer to her prayers. Ulysses is off her radar, at least for the time being."

"That's tough." The two of them looked at the sleeping woman. "It's a pity to wake her up, but I need to check her temperature again."

Michelle roused enough to take the thermometer in her mouth, smiling a bit as it slipped in, then fell back asleep.

"It's gone down a little. Sure I can't convince you to leave?"

Joe shook his head.

After Brian left, Joe prayed. "Lord, I know You have a purpose in this. I confess I'm full of fears, and I know they don't make much sense. Michelle isn't Dad, but I don't like seeing her so sick. And what will she do if she misses work and can't pay her bills?"

"There is no fear in love. But perfect love drives out fear."

I know, Lord. Help me to love her more perfectly. Driven by an inner impulse, he hunted for the Bible Brian kept in the waiting room and began reading the Psalms.

◆

Michelle didn't wake until the setting sun blazed through the west window, its warmth burrowing through the thin blanket. Joe occupied a seat to her right, an open Bible on his lap.

Joe's still here. Had he ever left? She shifted as much as the IV would allow and studied his achingly familiar profile. The sunset transformed his brown hair into copper and shaded his face a golden bronze. Waking to find him at her side made her feel cherished.

He looked up from what he was reading. "Good. You're awake. How are you feeling?"

"A little better. Still as weak as a newborn kitten. Is that a Bible you're reading?"

Joe nodded. "I've discovered some super things this afternoon." Enthusiasm leapt through his voice.

"What's that?"

"God reminded me that perfect love drives out fear. So I started looking for verses about love. I've found so many references to love in the Psalms, I stopped counting them. And not one of them is about the love between a man and a woman. How about this one." He flipped back a few pages. " 'Show me the wonders of your great love, you who save by your right hand those who take refuge in you from their foes.' " He scanned down the page. "Or this one: 'For the king trusts in the Lord; through the unfailing love of the Most High he will not be shaken.' " He continued turning pages and reading verses for several minutes.

Michelle smiled, basking in the warmth of his enthusiasm, the exuberance of a man emptying his toolbox in search of the perfect tool. She let the words flow over her, recognizing a familiar verse here and there.

He took her hand in his. "The only perfect love is God's love, of course. But our answer is here, in His word. I know it is. We just have to find it." His face beamed with the satisfaction of a child who had solved a difficult problem.

If only it could be that simple. What will happen if I can't go to work in the morning? She didn't qualify for sick days, not until she had been on the job for three months. "I know, Joe. But the answers have to make their way from my head to my heart."

Joe's face fell. Michelle hated to hurt him. "You're right. God will give us the answers, if we ask Him for wisdom. Give me my Bible, please." She pointed to where it lay next to her purse in the corner.

They read the Bible together all evening, finishing the Psalms then utilizing the concordance in the back of Michelle's Bible to find other verses about God's love. The study absorbed their attention, and queasiness bothered Michelle less and less. They hardly noticed Brian's comings and goings.

The sky outside the window turned black, and Brian came in. "Lights out. You need to go home, little brother. That's an order."

"I didn't realize it was so late." Joe ran his hand through his hair, creating uneven waves. He leaned over and kissed Michelle on the cheek. "I'll be back first thing in the morning."

Michelle didn't ask if she could leave. She no longer felt sick, but she knew she was too weak to leave in her condition. Hopefully in the morning.

Joe left, and Brian turned off the lights. "Judy and I will continue to check on you throughout the night. I can't promise you uninterrupted rest." She laughed with him, and he left.

She was alone in the unfriendly room. She missed Joe already. The verses they had read from 1 Corinthians 13 reverberated like a refrain in her head. *Love always protects, always trusts, always hopes, always perseveres.* The uncomfortable bed, the unfriendly environment of white and steel, faded in its rhythm, lulling her to sleep.

When she awoke early the next morning, she saw Brian sitting spread-eagle on a rolling stool. "How do you feel?"

"Much better."

"Glad to hear it." He smiled. "How does breakfast sound?"

"Wonderful." Michelle was ravenous.

"Mother will be here soon with food and clean clothes. And Judy will take out the IV. You should be set to go within the hour."

Michelle glanced at the clock. She wouldn't get on the road until almost eight, the hour she was supposed to be at the office. Nothing she could do about it, however.

Judy busied herself removing the needle from Michelle's hand. "Keep pressure on it." She placed a gauze pad on the puncture point.

"You're a good nurse. I hardly felt a thing."

"I wish I got to do it all the time. I spend half my time out front, scheduling patients, answering the phone."

Michelle cocked her head and looked at the couple. Might as well offer them the benefit of her human resources expertise. "Are you busy enough to hire an office manager?"

"Probably." Brian beat the pen on the clipboard. "In fact, that's a great idea. Are you interested in the job?"

Chapter 17

Before Michelle could answer, Joe and Nel entered the room. The aromas of hot coffee, sizzling bacon, and maple syrup filled the air, and Michelle's mouth watered.

"I brought you some breakfast, dear. Brian called to say you would probably be hungry this morning." Without fuss Nel arranged a plate and cups brimming with juice and coffee on the tray.

"Good morning. Feeling better?" Joe limited himself to a kiss on Michelle's cheek and handed over her overnight bag. "Mother washed your clothes last night. Brian has a shower here, or you can go back to the castle if you'd like."

Michelle looked at the circle surrounding her, all concerned for her welfare, and felt loved and part of a family that wasn't even hers. They had all been so kind. An hour later, showered, dressed, and fed, Michelle walked to her car, Joe by her side. He held her hand, their arms swinging slightly in a comfortable rhythm.

"I'd better call my boss. I'm an hour late for work already." Michelle dialed Chavonne's extension. She didn't answer. More worried than ever, she redialed the main number, and the operator connected her with Glenda Harris.

"Hello?"

Michelle heard the vice president's crisp tones, and her throat constricted. How could she explain her emergency to the supervisor, who gave the impression that she had no heart? But Michelle had to try.

"Miss Harris, this is Michelle Morris. I was calling to tell you I will be late today. I should be there in a couple of hours. I was sick—"

The woman on the other end didn't give her the opportunity to explain. "Michelle Morris. Didn't you just start working at Mercury?"

"Yes, two weeks ago—"

"And you couldn't call last night to let Miss Walker know?"

"I was too sick, hooked up to an IV—"

"We expect our employees—"

Was it Michelle's imagination, or did Miss Harris emphasize those words?

"—to keep us informed and to work their shifts except in the case of emergencies." Her voice held a severe reprimand.

"I'm sorry. I was sick." The words came out squeaky and uncertain. *I had an emergency. I couldn't help it. If I hadn't gone to Ulysses, I'd probably be at work by now.* Anger fought with humiliation, leaving her shaken.

"I'll make a note in your file. I'll let Miss Walker know that you will be in at noon today." The phone clicked in her ear.

Michelle didn't know what to make of the conversation. Had she been threatened?

"She was rough on you." Joe must have sensed her unspoken worry. "I'm sorry this had to happen, even if it meant I got to spend extra time with you. I'm glad you're doing better now." His fingers brushed a stray strand of hair from her cheek. "Quite a weekend, huh? Not what you expected when you came to Ulysses."

"Not exactly." She clenched her teeth against the acid in her throat. *Perfect love casts out fear*, she reminded herself, and it subsided.

"Willing to give it another try? Look at it this way. It can't be worse than this weekend." His smile could melt ice cream, and before Michelle thought about it, she agreed to return to Ulysses soon.

◆

The following Friday, Sonia's painting arrived at Joe's store without a hitch. In spite of his eagerness to view the work, he took his time opening the packaging, cutting the box ends with an X-Acto knife, and turning the frame with each layer of Bubble Wrap until the bright colors shimmered into view.

The power of the painting stunned him. Sonia had darkened the shadows on the valley side, sharpening the contrast with the bright colors of the garden that drew the eye to the light of the passage through the mountains. Her best work yet, it wouldn't look out of place in a museum.

He hung it on the back wall and fiddled with lighting to provide the right illumination. Finished, he poured a cup of coffee and studied its effect. The thrill of bringing great art to the public rushed through him. A part of him hoped he could keep it in his shop for a few weeks so as many people as possible could enjoy it with him. But that was impractical, and what was more, he had already contacted a potential buyer who was eager to see the painting firsthand.

Someone rang the doorbell. Stanford Dixon, a local lawyer who had built a career of defending DWUIs into a thriving criminal practice, had arrived. He was a Christian, and one of Joe's best customers. Setting down his coffee cup, he opened the front door. "Good morning, Stan."

"Is it here? I saw the truck." Before Joe could answer, Stan caught sight of the painting on the wall. He studied it without speaking for several moments, cocking his head this way and peering closely at different areas of canvas. He stepped back and made rectangular shapes with his hands, as if envisioning it on the wall of his office.

"You didn't do it justice. It's magnificent. You were right—this is one I have to have. A visual reminder for my clients that there's always light at the end of the tunnel."

Did all lawyers speak in clichés?

Stan whipped out his checkbook and wrote a check for the agreed-upon amount with a business-boosting number of zeros. "I'm having my office remodeled. Can you keep it here until then?"

Better than expected.

"I'd be happy to." Joe kept his enthusiasm in check. "I was just thinking it would look good in a museum."

"So that someone else besides my clients could see it?" Stan jabbed Joe in the ribs.

Now that you mention it, yes. "I was thinking about the larger number of people. No harm in dreaming big."

"You can't keep them all."

Although Joe couldn't understand why someone wanted to defend drunk drivers, Stan was a good sort, and he could afford the more pricey pieces. He wandered through the store, studying the new displays with calculating eyes. "Most of this is new."

"I had a successful run through Odyssey Days, had to put out new stuff."

"This is lovely." He admired dawn-gold blown glass, reached out his hands as if to touch, then stuffed them in his pockets. "Maybe another time."

After he left, Joe picked up his phone and dialed Sonia. "He bought it for the amount we expected. A little more, in fact."

"Great." The phone whined in his ear, and he pictured her dancing a jig in her excitement. "Can we get together for a celebration dinner? My treat?"

Go to Denver. Why not? See Michelle again. A flush of shame washed over him. Sonia had invited him, and the first person he thought of was Michelle. "Better wait until the check clears."

Sonia chuckled at the old joke. The first time Joe represented one of Sonia's pieces, the buyer gave him a check and left with the time-consuming project. The check bounced, and he never recovered the fee, although he reimbursed Sonia. Once stung, doubly careful. That buyer came from Denver. "I'll call the next time I'm in Denver."

"To see Michelle, I suppose. Not that it's any of my business. When do you think that will be?"

Joe regretted accepting her invitation to dinner. "I don't know. I haven't decided."

"Well, thanks for finding me a buyer." The conversation ended on an uncomfortable note.

Joe walked around the store, studying the balance of the display with the big painting in place. He decided he needed to move the abstract painting that Michelle had accused of giving her headaches farther away from Sonia's work and to hang the painting of the Maroon Bells that Michelle had liked so well there instead. While he straightened objects and adjusted their positions, he gave serious thought about going back to Denver.

Maybe he should consider opening a branch store in the capital. He knew a real estate agent who could help him find a reasonably priced rental, and of course, he would turn the day-to-day operation over to a manager. But even so, he would need to spend a lot of time in the city, especially at first. And he had made a promise to himself and to his family to stay nearby.

Face it, Joe. The only reason you're thinking about branching out is because of Michelle. He had thought about opening a second store someday, but not yet.

Perfect love casts out fear. He resolved to check into store sites the next time he went to Denver. Both he and Michelle would have to compromise if things were ever going to work out between them.

◆

The rest of the week passed smoothly for Michelle. Upon her arrival at work on Monday, Chavonne had inquired after her health, and Michelle's worries subsided. She must have caught some kind of twenty-four-hour bug.

Carrie, on the other hand, appeared to catch whatever bug Michelle had. She was sick every morning and didn't make it out of bed before Michelle left for work. Saturday was their first real chance to talk since Michelle's return from Ulysses.

"I know what made you sick last weekend." Carrie nibbled on a cracker and washed it down with hot tea.

"A flu bug, that's what."

"No, I think it was something else. You weren't in love when you were in Romania—only in love with the idea of love. Things are different now." Carrie grinned to let Michelle know she was teasing.

"I wish." Michelle didn't argue with Carrie using the word *love*. "Joe asked me to marry him on Saturday night."

"What?" The cracker broke in half in Carrie's hand. "And you're just telling me this now?"

Michelle squirmed. "I wasn't ready to share it."

"You don't seem happy about it." Carrie dabbed a bit of jelly on the cracker. "What did you tell him?"

"That God provided this job for me in Denver, and I have responsibilities I have to take care of. It's like the timing is all wrong." She stuffed a cracker in her mouth, mashed down on it once, and swallowed hard. "If only Joe lived in Denver."

Carrie's face paled, and she crunched crackers and sipped tea until color returned to her face. "We both know as well as anyone that it's useless to live our lives on the basis of what-ifs and if-onlys and whys. If God had let me adopt Viktor when I wanted to, I might never have fallen in love with Steve.

And there's more." She clasped her hands protectively over her abdomen. Dark circles under her friend's eyes underlined the pallor that had settled on her skin, and tired lines around her eyes made her look older than her years.

She's—

"I'm pregnant."

"Congratulations!" Michelle reached to hug Carrie but stopped short when her friend didn't seem as thrilled as she expected.

"Frankly, I'm a little scared. I saw what happened to Lila. Steve's first wife, you know. I was there when she died."

"There's no reason to think you'll have the same problems. And you'll be here in Denver, with first-class medical care."

"You're right. But the fear is still there. Steve, too, although he tries to hide it for my sake."

Michelle didn't know what to say. If she were in Carrie's shoes, she'd probably feel the same way.

"We didn't plan on having a baby right now. I wanted to work for a few years, and I am a little afraid. We could let our concerns control us. We could have decided never to have children, for instance. Or I could spend my 'confinement' in bed like an invalid—as it is, Steve coddles me. But we love each other, and we trust God to take care of me and the baby. And the timing. That's the bottom line. Going ahead, trusting in God's goodness, even when we don't understand it." She wrapped the stack of crackers back in the packaging and put it back in the box. "The morning I found out for sure, I read a terrific quote in my devotional book. Something about 'exercise your faith' and 'be not detained by self-doubt.' I think about that when I get a little scared."

That makes sense. Maybe Michelle should consider Brian's job offer. She shook her head. No, she didn't doubt God's leading to her job. Maybe God would convince Joe to open a store in Denver.

Chapter 18

Joe rolled down his truck window. He enjoyed the sensation of wind whipping through his hair, singing at the top of his lungs, the air rushing by swallowing up his voice. "Oh, what a beautiful morning." Not a cloud marred the bright blue sky, and nothing shadowed the asphalt that shimmered ahead like black crystals sprinkled in a straight line as far as the eye could see.

"I've got a beautiful feeling." *Michelle, Michelle.* His heart sang in rhythm with the rolling wheels. He had decided to make a short trip to Denver and drop in on Michelle unannounced.

She should be pleased to see me again in Denver. If not for Michelle, he would never have discussed the idea with Mum, and she would never have said to go for it.

Mile after mile of growing crops undulated in the light wind, the "amber waves of grain" immortalized by Katharine Lee Bates in "America the Beautiful." He pulled over at a historical site marker and read a panel about the Kansas Pacific Railroad. Taking a swig from his water bottle, he breathed in the scents of sweet-smelling hay and the moist earth, saying good-bye to the plains before the mountains appeared over the next ridge. He enjoyed the Rockies, but the plains gave him a feeling of serenity and continuity, endless variations of yellow and green and brown with an occasional splash of bright color.

His watch chimed, reminding him of the hour, and he jumped in the truck. He hoped to catch Michelle when she left work. The thought of seeing her again made his heart beat faster and his foot press down harder on the accelerator. The truck spurted forward.

The mountains climbed into view, snow still visible on the highest peaks on this clear August day. Colorado had the best of all worlds.

Soon the outskirts of Denver came into view. He slipped off the highway to avoid the rush-hour gridlock and wound his way downtown, arriving at Mercury Communications at five o'clock on the dot.

Employees left the building two or three at a time, but he didn't see Michelle. At quarter past, he was puzzled, and at five thirty he checked his watch against radio time. Impatience changed to worry after another fifteen minutes. Had he missed her somehow? He pulled out his cell phone and dialed the Romeros' number.

"Hello?" a man answered.

"Steve, this is Joe Knight. Say, has Michelle come home yet?"

"I haven't seen her." Joe heard a rustle that sounded like curtains. "Her car's not here, either. I'll tell her you called."

At that moment—precisely five minutes before six—Michelle walked out the front door.

"Don't bother. I see her." Joe closed the phone and jumped out the door. Racing to meet her, an idiotic grin on his face, he stopped a foot away from her. "Hi there, beautiful. Want a date tonight?"

"Joe." Her smile expressed her pleasure in seeing him. Her brief kiss on the lips made him shiver with delight. "What are you doing here?"

"I took advantage of some business to come to Denver. Are you free for supper?" They decided on a restaurant on the west side of town, and he escorted her to her car, pausing at the door long enough for another brief kiss.

A few minutes later they parked side by side at Gaetano's, an Italian restaurant converted from a Victorian house. The smiling waitress led them to a secluded spot. In the corner booth, Joe put his arm around Michelle while they studied the menu together. He already knew what he wanted to order, so he spent his time studying her profile. How he had missed her.

As if sensing his thoughts, she turned her head and smiled at him. "It's good to see you again."

All his reservations about opening a store in Denver fled at her smile. Surely he could find the right property, and then. . .and then Michelle would fall in his arms and marry him? Could it be that easy? He still didn't want to live in Denver, away from family, and she was committed to her job.

As soon as the waitress took their order—shrimp fra diavolo for Joe, fiorentina salad for Michelle—she started a minute-by-minute description of her activities for the week. Mercury asked her to develop training manuals for one of the departments.

"I spent Tuesday in Web Services. . . ."

She's only on Tuesday? Joe nursed his iced tea, squeezing the lemon slice for extra flavor, and inserted an appropriate comment when she paused for breath. "What's Web Services?"

She paused, as if surprised by his question, and her answer lasted through the salad course.

"After I spent Tuesday in the Web Services department, I started working on the manual today."

The waitress brought out the main course, Michelle's salad with perfectly grilled steak and Joe's shrimp over pasta.

When she talked about her job, Michelle's face came alive. Her voice sped up like a tape on fast-forward, high-pitched but clearly enunciated. He was excited because she was excited.

She hasn't asked about my store, my family, once. Joe wanted to ignore the thought as unfair and selfish, but it wouldn't go away.

"So you still haven't told me why you're in Denver." Michelle forked a bite of mushroom, artichoke, and steak and brought it to her mouth and chewed it thoughtfully.

You didn't give me a chance.

"Did you have business with one of the artists you met at the arts festival? Sonia?"

Joe caught a hint of jealousy behind the neutral question. *Maybe that's why she didn't ask. Afraid I came here to see Sonia.*

"No." He raised his glass in a mock toast. "Here's to Trojan Horse II, to open in Denver in the near future."

"Why, that's wonderful." The instantaneous smile lit Michelle's face like a sunrise.

"Yeah, I talked it over with Mum. Business has been going well lately, and I can afford to expand. Provided, of course, that I can find the right spot. Opening a store in Denver is bound to cost more than it does in Ulysses, and then there's the matter of inventory."

"It will be a terrific success. I know it will." Her eyes lost their glazed-over tiredness, and she turned serious. "Thanks for giving it a try. It means a lot to me." She took a drink of water. "Anyhow, let me know if there's anything I can do to help."

The evening ended soon after that, Michelle pleading the need for an early start in the morning. They made plans for dinner the next night.

The next day, as Joe paged through the commercial real estate section of the newspaper, he remembered her offer. He wished Michelle could spend the day with him, for her companionship if nothing else. He suspected she didn't have much experience in commercial rentals. He had an appointment with a Realtor that afternoon, but he figured there was no harm in checking what the paper had to offer.

With a Denver map spread before him, he circled those areas that interested him most and crossed out the areas he wanted to avoid. He doubted neighborhoods had changed much since he had moved away, but he would check with the local police station before he rented anything in any case.

One by one he evaluated the listings in the morning paper. He dismissed the ones that said "charming"—which could mean anything from "small" to "antique"—as well as ones that read "fixer-upper." He didn't want to have to reinvent the wheel. Some neighborhoods were just too pricey. In the end he marked four possibilities. *No time like the present.* A message at the first number he dialed gave the address. A quick glance at the map confirmed it was located in a bad area.

The next listing had already rented, and the third cost enough to bankrupt Fort Knox. That left the final listing, on the small side according to the square footage but a possibility depending on the arrangement of the rooms. He consumed a lonely sandwich and sought out the rental property. When he spotted an art gallery across the street, he decided against pursuing it.

The Realtor he met in the afternoon took his information but cautioned him he might not find an acceptable property in his price range. By dinnertime the hours of fruitless searching had taken their toll. Joe cheered himself up with thoughts of dinner with Michelle. After a brief stop at the hotel to freshen up, he drove to Carrie's house. Traffic everywhere in Denver seemed heavy these days, and the trip took longer than he expected.

When he arrived, he saw Steve playing catch with Viktor. Steve spotted him. "Hi there. Go on in." He passed the ball to the boy, and once again their play absorbed their attention. Joe wished he had a home like this to come to, with a wife and child waiting. He hurried up the steps.

Carrie met him at the door, wiping her hands on her apron. "Michelle called. She's trying to finish a project to show to her boss tomorrow. She said she'll be home by seven, eight at the latest. She told me to take care of you. Do you want to eat with us?"

Joe considered refusing, but he had eaten his lonely lunch hours ago, and he wasn't sure when he and Michelle would eat. "Sure." He headed back to the front door. "I'll hang out with the guys for a while."

"Great." Carrie flashed a smile in his direction as she stirred something on the stove.

Joe went back outside. "Mind if I join you?"

"Sure. If you'll catch, Viktor can bat the ball." He high-fived his son, who disappeared into the garage and reappeared with a plastic bat. "Let's go into the backyard."

"Nerf baseball?" Joe smiled.

"I have a softball when we can get to the park. Here we play it safe. Don't want any broken windows. Batter up."

Viktor took his place behind an old couch pillow that served as home plate. Joe crouched down behind the boy. He got in a day's worth of exercise chasing foul balls and Steve's pitches. By the time Carrie called them in to supper, he felt reenergized.

The meal was simple, spaghetti with salad. He sipped his iced tea, brewed, not instant—the way he liked it. He had never tasted Michelle's cooking, unless he counted the scones she made with his mother. He wondered if she existed on microwave dinners and restaurant dining, with an occasional home-cooked meal at a friend's house. He knew so little about her day-to-day life.

They finished eating, and Joe retired to the den with Steve while Carrie gave Viktor a bath. Steve turned on the television to a Rockies' game at seven. Michelle still hadn't arrived. *I hope she gets here soon.*

◆

Michelle left the office at 8 p.m. With traffic moving close to the posted speed limit, she made it home in a short fifteen minutes. Today's shift left her more drained than anything since some of her longer days in Romania.

Joe's blue pickup sat in front of the house. *I had almost forgotten him.* Her heart lifted, and a new boost of energy removed some of the tiredness. She walked in the house with a lighthearted step. Carrie greeted her at the door. "Steve and I will tuck Viktor in bed, so you two can have some privacy." She hugged her friend.

Michelle found Joe in the den. "Sorry I'm so late. What a mess at work." She sank down on the sofa next to Joe and kicked off her heels. "Oh, that feels good."

Joe massaged her shoulders, his strong fingers working miracles in her tense muscles. "Bad day, was it?"

She nodded. Under half-closed eyes she murmured, "Do you mind awfully if we don't go out? I'm sure we could scare up something to eat here."

"Yeah, sure." His mouth twisted in a funny smile. "Carrie already fed me. I hope you don't mind." He withdrew his hands from her shoulders and intertwined their fingers.

"I'll get some leftovers then." Michelle laid her head on Joe's shoulder, allowing herself to relax for a few minutes without moving. The longer she waited, the less she wanted to stir herself.

Joe loosened his fingers and brushed her hair back from her forehead. "I'll go fix something for you." He stood.

"No." Michelle struggled to a sitting position, but he shook his head.

"Let me." She heard the microwave door opening and closing. "Do you want coffee or tea?"

"Coffee sounds good." Maybe that would help her wake up. She had no energy left over for company tonight. *But this is Joe*, her conscience argued back. *The man whose smile makes your heart beat faster.* She got to her feet and joined him in the kitchen. "Did you have any luck today?"

"Zilch." His voice quivered with disappointment. "Nothing. Nada. Not a sniff."

The microwave chimed, and Joe brought her a bowl of spaghetti while he looked into the refrigerator. "Do you want the parmesan cheese?" He pulled out a bowl of salad and dressing.

"Sure." Parmesan might wake up her taste buds.

The coffee finished brewing, and Joe poured cups for both of them before joining her at the table. "I was hoping for some kind of lead. The Realtor didn't sound too hopeful that I could find something workable in the price range I can afford." He took a deep swig of his coffee. "And I have to return to Ulysses tomorrow."

"Go back?" The fork in Michelle's hand slipped. "But you just got here. I guess I was hoping you could at least stay through Friday night."

"Saturdays are our busiest days. I need to spend the night at home tomorrow so I can be up early Saturday."

Disappointment brought tears to the edge of Michelle's eyes. Work had robbed her of extra time with Joe tonight. She had counted on him staying in Denver through the weekend, but of course he had to be at his store.

"You are coming down for another visit this weekend, aren't you?"

Michelle remembered a vague discussion, but she had forgotten it in the press of work. "I don't know if I can. I might have to work Saturday." After missing that half day after her last visit, she had worked extra hard to prove herself. *Sorry, Ms. Harris, I made other plans?* Mercury expected commitment from its employees.

"What's so special about this job? It sounds like they work you nonstop."

Did he expect her to blow off her boss's demands in order to spend an extra day with him? He knew how important this job was to her. The pent-up frustration from the hard pace at work boiled out. She glared at Joe. "I don't understand what you have against my job."

Chapter 19

Joe wiped off his mouth and looked at her without blinking. "Just that it seems to always come between us. And why don't you understand that I have to be there for my mother?" He paused and took a deep breath. "I'm going to leave before I say something we'll both regret. We can talk about it later." He walked out the door without saying another word.

Go after him. Michelle struggled to rise from her chair. Discouragement and exhaustion as huge as a salmon fighting his way upstream threw her back on the couch. Nothing was going right—not with Joe, not at work. She could lose both.

Michelle put the rest of the spaghetti away without finishing it. She went to bed, but she stayed awake until well past midnight, replaying the evening in her mind. Two hours later hunger woke her up, demanding food. She slept in fits and starts for a while before heading to the kitchen for a quick snack.

She found Carrie placing banana slices on bread already slathered with peanut butter. When she saw Michelle, a surreptitious look passed over her face. "It seems morning sickness doesn't apply to the hours between midnight and five a.m. I was craving a peanut butter and banana sandwich."

Ugh. "So cravings aren't an old wives' myth." Michelle dropped a couple of slices of wheat bread in the toaster and poured a glass of juice.

"Apparently not." Carrie ran her finger around the edge of the peanut butter jar and licked it. "What's up with you?"

"Joe and I had an argument." Michelle stabbed a knife in the blueberry jam.

"That's good."

"Huh?" Michelle slathered jam over her sandwich.

"So you can learn how to resolve differences."

"Yeah right. He had a bad day. I had a bad day. And we took it out on each other. At least I think that's what happened."

"What are you going to do about it?"

"Call him, I suppose. But I'm still mad. He comes to Denver unannounced and expects me to drop everything."

"If you play a game of who's right and who's wrong, you'll both lose."

"I suppose you're right." Michelle nibbled on the toast. "I guess I could call." She reached for the phone then remembered the time. "I'd better wait a few hours, though."

The following morning, Michelle dialed Joe, but it went straight to voice mail. She frowned. Not a lot of time remained before she had to leave for work. She pressed the END button, and the phone beeped. Someone had left a message. She'd better check.

"This is Joe. Look, I'm sorry about last night. Please call me. I'll be at home until eight." His voice was ragged, as if he had slept as little as she had last night. *And it's my fault.* Her decision about the weekend was easy.

She hit the REDIAL button. Joe answered immediately.

"Michelle?" That one word expressed all of his regret and uncertainty and hope.

"Oh Joe." She stopped, unable to say any more.

"I was a jerk last night."

"No, I was out of line. I was so tired, I was only thinking of myself." Now the words came without effort. "But the solution is obvious. If I do have to work on Saturday, I'll drive down at night and come back on Sunday."

Joe's audible sigh held heartfelt relief. "That would be great. I have to be at the store most of Saturday anyway."

"I can't wait." Michelle hung up the phone and leaned against the wall, a warm feeling brimming over in her heart.

Although she worked as hard on Friday and Saturday as earlier in the week, the effort did not exhaust her to the same level. Saturday night found her barreling down the highway toward Ulysses.

◆

When Joe spotted Michelle's car entering the driveway to the castle, he ran out the door, meeting her halfway across the courtyard. He greeted her with a kiss as necessary as water for a parched man home from the desert. "I've missed you."

"Me, too." They walked into the castle, hand in hand.

Joe picked at the traditional English meal of lamb chops, peas, and potatoes. He'd rather feast his eyes on Michelle. He made a point of asking her about work.

"It's been terrible. Working ten- and twelve-hour days, checking and rechecking the facts for my training manual, running a beta test on it. And after all that work, the vice president didn't like big chunks of it and asked me to rewrite it. She thinks I'm working on it this weekend." Michelle tittered. Tiny tension lines appeared around her eyes that hadn't been there before.

"You must be exhausted. Thanks for coming." Joe resolved to help Michelle release the tension accumulated during the week and shifted the conversation to other topics.

"Have some more potatoes, dear." Mum handed the serving bowl to Michelle. "I heard from the Kildaires today. I wondered if you have met them, Michelle. They're missionaries in Romania. In Constanta."

"Rick and Kim?"

His mother nodded.

"Oh yes. They ran a guesthouse where we went for a vacation. Wonderful people. How did you meet them?"

"On the Internet. I read an article about them in our church's magazine that gave their e-mail address. Their work sounded interesting. I've thought about doing something like that with our home. I wrote a brief note, and Kim kindly responded."

"As they say, it's a small world."

"Actually, I write to people all around the world. They come to our church, or I read about them, and we start corresponding. I spent a small fortune in postage before computers came of age."

"What got you interested in missions?" Michelle leaned forward, one elbow on the table.

"It started with writing to my friends in England. Later my interests expanded, and I wrote to more and more people. My husband used to joke that we could make a trip around the world and never stay in a motel. Someday I'd like to make that trip."

"It was kind of like that for me. I always loved it when a missionary came and spoke at our church."

"You and Dad did make a trip to England when we were kids. I remember wondering why you would want to travel so far from home." Joe forked a potato.

"I know you hated staying with your aunt that summer. But I find that as long as I can get away now and then, there's no place like home. Which is in Colorado with my family." His mother stood. "Dessert anyone? I have bread pudding tonight."

"I'll take some," Joe said.

Michelle, who had polished her plate, demurred. "Instant access to the entire world. When I was in Romania, all I had to do was get online. How much harder it must have been for the early missionaries who had so little contact with home for years at a time." She bent over and reached into the bag at her feet. "Speaking of Romania. . .here is the scrapbook I promised you."

"Let me clear the table."

The three of them made quick work of clearing off the dishes and wiping down the table surface. Michelle placed the scrapbook in front of Joe, and the two women sat on either side. They spent the rest of the evening talking about Michelle's experiences in Romania. Joe thought he recognized the pictures of Pastor Radu, the national pastor Michelle had worked with, and the sister in charge of the orphanage was unforgettable. Joe took the scrapbook with him when he left for the night.

◆

In the Rosebriar room, Michelle discovered a pen she thought she had lost waiting on the nightstand. *They say you only leave something behind if you want to return.* If she kept coming for visits, they'd have to change the name of the room from Rosebriar to Michelle's Kingdom. The strange castle felt more like home all the time.

After Joe left, Nel had shown Michelle her office—named the Time Portal—with its dazzling array of the latest equipment. Thinking of electronic gadgets, she owed an e-mail to her pastor in Romania. She'd neglected answering his last message in the crush at work. One more thing to add to her to-do list of tasks neglected with her new schedule.

The high-canopied bed invited Michelle to recline, and she settled in. When she awoke the next morning, she felt more refreshed than she had all week.

After the church service, Brian and Judy invited Joe and Michelle over for dinner. "Our Bible study group is getting together. We meet twice a month."

Brian and Judy's home, an understated three-bedroom brick house, was located in a new housing development. Children, including Pepper and Poppy as well as numerous others from toddlers to adolescents, swarmed around the backyard play set and trampoline like honeybees.

Michelle had met most of the adults at Odyssey Days. The men congregated in the basement, shooting pool. Michelle joined the ladies in chopping vegetables and deveining shrimp. The informal atmosphere made her feel right at home. Conversation circled around work, children, and favorite books before taking a serious turn.

"That guy who murdered the pregnant mother was on the news last night," Judy said. "Something about his appeal."

"Why can't they fry him and get it over with?" Kit, the tall, muscular deputy sheriff, said.

"The longer he lives, the more opportunity he has to repent and receive God's forgiveness." Marge, a soft-spoken elementary school teacher, said.

"Those prison conversions don't convince me," Kit said.

Sheila Classen, a school social worker, spoke up next. "Well, I think—"

"We all know how you feel about the death penalty, Sheila." Kit slapped her knife down on the table as if in disgust.

A lively discussion ensued, exploring the question of the death penalty from all sides. Michelle hadn't taken part in such a spirited debate since college. She found it easy to share her own opinions.

Moments after Brian took steaks outside to grill, Joe rushed in. "I've got to go."

"What happened?" Michelle picked up her purse.

"The sheriff called. Someone's broken into the store."

Chapter 20

The way Joe drove, Michelle feared they might have an accident between Brian's house and downtown Ulysses. Joe must have broken every speed limit covering the three miles. Kit, the deputy, followed at a more reasonable pace. At each stop sign, he tapped the steering wheel nervously, and the car skidded through a yellow caution light. Michelle decided not to say anything until they saw the extent of the damage.

The sheriff directed them to the back door, which swung open. Joe hurried to meet him. "Have you been inside?"

"Just long enough to see there'd been a break-in." The sheriff shook his head. "I can't believe this happened. I was waiting on you and keeping guard."

Joe lunged for the door.

"Wait a sec." The sheriff dug a white handkerchief out of his pocket and pushed against the handle. "We'll have to check for any fingerprints."

Dust swirled in the shaft of light from the door, obscuring the room. After Michelle's eyes adjusted to the semidarkness, she saw construction paper and broken clay projects scattered across the floor, as if someone had brushed them off the shelves in an effort to find more profitable items. From what Michelle remembered of the inventory, she believed the thief had taken the expensive coffee table art books as well as several of the models—including the car Viktor had put together. She blinked back tears.

❖

Joe ignored the damage in the studio and pushed into the gallery. He stood at the door, and his shoulders sagged so low his disappointed bones could have pierced his heart.

The wood-carver's figurines—gone. Unusual blown-glass vases—gone. Numerous paintings, from pastel nature scenes to modern art—gone. He forced himself to turn to the wall where Sonia's painting had hung. The space gaped empty, as barren as Coors Field during hockey season. His hands balled at his sides. *This wasn't supposed to happen.*

Others came in behind him. Kit, who had followed them from the Bible study, checked the front door. "No sign of forced entry." She bent down to study a mark on the floor.

"We'll need a list of what was taken," the sheriff said. "You're insured, of course?"

"Yes." But the financial loss only represented a small part of the picture. Every stolen object, even a single pencil, tore a piece out of his heart.

Michelle wandered around, her face mirroring the shock he felt inside. "All those beautiful things." Tears misted her eyes.

Don't cry. Don't get me started.

Joe wheeled around on his heels and marched into the classroom. He went for a trash bag, wanting to get the destruction out of sight as soon as possible.

"Don't do that." Kit's voice was sharp. "Wait until we've finished our investigation."

But what can I do? Inwardly Joe wailed. Helplessness overpowered him. He slumped into a hard-backed chair and leaned over, his head resting between his hands.

He heard the quiet rustle of silk, and Michelle knelt on the floor next to him, her arms circling him, resting his head on her shoulder. His hurt ran too deep for words, but her presence gave him strength. In spite of his resolve, he allowed a few tears to fall. After a few minutes, they separated, their hands still wrapped together like a Gordian knot.

He drew a deep breath. "I've got to call Sonia. Her painting was the most valuable piece I had." Shaking fingers punched in her number.

"Hi, Joe. What's up?" The innocent laughter in Sonia's voice mocked his pain.

"Someone stole your painting, Sonia."

"What?"

"The store. It's been stripped clean."

"How horrible. Wait a minute." He could hear her pencil beating a rhythm against the phone. "I'll leave right away. Don't move until I get there. You're at the store?"

Joe swept his gaze across the shelves, the empty spots giving it the look of a lopsided checkerboard. "Yeah, we're here."

"An hour and a half, two hours tops. Is someone with you?"

"Michelle." He knew it might hurt.

"Good. You shouldn't be alone." She surprised him. "I'm on my way."

Joe went into his office and printed out an inventory list but found he couldn't concentrate. Time dragged while Kit and the sheriff combed the store for evidence.

Some time later, Michelle asked, "Have you let the buyer know? That lawyer."

"No." Joe punched in Dixon's phone number.

Before Joe could supply any details, Dixon cut him off. "Meet me in my office. Ten minutes."

"I—can't. I'm waiting for the artist who painted the picture."

"All the better. I'd like to meet her. And bring your insurance policy with you."

After he hung up, Michelle's hands made shooing motions. "Go on. If you're not back by the time Sonia arrives, I'll bring her over. Just tell me the address."

Outside, the street reflected the same peace and quiet that had lulled him into a false sense of security. The people of Ulysses didn't commit crimes like grand theft. A few supplies had taken flight over the years, but never anything of real value. He tried to calm his shaking insides when Dixon greeted him at the door to his office.

"I don't want to stay too long."

"Don't worry, the chief will call if he needs you to come back."

Inside the office hung several paintings Joe had handled for the lawyer. *Where can I get away from what happened?* He wanted to bolt. The sight of the lawyer in out-of-character Sunday-casual blue jeans and a Denver Broncos football jersey changed his mind.

"So what happened?"

Joe spelled out the few known details. The lawyer's pen scratched across the paper.

Joe took out his checkbook. "I'll return your payment, of course."

Dixon waved him aside. "Time for that later. They may recover the painting." He leaned back in his chair and looked toward one of Joe's favorite paintings, an abstract whose sharp lines and silver colors reminded him of the mountains. "You know I defend criminals. Over the years I have gained a little insight into how they think."

Is he saying he would represent the person who robbed the store? He can't. Conflict of interest.

"One thing that keeps me going—besides the concept that they are all innocent until proven guilty and they have the right to the best defense I can offer—is knowing the grace of God. When I represent them, I try to model His love and forgiveness. Every now and then someone listens and gets his life turned around."

Joe didn't want to think about the thief receiving grace. He should be punished.

"That's why I wanted the painting—a visual testimony to my clients that God is with them in what is for many their first brush with the law."

After that, Dixon spent time reviewing the insurance policy and going over the steps Joe would need to take. Some time later, someone knocked at the door, and Dixon let Michelle and Sonia in. He repeated his theory about Sonia's painting.

Sonia looked at Dixon with appreciation. "I agree. Maybe the thief needs the message of the painting more than any of us in this room."

Michelle squeezed Joe's hand, and he looked into the three concerned, hopeful faces, waiting for his reaction. Guilt, anger, fear—a multitude of emotions had washed over him at the invasion of his store. Most of all, he worried about how the robbery would affect the people closest to him, including these three people. Instead, they seemed to view the loss as an opportunity to trust God more.

Trust not in princes. . . . The Knight family motto came into his mind. All the information he had fed into his brain's computer clicked together and spit out the answer: his security didn't rest in time or place or people. It rested in God. Without God, he was crossing a high wire without a safety net.

Joy fizzed inside Joe and burst out in a bubble of laughter. He looked into Michelle's clear eyes, and his heart lightened, lighter than any time since the singing monk had taken Michelle's purse at the Renaissance Festival. If God—and the right woman—was for him, who could be against him? Amen.

◆

Michelle stayed through the long, difficult afternoon into the evening. How could she leave when Joe was so vulnerable, hurt, exposed? Once they had the okay, everyone returned to the store, and Sonia and Dixon made a list of missing items. The four of them shared supper at the steak place before going their separate ways.

"I'm glad you were here today." Joe held Michelle's arm as they walked up the driveway to the castle, gravel crunching underfoot.

She thought she heard all the things he didn't say. *I need you. You're important to me.* "I was glad I could help. Not that I did very much."

"You were there. That's what mattered."

"You're not as upset as I thought you would be." Something had broken loose during the meeting at Dixon's office. He appeared serene, for lack of a better word.

"God finally got it through my thick skull that my security comes from Him. It doesn't matter where I live or how careful I try to be. Bad things can happen. But God is always in control."

"God is always in control." Michelle repeated the words under her breath. She didn't fear for her physical safety—living on the edge for two years in Romania had cured any hint of that—but she did fear other things. Like failure. "I still need to learn that lesson myself. I'm glad you have peace about it." She lifted her hand to his face, as if to transfer his peace into her heart, and their faces drew together. They kissed, a joint affirmation and celebration.

By the time Michelle said good-bye to Nel and packed her things in her car, the hour approached nine o'clock. At this rate, Michelle would consider herself lucky if she got to bed before midnight. She shook her head and headed down the driveway. The car jerked over one of the stones lining the drive. A few yards later the rear end shimmied. *Oh no, not a flat.*

Michelle stopped the car and climbed out. Sure enough, the right rear tire wobbled in shreds along the ground. She opened the trunk and pulled out the spare and the car jack and hoped she could change the tire herself. She understood the concept well enough, but she hadn't changed a tire in years. Not since her father had first taught her how.

Light appeared at the castle door, and Michelle heard feet crunching on the gravel. She turned to see Nel approach. "I'll call Joe and tell him you have a flat."

Before Michelle could say no, Nel had gone back inside. A moment later, she reappeared at the door. "Come back inside while we wait."

Joe arrived about five minutes later and quick as a wink had the old tire off and had set the new tire in place. "When did you get this tire?"

"The garage that replaced my last flat had a spare on hand that they sold to me for ten bucks. I was grateful to get it." Michelle smiled as she remembered the Good Samaritan.

"I don't know how to tell you this." Joe sat back on his haunches. "But it's the wrong size tire. Almost right, but not quite. I'm afraid if I try to force it, I'll strip your lug nuts, and then you really would be in trouble."

What—

"Oh my." Nel pursed her lips in thought. "And the only garage that sells tires in town is closed for the night. In fact, I can't think of any place within fifty miles that would be open at this time of night."

Joe opened the door to the backseat and took out her overnight bag. "I'm sorry, but it looks like you're stuck here until the morning. Or I could drive you to Denver tonight, but you wouldn't have your car."

Morning—Michelle's mouth formed the syllables without uttering a sound. The thought of being late for work—again—squeezed her heart with fear. "When do they open?" The answer to the question held her chances of success on the job.

"Between seven and seven thirty."

And Michelle had to leave by six to get to work on time. She called and left a message for Chavonne, telling her she'd experienced car trouble but expected to get there by ten. She fought the urge to overapologize, deciding explained tardiness would look better than no message at all. During the long, sleepless night Michelle went over every scrap of her last conversation with Joe. *Trust not in princes—or employers. My security is in God. But why would God lead me to this job only to let me fail through no fault of my own?*

But what if He did? The question refused to go away.

Just in case, Joe drove her to the gas station by half past six in the morning. The first attendant appeared at 7:15. He moved slowly, or so it seemed to Michelle, adrenaline pumping through her veins like a performance-enhancing drug. She paid a small fortune for a new tire and a spare, and Joe took her back to the castle. Half an hour later, she merged onto the highway. She parked in the multilevel garage near the office at close to ten.

A sad-faced Chavonne intercepted Michelle before she reached her desk. "Come with me."

They walked past cubicles filled with coworkers, past the copier and office supplies, past the secretary's desk, past Chavonne's own office to. . .Glenda Harris, senior vice president of personnel. The nervous ball in Michelle's throat formed tentacles, strangling her ability to speak.

"Sit down, Miss Morris." Ms. Harris spoke in brisk but not unkind tones. Chavonne took the seat next to Michelle and looked straight ahead, avoiding Michelle's eyes.

"Let's see. You've been with Mercury Communications for what, a month?" She studied the folder in front of her as if to refresh her memory. When she looked up again, all traces of kindness had disappeared.

"During that time, you have been tardy twice. And frankly, your work has been below standard. Mercury can't afford to carry extra weight. Your employment with this company is terminated, effective immediately."

Chapter 21

Chavonne escorted Michelle to the exit, where the security guard took her ID badge.

"I'm sorry things didn't turn out better." Chavonne handed Michelle a box with the few personal items she had collected at her desk before disappearing behind a door that clanged like a prison. Only this jail locked her out, not in.

A security guard approached her. "Ma'am, you need to leave." She realized she was staring into empty space. She walked, almost ran, out the door and into the sunshine that mocked her pain.

She stashed her belongings in her car but didn't get in. She couldn't face Carrie with her failure yet. A right-hand turn brought her to the 16th Street Mall, and she meandered down the sidewalks. People in pin-striped suits hurried past, intent on business. Street performers—a saxophonist here, a guitarist there—plunked out tunes for a few coins in their hats. Giggling teenagers carried full shopping bags. She was the only one without a purpose, with nowhere to go.

She reached the end of the mall and wondered what to do next. In the distance she heard church bells ring, and she decided to find the place of worship.

Her steps led her up Colfax Avenue to a cathedral. A man with a weather-beaten face wearing too many clothes for the heat huddled on the front steps. A beggar's cup sat at his side, but he had focused his attention on a slice of bread he tore into pieces to toss to the pigeons gathered at his feet. "Beautiful day, ain't it?" His toothless grin held genuine warmth.

Michelle dug in her purse and tossed two quarters in his cup.

"God bless you, miss."

Michelle went inside. Perhaps a dozen people sat in the pews, causing her to wonder if she had interrupted a service in progress, but no one stood at the altar. They were probably people like herself, needing a quiet place to seek God's face.

The church must have seen every misery of the human condition, from the homeless man sunning himself on the front doorsteps to the oil barons who lost it all in the oil bust, from scared teenage mothers to senior saints who had outlived their children. Michelle's problem shrank back into perspective as she petitioned God not only for herself but for her fellow

239

worshippers as well. She poured out her feelings.

I failed, Lord.

"I love you, child."

I thought You led me to that job. Did I misunderstand, or did I screw it up all on my own?

"I will never leave you nor forsake you."

God never answered the "why" questions, Michelle mused. He said, "I am God. Trust Me." She slipped out of the church, found a phone, and called Carrie.

"I was just leaving to take Viktor on a picnic. He's bursting at the seams with energy."

Michelle checked her watch, surprised to discover the lunch hour had arrived. Her spirits lowered a fraction. If she ever needed to talk with Carrie, to get a good dose of her cheerful good sense, today was the day.

"Tell you what." Carrie interrupted Michelle's thoughts. "We can go to Washington Park. You should be able to meet me there and get back to work in an hour."

"Sounds good." Michelle would explain about the job when they met.

Carrie gave Michelle directions to the park, and they met fifteen minutes later. Carrie had packed an extra lunch for Michelle, and the three of them quickly polished off the food. Carrie also dug out a water bottle and a sun visor for Michelle.

"I don't suppose you have another job in your magic bag, do you?" Michelle sounded wistful, even to herself. "They fired me today."

Carrie stared at her. "Oh no. I'm so sorry." They started down the trail that circled the large pond, talking about odds and ends.

Not many people ventured outside in the heat of a summer afternoon, and they met no one on the trail. Michelle wiped sweat from her face. Viktor rode ahead on his tricycle and then waited for them to catch up. They paused by a flock of geese.

"This reminds me of the day the agency turned down my application to adopt a child." Carrie tossed a few remnants of their lunch to the geese. "I went to a park like this one in Bucharest. I almost kidnapped a baby that day."

"What?" Michelle had never heard this part of the story.

"Yup. I was so desperate for a child that I wanted to make things happen my own way. But God didn't let me." She took a long swig from her water bottle. "It's one of those old but true sayings. God never closes one door without opening another. Whatever God has for you will be far better than what you had at Mercury. Like God giving me both Viktor and Steve. So much more than I asked for. And He will supply your needs."

God always opens a door. Something triggered in Michelle's brain, a suggestion she had rebuffed at the time. God had already opened the next door. She had a lot of phone calls to make when she got home.

❖

What a week. On Thursday morning, Joe gave his store a final check. Because of the minimal structural damage, he had only needed to clean and restock his shelves. *Only.* The extra pieces he had bought at the Cherry Creek Arts Festival would come in handy. He called his bestselling artists and begged them to send some more soon as possible.

He had also installed an alarm system. Trust in God and be prepared. He should have done it before.

Joe studied the effect of the new display, disappointed in spite of his best efforts. The current pieces of art didn't quite reflect the quiet quality people had come to expect from the Trojan Horse. He had lost so much more than money.

I'm being too critical of myself. God will provide. He always has. Joe replaced the CLOSED UNTIL FURTHER NOTICE sign on the front door with GRAND REOPENING.

A steady stream of customers kept him busy all day. *There's no such thing as bad publicity, they say.* People curious about the break-in, businessmen worried about the prosperity of downtown Ulysses, concerned friends and neighbors—all those and more came through.

The last customers left after six, and Joe evaluated the day. Among the many well-wishers, serious buying had taken place, twice a normal day's business. *Thank You, Lord.*

He grabbed a can of Dr Pepper from the refrigerator and stretched out his legs, relishing the successful day. He could take the store in a new direction now, maybe work with the town council to develop an artist-in-residence program. He sketched out a number of ideas and cost estimates.

The phone rang. *Maybe it's Michelle.* Her week-long silence had surprised and hurt him. *Probably wrapped up in her job again.*

Judy was calling. "Something has come up at the office. Can you come by tomorrow morning about eight o'clock?"

"I'm going to see you at Mother's tomorrow night. Can't it wait until then?"

"No. It's rather urgent."

"Can I swing by tonight, then? I was planning on getting to the store early tomorrow."

"Sorry. We won't have the details until morning."

"I'll try to make it." He crossed fingers behind his back, not really intending to go.

"Promise me you'll be there." More than a hint of panic colored Judy's voice, intriguing Joe. What did his brother and sister-in-law have up their sleeves?

"All right, all right. I promise."

Because of the changed plans, he stayed late to get the store in order for tomorrow's business. At home he fell into a contented, if exhausted, sleep and woke late, putting on a T-shirt from Taos, New Mexico, with blue jeans. He made it to Brian's office a few minutes after eight.

The door swung open at his touch, but he saw no one. "Hi, it's me. What was so important?" He walked across to the room where he heard the whirring of a copier and pushed open the door.

Instead of Judy's red-gold mop, a sheet of hair as golden as corn silk swayed as the woman bent over the copier. *Michelle?* She pirouetted like a model on a runway, presenting herself for his inspection.

"Hi there, Joe. I'm the important business. Hope you're not disappointed."

"But. . .what? How?" Joe struggled to put his jumbled thoughts into words. "What are you doing here? In Brian's office? On a weekday? What about your job?"

"They fired me."

Joe opened his mouth to offer his sympathy, but contentment oozed from Michelle, as if the termination brought her peace.

"I soon realized I had unfinished business in Ulysses. I'm here in Brian's office because I accepted his job offer. I'm his new office manager so that Judy can concentrate on being a full-time nurse."

"You decided to move to Ulysses? Permanently?" Joe couldn't believe what he heard, like winning a contest someone else had entered on his behalf.

"I sure did. Like you, I realized my security has to rest in God, not the place I worked, and after that, details don't matter." She grinned. "Aren't you going to ask me what my unfinished business is?"

A wild hope sprang up in Joe, almost choking his voice. "Do you mean—"

"I do. Why don't you stop staring and kiss me, my beloved husband-to-be? That is, if you still want me."

"I do." Joe took Michelle in his arms, sealing their promise with a kiss, a song telling plainly of God's love and peace ringing in his heart.

KNIGHT MUSIC

Dedication

To the Lord who gives me songs in the night.
To the real-life Max, who brims with the glory of God—
and who happens to share my birthday.

Prologue

Bruce Wayne—at least that was the name he'd given to Kirby Kent—paced in front of the storage unit while his associate fiddled with the lock. He had a bad feeling about this. That puddle of water by the door suggested Kent hadn't taken care of the goods as promised.

With a *pop*, the door unlocked and Kent rolled it up. "Okay, Batman, go ahead."

Inside, hot air blasted him in the face. Dust motes danced in front of his eyes before landing on blown glass vases and delicate wood carvings partially wrapped against the elements. Who knew what damage the summer heat had done to the fragile objets d'art? "This everything?"

"Pretty much."

The shifty look in Kent's eyes made Bruce wonder if he had pocketed an item or two for sale on the side. If Kent had, Bruce wouldn't know; he didn't exactly have an inventory list he could check.

He picked his way among one-of-a-kind works of art peeking out of packing crates. After checking each one, he replaced them with more care than he had found them. His mother would love to see this stuff. "Where are the paintings?"

Kent pointed to the far wall, thick with quilt-wrapped bundles. Bruce removed one quilt to find several paintings stacked together, and his heart skipped a beat. Foolish, inept, careless. . .if any of the canvases had received so much as a scratch, Kent would pay, in more ways than one.

The first stack consisted of a trio of abstract paintings, impossible to judge for minor damage at a glance. He bypassed a stack of angel prints as sentimental. Or was it guilt? He snorted. He didn't want any angels looking over his shoulder on this day.

Another group included urban landscapes, reminiscent of the scenery he had seen on the light rail line into Five Points here in Denver.

Last of all he encountered one thin bundle. A single painting, perhaps the pride of the collection. He peeled the quilt away.

Tall mountains like the ones that greeted his sight whenever he stared west down a Denver street dominated the canvas. Dark clouds shrouded the peaks. In one tiny crevice Bruce spotted a handful of figures heading for a crack of light. He sucked in his breath.

"I've found us a dealer," Kent said.

Bruce jerked his head up. "No dealers. I told you that from the beginning."

Kent shrugged, his hands panning the assortment filling the storage unit. "It's a shame to let all this go to waste."

"You haven't been paid to *think*." Bruce took out a stack of hundreds and counted out fifteen bills.

Kent frowned. "That's not what we agreed on."

"And this isn't what I asked for." Bruce gestured around the unit. "Move everything to a climate-controlled environment, and I'll give you the rest."

"Yessir, boss." Kent tilted his cowboy hat back on his head. "How long we talking about?"

"A month to start with." Bruce forced his lips into a smile. "I'll know more as soon as I make a little trip."

Phase one in his plan to reinvent himself: completed.

On to phase two.

Chapter 1

Sonia Oliveira pivoted a full 360 degrees, not wanting to miss a single change. She took in the lighting—including a skylight—that reached every corner of the room, easels, plenty of shelf space, everything she had suggested and more. Her survey ended on the sign that read WELCOME, SONIA! She allowed her breath to escape in a long, drawn-out sigh. "It's perfect."

"So you have no regrets about accepting our offer." A small grin played around the corners of Joe Knight's mouth.

"None." Any hesitation on Sonia's part about the move fled in a moment of clarity. "I will gladly be the first artist-in-residence at the Trojan Horse Art Gallery here in Ulysses, Colorado." *And pray that over the next six months God gives me the peace that's been missing so I can return to work.* Already her fingers itched to break in the pristine brushes prepared for her use.

"Good." Joe rubbed his hands together and glanced at his watch. "We have a few minutes. Let me show you what I've done in the showroom." Without waiting for a reply, he led her to the sales area.

Sonia followed Joe through the door to the front of the store. He had an instinct for display, almost as important to a gallery owner as his ability to recognize good art. Splashes of vibrant color along one wall magnified the impact of several of her angel paintings, while small wooden figurines chatted together atop a pedestal and Indian pottery took up another corner. She explored every nook and cranny of the store until Joe turned her around and made her look at the back wall. Unlike the rest of the room, the space was blank, waiting for a canvas. "Your new painting will hang there."

Her mouth went dry. "God willing." She coughed.

Joe brought her a cup of water. "There's no rush. You'll turn things around here. I know you will."

She couldn't abide his compassion. "So when is Michelle expecting me?"

"Whenever you're ready." He glanced out the front windows at the small trailer she had pulled behind her car. "No moving van?"

Sonia shook her head. "I travel light." She didn't want to drag too many remnants of her past with her on the odyssey she hoped would mark a new start in her life.

"Michelle can't wait. She's been busy getting everything ready ever since you finalized the details of the offer." Even though Joe and Sonia had dated once upon a time, the glow on Joe's face and the matching trill of excitement in Michelle's voice when they had spoken by phone suggested everything was going well in the romance department for her two friends. But Sonia still wondered if her prior relationship with Joe would matter to her new roommate.

They left the store, and Joe locked the door behind them. While she followed his truck, she studied her surroundings. When she had visited Ulysses before, she had come as a guest. Now she looked around as a member of the community, at least for the short-term.

Late this Saturday morning several businesses were open. Joe turned a corner from the main drag, and she spotted a grocery store. She made a mental note to go shopping before sundown. Joe said the town closed for business on Saturday night and didn't open again until Monday morning, all except for a couple of restaurants that accommodated the after-church crowd. She didn't know towns like that existed anywhere in the United States anymore, but Ulysses was one of them.

Joe stopped in front of a small cottage, and she pulled into the driveway. Michelle, a lithe blond dressed in a pumpkin-colored sweater and sage-colored slacks, opened the door. "Welcome home!" She dashed forward and wrapped Sonia in an enthusiastic hug. "I have been so looking forward to your arrival. I've been missing middle-of-the-night girl talks Carrie and I used to have." She released Sonia and urged her up the walk. "This way."

"Carrie sends her love." Sonia had met both Michelle and her close friend Carrie Romero a few months ago, when Joe had wooed his now fiancée in a whirlwind courtship. For someone new to living in a small town, Michelle had adapted well. The cottage hummed with color and contentment, from fresh flowers on the table to the handcrafted items Sonia guessed were from Romania, where Michelle had served two years as a missionary. Michelle headed down a hallway and opened the second door. "This will be your room."

Sonia had stopped following. Hanging above the fireplace, in easy view of people entering the cottage and those sitting in one of the comfortable armchairs, hung a familiar sight.

"You have one of my angels." She leveled a look at Joe. *Why didn't you warn me?*

A grinning Michelle reappeared. "*Faith*. I couldn't resist. She was the perfect expression of the lessons God has been teaching Joe and me." The couple exchanged a look of pure longing, and Sonia turned away. She didn't begrudge them their happiness, but she felt like an unwelcome intruder.

"Anybody home?" a deep voice called.

The connection between Michelle and Joe broke. "Ty! Come on in. And I see you brought the rest of the gang."

A small army entered—two men, two women, and two small redheaded girls. "Sonia, you've already met my mother," Joe said.

"Nel." Sonia resisted the urge to curtsy, something Joe's mother always seemed to bring out in her.

"And my brother, Brian." He waved at a man who could be his double, as well as his wife and their two children.

"But I haven't met you before." Sonia approached the one man who was a stranger to her, as tall as the other men but dark. *Tall, dark, and handsome, just like my girlhood fantasies.* Her stomach flip-flopped.

Before Joe could introduce him, the stranger stepped forward. "I'm Joe's cousin, on our father's side. Ty Knight."

His voice held a trace of a gentle drawl. She considered. "South Carolina?"

"Virginia, actually. And you must be Miss Sonia Oliveira, the world-famous artist." He brought her hand to his lips.

A Southern gentleman. Her heart did that flip-flop thing again. Ty looked the part, even dressed as he was in comfortably fitting jeans and a T-shirt that stretched the letters of COLORADO across his chest. She bet he'd look even better in a football jersey. An interesting subject for a painting, if she could bring him to life. She'd think about that later. The time had come to move in.

"There was no need for all of you to trouble yourselves." With this crowd, they could almost unpack the trailer in a single load. She'd put most of her things in storage, packed and ready to move back into an apartment when she returned to Denver in six months' time.

The older girl—Pepper?—handed her a drawing of a house with the obligatory door, four windows, and peaked roof. "Welcome to Ulysses, Miss Sonia." She curtsied.

The younger girl handed her a bouquet of flowers that almost matched the carrottopped color of her hair. "Uncle Joe said you're the nicest lady." She threw herself at Sonia in a hug.

Sonia took a half step backward, into Ty's broad chest. His hands landed feather-light on her shoulders and settled her on her feet. "Whoa, there, Poppy. You almost knocked Miss Sonia down. Come on, I bet there are some things you can help carry." He chased both girls to the waiting trailer. Joe snagged the keys from Sonia and followed.

Sonia allowed herself a moment to enjoy the view of Ty's back before she joined them outside.

◆

So this was the famous Sonia Ty had heard so much about. The impression he'd formed from the descriptions he'd received led him to expect someone who looked like an urban gypsy, complete with head scarf and wrist bangles. The only hint of that vibrancy today was a bright-red scrunchie holding her dark hair away from her face.

Maybe she'd turned into a pale imitation of her old self after her best work was stolen and she lost her sense of direction. He had gathered that much from the little Joe had told him about the artist. His mouth twisted at the irony of it.

Sonia gazed west across the plains, in the direction of Denver. He joined her. "Not much to see, is there?"

"Joe would disagree with you."

Ty chuckled. "Joe thinks Ulysses is heaven on earth. But on my behalf, I would also say welcome to our humble town."

He received a shy smile in return. "Maybe what I've heard about Southern hospitality is true, if you feel compelled to welcome me when you're a newcomer yourself."

"I get the impression you don't have to be a six-generation Coloradoan to belong."

"Where does this go?" a girl's voice piped in. *Pepper*.

"Duty calls." Sonia turned in the direction of the trailer. Joe held a wooden crate. "Stop!" Sonia trotted over. "Leave that." She peered into the trailer. "Everything on the left wall goes to the studio."

Joe set the crate down and looked at Ty. "Come over here and make yourself useful, why don't you?"

Perhaps Joe meant it as a joke, but Ty gritted his teeth. He reached for a medium-sized carton, figuring it was easy pickings. When he lifted it, he discovered it felt like Sonia had packed small boulders inside. He adjusted the weight. "Where does this belong?"

"The kitchen. I brought my pots and pans." She shrugged. "I like to cook, and I prefer using my own things. I'll make everyone a thank-you dinner as soon as I get settled in." She looked straight at Ty as she said it, as if he would be her guest of honor.

He wanted to earn the title, so he pretended the box weighed next to nothing. "Good, I'll hold you to it." Planting his feet one in front of the other, he managed to get the box into the kitchen without dropping the contents.

"Oh good, that must be the cookware Sonia e-mailed me about. I cleared this space." Michelle pointed to a freestanding whitewashed cabinet before disappearing in the direction of the bedrooms.

Unpacking dishes? Ty shook his head. He should be used to it. He had helped plenty of people move around during his college days but usually that meant putting together beds or hitching up a washing machine. He dug out a pocketknife to open the carton and plunged his hands into the newspaper-filled container. Out of the corner of his eye he saw Sonia coming down the hall from the bedroom.

"How do you want to arrange your pots?" He had unwrapped the first item, a quart-sized glass measuring cup.

Her dark eyes lit up like blazing coals. "I can make almost anything with that cup and a whisk. In a pinch, I can make do with a stirring spoon." She took the cup in her hands, flicking off an invisible bit of lint. "I'd like to wash these before I put them up. I wonder where she keeps her kitchen linens." She set the cup in the sink and bent over to open the door underneath, pulling out a dishpan and a washrag. From the top drawer she grabbed a dish towel. "You can help me dry." He handed her pots from the box. She squirted dish detergent into the water and swished the dishrag around until bubbles formed.

If he was going to get all domestic, he might as well take care of the newspaper as he unpacked. In the drawer below the dish towels, he found trash bags and started working his way through the box, setting pans on the countertop and throwing paper away. Near the bottom of the box he found a smaller box.

"I'll take that." Sonia opened it and took out an assortment of cooking utensils, including some murderous-looking knives.

Ty whistled. "Remind me not to come around you when you're working in the kitchen."

"What, afraid of a little swordplay?" She whirled around, pointing a steak knife at his chest. "En garde."

He grinned. Here was the Sonia he had expected to meet—playful, flamboyant. In another century, she might have sailed aboard a brigantine with a pirate crew. "Maybe another time." He examined the knife more closely. "This looks like good quality stuff."

She shrugged, running the dishcloth over the knife and adding it to a growing pile in the rinsing sink. "For a time I wasn't sure if I wanted to become a chef or an artist. My father thought I should be a chef, since it seemed like a less risky career choice, and he bought the cookware for me."

Ty could see his face reflected on the glistening stainless-steel surface. "Some gift." He set it on the counter next to Sonia and dived into the box again. It seemed as bottomless as Mary Poppins's carpetbag.

"Are you just visiting Joe, or will you be here awhile?" Sonia looked at him over her shoulder while she rinsed a pot cover.

Ah. The inevitable what-are-your-plans question between two single adults interested in each other. "I'm afraid I'm in the doghouse with my family back in Virginia. I guess it's the twenty-first-century version of 'send a boy out West, and he'll come back a man.'" After emptying the box, he washed his hands and picked up the dish towel. "You're not the only one who hasn't followed the path laid out for them by their family."

Sonia grunted an acknowledgment while she scrubbed an invisible mark at the bottom of a sauce pot. A strand of black hair fell out of the scrunchie and curled around her ear. He considered stacking the pots after he dried them. Better not. He might scratch something, and that would never do.

"What are you chuckling about?" Sonia looked sideways at him, and the loose curl tumbled over her eyebrow. She brushed it back with soapy fingers.

"Wondering what your reaction would be if I scratched one of these pans. Like this." He held the bottom of the pot next to his mouth. "*Screeeech.*"

Sonia jumped, dropping a whisk back into the dishpan, splashing them both in the process. She grabbed the pot from his hands and turned it over and over. "Where's the chalkboard?"

"Got the teacher every time. I'm sorry, I didn't mean to startle you."

The look she sent his way said she suspected that's exactly what he meant to do. "And I apologize for soaking your shirt. So we're even. Sort of."

"No problem."

She dug in the linen drawer for two aprons. "These might help."

Ty eyed the ruffled item that would tie around his midchest and shook his head. "No thanks."

She put one away and slipped the other one over her head.

"Here, let me help you with that."

While he tied the strings, she asked, "So have you decided how you're going to get back into your family's good graces?"

That question went beyond getting-acquainted conversation and bordered on meddling. "Why do you ask?"

"I think my father hopes I'll stay in a blue funk and return to the chef's fold. I guess misery wants company, wondering how you handle it." She looked out the window over the sink.

Maybe she feared she would cave in and do as her father wished if she didn't turn things around. Ty's plan didn't involve telling anyone else, not even someone as charming as Sonia. "Michelle thinks I might be able to get some accounting work. She's even trying to talk me into building a business out here. She wants to make me a permanent fixture in the Ulysses community. If that's what I decide I want to do."

Sonia shook her head. "She's fallen head over heels in love with the town. She was determined she would work at her dream job in Denver, but then God changed her mind and brought her to Ulysses. With a little help from Joe."

God changed Michelle's mind? Was Sonia one of those Bible-thumpers who asked God what clothes she should put on in the morning? "Whatever happened, she and Joe seem happy together."

"Yes, they are."

Ty caught a wistful note in Sonia's voice, but she dried her hands and put away the pans with a minimum of fuss.

Aunt Nel entered the kitchen. "You've finished in here. Good. We're having dinner at the castle. I'm so glad you've come to Ulysses, Sonia. Joe has talked about little else since you accepted the invitation."

Without waiting for a response, Ty's aunt left the room. He chuckled at the stunned look on Sonia's face. "That's what you might call a command invitation."

Sonia nodded her head. "Joe did warn me." She grinned. "I guess that air of authority comes with the territory. There aren't too many people in Colorado who live in castles."

A bubble of laughter escaped from Ty's throat. "I know what you mean. My father told me about the 'castle' Uncle Brian built for his bride, but I guess I assumed he meant a fancy house."

"Instead of the entrance to Disney World, complete with turrets flying the American flag and the family's coat of arms."

"That's right, you've been there before. Aunt Nel's heart is in the right place, I'll say that for her. Always gracious, even to total strangers who find their way to the castle from the highway." His words trailed away as he studied the sunlight from the window that painted Sonia's cheeks a golden hue, turning a pale pink into shades of bronze.

Michelle gave Sonia a lift to the castle since the trailer was still attached to her car. After a splendid meal, Joe lifted a cup of apple cider. "Here's a toast to new beginnings—for both Ty and Sonia."

"Hear, hear," Joe's brother Brian echoed. Glasses clinked.

Over the top of his stoneware mug, Ty turned his dark gaze on Sonia. To new beginnings indeed.

Why did he feel like his success would depend on Sonia?

Chapter 2

A grandfather clock in the corner of the castle dining room chimed four times. Sonia set down her cup of English tea, with cream and sugar, and left a half-eaten scone on her plate. "I hate to eat and run, but I want to get to the grocery store before it closes."

Judy glanced at her watch. "Is it that time already? I need to pick up some things, too." Before Sonia knew what had happened, her simple suggestion had turned into a five-shopper, two-car event. She ended up in Ty's car, a battered secondhand Camry much like her own vehicle. Minimal transportation, not the sleek luxury car she imagined he would prefer. They both faced the same problem, making do and trying to move ahead when business turned sour.

He started the car and turned off the radio, a classical music station, leaving his left hand on the wheel. "What are you smiling about?"

"Picturing you in a lean, mean driving machine." She snapped her seat belt in place and settled against the headrest. "Black. With two-toned leather upholstery."

His laughter came out as a bark. "That ritzy, huh?" He glanced at her and arched his right eyebrow. "What kind of trim?"

"Suede, of course."

"How'd you guess?" The quirking of his lips softened the offended tone he'd used.

She shrugged her shoulders. "I'm very visual."

"The sensitive artiste." He drew out the word and nodded sagely.

"Not lately." Could she turn things around? She didn't want to defraud the good people of Ulysses. Eager to change the subject, she said, "But I didn't peg you as the classical-music type."

"You caught me." He flashed a grin at her. "I play violin in a small chamber orchestra back in Virginia. So you might say I'm a bit of an artist myself." They arrived at the grocery store. As she unbuckled her belt, Ty put a hand on her arm. "May I see you again, when you're not washing dishes?" Again, his lips twitched. "Are you doing anything tomorrow?"

Before she could answer, he continued. "It shouldn't take too long to unpack the few things you brought with you."

She shook her head. "No, but I'll be going to church with Michelle, and she said something about a young-adult group that meets on Sunday afternoons." She cocked her head. "Will I see you there?" She held her breath, as if his answer mattered.

"Maybe." The expression on his face disagreed with his words.

"Anyway, I don't think much happens here on the weekends after the sun goes down on Saturday night, besides church, that is."

"Things to do in Denver when you're dead."

What a strange thing to say. She eyed him dubiously. "What was that?"

"When I knew I'd be coming to Colorado, I checked out some old movies. Even watched a few episodes of *Dynasty*. I ran across this flick called *Things to Do in Denver When You're Dead*. Complete with the title lyrics by some singer I've never heard of. That's what weekends here in Ulysses remind me of."

"Never heard of it." She unlocked the door.

"Wait a moment." He dashed from the driver's side and opened the door for her. "After you, ma'am." By the time she locked and closed the door, he had fetched a grocery cart for her. Why was he being so attentive? Were all Southerners so gentlemanly?

Ty made no move to leave her side as they passed the cash registers inside the store.

Sonia stopped at the produce section. "I'm perfectly capable of shopping by myself."

"I'm sure you're capable of many things." Again his lips twitched. "But it's more fun if we do it together."

Sonia capitulated. "As long as you don't rush me."

He glanced at her shopping list: milk, butter, orange juice, cereal. A puzzled look crossed his face. "This doesn't look like it will take all that long."

"You'd be surprised." She moved forward, drawn by the scent of fresh fruit.

A nanosecond later, he followed her. "You won't find anything on your list in this aisle."

She shot him a look meant to say "I warned you" and caught mirth reflected in his brown irises. "You must have guessed that I take cooking very seriously. I want to see what they stock in this store. I intend to go down every aisle." She winked. "Even the books and magazines."

He didn't miss a beat. "You might miss the latest recipes." He grabbed a bag of grapes and ate one. "You're waiting to see *your* recipe in the magazine."

That drew a laugh from her, but she returned to her inspection of the produce on display. Several signs announced LOCALLY GROWN, and she spotted a number of more exotic items as well. They carried all the varieties of apples she could wish for in this fall season. She paused before a tempting display of Granny Smiths, only a dollar a pound. She went ahead and filled a sack then added a second of Jonathans. Apple pie? No, apple cobbler. Or maybe apple cake. . .

"Whatever you're planning will taste good." Ty tossed another grape into his mouth and licked his lips. She frowned.

"Don't worry, I'll pay for them. They're priced per bag, not per pound." As bad as a little child.

They turned the corner and headed down the bread aisle. She caught sight of Joe's sister-in-law Judy when they reached the end of the aisle. Pepper pushed the cart while Poppy put her head down on the handlebar. Sonia couldn't picture either one of those girls snacking on grapes in the store. Maybe it was just something boys did.

The next aisle featured pastas and packaged dinners, but they didn't carry her favorite brands. Of course she often made her own. She walked past jars of spaghetti sauce. That she always made from scratch.

Ty inspected a package of manicotti and stuck it back on the shelf. "Sonia. Is that an Italian name?"

She shook her head. "Brazilian. Several generations back. My sister says I'm a throwback to a previous generation."

Ty laughed. "That's a good one. Maybe I can tell my folks that the next time they ask why I'm not more like them."

"And what are they like? Let me guess." She studied him. "One of the first families of Virginia?"

"Close enough. Virginia blue bloods. But that's not me."

"So what are you like?" They had reached the cereal aisle. Her favorite brand, a high-fiber fruit and nut mix, cost more than she expected.

Ty wandered ahead of her and grabbed a box of cereal with a cartoon vampire on the front. "I'm like this cereal. Irresistible, but bad for you." He put the box back on the shelf and lifted his arms like a bat spreading his wings. "I vant your chocolate."

Sonia jumped then tittered a nervous giggle. "So you're from Transylvania. I see." After further investigation, she found a generic brand she liked. She sped up the cart and walked to the end of the aisle in a businesslike fashion.

◆

Ty tarried for a moment, staring at the figure of Count Dracula. What had possessed him to say such a thing? He hurried after Sonia. "Blame it on Aunt Nel. I thought I'd be the count of the castle." He attempted a ghostly laugh that came out sounding like stones in his throat.

She didn't turn around, instead inspecting the coffee selection. To his surprise, she chose a dark Colombian roast and added it to the basket before she looked at him again. "What is it about guys and scary stuff?" She smiled, her natural warmth returning. "I guess since you don't have to bring down mammoths with bow and arrow anymore, you find other things to challenge you. It's kind of sweet."

Baking supplies lined the next aisle. She whipped through the shelves, tossing flour, sugar, and spices into the cart. "Michelle probably has most of this, but I don't want to start baking and discover I'm missing something."

"Couldn't you just come back?"

She looked at him as if the answer was obvious. "Not before Monday."

"And you plan on baking before then?" Most women he knew would take a week to settle in before doing any serious baking.

"I want to take something to the Bible study tomorrow. It's potluck."

The Bible study. Oh yes. He suppressed a grimace. He could think of better ways to spend his weekend than enduring a whole day with church people, like spending more time with Sonia. Maybe he could do both. Joe had invited him, after all; only so far he had found excuses not to go. "Do you think I'd be welcome?"

Did he see approval in her eyes? "I've never seen a church turn someone away." She flashed a smile at him. "I want to fix something special to take tomorrow. I know I don't need to, since it's my first time and all, but I expect I'll be too busy to do much after that." A dark look darted through her eyes.

Ty knew a little bit about Sonia's current frustration with her work from Joe, but he wouldn't mention it if she didn't. "Joe has invited everyone in Colorado and half of Kansas to meet you next week."

"I saw the schedule. He's got me booked solid for the next week. Baking will help calm my nerves. It usually does. Grab that for me, would you?" She pointed to a package of powdered sugar on the top shelf. When he handed it to her, their fingers brushed. "Do you want to help?" She flicked her hair over her shoulder. "I could say it came from both of us."

"As long as you don't make me wear one of those aprons."

◆

"We'll be there in a couple of minutes." Sonia called ahead to warn her new roommate of her plans. Why had she invited Ty along? She had come to Ulysses to stop floundering, to recover and regroup so she could work again. Not to carry on a mild flirtation with Joe's devastatingly handsome cousin. And Michelle had expressed her desire for some girl time.

But her roommate was all grins when they arrived at the cottage, and Sonia could guess the direction of her thoughts. The newly affianced woman might believe a flirtation was just the cure for what ailed Sonia. Look what had happened between Michelle and Joe after their whirlwind courtship only a few months ago. Their relationship had transformed Joe in more ways than one. Now he was at peace and confident in spite of the theft that decimated his store; but after Sonia's initial brave words at the time of the robbery, she had withdrawn, prolonged grief at the loss preventing her from creating anything meaningful in the months that had passed since.

Michelle's mouth opened in a round O when she saw the number of bags in the trunk. "I bet I have a lot of this already."

Sonia shrugged. "I should have asked, I suppose, but I was anxious to get everything I needed before the store closed. I'm thinking about making apple raisin cake to take tomorrow. What do you think?"

Ty grabbed two bags filled with the fruit, and they headed inside. "Nothing beats good old apple pie."

Michelle shook her head. "Pie doesn't go as far though. I've got some chili ready to go."

Sonia's face split in a grin. "You haven't seen the size of my pie shells. And I have a utensil that will cut it into ten even slices." She made quick work of putting away all the ingredients except the ones she needed for the pie and grabbed a cutting board as well as an apple corer and a peeler from the cabinet where they had stored her things. Handing the apples and her largest bowl to Ty, she said, "Your mission, should you choose to accept it: Fill this bowl with apples from both bags. Cut them into thin slices." She held her fingers about a sixteenth of an inch apart and grinned. "Without nicking your fingers. Use the corer to help you get all the seeds out."

"Don't look so glum," Michelle chided. "She's left the hardest part for herself, the crust." She glanced at the freezer. "Unless you bought a frozen crust."

Sonia's lips curled at the mention of a frozen pie crust. "That *cardboard* stuff?"

"That's me. The cardboard queen." Michelle winked at them. "Have fun, you two." She left the kitchen, although Sonia could hear her humming slightly off-key in the den a few feet away.

Sonia winced. Ty caught her expression and put a finger to his lips. His gaze bounced around the kitchen until it rested on a clock radio. He turned it to a classical music station. The same one he had been listening to in the car? The low volume hid Michelle's voice.

"Thanks." Sonia mouthed the word. She flicked the oven on. "As long as I'm baking, I'll go ahead and make two pies. I'll send one back with you to thank Nel for the meal today." She paused. "Or are you staying with Joe? Or do you have a place of your own?"

"I'm the count of the castle," he reminded her. "I'm staying with Aunt Nel for the time being."

Sonia searched among her pans for her pie tins. Mixing bowl, pastry cutter, dry and liquid measuring cups. She *could* make almost anything with her quart-sized glass cup and a whisk, but she loved having the right tools for the job.

Water ran in the sink, and she saw Ty rinsing the apples. *Good.* He wasn't as inexperienced as he pretended. After washing them, he put the first apple on the cutting board and stuck his tongue in his cheek as he fiddled with the corer. "And *X* marks the spot." He pushed down, and a perfect rectangle slid out of the apple. He held the apple to his eye like a telescope. "Think I got all the seeds." Taking the peeler in his right hand, he eased into the top of the apple and unwound the peel in a single, circular piece.

He caught Sonia staring at him. "Bet you didn't think I could do that."

"I recognize someone who's had KP duty when I see him." Satisfied that he knew what he was doing, she returned her attention to cutting shortening into her flour mixture.

Within half an hour, two apple pies sat side by side in the oven. Sonia hung up her apron. "Care for some coffee?"

"As long as it's the real thing."

She removed the lid from the dark roast she had purchased. "Mom says the day will come that I can't enjoy a cup of good joe without spending a sleepless night." She grinned. "But until then, I intend to enjoy myself." She measured enough for half a pot and started the drip.

Ty studied her. "I'm surprised you don't grind your own beans."

She grimaced. "I like to cook. I'm not a coffee gourmet."

They sat down with their coffee—hers black, his with cream, no sugar—at the kitchen table. She smiled at the bouquet of poppies, the gift from Brian's girls, that graced the center of the table. The scent of simmering apples wafted from the oven. They sat in companionable silence, sipping their drinks.

"You make a mean cup of coffee." Ty saluted her with his cup and filled it a second time. "Do you want any more?"

"Maybe half a cup."

Ty's dark eyes peered at her over the rim of the mug. "So when should I pick you up tomorrow? For this Bible-study thing?"

She rolled her shoulders. "We'll go straight from church. You don't need to pick me up, I'm sure Michelle will give me a ride."

"It would be my pleasure. When does the service start? Eleven?"

Why didn't he know the time? Hadn't he gone there before with Joe? She pointed to a bulletin insert stuck to the fridge with a GOD LOVES YOU magnet. "Sunday school starts at nine."

"Sunday school?" He mumbled something under his breath. "You really take this whole church thing seriously, I can tell."

Chapter 3

Y*ou mean you don't?* Ty could almost hear the words, although Sonia didn't make a sound. He wanted to slap himself up the side of his head. Why did he think faith and church would be any less important than it was for his cousins? Because she was an artist? He thought about the painting of the angel hanging in the living room. *I should have known better.*

Sonia stood and peered in the oven. "Meeting with other Christians helps me to regroup. I even go on Wednesdays, to get my midweek fix." Grabbing an oven mitt, she opened the door and removed the aluminum foil from the edges of the pies.

Ty pursed his lips. "You don't need to go with Michelle. I'll be by at eight forty-five to pick you up." Maybe Joe would stop nagging him about church if he went one time—and he couldn't think of better company.

She rejoined him at the table. "It's really not necessary."

"No, I want to." He wondered what to expect. The last time he had gone to Sunday school, little white-haired Mrs. Brown had insisted he memorize the books of the Bible, and he did, right up until he got to the prophets. Those names got the better of him every time. "Do I need to take anything special?"

She looked at him, laughter in her eyes. "I haven't been to this church before, remember? Me and my Bible, that's all I plan on taking with me. Oh, and an apple pie." She stood and removed the pies from the oven. "Perfect."

He breathed in the aroma from the pies. They looked as pretty as they smelled. Probably tasted even better. He wanted to stick a finger in the middle like Little Jack Horner, certain he'd find a treasure. "I have dibs on the first piece."

She flashed a mischievous grin at him. "You'll have to ask Nel."

Ty glanced at the clock and stuck his hands in his pockets. "I'd best hie back to the castle before she sends the constabulary looking for me."

She stared at the side of his face, head tilted to one side, like a camera recording every feature.

He couldn't stand it. "What is it?"

"You have strong bones. I'd like to sketch you sometime, if you're willing."

When he didn't respond, she shook her head. "I shouldn't have asked. I might not be able to do anything worthwhile, even if you agreed. Forget I asked."

He smiled but didn't answer her question. "See you in the morning then."

"I'm looking forward to it."

After he returned to the castle, Ty climbed the steps to his room in the front tower. He passed a painting Joe had laughingly introduced as his ancestor, Sir Innis. The strength of character and reckless courage he saw in the knight's face remained stamped in the faces of Brian and Joe today.

If Ty had grown up with that for a role model, instead of a father who valued appearance more than character, would he have become a different kind of man? Shaking his head, he continued up the stairs. He doubted it. Even if he and his cousins shared the Knight name, all that chivalry came from Aunt Nel's side of the family.

At the door to his room, Ty reached for the light switch before he entered. The armored soldier in the corner gave him the creeps. Ty fantasized that the sword would fall and claim his head when he least expected it.

He prepared for bed before he remembered he meant to grab a Bible from the study. *What was a study called in medieval times?* he mused as he pulled his jeans back on and headed down the stairs. Did they even have such a room back then? Perhaps those so inclined had a resident priest who copied the biblical text with those fancy illuminations in the margins. Sonia's face flashed through his mind. But she would never have made a monk, for more reasons than her gender. He couldn't imagine someone that beautiful, that *alive*, cloistering herself away from others.

The study in this modern-day castle sat at the bottom of the staircase to his tower bedroom. Built-in bookshelves lined three of the four walls, complete with a rolling ladder to reach titles up high. The collection encompassed a wide variety of time periods and subjects, from something that looked like it could have been a first edition of Charles Dickens to the latest bestsellers. If memory served him correctly, religious titles were located next to the armchair by the window. He found a row full of Bibles.

He heard a light footfall behind him. Aunt Nel. "Are you looking for something in particular?"

"A Bible. I didn't expect you to have so many."

"Ah, yes. I think of that sometimes. What must God think about the abundance of versions of His word in the English language when some people still have none? But I can't bear to part with them." She took out a white leather-bound Bible with pages edged in gilt. "I carried this one at my wedding. And this blue New Testament—a gift when Brian was born." She went through and told the story of each copy. At length she pulled out a worn Bible with cracked leather that had pages drifting out of the binding. "This was my husband's Bible. I'd be honored if you use it." She handed it to him. "If you are seeking answers, this is a good place to start." She patted his hand and sat down before he could explain that he only wanted to borrow one for church in the morning.

Aunt Nel slipped on a pair of reading glasses to read from the Bible she had described as her "grieving Bible." Heading back to his room, he tried to imagine owning so many Bibles that he gave them nicknames and failed.

After undressing for bed a second time, he climbed beneath the quilts. In spite of the day's labor, he didn't feel sleepy. Sonia's face kept floating through his mind. *You're a fool, Ty Knight.* He couldn't let a woman come between him and his plan, especially not Sonia.

What was it Aunt Nel had said? He would find answers in the Bible? Mom said the same thing. Picking up Uncle Brian's Bible, a page fluttered out and he scooped it up. Strong block letters in blue ink were etched on the fragile paper. *Integrity = security.* He returned it to its place, Proverbs chapters 10 and 11. Arrows pointed to verses on facing pages. Ty read first one, then the other, to see what had impressed his uncle in the midst of the "greed is good" decade.

"Whoever walks in integrity walks securely, but whoever takes crooked paths will be found out."

"The integrity of the upright guides them, but the unfaithful are destroyed by their duplicity."

His mouth went dry. He closed the Bible without reading any further. If he wanted a sermon on the value of integrity, he could turn around and go home and listen to his father. Would the church services tomorrow bring more of the same?

He punched his pillow with his fist and lay on his back counting the beams in the ceiling. Tomorrow morning seemed a long time away. *I should never have offered to go to church with Sonia.*

◆

Sonia was buttoning her pajama top when Michelle knocked and opened the door. "Can I help you unpack anything?"

"I'm pretty well settled." She remembered Michelle's comments about late-night girl chats. "But I wouldn't mind a cup of cocoa." She wrapped a kimono-style robe around her body. "I even bought some at the store."

A few minutes later they entered the living room, hands wrapped around steaming mugs. Sonia stretched her neck and rolled her head around, loosening some of the kinks moving day had left in her spine. "This is the life." She joined Michelle at a card table that held a puzzle in progress.

Michelle picked up a piece but didn't place it. "I bet you're good at this kind of thing, being an artist and all that."

Sonia took the rejected piece and found its rightful place.

"See, I told you."

"Beginner's luck." Sonia chuckled. "Not all that good. When I'm painting, I can see the finished picture in my mind. At least I used to." Sighing, she brought the cup to her lips.

"You will again. Joe and I, we've been praying for you." Michelle strung together pieces of what looked like a large wooden door.

"Thanks. I know God is faithful. That's the only thing that keeps me going some days."

Michelle nodded in understanding. With a sideways grin, she handed Sonia the box top. "Here's what the finished puzzle will look like."

Sonia looked at miniature figures capering about a castle, everything from a cat standing on its hind legs wearing a plumed hat to a trio of pigs dancing down a road. She half laughed, half coughed. "Don't tell me. I bet Nel gave this to you."

"Joe did. As a joke. Said this was as close to a fairy tale as real life would ever get." She fit in a piece of Puss 'n Boots's tail.

"And what did you say to him?" Sonia pushed a couple of emerald-green pieces together, trying to make sense of the vines crawling up the castle walls.

"Why, I asked who needed a fairy tale when I was marrying my knight in shining armor." Michelle glanced at her engagement ring and lifted it to where she could see it flash in the light.

Emotion clogged Sonia's throat, and she found the spot for the vines on the wall. "So everything is going well between the two of you?"

"Better than good. Fantastic." Michelle connected the door to one of the castle turrets. "You and Ty spent a lot of time together today."

Sonia squirmed. Was Michelle going to become the latest in a long line of acquaintances to play matchmaker once they had found that special someone? "Well, you know, after you and Joe, Brian and Judy, that left Ty and me." She laid down the piece she held in her hand. "Are there half a dozen eligible bachelors waiting to meet me at church tomorrow?" Michelle threw back her head and laughed. "There might be that many in the whole town. I'm not sure. But Ty is. Eligible, that is."

Sonia took the time for a long swallow of her cocoa. "Okay, roomie. Ground rules: no matchmaking." She smiled to lighten the complaint.

Michelle's green eyes widened in mock surprise. "Of course not."

Michelle was a good sort, Sonia decided later as she went through her bedtime stretching routine that the doctor said might help her relax enough to sleep. Sleep had never been an issue until the day someone stole her most ambitious painting to date straight out of Joe's art gallery. She mourned the loss as if her firstborn child had been killed. When she added the theft of the angel pictures, the theft of so much of her inventory created a void she struggled to refill. She opened the window a crack, letting in a thin stream of the cool September air, redolent with the smell of hay and the music of crickets chirping instead of exhaust and honking horns.

She dug into her suitcase for her latest prayer journal, although few glancing through the pages would guess its purpose. As an artist, she thought less in words than in images, and that's what filled the pages. When everything had fallen apart and she felt herself slipping into a dark void where God seemed absent, she challenged herself to examine each day for signs of God's presence and record them.

She leafed through the pages. Some things she recorded so frequently they had become a kind of personalized hieroglyphics: the sunrise and sunset, rain and rainbows. She thought today about her drive from Denver and reached for a dark yellow colored pencil, sketching a tree in the process of changing color. Next to that she drew an empty cross and open tomb—a reminder that life follows death for the believer.

An orange-red pencil created a bundle of flowers in a small girl's hands. The many hands that had carried boxes into the house today. Michelle's carefully manicured hands. Brian's slender fingers fit for a surgeon. The small pudgy fingers of a child.

At least she could still sketch. If only she could do *more* than sketch. The ability to add piece to piece, image to image, to create a meaningful whole, had fled.

The next hands had just the hint of ink smudged on the fingertips. Black hairs crisscrossed the back of the wrist, poking out around the edges of the watch with the simple leather strap. To the hand she added an arm. . . shoulder. . .profile.

She started over again, this time in three-quarter profile. Eyebrows arched over lips barely parted in a smile, an aura of mystery behind his charming facade.

Ty was charming all right. But was he hiding something? And what right did she have to pry? His family didn't share her doubts. She added shadows beneath his eyes, suggesting someone with a weight on his shoulders— someone who hadn't yet learned that Jesus' yoke was easy and His burden was light.

She drew another pair of hands, mimicking Dürer's praying hands, asking God to open his eyes and his heart at the church service tomorrow. When she finished, she snapped a rubber band in place around the book and tucked it back into her suitcase. The pictures in that book were a private conversation between her and God, but it always surprised her how many people couldn't resist the urge to look through an artist's sketches. She zipped it in the compartment built into the bottom of her suitcase, as close to a hidden compartment as she had.

◆

People mobbed Sonia and Ty before they could leave the pew. When they came in the sanctuary, he had grabbed the seat next to her. Now she hugged a few parishioners like old acquaintances—maybe they were, or maybe her natural self was peeking through. People welcomed him as a Knight cousin and thronged Sonia as the new artist-in-residence. No one with two eyes could have missed her entrance today, all shades of yellow swirling around her like molten gold, bringing out the sheen of her dark hair, a strand of beads sparkling against her chest. . . .

"And you must be Ty." A woman with a head sprouting a thousand curls held back by a hair clip came around to the pew in front of them to shake his hand. "Joe has told us so much about you." Her voice sounded unnaturally high, like a child's, but more musical, like a high C on a violin. She beamed. "I'm Janice Perkins."

"The pastor's wife." He had seen the name on the bulletin.

Her smile grew wider. "We're delighted to have you here. Do you expect to be in Ulysses long?"

Ty made some offhand remark while he strained to eavesdrop on Sonia's conversation. Something about her classes and how everybody was looking forward to them. His mouth twisted. Perhaps he should sign up for a class. He grinned at the thought of Sonia guiding his hand through some elementary art lesson.

"Good. We'll look forward to seeing you there."

Ty blinked. What had he missed? Mrs. Perkins had taken his facial expression as assent. "And when is it?" And what and where? Although he didn't voice those questions.

"Why, I didn't tell you, did I? The choir meets on Thursday nights. You won't need to take your violin until the orchestra rehearsal. It's starting up again next Sunday afternoon."

Choir? Rehearsal? *Violin?* What had he agreed to?

Mrs. Perkins snagged Sonia before anyone else greeted her, and this time Ty listened as the pastor's wife made her way through the welcome. "Ty here has just offered to play his violin in our orchestra. And he's going to check out the choir as well. Wasn't that sweet of him?"

Sonia widened her eyes and looked at him. He shrugged. Might as well.

"We'd love to have you come, too. To either choir or orchestra."

Sonia was already shaking her head. "I'm afraid I don't sing." As if sensing the next suggestion, she said, "I don't play an instrument either." She put a finger to her lips. "I have worked with audiovisual equipment before."

"Wonderful! The lady who ordinarily does that has just had a baby. I'll have Josh call you, shall I? Did you fill out a visitor's card today?"

Joe came up behind Michelle. "Mrs. Perkins, I'm sorry to interrupt, but we're expected elsewhere."

The sanctuary had emptied except for the four of them. She blinked. "I'm sorry, I didn't mean to keep you so long. I'll look forward to seeing you both on Thursday night then." Beaming, she headed away from the entrance, perhaps in the direction of the church offices.

Joe bustled them toward the exit. Once they were outside, he apologized.

"She's a great believer in getting people involved. But if you don't want to go on Thursday night, she won't be offended."

Ty thought about it. He *had* brought his violin with him, after all, and he loved to sing. "Oh, why not? I get to make music. It'll be fun."

Only later did he make the connection that committing to choir also meant committing to regular attendance at church. What had he signed himself up for?

Chapter 4

Ty picked up the familiar weight of his violin case and stared at the church building. Janice said tonight was choir rehearsal, but he wanted to be prepared. A family—father, mother, two teenage girls—walked by, laughing, music clasped in their hands. Why was he nervous? He opened the car door and took a deep breath.

He straightened his shoulders and allowed his mouth to fall into his most heart-warming smile. His Southern charm made him welcome in most groups, and this should be no different. He was only adding a wrinkle to his campaign to make a good impression on his family.

The church door opened before Ty reached it. "There you are." Joe held it for him. "I began to wonder if you had changed your mind. Right this way." He glanced at the violin. "Choir rehearsal's tonight. The orchestra practices some other time. Sunday afternoons, I think."

"I don't know if this is such a good idea." Ty hung back.

"But as long as you're here. . .another baritone is always needed." Joe clapped him on his back and crossed the foyer to the sanctuary. So, the choir didn't practice in a separate music room, not surprising in a church this size.

Up in the sound booth, a familiar figure waved to Ty. He turned to Joe. "I'll join you in a minute." He climbed the stairs and knocked on the door. Sonia let him in. "How's it going?"

Sonia squinted at the console. "It's a little different than what I'm used to. But Barb left excellent notes. I'll get the hang of it."

The music minister—Josh Redding—called the choir to order.

"You'll have to tell me all about your first week on the job later." Ty found a spot next to Joe in the choir loft—one of only five men. Down in the first row, he spotted Mrs. Perkins and a couple of women from his Sunday school class. "Michelle's not in choir?"

"She doesn't like to sing." A faint smile crossed Joe's face. "Unless it's country karaoke." Ty must have looked surprised because Joe said, "Long story. I'll tell you about it sometime."

Josh handed out music, simple SAB arrangements. Ty leafed through the pages and found a few places where the men split into two parts. Easy enough. An older woman took her place at the piano. Did the orchestra play for the choir? Did they use a recording? Piano? He couldn't imagine anything too elaborate with this group.

"Joe, why don't you introduce our guest."

Ty looked up as two dozen pairs of eyes fastened on him. He smiled as Joe put his hand on his shoulder. "This is my cousin, Ty Knight. He's here for a visit, but we're hoping to convince him to make Ulysses his permanent home." Murmured greetings welcomed the announcement.

"I understand you play the violin?" Josh tilted his head at him.

"I have my instrument right here." Ty patted the case.

"Wonderful. Now we have a string quartet." Josh smiled and handed out the rehearsal schedule for the night.

The man next to him extended a hand. "I'm Hugh Classen."

"He teaches art at the high school," Joe said. "He's one of my best customers."

"Pleased to meet you." Ty turned his attention to the rehearsal schedule and arranged his music in the order listed.

"And my name is Max," a bearded man on Joe's other side said.

The choir, though smaller in number than most he had heard, held a good blend of voices. One of the men tended to hang on to the melody line about two octaves below the sopranos, but everyone else sang their parts. Ty had forgotten how much fun choral singing could be, although he still played with a small community orchestra back home. That is, he had until he moved out West for his new start.

The choir special for Sunday included a solo, and Ty watched Sonia through the glass to the sound booth. She was cute when she concentrated that way, puckering her lips and scrunching her eyebrows close together. The choir stood for a final run-through of the number before they dismissed.

◆

"So you favor a hands-on approach to teaching." Ty walked with Sonia to her car after the rehearsal.

She flung her hands upward, as if to say, *What else do you expect?* "It *is* art, after all. How else can someone learn to draw? Timid students, who make a few lines here and there before asking for reassurance, often don't continue. It's easier to teach someone who has a little more confidence."

They reached her car. Ty shifted his weight from one foot to the other. "I was wondering. . ."

Sonia paused in unlocking her car door, the light September wind curling dark strands of her hair about her face. "Yes?"

"I have discovered something to do in Denver when you're dead. More precisely, something to do here in Lincoln County on the weekends. Believe it or not, there is a wetlands sanctuary near here, over in Limon."

She caught her breath. "Wetlands? Really?"

"Would you like to check it out with me this weekend? Maybe find some Canadian geese settling into their winter digs?" He looked away, across the parking lot in the direction of the highway. "I thought it might be a good place to sketch. Practice that assignment you listed for your class."

A smile ghosted Sonia's lips. "I saw your name on the class list for Saturday morning. Have you bought all your supplies?"

"Yup. Paper, pencils—drawing, charcoal, *and* colored—ruler and eraser. I can't wait." He rubbed his hands together. "So, what do you say? Can we go on Saturday? Or if you'd prefer, we can go on Sunday afternoon. There's no Bible study this week."

"Saturday afternoon sounds good, after the adult class." *Did I just agree to a date?* A pleasurable tremor passed down her arms.

"Great." When Ty smiled like that, he could run for man of the year. "I guess I'll see you again at class on Saturday morning." He walked away, whistling the tune of the choir's Sunday selection, his violin case gently bumping his thigh in time to the music.

Seeing him in choir sharpened some of her questions. Would someone who wasn't a Christian do that? Sonia sensed Ty didn't know the Lord and decided to make it a matter of prayer.

On Friday, Sonia sent out information to her Denver contacts about a master's studio she would hold on Tuesday nights. She also went over her plans for her Saturday classes one last time, the first for children, another for teens and adults. The high school art teacher, a guy named Hugh Classen, had signed up with several of his students. Other names she remembered from church. She was touched to see Nel among the registrants and pleased beyond reason that Ty had also decided to take part.

Was Ty a renaissance man—one who could claim some degree of skill in every area, from finance to music to art—or did he have a personal interest? She pushed aside the question as ridiculous. Since he was new to the community, as she was, he might want to meet as many people as possible.

Someone knocked on the door to the studio. "Come in."

Joe entered. "Are you all ready for your big debut?"

"So-so." She twiddled her hand. "I think I was less nervous the last time I had a booth at the Cherry Creek Arts Festival." Which was why she planned to wear her brightest red paisley skirt with a yellow peasant blouse tomorrow. She wanted to look confident even if she felt intimidated.

"I get that way the first time I offer a new class." He walked around the room, taking in the child-sized art easels with jars holding tempera paint. A stack of plastic aprons waited on the shelves. In one corner she had assembled a rainbow of children's toys, everything from brown teddy bears to red trucks to yellow balls. "Interesting setup you have here."

Sonia flashed a smile. "For this first session, I just want them to have fun. They get to choose something in their favorite color and paint that. And I'll talk some about color."

He nodded. "Fun is the key ingredient." He placed his hands on his hips. "I know there are some parents who would love to take a class as well, but they have no one to leave the children with. Would you mind if I taught a second class for children so their parents can come to the adult sessions?"

"Good idea. I know you were doing that before I arrived." Sonia turned around. "But where?"

"I have some ideas." He explained his plan to remodel part of the back room, and they agreed to have it ready before the second session started in six weeks.

On Saturday morning, the children arrived early and stayed late. When they got to hang their paintings on a clothesline to dry "just like grown-ups," Joe's niece Poppy danced with excitement. Sonia wondered if she had allowed enough time between classes.

She was putting away the last of the children's easels when Ty walked in. "Can I help?"

Sonia felt herself smiling. "I need to set up for the adult class. Just a table and chairs today. The round one, over there." She grinned. "The only Knights I'll allow in my class have to sit at a round table."

"Hardy-har-har." He lifted the table as if it weighed no more than two soda cans and soon put the room in order.

Sonia had asked the students to bring examples of their work, if they had any. Although no experience—or talent, for that matter—was required for participation, it helped to have some idea of her students' beginning skill levels. If she discovered a variety of abilities, she might expand to beginning and intermediate classes in the next session.

A couple of the high school students showed real talent. Perhaps these classes would inspire them to explore a career in art and not feel it necessary to pursue other dreams. If she could provide that ray of light and encouragement, she'd consider the class a success.

Even though she felt like her own career had stalled. *No.* She refused to think of it as anything more than a temporary stumbling block.

At the table, Ty sat next to his aunt, holding his pencil with a violinist's grace but without moving it. Nel's hand flowed in a steady line across the page. He caught her gaze and smiled. Maybe their trip this afternoon would encourage both of them to sketch without inhibition.

◆

"I looked up the wetlands on the computer last night." Sonia opened up a notepad where she had written a few bits of information. "Colorado originally had two million acres in wetlands. Can you imagine? Now it's down to one million. Cut in half." She looked out the window at the fields greening toward harvest. "Colorado isn't a place that jumps to mind when you think of the rain forest."

"Are you into all that environmental stuff?" Ty cocked his head at her. "Liberal artist and all that?" He grinned wide white teeth to show he meant it as a tease.

"Not really." Sonia shook her head. "I recycle my pop cans when I can and buy recycled unless the price is outrageous. But I never imagined Colorado as having a big problem. There's little law to protect the wetlands and not much by way of enforcement." She sighed. "Something to think about. I'm looking forward to seeing what wildlife lives there."

"Flora and fauna." He nodded his head. "I have no idea what the situation is like in Virginia. Probably a lot worse than in Colorado. Europeans came and cut down the forest." He rolled his shoulders and pointed ahead. "There's a sign for Limon. How many acres are they preserving in Limon?"

Sonia brought up the website on her smartphone. "All of fourteen acres." She shrugged. "That's pretty small. But I guess it's a start."

"Ah. Here we are." Ty exited the interstate. "We're looking for the Doug Kissel Fishing Pond."

"What is that?"

"I don't have a clue." He grinned. "But once we find it, we follow the pedestrian trail under the railroad south about fifteen hundred feet."

"I'm glad Joe let us borrow his binoculars. I suspect looking for the wildlife will be like a hidden-picture puzzle, only without the key to check for answers."

"That's not a problem when you have eagle-eye Ty Knight with you." He narrowed his eyes and gazed at the passing landmarks. "Aha! There's a sign pointing the way. It says it's funded by CDOT. What's that?" He found a parking place and turned off the engine.

"CDOT is the Colorado Department of Transportation." Sonia scrolled down her computer screen. "They're trying to transform a retired sewage lagoon into a wetland basin."

By the time Sonia had closed the phone and replaced it in her bag, Ty was opening her door. The binoculars hung from his neck. He whistled at the marsh grass waving in the distance. "Hard to believe this was once a sewage dump."

"They even have four different unique wetland environments, all in this tiny space."

"Different kinds of wetlands, huh?"

"Different kinds of plant life, in any case. Everything from willows to cattails to pondweed."

Ty arched an eyebrow at that. "I didn't know weeds were ever encouraged."

Sonia returned a ghost of a smile. "But we're not here as naturalists. We'll draw however fancy strikes." She smirked. "Even if it's a weed."

They walked the pedestrian path. "Passing on the right." A bicyclist, dressed in lime-green biking shorts, passed them. Moisture weighted the air, and Sonia breathed deeply of the scent of mossy earth and moist dirt.

The surface of the pond looked as blue as it might have on the day of Creation, intermixed with shades of green with dashes of gold, red, and pink. Sonia reviewed her choice of colored pencils, but decided to stick with a black-and-white pencil sketch. Something plopped in the water, and she checked her list. "A green-winged teal, or duck to ordinary folks like you and me."

Ty put his finger to his lips and pointed in the direction of a white ibis standing only a few feet away from them. The bird stared down his long pointed beak at some spot in the water, probably searching for his next meal.

"If we're lucky, we might get to see coyotes and muskrats as well as mule deer. Although I don't know if the deer will show up before dusk." Sonia danced down the path a bit farther. "I wonder if we'll find places to sit." She wrinkled her nose at the trees lining the pathway. "Nothing I read mentioned poison ivy, but I wouldn't know it if I saw it."

"There's a seat up ahead." Ty pointed to a wrought iron bench, where a white-haired gentleman helped his wife to her feet.

"Beautiful day, isn't it?" the woman said.

"I keep telling her any day we're still together is a beautiful day," her husband, tall and straight in spite of his shock of white hair and speckled skin, said.

How sweet. Will any man ever feel that way about me? Sonia glanced at Ty, and he reached for her hand. They walked to the bench with their hands clasped.

Ty didn't sit down. "I expect the path circles the wetlands. Do you want to go all the way around first or stop here?" The lazy look in his dark eyes suggested he'd rather spend the time enjoying a quiet stroll than sketching.

As much as the prospect appealed to Sonia as well, she needed to work. Time for both, she decided. "Let's keep going. See if we can figure out where one kind of 'cell'—that's what they call the different environments—becomes another."

◆

A breeze blew across the water, and Sonia shivered ever so slightly. Ty used it as an excuse to slip his arm around her shoulders. Why this woman of all women drew him, he didn't know. Perhaps he relished the knight's ideal of a challenge. His lips curled a little at the thought.

Sonia broke away from him by a couple of inches, and she knelt by the shoreline. "Here are the cattails."

The slender reeds did resemble the tail of his mother's Siamese cat, soft, brown, and furry, swaying back and forth like a cat on the hunt. Sonia's fingers tapped her sketchbook, and he could almost see the images forming in her mind.

If today's trip renewed Sonia's eagerness to create again, Ty's trip out West would double in value. Once he had seen her work, he knew her heart—a heart given over to beauty but sullied by the robbery at Joe's store. He picked up a stone and skipped it across the water, waiting until it sank beneath the surface and ripples spread out from the point of impact. Actions always had unintended consequences.

They walked a little farther and reached an area where the vegetation grew thicker, less marshy. Across the pond, he saw a flicker of yellow on the ground before white wings fluttered and a brown neck stretched out of the water. Sonia's fingers beat her sketch pad in a march tempo.

"Why don't we stop here?" Ty sat on the closest bench and patted the spot next to him. "I see two, maybe three different birds out there."

Sonia joined him. "It's so peaceful here." She lifted her face to the breeze for a moment, and it lifted tendrils of her dark hair away from her face.

"And beautiful." But Ty looked at her, not at the scene in front of them.

Ty had always admired beauty.

Chapter 5

Ty opened his sketch pad. In class that morning, he had drawn the candle and goblet Sonia had put on display. But his attempt was as childish and immature as "Chopsticks" on the piano.

"Don't think. Just let your fingers follow what your eye sees." Sonia spoke without looking at him, her own pencil flashing over the page, at ease.

Ty moved his pencil in a choppy, semicircular line, the water rippling across the pond. He hummed to himself, the theme from "Suite No. 1 for Hornpipe" from Handel's *Water Music*. His hand moved in time to the rhythm of the lively Baroque melody. By the time he had finished the first movement, he had produced an approximation of the movement of the water in front of him. Better than he expected.

Maybe he should always draw to music. During one of his favorite classes, years ago in middle school, the teacher played Beethoven while they drew. His school required art but made music optional, an anomaly that always seemed unfair to him, since he loved music but only tolerated art.

Half a dozen sketches covered Sonia's sketch pad: a bird landing on the water, another taking off, another diving for food, yet two more idling side by side. The breeze lifted the corner of the page, and she flipped it over, securing it in place with a rubber band. "Looking good." He nodded at her page.

"What? Oh, thanks. I've never done anything quite like this before." Her pencil drew a suggestion of wiggling tail feathers. "I've spent a lot of time in the mountains, but never out here. I never thought there was much to see."

"The change of scenery must be doing you good."

"Oh, I hope so." A few lines added the duck's body and head. "We'll see." She said the last words to herself.

Ty laid his hand on top of hers. "Look at me."

Her brilliant dark eyes sought his, and his heart ached at the doubts reflected there. "It will get better. It already is. I know it."

"From your mouth to God's ears." A slight smile formed around her mouth. "And the same thing will happen for you. You'll return home in a blaze of glory. . .or perhaps find what you're searching for right here."

"I think I already have." Refusing to consider consequences, Ty leaned forward and kissed Sonia's full red lips.

◆

Ty's lips feathered Sonia's own, as light as the down on the ducks in front of them, and then he pulled away. Her breath caught, and she cleared her throat. "That's not quite what I meant." The intended mild scolding came out like an ingenue's hesitation.

"I know." He settled back against the bench. "Starting next week, I will be looking for a temporary job. Joe's going to ask around if anyone needs an accountant."

"It's hard to imagine you as a number cruncher."

"Number-one bean counter, that's me." He shrugged. "It pays the bills."

Ty said the last with such wistfulness that she wondered what unexplored dreams lay in his past. "If you could do anything in the world, what would it be?"

He arched his eyebrows at her. "You mean, besides sitting here in Limon, Colorado, with a lovely woman?"

Heat stained her skin. "Yes."

"Oh, I have a few things on my bucket list. Hike the Appalachian Trail. Climb Mount Everest—or at least Mount McKinley. Play at Carnegie Hall." He hesitated. "But that's not what you're asking, is it?"

"What's your calling, for lack of a better word? Music?"

Ty blew out his cheeks. "No." He drew out the word. "In spite of what I said about Carnegie Hall. I love music, but I don't want to live in that world." He leaned against the corner of the bench. "I think I might have done well on a plantation, or maybe as a squire taking care of his tenants. Not that I know the first thing about farming. I guess I'm out of luck."

Sonia gazed across the pond and thought about the fields they had passed on their way to Limon. "Perhaps you could plant a garden at the castle. It's a start, in any case."

"It's the wrong season of the year for that."

She waved away his excuse. "You know, plant bulbs for next spring, prepare the grounds for the winter. There must be something that you can do to get your hands in the dirt." She reached down and scooped a handful. "Something elemental about getting your hands dirty."

Something flickered in Ty's eyes before disappearing. "I'll look into it."

◆

"I'm glad you're coming over to the castle for dinner today." Ty walked with Sonia from their Sunday school room. "Nel would be dreadfully disappointed without guests."

"Does she always eat in the dining hall?" Sonia shuddered at the thought of eating all her meals in the large room hung with tapestries suggestive of the family's medieval origins.

Ty laughed. "No, when it's just the two of us, we eat in the kitchen. But she loves to serve elaborate dinners."

Sonia spared one last thought to the leftover spicy stew she had intended for lunch today, but gave way graciously. "I wonder if she gets lonely rattling around in that place by herself. I bet she's glad to have you there."

They parted ways, with Ty headed for the choir. After their special, he climbed the stairs to the sound booth. The congregation sang "Joyful, Joyful, We Adore Thee," which she thought was written by some well-known composer. She checked—Beethoven, sure enough. Ty sang the bass line as if he had memorized it.

When the pastor directed them to turn to the Gospel of John, she noticed Ty peeked at the index. Who didn't know how to find the book of John in the Bible? Someone who didn't do much Bible reading, that's who. She turned her attention to the monitor in front of her, making sure she kept the points of the pastor's sermon in sync as he moved through the passage of scripture.

Stop it, she scolded herself. What better place for someone who didn't know God's Word than church? To expect anything else was like asking a man to become perfect before he became a Christian.

Again, the question rose in her mind. Was Ty saved? Until she knew the answer, she had no business thinking about yesterday's kiss as much as she had, no business at all.

Pastor Perkins preached about the abundant life Christ came to give, contrasting it with the thief who stole away what was good and right about life. Abundant life made her think of the wetlands. Ty had given her much more than a day off; he had renewed her excitement. Her fingers itched to bring the wild elation and reclamation of beauty from ugliness that had transformed the former sewage pond to life on a canvas. Perhaps she had turned the corner from grieving the past to experiencing what lay ahead in her future.

How could she return the favor? Bring the smile from his lips to the eyes that sometimes looked so sad? She saw him now, staring at a print of Sallman's picture of Christ standing at the door and knocking, a wistful expression on his face.

Then the sermon ended, and once downstairs, people greeted them as if they had known them forever.

Hugh Classen, the high school art teacher, came up with Joe and Michelle. "It's good to see you both active in the church already. I always like to jump right in." He nodded at Michelle. "Like this one did, judging the pie contest at Odyssey Days her first weekend here."

"I'm still not so sure that was a good idea." Michelle grunted, but Sonia could see the memory was a happy one. "I don't think Esther has ever forgiven me."

"Nonsense." Nel joined their circle. "You judged fairly, and Molly's business received some well-deserved recognition." She turned to Ty. "I thought the choir sounded well today. It's always pleasant to hear men's voices raised in song."

Ty bowed. "My pleasure, Aunt Nel." He turned to Sonia. "May I give you a lift to the castle?"

"We'll meet you there." Michelle didn't wait for her response.

"If you keep this up, people will say we're a couple." Sonia hovered between jest and serious complaint.

He opened his eyes wide. "Would that be so terrible? No, I just wanted to show you something. Come on." He cocked his head in the direction of the doors, and she followed him to the spot where he had parked his Camry at the far end of the parking lot. "I thought about taking one of those convenient visitor spots near the door but decided a member of the choir might not qualify as a visitor." He smiled.

"My doctor tells me to park as far as possible from the doors and make myself exercise."

"Then we'll both be really healthy." When they reached his car, he popped open the trunk. "Take a look."

She noticed several gardening implements: a rake, a bag of bulbs, a spade, as well as several other things. "What's all of this for?"

"I took your advice to get my hands dirty and see how I like working in the soil. And there'll be plenty of leaves to rake before long, I'm sure." He took a shiny spade in his hand and turned it over. "Besides, Aunt Nel could use the help. I want to earn my keep."

Sonia clapped her hands together. "I'm so pleased. I'm sure you'll enjoy it. It might even help when you're thinking through things. I know housekeeping does that for me."

He closed the trunk and opened the door for her. "What does your schedule look like this week?"

She buckled her seat belt and flexed her fingers. "I can't wait to work on what I brought home yesterday. I can't thank you enough."

"Excellent. It sounds like we both found some inspiration on our date."

The word closed Sonia's mouth. She hadn't allowed herself to think of the trip to Limon as a date, although what other word applied? She nodded. Admit it, it *was* a date, and they'd had fun. Before she thought further about it, she invited him to join her on her trip to Denver later that week.

"Sure. I'd like that." He grinned. "Tomorrow? Tuesday?'

"Not so fast. Tomorrow is my day off, and I have my first master's class on Tuesday night. How about Wednesday morning?"

"It's a date."

◆

Coming to Denver with Sonia was either a smart move or a big mistake. Ty couldn't decide which. Sonia relaxed as she drove, her hand resting on the steering wheel, guiding her car through the maze of Denver traffic that seemed heavy after his few weeks in Ulysses. *Stop worrying*. He planned to enjoy the next few hours.

"I can't stay all day, but I wondered if you would like to toddle around downtown for an hour or two. Say, the Colorado History Museum—or the Denver Art Museum?"

"Sure, since this looks like it's going to be my last day of freedom for a while."

"Don't tell me. You got a job."

"I'm filling in for Barb—the same one you're pinch-hitting for at church—until she comes back from maternity leave. Payroll and general accounting. It's not much, but it should tide me over until I figure out my future."

"Wonderful! God is opening doors for both of us. It's exciting to know God directs our lives, even the bad times." She thrummed her fingers on the steering wheel. "But I confess it's easier when I can see it happening."

He made a noncommittal grunt. *God again.*

"And there's my exit." She turned off the highway and headed downtown, parking beneath a building called the Denver Pavilions. He noticed a gigantic bookstore and a number of smaller stores and restaurants, as well as a movie theater.

They stopped by the bookstore to get the parking ticket validated. "If I start mooning over the Monet prints for more than five minutes, promise you'll drag me away."

Ty studied the portraits of Walt Whitman, William Shakespeare, and Willa Cather that adorned the walls. "As long as you promise to tear me away from the music."

In the end, they dallied long enough to enjoy a cappuccino in the bookstore's café before purchasing the latest book by Debbie Macomber for Sonia and a Clive Cussler action yarn for Ty. "Cussler lives in Denver. Did you know that?" Sonia asked.

"Can't say that I did."

Ty opened the door when they exited the bookstore. "Which way to the art museum?"

"A couple of blocks in that direction." She nodded away from the 16th Street Mall that ran like a ribbon through downtown Denver.

"Lead onward." The sky overhead sparkled a clear blue with a few puffy clouds over the mountaintops he could see when he faced west. He hadn't known what fall in Colorado might entail—he had heard tales of days when he might experience all four seasons in twenty-four hours—but so far September had been a pleasant surprise. The temperatures did dip into jacket weather at night. Often the temperature swung forty degrees in a single day. Natural beauty, temperate climate, pleasant people—Colorado might not be such a bad place to call home, not at all.

He almost changed his mind when a yellow broom and blue dustpan—as tall as a building—came into view. "What on earth is *that*?"

Sonia's lips curved in a smile but then she straightened them. In a serious voice, she said, "That is the 'Big Sweep,' created by Van Bruggen and Oldenburg. They say it was inspired by the way the winds meet the mountains in Denver."

"Hah." He let the word express his derision. "It looks more like Jack and the Beanstalk's giant decided to do some housecleaning."

She giggled. "The museum is straight ahead."

As they passed through the turnstiles into the museum, Ty spotted someone who seemed familiar, but out of context and unexpected. The man saw him at the same time. The man's steps faltered for a moment, and then he increased his speed and headed toward the exits.

"Something the matter?" Sonia looked up from the museum map.

Ty shook off the feeling of unease. "I saw someone who looked familiar." He forced a laugh. "But I'm not likely to run into someone I know in downtown Denver, of all places. It must be someone's doppelgänger."

"Stranger things have happened. Where is he?" Sonia glanced around the lobby as if she could identify Ty's elusive acquaintance.

"Whoever it was, he's gone." Ty glanced over his shoulder one last time and then made himself study the museum map for inspiration. "I'd like to see the Indian art exhibits. We don't get much Navajo and Hopi art back in Virginia." His cell phone vibrated in his pocket, but he ignored it.

"And I'd like to check out the special exhibit. But I don't think we have time to do both. I'll go upstairs with you."

Ty's phone vibrated again. "No, you stay down here and enjoy the traveling exhibit. It might not be here when you get back. I'll go upstairs for a look-see and join you in the cafeteria in, say, forty-five minutes?" He edged his way toward the elevators. The last thing he saw as the doors closed was Sonia's questioning face.

Chapter 6

W hen can we talk?" Kirby Kent's voice came through loud and clear. "I'm getting anxious, sitting on the merchandise."

"I told you. I'll call you when everything's in place," Bruce Wayne said.

"I gotta tell you, I have some customers primed to buy." Bruce heard papers rustling in the background. "Good money."

Bruce pushed aside the feeling of panic. "You've been paid for the work you did. The merchandise belongs to *me*."

"I'm just saying, if you're not ready to move on it sometime soon, a guy's gotta do what a guy's gotta do."

"Don't do anything foolish until I talk with you again. Don't call me. I'll call you."

"I'll wait." Kent waited a beat. "For now."

◆

That was strange. Sonia fought the urge to follow Ty into the elevator. He acted like he didn't want her to accompany him upstairs. But his suggestion would allow her to check the traveling exhibit. When it didn't hold her interest, she slipped into the cafeteria early.

The high prices must help underwrite museum expenses, she decided as she studied the menu. Still, due to the exorbitant prices, she ordered only a plain coffee while she waited for Ty. She could join him at the Navajo exhibit, but his behavior had troubled her, and she wanted to think about it before she saw him again.

What did she really know about Ty Knight? Only what little he had told her. She flipped her phone open and logged onto the Internet. Googling "Ty Knight Virginia" spat back a variety of listings, everything from a Facebook page to community orchestra concerts to a business called Knight Industries where he worked as the chief financial officer.

A headline reading SCANDAL ROCKS KNIGHT INDUSTRIES caught her eye, and she clicked on the link. An audit had revealed funds missing from employee retirement accounts. She set down the coffee cup and drummed her fingers on the table. No accusations were made, but a statement released to the press stated that CFO Tynan Knight was taking a leave of absence from the family firm.

"Is the coffee any good?"

Ty's voice interrupted her reverie, and she flipped the phone closed. "Not four dollars' worth." She gestured with the cup. "Did you enjoy the exhibit?"

"I liked the sand painting. Don't the shamans usually destroy them when they're done?"

Sonia nodded. "But from what I understand, the artist changed the design so that it's not something used in one of their rituals." She thought of her own prayer journal, filled with images meant for private communication between her and God. "I can appreciate their point of view. Some things should be private. Not that I believe in their religion." As she said the words, she decided that if the man across from her wanted to keep his past private, she would allow him to do so. "So, shall we order lunch here or go somewhere where it won't take a day's work to pay for lunch?"

◆

Later that afternoon Sonia stood in front of her easel. A drop cloth covered the canvas like an inactive computer, hiding the lack of progress. She glanced at the sketch on the table and took a deep breath. *God, help me.* If God's image imprinted creativity on her, in recent days she wasn't reflecting Him very well.

Today she had determined to make a start. Something, anything—it didn't have to be good. She only wanted to conquer her fear of the blank canvas.

God had stared into the formless void and created an entire universe, and she took courage. She removed the covering and studied the canvas. Next she closed her eyes and envisioned the scene at the wetlands, cropping edges to the far end of the pond with a strip of sky on the horizon, focusing the lens of her memory on the intricate detail of two killdeers waiting side by side in the marsh grasses. She opened her eyes. The bright white surface blinked at her, threatening to erase the image from her mind.

"Not this time." She dipped her brush in the palest of golden oils and brushed broad swirls across the surface, creating a wash that would form the basis for the rest of the painting. Light rolled and bounced and fed the beauty of the scene. She moved methodically from the top left-hand corner to the bottom right, like a reader committing a page to memory. Only when at last had she filled in the last tiny bit of space, where her name would appear, did she put down the brush.

The light outside the studio blazed with the late afternoon sun. She stretched her arms over her head, working out the kinks. Someone knocked and turned the doorknob behind her. Joe entered. "Am I disturbing you?"

"Is it that time of day already?" Sonia glanced at the clock. "I guess so. Come on in." She rolled her shoulders and took a drink from a water bottle.

Joe came around and looked at the canvas. He nodded, smiling, but didn't make any comments. "Are you ready to call it a day?"

Sonia glanced overhead. "The light's almost gone. And I need to let this dry." Reluctantly she put away her paints, hoping that inspiration would continue to carry her forward tomorrow. Putting on her jacket, she headed for the exit.

Joe followed behind her, checking doors and setting the alarm. "It's good to see you working."

"Mm-hmm."

They paused on the back doorstep, where her car awaited. The parking ticket from the Denver garage was plastered to the front windshield, reminding her again of Ty's unusual behavior at the museum. "Do you mind if I ask you something?"

"What?" Joe pulled the door shut behind them.

"Do you know what happened with Ty in Virginia?"

Joe checked the lock and shook his head. "All I know is that Uncle Thomas—Ty's father—asked if he could come for a visit, and Mum said yes." He pulled his keys out of his pocket. "You like Ty, don't you?"

Sonia turned aside to hide the heat rushing into her cheeks. "Yeah, maybe."

"Ever since he's arrived, he's been a godsend for Mum. He's doing all the things I never got around to. This week he's preparing the gardens for winter. Makes me a little ashamed of myself, to be honest."

Sonia paused by the door to her car, fiddling with the bracelet that held her key ring. "Do you know if he's a believer?"

Joe sucked in his breath. "That I don't know. He's a good guy, but. . ."

That matched her impression, and she nodded. "We'll just have to pray him into the kingdom then." She opened the door.

"Do you want me to ask Mum if she knows anything more about what happened?"

Should she? Sonia shook her head. "No. He's entitled to a fresh start. That's why I'm here, after all." *Ulysses, headquarters for extreme career makeovers.* She'd keep her concerns between herself and God for now.

◆

Ty wondered if he should have purchased extra trash bags when he had the chance. Autumn had begun to drop its canopy onto the ground. He pushed his hair back from his forehead and looked at the jumble of golden leaves piled in front of him. He'd bag this last pile and call it quits for the day. His muscles might ache in the morning, but for now he was riding an endorphin high that came with fresh air and exercise.

That, plus the anticipation of seeing Sonia again at choir rehearsal tomorrow night. Would she object if he stopped by the studio during the day? He wanted to see for himself if she had made any breakthroughs. She deserved better than teaching classes to local yokels in a small town like Ulysses.

He raked up a forkful of aspen leaves, still damp from an afternoon shower yesterday. Like it or not, he had earned whatever hard times came his way. He hadn't mishandled the funds from the retirement accounts at Knight Industries, but neither had he performed a thorough audit. He had allowed the fraud to happen, and even worse, he'd been caught, bringing shame on the family name, and that was enough for his father to banish him.

Whereas all Sonia had done was create a magnificent painting and commission his cousin to sell it for her.

Ty tugged a few stragglers off the rake with his hands. Too much yard work would leave his office-pampered hands raw. Unable to play the violin, which he enjoyed even more than playing lord of the manor. Tomorrow he would invest in a pair of work gloves.

Of course, the robbery had affected Joe and the rest of the family as well. Ty regretted what happened to all of them. He dropped another pile of dripping leaves into the trash bag. Why else would he try so hard to be everything the Knight family could want or need?

He dumped the last bit of leaves into the bag and tied it shut. The satisfaction he felt in joining the choir and raking leaves faded when he remembered the spark he had seen in Sonia's eyes at Limon. He had caught a glimpse of the real woman at last.

He carried the bags to the castle's Dumpster. He gritted his teeth. Whatever it took, come what may, he would ensure that spark remained in Sonia's eyes permanently.

◆

A light knock rapped at the back door. Sonia ignored it, hoping whoever it was would leave. When the knock repeated, she swept the sketches she had spread across the table into her folder and threw a drop cloth over the easel.

Ty stood at the door, holding a bunch of fresh-cut asters and chrysanthemums. "For you. I begged Aunt Nel's permission." Ty hesitated before smiling, as if uncertain of his reception.

"Come in." She couldn't remember the last time someone had brought her flowers. She took an empty paint jar from the shelf.

"Let me." Ty tore open a florist's packet and stirred it into water before adding the flowers. "That should keep them fresh." He looked around the room for a good resting place, settling on a spot between two art books on a shelf about shoulder high.

He sat at the table where she had laid her folder. "Are you free for supper?" He glanced at the folder and the covered easel. "How's it going?"

"It's going well." *Until you interrupted me.* "In fact, I'm hoping to work right up until choir. I should have natural light until then." She glanced at the skylight, afraid a thundercloud might appear as it so often did in the late afternoon.

Ty spread his hands in front of him on the table. "Don't let me stop you."

"Ty." Sonia let her agitation show. "I prefer to work alone."

A flash of something—anger? hurt? confusion?—flashed in Ty's dark eyes. Then he regained his charming demeanor. "I want to help you if I can. To find that tiny fissure of light that will lead through the dark mountains of despair."

Sonia froze. He had given a good description of the stolen painting, one he had never seen. "How did you do that? Describe my painting, the one that was stolen?"

Ty tipped his chair on its back legs and blinked. A vague expression dampened the light in his eyes. "Joe must have shown me a picture. Or maybe I saw it on your website."

"Maybe." But not recently. She had deleted it right after the robbery, as if removing it from public view could erase the pain and memory from her heart.

"I know it made a big impression on my cousin." Ty grimaced. "I wish I could have seen it on display in his studio." His facial expression turned into an infectious grin. "I may not be able to draw a straight line, but I appreciate fine art when I see it." He stood. "Sure you won't change your mind? I could serenade you with my violin while you work."

Against her will, a smile curved Sonia's mouth. "No, really." He looked so chagrined that she relented. "But maybe you can come over to the house after rehearsal. We've got a mean jigsaw puzzle going."

Ty let loose a loud laugh, a sound that brightened the air in the studio as much as sunrise. "Now there's an offer I can't refuse. Au revoir." He winked and left.

Sonia glanced at the clock. Half past five. Joe would close up shop soon. Ty's interruption had eaten valuable time. She sighed, shook her head, and rubbed her eyes before opening her folder, studying the pages in the order she wanted to use them. Several sketches of a green-winged teal in flight chronicled the rise from earthbound creature to the freedom of flight. A transformation that resonated within her heart as she longed to leave behind the despair that weighed her down and once again float weightless in the freedom of God's creativity.

That one appealed. But so did the V formation landing on the water, the beauty, unity, security of migrating birds. Or the killdeer nuzzling the neck of its mate.

I need to paint more than one picture. She would start with a series of small watercolors. If they turned out well, she could turn them into limited print runs which would generate income and prove she'd broken out of her slump. Six months allowed plenty of time to work on the large canvas later.

As Sonia tacked her paper to the easel, she checked her spirit. Had she made the right decision? A shadow appeared in the skylight, and she glanced up to see a dove peering through the glass, checking out the human below. God had sent a dove to look over her shoulder; Sonia didn't need further affirmation. She prepared her palette and selected her brush. Choosing a heron for the subject of her first painting, she began working.

When Sonia arrived at the church about a minute late, Josh was already leading in prayer. So, he was the punctual type. She would keep that in mind, since she tended to lose track of time when she got into a project.

The prayer ended, and Joe made a joke, something about singing in falsetto because the men's part went so high. After that the choir settled down to work. Sonia didn't have anything to do until they practiced with the tape. While she waited, she studied the choir members, matching names to faces. She knew most of the guys—Joe, Ty, the jovial Max who had taken Ty under his wing, Hugh, Andy, the guy who sang with the praise team. The gal sitting next to Ty came to their Sunday school class. She offered him her copy of the music.

"Sonia?"

She raised her head. Ty wiggled his eyebrows, and she wondered if Josh had called her name more than once. She checked the controls in front of her. "Ready." At a nod from Josh, she turned it on, but it only spit and sputtered.

She pushed the EJECT button and the CD slid out, looking unharmed. "Let me try again." At Josh's nod, she pressed PLAY one more time. This time the monitor screen in front of her went blank. A cold dread washed over her. "Something's wrong."

"Let me see." Josh dashed up to the sound booth and ran his hands expertly over the keyboard, but nothing changed. He frowned. "It's given up the ghost at last." He sighed, pushing his glasses back up his nose. "Not to worry, there was nothing you could have done." He walked back to the choir. "It looks like we'll have to sing with the piano on Sunday." The pianist ran through the piece like a true professional, and the choir rewarded her with a round of applause.

At least the choir mics still worked, so Sonia felt like she contributed something. After dismissal, Josh approached her. "Can you come to the next orchestra rehearsal? We're performing a week from Sunday and need to check sound levels."

"Of course." She'd love a chance to hear Ty play. She gestured to the silent computer. "Do you expect to have this repaired by Sunday?" The outline for the pastor's sermon, music lyrics, videos that played during the offering and Lord's Supper—so much of morning worship depended on it.

Josh shook his head. "Barb warned us this might happen. She's been holding it together by a shoestring. We've budgeted money to replace it for the last couple of years, but we keep running out of year before we get the money." He shrugged. "Could you run it from a laptop?"

◆

Ty pulled into Sonia's driveway and jumped out of the car. She opened the door before he had a chance to knock. "I'm fixing myself a salad. Do you want anything to eat?"

"I almost forgot." Ty returned to the car and picked up a wrapped package. "Since you refused to join me for dinner, I picked up a club sandwich for you. Figured since it has a little bit of everything, there was bound to be something you liked."

"You didn't have to do that." But Sonia took a bite.

Michelle wandered into the living room. "Hi there. Sonia told me you were going to join our puzzle team." She looked over his shoulder. "Did Joe come with you?"

Joe? Ty blinked. "Uh, no. He slipped out a few minutes before I left."

Michelle shrugged. "That's okay. It's a late night."

"I promise I won't stay too long. Lead me to this killer puzzle."

Chapter 7

Don't tell me. Aunt Nel gave you this puzzle," Ty quipped when he saw the fairy-tale-themed picture. "Even the castle looks familiar."

Michelle giggled. "No, Joe gave it to me."

Sonia turned on an overhead light. "I want any red pieces you find. I'm trying to piece together Little Red Riding Hood."

Ty slid onto a chair on the opposite side of the folding table. "I'll tackle the Big Bad Wolf. Which means I need gray." He found the figure on the box cover. "And white. Grandma Wolf. What big bad teeth you have." He pulled back his lips and flashed his teeth in a snarling smile.

"That's not quite white." Sonia stared at the picture. "There's a tinge of yellow. More of an ecru."

He looked at Michelle, and they both laughed. "Only an artist would worry about that." Ty pointed to Red Riding Hood on the box cover. "Is her cape really red? Or is it crimson or vermilion or, I don't know, cherry?"

"Just plain red will do."

Ty took the box that held the spare pieces and checked them one by one. "What was Josh saying about needing to replace the computer?"

Michelle looked up. "What's that?"

"The computer died tonight," Sonia said. "Barb's been holding it together with a shoestring, but my capabilities don't extend that far. I know how to run it, not fix it."

"Oh dear. Hey, I need that piece." Michelle grabbed a bit of yellow from the box lid and stuck it into the plume of Puss 'n Boots's hat.

"So why don't they replace it?" Ty found what looked like a gray paw enclosed in frilly white lace.

"Not enough money. There's been a shortfall between budget and offerings since I've been here. Bills and salaries take priority."

Ty matched the paw to an arm encased in white linen. "So they plan on replacing the system but haven't raised the money yet."

"That's it in a nutshell." Michelle gave a cry of delight. "Oh look, there's the missing edge piece." She snapped it into place.

"I guess her cape is more of a cranberry color." Sonia tried piecing a couple of pieces together but had to pry them apart.

"Are there other projects like that? Things the church has had to put off doing for lack of funds?"

Michelle shrugged. "Probably. I could get a copy of the budget and find out, or Joe might know. Why? Do you have a small fortune you're looking to donate?" She grinned as she snapped Puss 'n Boots in place at the point where his paw held the foil.

"No." Ty found the puzzle piece with the wolf's not-quite-white teeth. Snagging it into place, he contemplated the situation. He might not have money, but he knew how to raise it.

◆

Between them, Ty and Sonia finished enough of Red Riding Hood and the Big Bad Wolf to join the two figures together and position them in the puzzle.

After that, Ty excused himself without extending an invitation for a future date. Sonia fixed herself a cup of Goodnight tea and told herself it didn't matter.

Michelle joined her in the kitchen. "What's happening with you and Ty? I don't know many guys who would spend an evening working on a jigsaw puzzle."

Sonia took some carrot sticks from the fridge. "He's funny and charming and considerate. But. . ."

"But what?" Michelle opened a cabinet and removed a box of crackers.

"How much do you know about him?" *Like why his father sent him away.*

"He's Joe's cousin." Michelle made it sound like that was all that mattered.

"I know that. But have they spent much time together before now? I mean, it's not like they could hop in a car and get together for weekends when they were growing up." Sonia thought of her relatives in Brazil, people she had met in person only once.

"I'm not sure. But they've grown pretty close in the short time he's been here. Like another brother, Joe says." Michelle snapped a cracker in half. "Why all the curiosity? Considering him as husband material?"

Heat seeped into Sonia's cheeks. "Sometimes Ty says something that doesn't add up. And I know there were problems in Virginia." She munched on a carrot. "I'm not even sure if he's a Christian. I don't know, maybe I'm looking for trouble where none exists."

"Enter the dark knight." Michelle grinned at her roommate. "Tynan. When someone commented on how dark complected he was compared to Joe and Brian, he told us his name means 'dark.'" She placed the crackers back on the shelf. "Nel is crazy about Ty, and she's a pretty good judge of character."

Alone with her prayer journal a few minutes later, Sonia sketched Ty piecing together the Big Bad Wolf. Then she added a figure in a chain mail suit. Wolf or dark knight? Both possibilities left her uneasy.

◆

When Saturday morning rolled around, Sonia tucked away the completed heron watercolor. Her Limon Wetland series was off to a good start.

But she wasn't ready to share them with the world, so she put them in her cabinet and locked the door. Today's lesson in the children's class revolved around mixing colors. The fact that blood red and serene blue became regal purple when combined never ceased to amaze her. The transformation of sky blue and sunshine yellow into green, the color of growth, seemed a little more predictable.

Watching children discover the magic for the first time reawakened the wonder in her spirit every time.

In addition to paint, she offered Play-Doh in primary colors. She remembered her shock the first time red and blue Play-Doh became lavender when she rolled them together. Unfortunately, after she added yellow and green and every other color she had on hand, it became a muddy brown.

Another time she might bring homemade play dough and let the kids add their choice of scent and food coloring. Youngsters seemed to love that.

Today the kids would choose the medium they wanted to use, paint or Play-Doh. Rolling the mushy substance with their hands kept some kids engaged whose attention might otherwise wander.

The door opened behind her, and Joe joined her at the table. "All set?"

"Yup." She took the paintings the children had finished last week and set them out, one by each chair.

"I'd separate those two." Joe pointed to paintings signed by Tommy and Jared. "They're both sweet but get them together and. . ."

"Thanks for the warning." Sonia slipped one painting three seats down from the first.

"And here they come." Joe opened the door. His nieces Pepper and Poppy raced through. Soon two dozen chattering children filled the room. Joe's help was a godsend. Sonia didn't know how he managed children's classes on his own.

Tommy turned out to be a gap-toothed boy of six or seven. He chose paint and took pains in mixing yellow and blue together. After he finished, he painted a yellow sun with rays in one corner and added a band of blue sky across the top and green grass at the bottom before outlining a couple of fleecy clouds with blue paint. He tugged on Sonia's elbow. "I need black paint."

"We're not using black today." Sonia bent over and studied his painting. "That's such a pretty day."

"I want black paint." Tommy raised his voice, and his lower lip trembled.

Sonia tried to distract him. "I bet some yellow flowers would look nice on your grass."

The door opened, and Sonia caught a glimpse of Ty entering.

"I don't want yellow flowers. I want a soccer ball." Tears glistened in Tommy's eyes.

"Did I hear someone mention soccer? I happen to know a thing or two about soccer." Ty winked at Sonia over Tommy's head. He put his hand on the boy's shoulder. "I coached a soccer team once. And guess what?" He produced a jar of red paint and placed it in the paint tray in front of the boy. "My team always used red-and-white balls. They thought they were cool."

Tommy pushed his tongue through the gap between his teeth while he thought about it. Then he nodded, swished his paintbrush in the water jar to clean it, and painted a circle with red splotches rolling down the grass.

"Thanks." Sonia mouthed the word to Ty. A glance at the clock confirmed that class time was drawing to a close. The crush of departing parents and children and the influx of her adult class occupied the next few minutes.

Sonia gave the adult class a study in perspective, providing them with an enlarged photograph of the town park with the pagoda at the center. While they worked, she reviewed the sketchbooks the students had turned in.

She left Ty's for last, curious as to what she'd find. She suspected he was better than he claimed. Had he focused on the wetlands or something else?

The first page featured a reasonable facsimile of the Limon pond—not bad. The next page surprised her: a sketch of her profile. He had added a red tie holding her hair back as well as splashes of color in her skirt to the otherwise black-and-white sketch. In spite of the problems with proportion and other inadequacies, he had captured her attitude of intense joy. Her hand trembled. She felt like he had exposed her soul.

Sonia circled the room one by one, making suggestions on the day's assignment and discussing their sketchbooks. She didn't get to Ty before the time expired and apologized.

"Maybe we can discuss it over lunch?"

Sonia clamped her jaw together. Did he think she would drop everything when he called? "I can't do lunch today." She felt a twinge of guilt. He paid for her class and deserved her input. "Can you stay a few minutes after everyone leaves?"

A hint of disappointment flickered in Ty's eyes and then disappeared. "Sure." A few people lingered, anxious for a final word with the teacher. Eventually the door shut behind Hugh Classen and his high school students, and only she and Ty remained.

Sonia came to Ty's easel. Hmm, here she saw evidence that he couldn't draw a straight line. The vanishing point of the pagoda had shifted slightly to one side, a skewed, almost astigmatic perspective.

Ty waited beside her, his arms folded across his chest. "Don't sugarcoat it. It's as crooked as a trapezoid."

"Maybe you'll start a new trend." She retied her hair. "If I had to guess, I'd say it might be a problem with your vision."

Ty's eyebrows rose. "I've never needed glasses."

She shrugged. "It doesn't have to be much. But do you see how the center drifts left?" She traced where the lines faltered. "Maybe use a ruler and pencil to pinpoint the exact center next time. Try it before next week's class, with a street or a field or Nel's garden."

"I can do that." He pointed to the sketchbook she held in her hands. "What did you think of that?"

Heat bubbled into Sonia's cheeks. "I was surprised to see myself." She forced a laugh, a self-conscious sound. "I asked for landscapes, not portraits."

"What can I say?" Ty shrugged, but his eyes twinkled. "You were the most interesting thing around." His grin widened. "Didn't you tell us to draw whatever sparked our interest?"

Be professional. "It does show more promise than your nature sketches. It definitely conveyed emotion." Her cheeks flamed, but she persevered. "The use of red draws the eye in."

"It's impossible to picture you without color. Bright, vibrant, eye-catching colors—never pastels." Ty pointed to her outfit, a henley shirt with a riot of fall leaves against a green and brown background, matched with russet-colored corduroy pants.

"Whereas you like to wear black."

Ty wore a black cable-knit sweater with a gold chain dangling around his neck. "Yeah, me and black go way back."

◆

Ty decided to change the subject before things got any deeper. "May I escort you to the Bible study group again tomorrow?" He held his breath. She had already refused his invitation to lunch.

She hesitated an extra beat before she answered. "Sure." They worked their way around the room, putting away easels and the other supplies. "It'll be a long day, since we'll go straight from there to orchestra rehearsal."

Ty had almost forgotten about the orchestra rehearsal. He shook his head and laughed. "My father wouldn't believe it if he heard all about this. Me, at church from nine in the morning until nightfall." He looked around, curious about Sonia's progress, but didn't spot anything. "Then again, there aren't a lot of things to do in Ulysses on Sundays."

"You make it sound like church is a chore." Sonia washed a few dishes at the sink. "Are you a Christian?"

Of course Ty was a Christian. He believed there was a God, and he agreed with the principles Jesus taught. "Better than some, worse than others." He found the broom and swept the floor.

With her back to him, Sonia dug beneath the sink for a dish rack. "God doesn't grade on a curve. It's a pass/fail system. Either you're a Christian, or you're not. Either you've accepted Jesus' sacrifice for your sins, or you haven't."

"I never said I was perfect." Ty swept the debris into a dustpan. "But I'm no Hitler either."

"That doesn't matter. Pass or fail. Me. Joe. Josh. Michelle. Even Osama bin Laden." Sonia swung around to face him. "Even you. Jesus came into the world to redeem sinners from the penalty of their sins."

Redemption. That sounded like the reason Ty had come out West. Could that redemption take a different form than his carefully laid plans?

Ty shook himself internally. It couldn't be that easy. Not after what he had done.

Chapter 8

Ty listened as the oboist played an A before tightening the first string. He lifted the violin in place and played a chord, grimacing at the disharmonies. He hadn't played for so long that his instrument had gone seriously out of tune.

Around him his fellow musicians did the same. Instrumentalists ranged from a high school flutist to an octogenarian trumpeter who could still sound reveille. Ty relaxed. The magic elixir of music drew people of all different walks of life together. He felt more at home in a musical ensemble than anywhere else on earth.

Sonia watched from the sound booth, and he waved to her. An audience of one, and he was glad she was there.

Once he had tuned his violin, Ty spoke to Josh. "Say, can I have a few minutes at the end of rehearsal? There's something I'd like to discuss with the group."

"Of course. Remind me if I forget." Josh dropped his gaze to the score in front of him and made a note.

The orchestra ran through the piece scheduled for next Sunday—a catchy tune Ty hadn't heard before, perhaps one of the songs that brought the congregation to their feet during Sunday worship. The group had a pleasant if not robust sound, any missing instruments rounded out by keyboard synthesizers that could mimic almost anything.

The practice ended as they all did, with a call for prayer requests. Josh asked how Ty's first week on the job had gone. Back home, no one would have bothered. Others reported on safe travel and cancer scares, troubled marriages and births of grandchildren. This group seemed to genuinely care for one another.

Max—who played an enthusiastic tambourine when called upon—led in a closing prayer. Josh motioned for the orchestra to remain in place. "Ty has something he wants to discuss with us."

Ty stood. "After the computer died last week, I checked into options for getting it fixed." Curious glances aimed his way. "No, I'm not a computer tech, but I do work with finances. So I checked the church budget. In addition to a new computer, I noticed a number of other projects: resurfacing the parking lot, upgrading the playground. I even saw a suggestion to open a free clinic once a month."

Around him people exchanged uncertain glances.

"Look, I know times are tough. But I have an idea on a way to raise money."

"We've always trusted God to provide. If we don't get the money, I figure it's not God's will." Max's strong voice boomed from the percussion section.

Josh raised a cautionary finger. "Let's hear him out, Max. After all, the youth group raises money for mission trips."

Ty stroked his chin. "I know I haven't been here long, but I do know something about music. And you guys—both the choir and the orchestra— are great." The compliment hit home as people nodded their heads in agreement with him.

"I think if we're willing to commit to extra rehearsals, we can put on a concert in time for Thanksgiving. Some church music, sure, but also some pop and some classical." He flashed a smile. "We may even get some outside talent. My cousin Joe thinks he can get his friends who were with the Victory Singers to come."

"A concert. You mean, like charge for tickets?"

Ty shrugged. "Call it a suggested donation."

"Classical." Josh looked thoughtful. "Do you have any suggestions?"

"I'm a big fan of Mozart. Anyone interested in *A Little Night Music*?"

After they dismissed, Sonia danced down the aisle in front of Ty. "What a great idea. Maybe I can create backdrops for the different sets. Make it a class project."

"Whoa there, wait a minute." Sonia's imagination ran faster than he could keep up. "We're talking about a lot of work to finish in just five weeks. We haven't even decided on the music yet." They'd scheduled the Ulysses Harvest Concert for the first Saturday in November. By then Ty hoped to know how much longer he needed to stay in Ulysses. Perhaps he could even head home.

His caution didn't dampen Sonia's enthusiasm. "Oh that doesn't matter. If you can get the music ready, we can do our part."

Oh yes, he needed to set a departure date, or else he might never escape the dark-haired beauty with sparkling eyes. "You must be feeling better about your work."

The sparkle in her eyes caught fire. "I think this is just what I need to get my creative juices flowing. Thank you!" She threw her arms around him and kissed him on the cheek. Ty caught her face in his hands and turned it toward his. Time stopped as he gave her a chance to back away. Their lips brushed, and something inside Ty broke.

◆

Sonia relived the kiss a dozen, a hundred times. She couldn't, mustn't, allow herself to feel so strongly about a man who wasn't a Christian. No more intimate dinners. No more shared rides, even to go to church. She must stay alone. . .aloof. . . . Why did that prospect leave her cold when nothing had really changed?

Nothing had changed except Ty's presence in her life. *Oh, God, help me and open his eyes.*

Sonia kept her distance for two long weeks. When she saw Ty at class, she made sure she treated him like everyone else. At Sunday school the next day, she found a seat between two others so that Ty couldn't take the place next to her. She stayed in the sound booth as Ty put away his violin and waited until he gave up and left, his shoulders slumped in disappointment.

Josh gave her the complete list of music for the concert, and Sonia planned the backdrops. Whenever she thought about Ty, which was only ten times a day, she threw herself into her work. The Limon watercolors flew from her brush, their joy and delicate beauty making a mockery of her heaviness of heart.

No, that wasn't quite true, she decided as she added a dash of color to the coyote's tail, the last watercolor she planned. Her work provided a refuge, a place she could experience joy and escape the disappointment about Ty. She allowed herself an ironic smile. Who would have expected one kind of heartache to ease another?

Friday night, Sonia fixed herself shrimp pasta in preparation for a solitary evening. Michelle had gone out with Joe, working on wedding plans. Sonia steeled herself against the loneliness that hammered her heart.

Halfway through the pasta bowl, the front doorbell rang. Ty stood outside, a dozen red roses in hand. "May I come in?"

Sonia worked her mouth, unable to find a reason to refuse. "I'll join you on the porch. It's too nice a night to stay inside." Maybe if she stayed in full sight of the neighbors, she could keep an emotional distance from Ty. "I'll be right out." She accepted the roses with a smile, put them into a vase, and set it in the front window where he could see it. To dishonor his gift seemed churlish. She took a couple of more bites of her pasta before pouring iced tea and arranging gingersnaps on a tray for both of them.

Ty lounged in a wicker chair. When he saw her, he stood and smiled. "Tea and gingersnaps. Yum." He held the chair for her and then took the seat next to her.

They sat for a couple of minutes, silent except for the crunching of cookies. Ty ate two, wiped his mouth, and leaned forward. "Look, it doesn't take a genius to figure out you've been avoiding me. What I want to know is, why?" Pain darkened his eyes. "I thought things were going well between us. Is it something I did?"

I haven't been fair to him. Sonia agonized. Did she have enough strength to let him down gently? She wrapped her arms around her chest and rocked back and forth once. "No, it's nothing you did. It's something I did." What could she say that wouldn't sound holier-than-thou? "I made a mistake. I assumed you were a Christian, and I let things get too far."

"We didn't do anything wrong." A puzzled look twisted Ty's face. "It was just a kiss."

Sonia shook her head. "No, that's not it." She took a deep breath and swallowed. "The Bible says Christians shouldn't be yoked with unbelievers." Tears jumped into her eyes. "I like you, Ty, I really do. But I have to obey God."

Ty's face cycled through a half dozen expressions. "You're saying I'm not good enough for you."

"No, it's like I've tried to tell you. I'm not any better than you. Maybe worse, since I've hurt you and I never wanted to do that. I need Jesus as my Savior. But you. . ." A sob escaped her throat. "You don't know that yet."

Ty looked at her, an inscrutable expression on his face. "Maybe I do. More than you know."

❖

Ty stared at his hands as the fading light cast his profile into long shadows down the length of the porch. Sonia allowed the silence between them to lengthen.

"It can't be that easy." Ty broke the silence. "Redemption. Restitution. Forgiveness. All for free. At no cost to me." He shook his head. "You don't know what I've done."

"Don't misunderstand me. I'm not saying we won't suffer consequences for the things we do here." Her mouth twisted. "Like me hurting you, when you did nothing wrong. But the good news is that God wipes the slate clean when it comes to eternal matters. Life and death. Heaven and hell. And He will forgive anyone for anything when that person trusts Him."

The need to relieve himself of his burden of guilt almost overwhelmed Ty. He took a gingersnap, broke it in half, and bit down on it. It tasted like straw in his mouth, and he coughed. "You've given me a lot to think about. Can we get together tomorrow, after class? Please say yes."

Sonia looked at him as if weighing his intentions. "Yes."

They both stood, and Ty stepped off the porch.

"And Ty?"

He turned.

"I'll be praying for you."

Warmth flooded his heart. Maybe he'd get through this after all.

❖

Ty spent a lot of time finding a place to spend Saturday afternoon. When he unburdened his heart, he didn't want anyone to overhear.

In the end, Max, a choir member who had become a good friend in the short time Ty had been attending the church, suggested the perfect location—the church library. With no activities scheduled and no one expected in the building, Ty knew he had found his confessional. Would Max still want to be his friend if he knew the truth? Ty couldn't guess.

They stopped for hamburgers after class and took them to the church. Walking down the hall, they passed a poster that read THE TRUTH SHALL SET YOU FREE with a reference from John. Ty hadn't known that saying came from the Bible. Today he hoped to prove its validity.

Ty held the library door open for Sonia. He gestured to a grouping of armchairs clustered by tall windows and low bookshelves. When he shut the door behind him, he felt his last avenue of escape disappear.

"I have to say, I've never gone on a date in a church library before." Sonia sank into the nearest chair.

Ty twisted his hands in his lap. "Well, I don't know if this qualifies as a date. I need to talk with someone, and you're it."

She smiled, genuine openness lightening her features. "I'm listening."

"I haven't been entirely up front with you. I've been to Colorado before."

"I guessed as much." Sonia's answer surprised him. "But why the secrecy?" She leaned back, her hands on her knees.

So, she had guessed part of his secret. "My reasons for being here weren't exactly honorable." He felt in his pocket for a worry stone he used in times like this and rubbed his thumb over the smooth surface. "The truth is. . ." He paused. Once he said the words, he couldn't stuff the rabbit back down the hole. He hedged. "Will you promise to keep what I say between us?"

"That depends." Sonia crossed her legs. "But I won't betray your confidence just for the fun of it."

"That's fair enough." He stood abruptly and turned his back to her. "I hurt you the most of all, and I didn't even know you. I didn't think about the consequences of my actions, as you described so eloquently last night."

"What are you talking about?" Her voice strained against the dead air. When he turned, he saw the color in her cheeks had faded.

"I came to Colorado a few months ago to do some business with a man I met over the Internet. He was a criminal. A thief who specializes in stealing art." He took a breath and added the rest before he lost his courage. "I paid him to rob Joe's store."

◆

Disbelief froze Sonia's throat. In her worst flights of imagination, she had never guessed this. She had suspected Ty might have committed fraud at his father's company. But he was behind the robbery? A squeak escaped her lips. "Why?"

"Does it matter? It happened."

He had kept the painting hidden from her all this time. "It does to me."

"I asked the thief to store everything in a safe place."

"The man you saw at the museum." Sonia's voice thinned to not much more than a whisper.

"Yes. My plan was to 'discover' it and restore it to Joe. Restore my reputation at the same time, and return home a hero." He turned from the window and plopped down in the chair.

"And just when were you planning on doing that?" Sonia clasped her hands together but didn't meet his eyes.

"After I made myself indispensable to the family. I wanted the western branch of the Knight family to like me, you see. To give a good report back to my father."

"It seems to me that committing a crime is a strange way to get back in your father's good graces."

"What can I say? I figured no permanent harm would be done. I knew Joe would have insurance." He resisted the urge to squirm. "I didn't know the people involved."

Sonia made no attempt to suppress her emotions. She shook her head so hard that her whole body shuddered. "You've known where my paintings were this whole time." Her voice shook to the point where she stuttered. "You knew how I was struggling, something you could have ended at any time, and you did nothing." She stood and searched the room, grabbing a box of tissues. "I thought we were friends, maybe more. I can't believe I was falling in love with you."

She blew her nose and sat down. When she pulled out her cell phone, Ty looked alarmed. "Who are you calling?"

"Michelle. To come pick me up."

"No. Wait. I'll take you home or back to the store or wherever you want to go."

"Will you take me to get my painting?"

Ty didn't move.

"I didn't think so." She gawked at him, the tears on her cheeks magnifying her anger. "So you want me to act like nothing happened."

"Aren't you the person who's been preaching to me about forgiveness and redemption?" His voice turned cold. "I told you some things are unforgivable." He clenched his teeth. "Do what you want. I'm heading out to my car. I'll wait for you out there."

◆

Oh Lord, help. Sonia could only lift up a simple prayer. How had her efforts to share the Gospel with Ty turned into this painful quagmire?

She stared at the open cell phone in her hand and closed it with trembling fingers. She would wait, for now. On her way out, her gaze fell on the TRUTH SHALL SET YOU FREE poster. Jesus' promise mocked her hollowness of spirit. The slavery of ignorance had at least been a familiar prison.

Ty waited where he had promised. She slid into the passenger's seat, and he drove her to the parking lot behind Joe's store. "Is there any point in asking for some time before you tell the world?"

Will you promise not to tell anyone? Ty's earlier request made sense now. Sonia took a deep breath. "I don't know. I have to think about it." She looked at him directly for the first time since she had climbed in the car. "I will tell you first if I decide to talk to anyone else about it. I'll do that much."

"Thanks."

She slipped out of the car without waving good-bye and waited while he pulled out of the parking lot. She studied her hands, which had stopped trembling. A cold numbness spread through her body, enabling her to move. That was good.

Driving might clear her mind. She popped into the store and grabbed her sketchbook. She'd rather have her prayer journal, but she didn't want to stop by the house and risk running into Michelle. Pencil, sketchbook, and purse on the passenger's seat, she filled the car with gas and headed to the interstate. East, where nothing but mile after empty mile stretched? Or west, to the mountains, but also the hustle and bustle of the city? East, she decided, to an undiscovered country. Undiscovered by her, in any case.

She picked up a cup of coffee at a drive-through and headed down the road. She turned her radio to NPR, which was broadcasting classical music. She sipped her coffee, accelerated to the speed limit, and let the miles slide over her shoulders and mind while the music breathed beauty into her soul.

She saw an exit sign that promised an RV park and a restaurant nearby when the DJ announced, "Next we'll hear a performance of Mozart's *Eine kleine Nacthmusik* by the Boston Symphony Orchestra."

A Little Night Music. Tears she had held at bay jumped into Sonia's eyes, and she left the highway and found a charming town park. She turned off the engine and let her tears flow. When at last she finished, she fished tissues out of her purse, dried her nose, and gave another sob. *Enough.* Sketchbook and coffee in hand, she found a picnic table underneath an aspen that carpeted the ground with yellow leaves.

She flipped past the pages where she had drawn sketches for the backdrops at the concert. She sniffled and found a blank page, where the planned murals wouldn't mock her mood.

She drew outer space, the moon and beyond. The moon's face took on Nel's aristocratic features. She left a space for Mars, drawing Saturn and its rings that shimmered in anticipation for Joe and Michelle.

She returned to Mars, the red planet. The angry planet? Full of craters and closest to earth. Craters grew into black holes that suggested Ty's eyes and hair and mouth—silent, unknown, menacing. She pressed down with the pencil hard enough to break the lead, shocking herself in the process.

Oh God, forgive me. I don't want the sun to go down on this anger.

"But I have a right to be angry. He betrayed me. He used me." Sonia said the words aloud into the cooling afternoon air.

"But God demonstrates his own love for us in this: While we were still sinners, Christ died for us." Paul's word in Romans ran through her mind. She bit her lip.

But neither could she just let it go. She had more people to consider than herself. How about Joe, and the lawyer who had paid for her picture, and all the other artists whose works had been stolen?

And did keeping quiet really help Ty? She shook her head. Even if she removed herself from the situation, she didn't see how it helped him to benefit from a crime.

Let Me handle it. Sonia looked up at the aspen, and a breeze knocked a few leaves to the ground, the dead leaves falling so that in the spring new life could burst forth.

Maybe God wanted to do something like that with Ty. She would wait, for now.

Chapter 9

One long week passed. One where once again Sonia stayed as far away as possible from Ty, although for different reasons than the previous occasion. One when every day she prayed, "What should I do?"

She received the same answer: *Wait*.

That Saturday afternoon she scheduled the first of two planned workdays to finish the backdrops for the concert. She had sketched out large sections, making it easy for people of any skill level to slap paint on the scenes. Her adult class planned to attend, as well as a few choir and orchestra members. She had assembled all the supplies in the fellowship hall.

As people arrived, she put them in groups of two to four people. Joe, Michelle, and Nel volunteered to work on the gigantic flag that would accompany the orchestra's patriotic fanfare. Classen and his students painted a harvest cornucopia of goods produced locally. Max had volunteered as well, but so far he hadn't showed. And as for Ty—well, she didn't know whether he'd dare show his face or not. He hadn't come to the morning's class. She had seen him at choir practice, but they didn't speak.

After work began, Max came through the door, followed by Ty. "Sorry we're late, but Ty accepted my invitation to be my partner at the last minute."

Ty glanced at her. "If that's all right with you."

"Why not?" Max chortled. "Many hands make light work, my ma used to say."

Ty's dark eyes sought hers, a silent plea for acceptance evident in their depths.

"Certainly. Thank you for coming," she found herself saying. She sounded like a principal on the first day of school, but she couldn't manage any warmer welcome. "You'll be working on the Easter scene. Here is your guide." She handed them a sheet with numbers indicating the colors needed for each section of the backdrop.

Ty glanced at the sketch of three crosses on Calvary's hill and arched an eyebrow at her. *Are you preaching at me again?* he seemed to be saying. But he set to work without comment, answering Max's question about applying the paint.

Sonia moved among the volunteers, replenishing paint, making an occasional correction or clarification. Her ears tuned in to Max's hearty laugh in response to Ty's quiet murmur. She bit the inside of her cheek to keep from crying in frustration. Ty had no right to seem so happy, calm at least, not after the stunt he had pulled.

Sonia called a halt to the work at half past four. "We've made good progress today. More than halfway done. Next week we should finish early. Thanks to all of you for your help."

"No, we should be thanking you for all your work." Josh had arrived late with a few more choir members. "You and Ty." He clapped Ty, who almost dropped a dripping paintbrush, on the back. "You've both brought excitement to our town. I thank God every day for sending you here."

The blank expression in Ty's eyes gave nothing away, and the group dispersed except for Max and Ty. When Ty left the room for a moment, Max said, "Look, I don't know what's going on, but it's plain as snow in August that something's wrong between you and Ty. Give him a break, for my sake." He patted her shoulder and left as Ty returned.

Ty rubbed his chin, where a beard had grown. He looked roguishly handsome, in a serious, thoughtful kind of way. Tiny lines had appeared at the corners of his eyes, and shadows darkened the pockets beneath his eyes.

Why, he's as miserable as I am. When the realization hit Sonia, she looked at him with new eyes. "We need to talk."

◆

Sonia's words made Ty uneasy. *"I'll let you know before I tell anyone else."* Did she want to spill his secret? His mouth went as dry as the Santa Ana winds. "Yes, we do." The words scratched with static.

"Did you come with Max? Or can you stay a few minutes?"

"I brought my car, so I can stay."

Sonia went to the gym doors and looked out as if checking for unexpected company. Ty found a couple of folding chairs in a closet and set them up by the kitchen window.

When Sonia took a seat, Ty couldn't face her. He stayed standing, looking down the hallway that led to the rest of the church building. "How long do I have?"

Sonia shifted in her chair, not answering. When he allowed himself to look at her, he saw her hands folded, her eyes closed, and her mouth moving without making a sound. At length she opened her eyes. "Until the concert. God has reminded me that He can bring good out of evil, and this concert is definitely a good thing." She started to reach for him then stopped when he didn't move toward her. "After that, it's up to you. Either you tell them, or I will."

The concert. Two weeks. How could he bring his plan to fruition, as busy as he was between rehearsals and his job? *Stop making excuses.* He nodded his head. "I understand."

◆

Josh faced the sanctuary, where they had set up folding chairs to accommodate the overflow crowds. The audience remained on its feet, the applause not yet dying down. Behind the orchestra, stars and moon glittered against a night sky that reminded Ty of van Gogh's *Starry Night*. Too bad they didn't plan for an encore. Ty didn't want to play all the way through *Eine kleine Nachtmusik* again.

At length the applause died down, and Josh took the mic in his right hand. "Thank you all for coming to our Harvest Concert. Didn't our musicians do a great job?"

Again applause and cheers, and one teen—Ty recognized him from Sonia's class—shouted, "Encore!" Josh quieted them again.

"But we wouldn't have done any of this, wouldn't have dreamed of it, if it wasn't for our concertmaster Tynan Knight." He gestured for Ty to stand.

His fellow orchestra members clapped. "Speech, speech!" Max called from the percussion section.

Ty willed his hands to stay still. He didn't deserve their praise or thanks, not with his less-than-pure motives. But the audience didn't know that. Josh handed him the mic. Ty turned on the Southern charm. "I may have suggested the idea, but it's these good church folk who have done all the hard work. And Josh, who put it all together. The Romeros, who were kind enough to share some of their Victory Singers music with us." As he named each group, he paused for renewed applause.

He wanted to thank one last person. "Not to forget artist-in-residence, Sonia Oliveira, who designed and created these amazing backdrops with the help of her talented students." He saw her shake her head from her seat in the sound booth.

A wild idea occurred to him, and he turned to Josh. "I'm sure we've raised a lot of money here tonight, but I know this church has even bigger dreams. What would you folks say to an encore performance? Same time, same place, next Saturday?"

Thunderous applause greeted his suggestion. Josh's surprised expression morphed into a grin. "What say you, orchestra? Choir?"

Their smiles indicated their agreement.

Maybe Sonia would give Ty a reprieve from telling all. He risked a glance at the sound booth. She gave him a thumbs-up, and his heartbeat slowed to a normal level.

◆

Sonia looked out the window at the passing highway miles. She couldn't believe she had agreed to this expedition with Ty.

Maybe she could blame Max, who had sought her out. "See, I told you everything would work out fine." When they totaled the money raised, they had enough to replace the AV system as well as resurface the parking lot before winter weather set in. A second concert might well raise the rest of the money affected by the budget shortfall.

Whatever the reason, when Ty had invited Sonia to try out the Kit Carson County Carousel in Burlington to celebrate the success of the concert, she had agreed. What else could she say when he made arrangements for a special ride in their off-season after he learned about her passion for carousels from Joe?

"There's the exit for Burlington." From Ulysses, the interstate continued its eastward march into Kansas. Burlington was one of the last stops in Colorado.

"Good. I began to wonder if I'd missed it." They found the carousel without difficulty.

"Did you know there is a carousel inside one of the malls near Denver?"

"Joe might have mentioned it. He said you rode it every time you went to the mall together." Ty sounded amused.

"With bells and whistles on. It's as close as I get to being a cowgirl. Ride 'em, cowboy." She made an imaginary loop in the air before giggling. The levity felt good.

Sonia paused to read the sign outside the carousel. The Burlington carousel was one of only one hundred fifty carousels of the four thousand built between 1885 and 1930 still in existence. A speedster, it went twelve miles per hour instead of the more normal eight. The three rows remained stationary. The animals—described as a *menagerie*—didn't move up and down.

Ty bought tickets. "Maybe we can find a little bit of Mary Poppins's magic and ride off into a chalk drawing."

"But I didn't bring my chalk." Sonia fought to bring herself back to reality. Exchanging lighthearted banter with Ty as if nothing had changed between them bordered on ridiculous. She headed for the entrance of the twelve-sided building, but Ty whipped ahead of her and opened the door.

Sonia took her time walking around the carousel. *Menagerie* described the ride perfectly. In addition to horses, she spotted a giraffe with a snake wrapped around its neck, a zebra ridden by a gnome, even a cupid and an Arabian sheikh. She could spend hours studying the intricate carvings and delicate paint, but the operator tapped his watch.

She chose an Indian pony, complete with horseshoes it would never have worn in real life. Ty helped her onto the seat before climbing aboard a snarling black stallion next to her.

The calliope music—a Wurlitzer organ, the brochure had said—started an unexpected rendition of "Stars and Stripes Forever." She held onto the pole and leaned back, riding a bucking bronco. The tie slipped out of her hair, and dark waves cascaded down her neck and swept across her face. She glanced at Ty and saw his laugh. He raised one hand, like a rodeo rider seeking balance.

Sonia leaned forward on her horse. "Wanna race?"

"Sure."

"And they're off. . ."

The music ended before Sonia was ready.

"Who won?" Ty asked.

"Why, I did of course." They bought two more tickets and sought new mounts. This time she chose a lion while Ty stretched his long legs over a giraffe's back.

"This time I want to touch the brass ring." Ty pointed to the dispenser at the center of the carousel. "It takes courage and daring"—he swiped at it as they passed it—"to go for it." His hand landed short, and he slipped a bit in the saddle before he righted himself.

Sonia craned her neck to see. "Too bad I can't reach it from here."

Ty made three unsuccessful attempts before the music—"Turkey in the Straw" this time—ended. Mischief danced in his eyes as he turned to her. "One more ride?"

Sonia glanced at her watch. "We can if we grab some fast food and eat in the car."

"Yeah, I didn't know Burlington was quite so far away. We can't afford to get back late, not with the encore tonight."

When Ty succeeded in grabbing the ring, he whooped loud enough to be heard all the way to Ulysses. After the carousel stopped, he helped Sonia dismount. "I'll take the ring as an omen of good things to come." He took something from his pocket and flipped it into the air and then caught it in his palm.

"What's that, your good-luck charm?" Not that Sonia believed in luck, but Ty might.

"No." The laughter in his eyes died for a second. "A worry stone." He handed her the rock, granite stone polished smooth and painted with a cardinal.

The paint had almost worn off, worked by his thumb on many occasions she presumed. A worry stone made about as much sense as any other effort to find peace apart from Christ. "Does it help?"

◆

Ty took the stone back, rubbed his thumb over the surface in a single reassuring movement, and tucked it into his pocket. "Sometimes." But not today. Although the carousel provided a happy oasis, he felt the goodwill created by the day slipping away before they reached the car. He shook himself. "What do you want to eat?" He looked down the town's main street. "It looks like we have a choice of hamburgers or. . .hamburgers."

Sonia's laughter bubbled over him. "Then by all means, let's have hamburgers. Some of those square ones." She pointed to the entrance for the drive-through, and soon they returned to the highway.

They ate in companionable silence. Sonia stuck the empty containers in the trash bag Ty kept on the front seat. She settled in the passenger seat, half-turned to face him. "Are you ready to tell Joe what happened?"

The question he had avoided for a week. "Not really." Ty's right hand slid down to the pocket holding the worry stone. "But I don't think I'll ever feel ready." He swallowed. "I've left a message for my associate, to make arrangements to pick up everything. But he hasn't called me back yet." She looked at him without blinking. "Not to put you off, but it might be another week before I can get away to Denver. To bring it back."

She finally blinked and nodded once. "I can live with that. Just let me know once you've made the arrangements, okay?"

Her request reminded Ty how fragile the veneer of trust between them was. "I'll do that."

She relaxed, a hint of a smile playing around her lips. She laughed. "You don't have to look so worried. Right now focus on that brass ring and tonight's concert. I've prayed for you, and whatever else happens, I know this much: God is doing His best to shower you with His love. And I don't think you can resist Him much longer."

Then Sonia did the most astonishing thing of all. She leaned across the seat and kissed his cheek.

Chapter 10

After the kiss, Sonia retreated to her side of the car, her face turned forward so that even though Ty must see the flush spreading across her cheeks, he couldn't read her expression.

How much more foolish could she act, after her determination not to get involved with an unbeliever and after his hurtful confession of betrayal? So why did her heart feel lighter than it had for weeks?

"What was that for?" Ty's voice sounded as strangled as her throat felt.

The burn in her cheeks went up a degree. "That was meant to encourage you that you are headed in the right direction."

"Huh." He whistled a couple of measures, a tune she recognized as part of the concert's showpiece by Mozart. "I hope so. I certainly hope so." He smiled at her then, and the world tilted in the right direction. It hadn't made it all the way yet, but it was headed there.

They arrived in Ulysses with half an hour to spare. Sonia went straight to the church, while Ty stopped by the castle to change into the black-and-white attire required for the musicians. More likely, he would wear black-on-black, his preferred colors. Since Sonia hid away in the sound booth, she could wear whatever she wanted.

She grinned. People who didn't know her well sometimes accused her of dressing to draw attention to herself. But she dressed to please herself, often with colors and bling that expressed her joy. Like today. She checked the golden hoops dangling from her ear lobes and then adjusted the red knit scarf draped across one shoulder. At the church, she exchanged her ponytail for a loose chignon held in place by a large red hair clip. Her outfit had nothing to do with her date with Ty. Of course not.

Ty left her more confused than ever. She didn't understand herself. She had no business entertaining romantic notions about him. So why did she still hanker after him? She had never been the sort to fall for a bad boy, so why did she find him so attractive now?

She climbed the stairs to the sound booth and unlocked the door. Once again, she resolved to keep away from Ty and prayed for strength to follow through. Did knowing about his crime make her some kind of accessory? The thought kept coming back to plague her. She opened a bottle of water she had brought with her and took a deep drink.

Someone knocked on the door, and Josh entered. "Are you ready to check the mics?"

"Sure." Sonia glanced at the clock. Ten minutes to go before the musicians would arrive, yet already guests were filtering into the sanctuary.

Josh disappeared down the stairs and reappeared on the platform. She made minute adjustments to the mic settings until Josh flashed an okay sign. During the break, she made a bathroom run before returning to her upstairs sanctuary. From her aerie in the balcony, she watched the congregation assemble week by week. Who claimed which self-assigned seats? Which boy changed places to sit next to which girl? Which parents struggled with their babies instead of taking them to the nursery? Not that she blamed them. If she ever had a baby, she'd probably want to keep her nearby as often as possible. A baby with Ty's expressive dark eyes.

The concert had drawn many people Sonia hadn't met during her brief stint in Ulysses. Brief. She couldn't believe that a third of her six-month residence had already passed. The thought of leaving saddened her. Tonight she saw new faces, people who hadn't attended a week ago. Others had returned, bringing new people with them. People would be packed even more tightly than last week.

One man entered, alone, accepted a program, and walked down the aisle on the left-hand side of the sanctuary to the front row where he sat directly in front of the string section. Something about him tickled her memory, but then the arrival of the extended Knight family distracted her attention. A dark-haired boy joined the two girls on the pew. He looked like he could be Ty's son, and Sonia's heart faltered. Then she spotted Carrie and Steve Romero, Michelle's friends, and she recognized their son, Viktor, adopted from Romania. The couple had gone the extra mile, agreeing to return for a second concert.

The lights flickered twice, the house lights dimmed, and the spotlight landed on the cornucopia on display behind the choir. Ty and Joe, the two tallest men in the choir, centered the back row. The pianist struck the opening chords, and the second Harvest Concert opened with a medley of Thanksgiving favorites.

◆

Ty let his eyes adjust to the dimmed lights and focused on Josh's hands as he directed the choir. He did a better job of bringing them in than at cutting them off, and Ty winced as he heard multiple hisses when they sang "Jesus." But the audience didn't appear to care, clapping at the end of the medley as if they were listening to the Brooklyn Tabernacle Choir.

The lights dimmed again, and several teens exchanged the cornucopia for the Easter scene Ty had painted with Max.

As far as Ty was concerned, crucifixion ranked right up there with chopping off a thief's hand as cruel and unusual punishment. He changed the music in his folder, glad they didn't go in for that today. Or else he would never confess his misdeeds.

But these church people believed Jesus was more than an innocent man put to death for a crime he didn't commit—a fate endured by thousands before and since. They insisted Jesus came to earth to die on that cross and somehow by doing so He made it possible for God to forgive sin—all sin. Oh and by the way, He had risen from the dead and lived still today.

It didn't make sense, nor did the songs they sang, although Ty enjoyed the gospel feel of "The Old Rugged Cross." But when he saw the faces of the people around him, he sensed their sincerity. They meant every word.

They ended the section with a song called "Because He Lives," and he envied the rest of the choir for the peace they radiated. Some of them faced tough times. He had heard the prayer requests. Yet they faced the future with an unbelievable certainty and peace.

When the set ended, he felt relieved. The choir filed from the stage while the Romeros set up for their section. Ty fetched his violin and lingered near the door as Steve and Carrie sang a couple of duets before inviting their son to join them. Next Viktor performed on a child's recorder with his father's accompaniment. The boy played the simple instrument with a pure, clear sound. He had the makings of a fine musician.

When the Romeros finished their music and the audience rose to its feet, Ty prepared to take his place with the orchestra waiting to file onto the stage. But while he still stood in the door, a man turned in his direction and smiled.

Kirby Kent.

"Go ahead." Josh motioned for the orchestra to enter.

Ty shook himself. Later he could ask questions. For now he had to keep up the pretense and deliver the performance of his life. He smiled at Josh and took his place in line behind the viola player. From his seat at the edge of the platform, he could see Kirby Kent clearly.

During the intermission, the prop handlers had exchanged the Easter scene for the large flag, so well executed that it looked like a stiff Colorado wind rippled through it. The orchestra embarked on a set of patriotic songs. Four of the church's veterans carried the colors during "It's a Grand Old Flag"; a children's choir joined them for a song that ran through the capitals of all fifty states; and the congregation joined in singing "God Bless America." The music featured the brass section—that octogenarian trumpeter blew his horn like he was twenty years old. Max exchanged his tambourine for a triangle during several songs.

The fanfare kept Ty from worrying about Kent until the next break, when they exchanged the flag for the night sky. Kent spoke with the people to his left—no one Ty recognized, people who had squeezed in as the concert started. On Kent's other side sat Pastor Perkins and his wife. Mrs. Perkins might wrangle the story from Kent, something Ty hoped to avoid.

Ty fixed his attention on Mozart's *Night Music*. Josh lifted his baton, and within the first three notes, the magic of the music carried Ty to a place where nothing existed except beauty and wholeness.

At the end of the concert, the pastor welcomed the guests and extended a low-key invitation to return for Sunday services. Expecting a request for an encore this time, the orchestra reprised the last section of *Night Music*. Then the full houselights came on, and relief and exultation flowed through the group in equal measure. Ty didn't move. Max stopped by his chair. "Thank God He sent you our way, brother. It's sure been good to have you here."

By Max's own admission, he had once been a drunkard and "the worst of sinners." If Ty could believe that transformation, maybe there was hope for him after all.

Then he saw Kent talking with the pastor and pointing to him, and Ty recognized the futility of those hopes. There would be no second chances for him.

❖

Sonia watched as Ty stepped down from the platform and spoke with the pastor and the same man she had noticed earlier. A memory shifted, and she remembered where she had seen the stranger before: at the art museum in Denver. The thief.

For a wild moment, her heart sped faster. Perhaps he had brought the artwork to Ulysses. Perhaps even now her painting waited in a van in the parking lot. But then she saw Ty's face. His charming facade slipped for a moment, replaced with ill humor. The stranger was all smiles, chatting with Pastor and Mrs. Perkins. When Ty made to leave, the stranger barred his way, still smiling while he gestured outside. Ty nodded before following the other musicians out the side door.

"Pray for him." The Holy Spirit whispered the words into Sonia's heart. *"He's in danger."*

Sonia closed up the sound booth, saying short prayers with each step. Turning off the sound board, she asked, "Lord, silence the tempter's schemes." Shutting down the lights, she said, "Lord, lead him into Your light." As she locked the door behind her, she cried, "Let him open the door to his heart when You knock."

A handful of people stopped her to praise the magnificent backdrops. Sonia forced herself to civility while her eyes roamed the sanctuary, but Ty and the stranger had disappeared. Her high school students carted the backdrops back to the fellowship hall under Hugh Classen's supervision. He asked, "Do you think we could take these to school?"

"I don't know why not, but check with Josh. And guys? Thanks for all your help." The kids had saved the day in the props department, and she wanted to recognize their contribution.

Michelle found her. "Hey, Ty stopped me on his way out and asked if he could have a rain check. And I said I'd be happy to take you home with me."

Sonia closed her eyes and sent up another plea for help.

"Sonia?"

She opened her eyes. "Sure. That sounds fine." Let her get home and start filling the pages of her prayer journal.

◆

Ty arrived at the motel first, located on the way out of town. He climbed out of his seat and then realized he didn't know which room Kent had rented, so he leaned against the hood of the car.

Kent arrived a couple of minutes later and took his time getting out of the car. He laughed as he opened the door with an old-fashioned key. "You got quite a gig going on here. You could have knocked me over with a feather when I heard about it."

"How did you find me?" Ty had never told Kent his real name.

"Please. Give me some credit. I've known who you were almost from the beginning, but I played along." Kent chortled. "Bruce Wayne, or should I say Ty Knight, sitting as concertmaster for a church orchestra." He threw his head back and laughed. "Gotta love it."

Ty gritted his teeth. He didn't need more reminders of how ridiculous his grand scheme appeared. "What are you doing down here, Kent? I don't think you came all the way to Ulysses just to laugh at me."

"Why no, compadre. You called me, remember?" Kent fished around in the refrigerator. "Care to join me for a drink?" He pulled out two longnecks. "Champagne might be more appropriate, but I don't think this place offers room service."

All Ty wanted was to leave as soon as possible. He shook his head.

"Bruce, my friend, you need to relax." Kent sipped his beer. He opened the second bottle and thrust it at Ty.

"I said I don't want any. I'll take club soda, if you have it."

"Since when have you become too good for a drink?" Kent rummaged through the refrigerator and pulled out a bottle of water.

"Since forever. That's one vice I managed to avoid."

"Take a seat and sit a spell." Kent suited his action to his words.

"I'm not here on a social call, Kent. Cut to the chase."

Kent's bonhomie vanished. He unzipped the suitcase lying on the luggage rack and dug into one of the side pockets. Ty saw a stuffed envelope, and the dark feeling that had dogged him all night crept as high as his eyeballs.

"Here you go, partner. Ten thousand smackers. I found a *very* accommodating buyer." Kent thrust the envelope at Ty, but he didn't take it, and it fell to the floor, raining hundreds on the way down.

"What did you do that for?" Kent bent over to pick up the cash.

Ty grabbed him by both arms and made him look at him. "You sold the pieces?"

"Every last one of them." Kent licked his thumb and counted the bills in his hand. "Found someone who made me an offer I couldn't refuse."

Blackness closed Ty's eyes, and he grabbed the edge of the desk to keep his balance. "That wasn't our arrangement."

"The way you've been dragging your feet, I had to do something. You told me one month, and it's been two already with no end in sight. What with you insisting I pay megabucks for a climate-controlled environment, every month that passes cuts into my profits."

"I paid you plenty." Everything Ty had saved plus a little bit more.

Kent shook his head. "Never would have agreed if I'd known you would take so long about it." He slapped Ty on the back.

Ty fought the urge to punch him in the nose. "It was never about the money, you fool. You've ruined everything I set out to do." As angry as a caged tiger, and feeling as deadly, Ty paced the room. He turned a murderous glance on Kent that had none of the forgiveness Jesus preached. "I don't want your money. And God help me if I ever see you again. You'd better pray to whatever god you believe in that never happens." He clamped his jaw shut and walked out. He slammed the door behind him and fell behind the steering wheel of his car before he buried his head in his hands.

◆

Michelle couldn't stop talking about the success of the concert and didn't seem to notice Sonia's quiet demeanor. "People raved about the backdrops."

"That's nice." Sonia uttered a variation of the same response she had made to Michelle's numerous observations and comments ever since they had arrived home. She wished her roommate had gone with her fiancé to celebrate, but they had decided to call it an early night because of church in the morning.

The worst is over. The same Spirit that had urged Sonia to pray for Ty earlier in the evening spoke words of reassurance, and the heaviness in her heart lifted. With her first genuine smile of the night, she said, "I'm glad it went so well. I wish I could be here to see all the changes happen." Although she hoped to return to her life in Denver, she had rarely invested so much of herself in something—in someone.

"I know what you mean." Michelle beamed. "When I think how close I came to turning up my nose at everything Ulysses—and Joe, mostly, of course—has to offer, why, I could die inside." She sucked on a flexi-straw she put in her glass of tea. "Have you considered moving out here? We'd love to have you."

The possibility had crossed Sonia's mind more than once. But she'd be an even bigger fool if she entertained thoughts of staying in the same town with one old boyfriend and one new, both of whom had hurt her in his own way. "I don't think that's a good idea."

"Oh well." Amusement glinted in Michelle's green eyes. "No harm in asking." She emptied the ice in her glass into the sink and threw away the straw. "I think I'll take a shower and get to bed. Otherwise I'll never wake up in the morning."

"Sleep tight." Sonia shifted in her chair. No point in going to bed just yet. She wouldn't sleep. She headed for the kitchen. Maybe baking brownies would calm her down. The simple task wouldn't keep her up much longer. An hour later, she removed the pan from the oven. She cut a small wedge and carried it into her bedroom, ready to take out her prayer journal until dawn's early light broke in the east. In the end, her prayer centered on a single image, Ty kneeling before the cross.

◆

"So now you have no idea who this Kent guy sold the pieces to?" *Should I have spoken up earlier?* Sonia didn't get a moment alone with Ty until Sunday afternoon, when she caught a ride with him to the castle after church.

Ty's hands gripped the steering wheel. "No. I asked, but he wouldn't say. Offered me money instead." He rubbed the smooth surface like his worry stone. "I didn't take it, if you're wondering."

Sonia grabbed onto that ray of hope. First her paintings were stolen. Then she thought she had found them. Now they were lost again. She reminded herself that peace came from the Lord and not her circumstances. "What do you plan to do next?"

The tortured look on Ty's face tore a hole in Sonia's heart. "I don't know. What can I do?"

"Tell Joe." So far, hiding the truth had brought them nothing but pain and hardship.

"I would, if I thought it would make a difference. At least, I think I would." Ty's laugh sounded forced. "But what good would it do? The insurance company has already paid him. His store is thriving." He shrugged. "It might help me if I confess, but I don't see that it helps anyone else."

"Oh, Ty. You still want to be the knight that rides in and saves the day, don't you?"

Chapter 11

I s saving the day like a knight of old such a terrible thing? I have an aunt who lives in a castle. My dream seems tame compared to that." Ty parked the car in the castle drive.

Sonia didn't open the door. "You're trying to change yourself on the outside, but it won't work that way. Only in Christ can you be that shining new man—a change that happens from the inside out."

"Yeah, yeah, that's what you keep saying." Ty shook his head. "But it's not for me. Even if God could forgive me, I've hurt too many people." He looked at Sonia, and she said a quick prayer. "What I want to do is to find out who has the stuff and try to get it back."

His suggestion had merit. "Very well. I will help you look. For now."

"Thank you." Ty relaxed his grip on the steering wheel. "I want to make this right, if I can." He looked at Sonia sideways. "When and where shall we meet to discuss our strategy?"

Good question. They couldn't go to the church library every time they wanted a private conversation. She bit her bottom lip. "Joe will be gone on Thursday afternoon. That might be a good time." She returned his gaze. "But if you don't have some kind of lead by then, I'm going to tell Joe." She thinned her lips into a smile. "Correction. *You're* going to tell Joe, but I will go with you."

He huffed out a breath. "Fair enough." He scampered from his side of the car to open the passenger door and offered her his arm. "For now let's celebrate the success of the concert with the others. That seems to be all anyone wants to talk about these days."

"Absolutely." Sonia accepted his arm, and they walked through the doorway together.

❖

Monday morning Ty was tempted to call in sick. He woke up feeling queasy, although he suspected no antibiotics could make him better. But as a temporary employee who barely kept up with the workload, he felt a responsibility to report to the office. At the end of a long day, Ty headed straight for the castle. He would spend the evening hunting down Kent's contact. Since Aunt Nel had wireless Internet, he could check out the web in the privacy of his room.

Leaves once again lay scattered across the ground, and Ty had told Aunt Nel he would take care of the lawn. He groaned at the delay, but he refused to renege on his promise.

He chuckled. When had he become so responsible? Perhaps he was more worried about the questions his failure might raise. *What were you doing all alone in your room all night, Ty? Oh, I was just looking for fences who handle stolen artwork, that's all.*

And suppose the predicted snow did fall? Frowning, he looked down the sweeping drive. Would Aunt Nel expect him to shovel the long driveway? Did she engage a service? Own a snowblower? He should find out.

He couldn't complain though. He liked helping Aunt Nel. Who would have guessed? The son who rarely initiated a phone call to his own mother found pleasure in doing little things to help his aunt quite apart from any benefit to his master plan.

Between raking leaves, eating supper, and engaging in small talk with Aunt Nel, Ty didn't make it to his room before the evening news came on at ten. HD television, another luxury that Nel provided in the anachronistic castle. Ty grinned to himself. Any modern monarchs who lived in castles would insist on the latest technology. He turned to The Weather Channel, hoping he might catch a prediction covering eastern Colorado rather than the Denver metropolitan area. While he waited, he booted up his computer. He rubbed his eyes and plugged in a coffeemaker that made two-cup servings. It was going to be a long night.

While the computer hummed to life, the weather forecaster predicted freezing temperatures with the possibility of snow flurries. Ty debated how best to attack the problem in front of him. Locating a thief had proved surprisingly easy. Ty contacted frat buddies who adhered to the same moral code he had—or lack thereof. Within days, he had located a friend of a friend who put him in touch with Kent.

Given the way things turned out, Ty wished he had examined Kent's bona fides more closely. Maybe he would have discovered the man couldn't be trusted, or perhaps there was no such thing as honor among thieves. He couldn't worry about that now; today's problem required his attention.

Ty considered his dilemma. Could the same friend of a friend direct him to the party he sought? Would he ask uncomfortable questions? Question his motives?

Ty stared at the computer screen and debated about Googling pawnshops. He couldn't imagine a neighborhood pawnbroker handling high-end art, but neither would any reputable art dealer deal in art with a questionable provenance. So he needed to locate someone willing to deal under the table. But how?

Perhaps he could pretend to be a buyer. Ty shifted in his chair uncomfortably. He'd had enough of pretense to last a lifetime.

And could he locate that person without going to Denver? Something he couldn't do before his meeting with Sonia on Thursday. She wouldn't accept another delay.

Ty thought back to his circle of so-called friends from college and the ones whose homes he had visited. Did any of them display pricey art on the walls?

He shook his head. He remembered a few collectors of European art, but no contemporary Western artists. For most of his friends, the United States ended with the Appalachian Mountains for all intents and purposes. Until he came out West, he had been the same way.

Something snagged his memory though, someone who might know a friend of a friend who could point him in the right direction. It was there, and then it wasn't. He didn't waste time trying to pull the memory back. Either he would remember or not. If he forced it, he'd only push the memory further away.

For now he checked out the few pawnshops that had web pages. Something there might point him in the right direction.

◆

Sonia had taken Monday off, as she often did. Between the hurried pace of concert preparation and her worries about Ty, she needed the break. She returned to the studio on Tuesday, concerned that the revelations of the weekend might force another artist's block on her.

She arrived at the studio before Joe opened his store for business. Glancing at the folder holding her watercolors, she considered going through them. But no, that would only postpone the moment of truth. She set up her easel and went to the back room where the canvas she had prepped awaited her. Leaving it in its wrapping, she carried it to the studio and placed it on the easel. After a prayer for courage, she removed the cover.

Pale golden light emanated from the skylight overhead and on the canvas, and Sonia's mind filled with images of ducks in flight. Satisfied she had the shape and shades of the marsh vegetation fixed in her mind, she dabbed several shades of green on her palette.

She worked without stopping, painting each stalk of grass, creating layers over and under and around the swaying grass, until she completed the near side of the pond. She didn't feel the passage of time until Joe knocked and came in, as he ordinarily did before he left for the day. Hastily she pulled the covering over the painting.

He smiled. "You don't need to do that. I know better than to look. Do you need anything for your master's class tonight?"

He always asked, and she always gave the same answer. "No. I'm all set. I'll close up for a few minutes while I grab a salad at home."

"If I didn't know about that pumpkin cheesecake waiting for your class, I'd worry about you getting enough to eat." He shook his head.

"Don't worry, I'll try to save you a piece."

"Good. Make it two if you can. I'd like to share it with Michelle."

"It's a deal." In fact, Sonia had taken to making double batches of whatever she brought to class—one for her students and another for the various members of the Knight clan who wandered through from time to time, always eager to sample one of her creations. Joe left, and she ran home for a quick bite to eat.

The master's class made for a long day, but she looked forward to the gathering. Most of her students in Denver chose to make the weekly commute to Ulysses, and they often stayed late into the night for coffee and a chat.

The late nights were well worth it. The participants came from Denver's burgeoning art community, more her peers than her students. But she took pleasure in passing on what she had learned, even when that included her struggles. They had supported her through her recent struggles, and she had shared the watercolor series with them. Next week, maybe, she'd have something to show them on the larger canvas. Or not. She didn't know when she'd be ready to show that to anyone else.

Sonia was eating a chef's salad when her first student arrived—Lydia Costillo, one of her oldest friends. Generally as mild-mannered as Sonia was flamboyant, tonight Lydia shimmered with excitement as she burst into the room. "Brr, it's cold out there." She hung her coat on one of the pegs along the wall where the children's art was stored.

She poured herself a cup of coffee and took the seat across from Sonia. "I couldn't wait to get here tonight. I'm so excited for you. I almost called but decided nah, you were probably busy."

Sonia tilted her head, trying to guess what had her friend so excited. "I didn't think you knew about the concert."

"Concert? What concert?" Lydia shook her short brown curls. "I'm talking about your painting. I saw *Light Shining through Darkness* hanging at a very prestigious address yesterday when I went there trying to sell one of my pieces. No luck."

Sonia blinked. "You saw my painting? Where?"

"Oh, come on, Sonia, you don't have to be shy with me." Lydia patted her arm. "It's me. Your God came through for you big-time." She buried her nose in her cup. "You must have known the police had found it when we were here last week. I'm surprised you didn't tell us—me at least—about it." Shadows darkened her gray eyes.

"But Lydia." Sonia stood and circled the room before turning around and glaring at her friend, who deserved better. She softened her stance, but her hands fiddled with the broach that kept her scarf in place around her shoulders. "I didn't know about it. As far as I'm aware, no one has solved the crime."

Confusion clouded Lydia's eyes "But then how. . .when. . .did Mr. Big Bucks Jones acquire it?" The patron she mentioned was well-known in Denver and beyond, his nickname earned by his generous support of the arts. "That doesn't make sense." The man had earned a reputation for acumen and honesty. "He was so pleased to have an original 'Sonia.'" Lydia blinked several times as if she could clear up the confusion.

Sonia clicked her tongue. "So he shouldn't mind answering a few questions for me." She leveled her gaze at Lydia. "Please don't mention this to anyone else, okay?"

"If you say so." The conversation ended when the door opened and two more students came in.

Tonight Sonia's pleasure in the master's class flagged. Her attention wandered so far from her students that she wondered if she should refund their money. Paying for classes plus driving the hundred-plus miles each way represented a serious investment, and she regretted giving less than 100 percent.

Maybe they sensed her distracted manner, because the normally lively after-class discussion lagged. One by one, they made their excuses due to cold and snow flurries—more expected in Denver than here in Ulysses—and took their leave.

Lydia lingered after the others. "Man, Sonia, I feel terrible about what happened. Like maybe I should report it to the police or something."

"Don't do that." What a mess that would create. "I'll talk to Mr. Jones myself. After all, we don't want to upset one of our best customers, do we?" She managed a laugh. "And I'd like to get a look at the painting, to make sure it's really mine." She sighed. "Although I'm sure you're right."

"If you say so." Lydia reached for her coat. "Well, I'd better get going down the road with the others. Please let me know what happens, won't you? I feel kind of responsible."

Sonia hugged her friend, another acquaintance so close to coming to know the Lord and yet still so far. "I'll tell you when I can. I appreciate your friendship." When Lydia left, Sonia sagged against the table. She fought the urge to call Ty with the news. Why trouble him until she was certain? He couldn't take the day off to go to Denver tomorrow, but she could. She'd hunt down the man who was so happy to have an original and do some snooping of her own.

Sonia left a message for Joe not to expect her on Wednesday morning and that she didn't know when she would return. As long as she was in the city, she'd buy a few supplies Joe didn't carry in stock. Maybe she could stop by the facility where she had put her things in storage. *No.* When she left in September, a thundercloud had taken up permanent residence in her spirit. She didn't want to risk rekindling the nightmare.

In spite of the late night, she awoke early in the morning, and she timed her drive to avoid the morning rush hour. She called Mr. Jones, introducing herself and requesting an appointment before she left. While she drove west, she counted the mile markers and pondered her approach to her painting's new owner. She couldn't exactly ask, "Who sold you the painting?" He'd expect her to know. Could she imply more than one dealer had handled it?

Sonia battled her conscience. She didn't have to lie outright. She'd be speaking nothing more than the truth if she said she didn't know which dealer had handled the sale.

Denver traffic slowed her down a couple of miles after passing the exit to the airport. Mr. Jones wouldn't believe her. He would expect the dealer to have confirmed the sale with Sonia before closing the deal.

Her phone buzzed, and she wondered if Mr. Jones had returned her call. Before she hit the Mousetrap, where the east-west interstate crossed the north-south corridor, she pulled off the highway and found a parking lot before opening her phone.

Mr. Jones had indeed called and left a message. "Miss Oliveira, how delightful to hear from you. Mr. Cipoletti indicated you were a shy sort, although I dearly wanted to meet you. Yes, please do come by my house." He gave the address. "I shall be home any time after one."

And just like that, Sonia knew the answer: Tony Cipoletti, a flashy new dealer, had set up business in LoDo, lower downtown Denver where a lot of galleries operated, a couple of years ago. He had appeared on the Denver scene shortly after Joe left the city for Ulysses. She didn't especially like him; he treated the artists themselves like contestants on a game show. However, a lot of buyers loved him, and he had built a loyal clientele. No whisper of scandal had attached to his enterprise as far as Sonia knew.

So Mr. Cipoletti had told Mr. Jones that Sonia was shy? She looked at her apparel for the day—a fairly conservative outfit, suited to the nature of the day's business. But she still chose her trademark colors: a silky gold blouse tucked into cinnamon-brown slacks over Italian leather boots—the footwear a rare indulgence for her. What impression would she make on the collector? She touched the opal earrings in her ears. After she checked her makeup in her compact mirror, she reapplied lipstick. Two hours remained until one— enough time to pick up the supplies she needed and get a bite to eat.

◆

"You saw your painting? In this guy's house?" Ty couldn't believe his ears. Sonia had spilled the news as soon as he picked her up for dinner before choir rehearsal on Thursday night.

Sonia nodded. "I didn't tell him anything was wrong. I'm not sure what the right thing to do is."

Conflicting emotions raced through Ty. Relief surged because Sonia now knew what had happened to her painting. Worry intruded when he wondered whether all the rest of the merchandise had already been sold.

"I know who sold it." Sonia's eyes sparkled.

"Tony Cipoletti would be my guess."

Chapter 12

Ty allowed himself a satisfied smile when his answer surprised Sonia. "How did you find out?" Concern darkened her eyes. She could never hide her feelings as long as anyone could see her face. Her eyes said more than her words did.

"You gave me an ultimatum, remember?"

"I remember." Her voice was soft and low. "But I didn't think you could pull it off."

"I wasn't sure, not until you confirmed my guess." He found himself shy about explaining. The old-boy network that engaged in business by any means, both fair and foul, didn't reflect well on him. He chuckled inwardly. He had lost the right to worry about that when he engaged Kent to rob Joe's store. "I knew a guy in college. Old money. Always had an eye for art. When I was at his house for an alumni event, I commented on some truly remarkable pieces hanging on his walls." He shrugged. "He gave me a wink and a nod and said I'd be surprised what I could manage if I didn't worry too much about legal niceties."

Sonia nodded, her expression not changing. "And he knew Cipoletti."

"Well, he started me on the path that led me to him. I, uh, indicated I might be interested in attaining some American Western art."

Sonia grinned as if he handed her diamond earrings. "We've found the fence. Things are looking up. We just have to decide how to handle Cipoletti." Some of her enthusiasm dimmed. "It's still a mess, Ty. The time has come for you to tell your family."

My family. How dear they had become to him, to the point where Aunt Nel's stubborn cough worried him. Although Ty looked at Sonia, tears clouded his vision and he couldn't read her expression. "Will you be with me when I confess?"

She stretched her arm and touched his elbow. "Of course I will. I wouldn't ask you to do it on your own."

"The family is getting together for dinner at the castle on Saturday night." He took a deep breath. "I'll tell them then."

Pride and confidence shone from Sonia's eyes. With her by his side, he might survive admitting his wrongdoing after all.

◆

On Friday, Sonia threw herself into her new painting with a passion as excessive as the depression that had dogged her for the past few months. Coming so close to resolving the robbery and Ty's part in it freed something in her. She spent a few hours experimenting with colors to get the right hues of blue and green and gray that mottled the water in the wetlands. Sky and bracken, birds and soil all contributed to the color that tinged a clear liquid, a phenomenon that never ceased to amaze her. Only God would, *could*, create such beauty out of nothing.

At last, after her lunch, she dipped her brush in white paint and placed the first brushstrokes of a duck paddling in the water to the canvas. Years ago, she had read "ducks don't get wet" in a children's book. The oil on their feathers kept them as dry as a rain slicker. God made each creature suited to its unique environment, another miracle.

She was adding the distinctive teal stripe to the duck when Joe appeared in the doorway. Was it closing time already? The skylight suggested midafternoon.

"Sonia. I gotta go, but I thought you would want to know." He was stuffing his arms into his coat sleeves as he talked. "It's Mum. Brian's worried she has pneumonia—he's taking her to the hospital."

"Oh no." Sonia put her hand to her heart. "Is there anything I can do?"

"Pray." The grim look on his face tugged at Sonia's heart, for both Nel and Joe. Joe had returned to Ulysses to look after his mother. If anything happened to her, he would be devastated.

And not only Joe. "Have you called Ty?"

The shamed look on Joe's face gave her the answer. "Call him for me, please?" He headed for the door.

"And where's the hospital?" Ulysses had an urgent care clinic at Brian's office, but patients needing hospital care had to go elsewhere.

Joe gave her directions. "Michelle is calling Brian's afternoon appointments to reschedule. She'll drive over later. You can catch a ride with her if you like. You'll lock up for me, won't you?"

"Of course."

Joe whisked out the door, and his car disappeared from view seconds later.

Sonia picked up her brush to finish the duck, but she couldn't get Nel out of her mind. She covered the canvas and called Ty's work number.

"Ulysses Home Furnishings, Ty Knight speaking."

"Ty, it's Sonia."

"Hey, beautiful, what's up?"

"Brian is sending Nel to the hospital. He thinks she has pneumonia."

◆

"Pneumonia? I had no idea it was that bad." Ty slumped down in his chair. "I told her not to go out in that snow yesterday. But she was determined to get to her ladies' meeting." His throat went dry. *Aunt Nel, sick.* It couldn't happen, shouldn't happen, to such a good person.

"You sound like a mother hen."

He grimaced. "Well, Aunt Nel brings that out in people. I don't know why." He twisted the phone cord with his free hand. "Look, I leave work in an hour. Do you want to come with me to the hospital?"

"Yes. I'll head home and fix us a sack supper. Pick me up there."

They said good-bye, and Ty stared at the unfinished spreadsheet in front of him. He had hoped to finish inputting the data from the week's sales to get a head start on Monday's work. He riffled through the remaining files on his desk. Not possible without overtime, and tonight he would leave at four on the dot. He checked the computer clock. Forty-seven minutes to go, forty-two if he stopped five minutes early to close up shop. He hadn't resorted to that trick since starting this job.

He glanced over his cubicle wall. The sales manager brought out upholstery swatches for a prospective buyer to examine. What would Rob say if he had met Ty in his old life, where his expected forty-hour workweek as often as not turned into thirty-five hours or less; and he spent his time in the office on the phone or playing with Facebook. No wonder he had overlooked the fraud. He shook his head. Rob praised Ty for his diligence and work ethic and hinted at a permanent job even after Barb returned from maternity leave.

But Ty doubted they could handle another salaried position over the long haul unless business picked up. He entered data as fast as he could and then verified the numbers. Rob stopped by his desk and added another file to the stack. "Closed the deal. It's time to close up shop. Or are you staying late again?"

Ty glanced at the clock—3:59. He shook his head. "Not tonight." He logged out and turned off the computer.

"Do you and Sonia have plans?"

Everyone seemed to know every step he and Sonia made, one of the disadvantages of small-town life. He smiled. Not that he wanted to hide his relationship with Sonia. "We might." Then his smile faded. *Aunt Nel.* He considered telling Rob but decided against it. If he did that, everyone in Ulysses would know before midnight via the town grapevine.

"See you Monday then." Rob waved good-bye.

Just in case Joe hadn't called the church, Ty checked the numbers stored in his cell phone and dialed Josh's direct number. He left a message, explaining what little he knew about Nel's condition while he made his way out to his car.

Ty closed the phone as he slid into his seat. Shaking his head, he inserted his key into the ignition. How he had changed, indeed, to call on a church for prayer. Among this lot, the response came as naturally as breathing. He had seen enough answers to prayer in his brief time here not to dismiss its power. Aunt Nel deserved that much, even if he didn't.

Minutes later, he arrived in front of the house Sonia shared with Michelle. Sonia hurried out the door, a cooler in her hand, and tucked it away in the backseat before she joined him in the front. "All set." She buckled her seat belt. "Head south on the main drag, and turn east at the first intersection out of town."

He swung the car onto Main Street.

She uncapped a bottle of cherry cola—his favorite—and placed it in the cup holder before adding a bottle of water for herself. "Which do you want, ham or turkey?"

"Ham." He peeked into the cooler. "With some of those cheese curls. Looks like you packed enough for an army."

She tore open the cheese curls, and he grabbed a couple. Unwrapping a sandwich, she handed it to him. "I figured that everyone would be hungry by now, and they won't want to leave."

"Good idea." He bit into his sandwich. Sonia made an art form out of sandwich fixings. Her father was right, she'd make a great chef—a great quality in a wife.

Sonia made a phone call and took a couple of small bites when they placed her on hold. "Is Nel Knight still in the ER? She's been admitted to the hospital? What's her room number? 312? Thanks." She closed the phone.

"She's already been admitted? That doesn't sound good." They covered the thirty miles to the hospital in twenty minutes. Ty followed the H signs and found the facility with minimal fuss. He had to park at some distance from the entrance. He jumped out and took two steps before he remembered Sonia. The door closed behind him, and she caught up with him.

"I hope we don't have to worry about visiting hours." Sonia tugged the lapels of her red woolen coat together.

"We're family. Those are usually magic words."

"Sounds good. As long as they don't ask me about a wedding ring."

Wedding ring. He could see it now, a marquis-cut diamond surrounded by rubies. He covered his confusion by stepping ahead to open the doors, but they slid open automatically. No one manned the information desk at the center of the lobby. A sign announced DIAL 0 FOR INFORMATION AFTER 4 PM.

Sonia held the cooler.

"Here, let me take that." Ty wasn't shining in the courtesy department tonight, and he resolved not to let stress take over.

"The elevators are that way." Sonia pressed the Up arrow.

The hospital was small compared to the few he had ever visited: three stories, with a slightly taller doctors' building next door. They would have more facilities than Brian's clinic, but was it enough? Aunt Nel deserved the best of care.

The elevator parked on the second floor without moving. "Let's take the stairs." Balancing the cooler against his chest, he opened the door to the stairwell. Sonia entered ahead of him, her heels clattering on the concrete steps. The two sets of stairs were no worse than the climb to his turret bedroom every night.

They opened the door to the third floor. "There's the nurses' station." Sonia headed to the right, and he followed. "We're looking for Nel Knight."

She spoke to a young woman with a friendly face who wore a loose tunic with cuddly kittens printed against a pink background. Her name tag read WENDY. "Mrs. Knight is having a breathing treatment right now. Her family is in the waiting room—that way."

"Thanks." Ty spotted Joe's broad back ahead, and his steps sped up.

When they entered the room, Michelle turned a tear-stained face in their direction. "Ty, Sonia. You made it." Only Brian was absent, probably supervising his mother's breathing treatment. "This is so awful."

"What's the verdict?" Michelle's demeanor scared Ty.

"Mum would say we're making a big ado about nothing." Joe had wilted. "She insists it's just a winter cold."

"That's what she said to me, even when I heard her coughing hard enough to bring down the Grand Canyon." Ty shook himself. "I should have insisted she go to see Brian earlier."

Judy glanced up from the book she was reading to her girls. "Oh, Ty. Joe. No one can convince Nel of anything once she's made up her mind. Believe me, Brian has tried."

Poppy, the younger girl, removed her thumb from her mouth. "Is Grannie going to be all right?"

"Of course she will, honey. Daddy is taking good care of her."

"I'm hungry." Pepper stared at the cooler in Ty's hand. "Did you bring something to eat?"

"I sure did." Sonia took the cooler from Ty. "I figured two growing girls like you and Poppy would be hungry, so I brought sandwiches and crackers."

"And chocolate chip cookies!" Pepper reached for one.

"Better eat your sandwich first. I have ham or turkey."

Ty wanted to laugh at the expression on Pepper's face.

"Or. . .I made a couple of fluffernutters."

"I want a fufnutter." Poppy looked puzzled. "What's a fufnutter?"

"Peanut butter and marshmallow fluff. It was one of my favorite sandwiches when I was a girl."

"I want a fufnutter." Poppy bit into it. "I like it.'

"Me, too." Pepper ate hers quickly. "Do you have another one?"

Laughter rippled through the adults, easing some of the tension.

Michelle shook her head when Sonia offered her food. "I'm not hungry." Still, she accepted the turkey sandwich Sonia placed in her hand. Soon the food had been consumed.

Sonia had known how to help the girls. Ty had observed the same quality in the kids' class. She'd be a great mother someday. He cleared his throat. Why did this family emergency make him think of Sonia in terms of family—their own nuclear family?

He helped clear the trash from the meal. Brian joined them and looked into the empty cooler. Ty felt a sting of guilt for the second sandwich he had consumed.

"I brought you a ham sandwich. That's all that's left. I hope it's okay." Bless Sonia for setting it aside before they devoured everything.

"Thanks." Brian took a bite, chewed, and swallowed. "Mum is breathing better. She's asleep for now. I don't want anyone to bother her, so let's stay out of her room." He ate another bite of sandwich. "Ty, Sonia, thanks for coming—and for the food."

"How is Aunt Nel?" Ty glanced at the girls, their attention centered on a cartoon. He lowered his voice. "How serious is it?"

"We've established that it is a virulent strain of pneumonia. Unfortunately, she's allergic to a long list of antibiotics, but she handles penicillin without a problem. We'll X-ray her lungs again tomorrow to check for any improvement."

"Her lungs. Is there a pulmonologist on staff here?"

"Yes. I've been in touch with him. He's on call. If Mum takes a turn for the worse tonight, he'll come in. Otherwise, he'll check on her tomorrow." Brian passed a tired hand over his forehead. "We went to med school together." He turned to his wife. "Judy?"

"I know. I'll take the girls home to bed." She hugged her husband. "Call me, though, if there's any change in Nel's condition."

"Of course." He held her against his chest before releasing her with a kiss.

"See you later, folks." Judy took the girls' hands and headed for the elevator.

Brian sat down next to Ty. "I'm sorry you came over here, and now you can't see Mum."

"We understand. There's a reason these are called waiting rooms." Sonia settled next to Michelle, who was holding Joe's hand. Leaning forward, Sonia leafed through the magazines on the coffee table. "Preseason college football. How. . .current. Ah, here's a one with suggestions on how to free your creative spirit. Should be interesting." She turned to the table of contents.

Ty picked up the sports magazine she had discarded, but college football didn't interest him, especially preseason predictions about teams that by now were either headed home or to conference playoffs. Joe changed the TV channel to a Nuggets' basketball game. Brian closed his eyes, and within minutes his chest rose and fell in a steady rhythm. How could he sleep, Ty wondered. Maybe he had developed the knack for taking catnaps during his residency.

Ty didn't want to read or watch television, and he couldn't sleep. Restless, he stood. "I'm going downstairs for a little while."

Sonia looked up from her magazine. "Do you want me to come with you?"

He shook his head and headed for the elevators at the end of the hall. In the lobby, a small sign pointed to various departments. His eyes landed on CHAPEL, and he moved in that direction. A note read, FOR THE CHAPLAIN, DIAL EXT. 223. Ty didn't want the chaplain, so he opened the door.

Light bounced off serene blue and green walls. One of Sonia's watercolors from Limon would do well on these walls, leading a person to worship. He knew decorators used blue and green to create calm environments. This place would sooth the spirit of petitioners beseeching the Almighty for a sick loved one.

A simple wooden cross adorned the podium. He glanced at the brochure he had picked up by the door, which listed nondenominational services on Saturdays and Sundays for any who wished to attend. He was grateful for the solitude, with no other voices competing for his attention. He and God, talking about Aunt Nel.

The problem was he didn't know how to start. He stared at the cross. Sonia would know what to say. So would Max. For that matter, probably everybody in the choir would know what to do, except for him.

How had Sonia described prayer? A conversation, talking to God and listening for His answer. Posture didn't matter, even though whenever they prayed at church, everyone closed their eyes. He didn't have to speak aloud because God knew his thoughts.

That was a scary thought. He didn't want anyone listening to his private thoughts, and certainly not God. Okay. He could also pray out loud or with images—something Sonia described as hurts too deep for words.

Checking the hall to make sure no one else wanted to enter, Ty closed the door behind him. The sound of the door opening would alert him if someone else entered the chapel. He sat on the front pew and stared at the cross again.

"Okay, God, Sonia and Joe and even Max all say You want me to come to You with my problems. That it doesn't matter how bad I've screwed up. In fact, they say You don't have much patience for people who think they're A-okay. Maybe You're like AA that way, huh? I have to admit I have a problem before I can change."

He stopped, not certain what to say next. "But even You must know Aunt Nel is one of the best people on this earth. If You were ever going to pay attention to someone because she's a good person, well, that would be Aunt Nel." He paused. "I might as well say what I'm thinking, since You already know. I wonder if I would be a different man if I had grown up with Aunt Nel and Uncle Brian. Not that I blame my parents for my own bad choices."

He heard the door open, and he stopped speaking out loud, hoping his words hadn't carried through the wall. He shut his eyes, his thoughts a rambling morass of doubts and pleas. He felt a weight settle next to him on the pew.

Chapter 13

I thought I might find you here, brother."

Max. Ty's eyes flew open.

"I came as soon as I heard Nel was in the hospital."

Funny, Ty didn't peg Max as the type to hang out in hospital rooms.

"I figured you'd be here and you could use a friend right about now."

"You got that right."

Max didn't say anything more for a moment but took in the room with his usual wide-eyed interest. "This is a pretty place. A good place to come and meet with God." He put his hand on Ty's shoulder. "Is that what you're doing here, son? Meeting with God?"

Ty turned to the man who had become a good friend in a short time. "I think maybe I am."

"You can't fool me, not when you've been where I've been. You got something weighing heavy on your heart. And if I had to guess, I'd say you've never even crossed the starting line. That you're still fighting it out with God as to whether you need saving or not."

"That's not the question. I know I'm—to use the word I've heard at church—a sinner." Ty looked at the cross. "And I know that you believe Jesus died for everyone's sins. That's the sticking point. Some things are just plain unforgivable."

Max didn't speak for a minute, and Ty wondered if he was marshalling arguments against Ty's disbelief. But Max took the conversation in a different direction. "You know I used to drink."

Ty nodded. "So you say."

"I drank for years. Pretty near died from it. Couldn't hold down a job. My wife had the patience of a saint, but finally she had enough and went to her mother's when the bank threatened to foreclose on our house."

"I don't need to hear this." Ty shifted uncomfortably on the pew.

"I think you do." Max dropped his hand from Ty's shoulder. "The day I got the foreclosure papers, I took my first drink at daybreak and didn't let up all day. I tried to start a blaze in the fireplace. When the kindling didn't catch fire, I poured lighter fluid over the pile and lit a match." He scratched his chin. "Well, it don't take much imagination to guess what happened. By God's grace I got out of there, but we lost everything." He stared at the cross without seeming to see what was in front of him. "Amazing grace that saved a wretch like me."

Ty didn't respond, not sure what he would say. Back in the day, Max didn't only have a problem with alcohol, he'd almost killed himself and his family in the process. Ty found it hard to believe, knowing the man he was today.

"So I don't know what's on your heart, son—and I don't need to know, that's between you and God—but you can't tell me you've done worse than I done. And then there's another story. From the Bible. The apostle Paul."

"The guy who wrote all those books of the New Testament?"

"The same guy. Only before he became a Christian, he made it his mission in life to hunt down and kill as many Christians as he could. After God got ahold of him, he called himself the chief of sinners, and I guess he figured he had a claim to the name after what he done." Max wagged a finger at Ty. "And you can't tell me you've killed bunches of people for believing in Jesus."

Ty shook his head. "No, I haven't."

"So you see? God forgave Paul, and He forgave me. He'll forgive you, for sure. All you have to do is ask."

A light turned on in Ty's soul. *All I have to do is ask.*

"Will you. . .pray with me?"

"That I will, son. That I will."

In the most natural way in the world, both men got to their knees and went before God.

◆

After Sonia finished reading the magazine cover to cover, even filling out the crossword puzzle, she joined Joe in watching the basketball game. Halftime arrived, and Joe turned down the volume. "Ty's been gone a long time."

Sonia shifted in her chair. "Yes, he has. I wonder what's keeping him. I'll hunt him down." She stood, stretched, and walked in the direction of the elevator. The door opened and Ty came out, followed by Max. The two men beamed with an enthusiasm that could have lit a thousand-watt bulb if they could have found a way to plug it into a socket.

"Max! How kind of you to come. And Ty—you look—I don't know. Happy."

The two men looked at each other and laughed. Ty's smile widened to the point where his facial muscles must hurt. "I asked Jesus to be my Savior."

"Oh, oh, oh." Her voice rose higher with each syllable. "I'm so happy for you." She hugged him. "Come on, you have to tell the others." She giggled. "What wonderful news!" She danced ahead of them down the hall, holding Ty's hand the whole while.

They burst into the room. Joe glanced up, curious, and stood. "What has you so excited?"

Their joy must seem strange given the reason for their presence at the hospital.

"This is what the Bible means when it talks about confessing the Lord before men. Tell the world." Max grinned.

"I just gave my life to the Lord." Ty showed no hesitation in saying the words.

Joe jumped in the air. "Hallelujah!" He hugged his cousin. "That's the best news I've heard all day." Michelle added her congratulations.

Brian returned from his latest check on Nel. "Mum's awake now, and we can visit for a few minutes."

"Let's go tell her your news." Nothing could equal the thrill of a new baby Christian. The news would perk up Nel for sure. Sonia tugged Ty's arm, and he trotted behind her down the hall. The others followed. They tiptoed in. Nel looked drained and scary, the way people did when hooked up to IVs and monitors. An oxygen mask hid Nel's nose and mouth, but her face looked serene. She flicked her hand, gesturing them closer to the bed. Max came in with the other family members. "It's good to see you, dears." The mask distorted her words.

Joe took his mother's hand on one side while Michelle stood on the other. Brian checked the monitor and nodded, apparently satisfied with the readings. Sonia and Ty hung back with Max.

"Is that you, Max Collier?" Nel pressed a button and brought her bed to a sitting position. "How kind of you to come."

Max approached the bed. "It's my pleasure, Nel." He winked. "We have some good news for you."

She smiled, a little weakly. "Do tell me. I could use some good news." She coughed, a horrible hacking sound, and then sipped on her water jug. Her eyes swept the room and landed on Ty. "Tell me, Ty."

Sonia saw him hesitate, a childlike shyness creeping over his features. She gave his hand a reassuring squeeze. "Go ahead. Tell her."

"Are the two of you. . ."

Sonia and Ty looked at each other and laughed. Michelle giggled.

"Very well. What has happened?"

"Oh, not much." Ty's grin burst out again. "I just asked Jesus to be my Savior tonight, that's all."

"Oh, praise God, praise God."

A nurse—Wendy, the one with the kitty-cat tunic—stuck her head in the door. "You folks are having entirely too much fun."

Brian lost some of his professional demeanor and grinned at her. "Well, you see, we just learned my cousin here"—he slung his arm around Ty's shoulders—"has made things right with God. And we're all rejoicing."

"Well, praise the Lord and hallelujah." She winked. "You bottle up some of that good feeling and take it again tomorrow, Mrs. Knight. That's good news indeed."

God had blessed Nel with a Christian nurse.

"Ty. As my new Christian brother, I'm going to ask a favor of you. Please find the Bible I'm sure is in that table drawer and read me Psalm 34." Nel's voice grew weaker with each word, and Sonia worried they had tired her out.

"Sure thing." The drawer was empty but for the Bible. "Psalms is in the middle, right?" He stuck his thumb in the center and turned a few pages. "Here it is." He positioned the volume in his hands like a piece of music and began reading. " 'I will extol the Lord at all times; his praise will always be on my lips.' "

Sonia glanced at Nel and thought she saw her lips moving underneath the oxygen mask.

Ty continued through the end of the psalm. " 'The Lord will rescue his servants; no one who takes refuge in him will be condemned.' "

"Amen. 'Therefore, there is now no condemnation for those who are in Christ Jesus,' and that means you, brother." Max clapped Ty on the back. "I'd best be heading home. But I'll check back with you tomorrow. You know the whole church is praying for you, Nel."

"I know."

"Thanks for everything." Sonia hugged the friendly bear of a man.

"Sure thing." He left.

Sonia glanced at the clock. The time neared eleven; she had class in a little more than ten hours.

"Do you need to go?" Ty asked.

Sonia looked at Nel, whose eyes closed for a second before she forced them open again. Sonia nodded.

Brian frowned at the group. "All of you, get on home and rest. I'll call you if anything changes." The fact he would stay the night with his mother went without saying.

Nel roused herself long enough to give Ty one last smile before he left, and then he and Sonia waited at the elevator with Joe and Michelle. Michelle stood in the shelter of Joe's arms, their burden halved by sharing it together. Perhaps someday she and Ty. . .now that he was a Christian. . .Sonia shook her head. It was far too soon to think such a thing, not with the issue of the stolen artwork still unresolved.

The temperature had dropped twenty degrees since their arrival earlier in the evening, and Sonia skipped ahead to the car as fast as she could. Closing the door cut the windchill even before the heater kicked in. "Brr."

Ty turned the engine on and let it idle for a few moments until the hot air began circulating. "I know I need to tell the family about what I did. And I'm ready to do it. I figure it's what Jesus would want me to do." He threw his head back against the headrest and grinned. "I can't believe I just said that. If you had told me when we drove over here tonight that I would be asking 'What would Jesus do?' before the night was over, I would have laughed."

"I know. Isn't it wonderful?" Warm air filled the car, and drowsiness crept over Sonia. But first, Ty's concern. "But with Nel being sick. . ."

"It's not the right time." Ty shook his head. "What's the saying, take one step forward, two steps back? That's what this whole business with the robbery feels like. I want to do the right thing, but does it have to be so difficult?" Some of the joy that had poured out of him all night dimmed.

"God's ways aren't ours. But His timing is perfect." *Cliché, Sonia, cliché.* "You'll know when the time is right, and now I bet you'll have the courage, too."

"I sure hope so." He put the gear in reverse and backed out of the parking space. "I guess I have a lot of praying to do."

"If it means anything, I'll be praying, too. I have been all along."

"I know." He turned his face to her, the smile back in place. "And it does mean a lot. More than you know."

◆

A phone call from Joe before the children's class reassured Sonia that Nel remained in stable condition, if not making rapid progress. She put aside her concerns for her friend as she worked with the children. Today was the third class of the second session, and she asked the class to use shapes to create pictures. Last week she had provided cutout squares, diamonds, and circles for them to paste onto paper. This week she encouraged them to paint using the shapes they had studied.

When the class ended, she missed Ty's help in setting up for the second session. Parents picking up their children asked after Nel, and Sonia repeated what little she knew. Nel remained in serious, but stable, condition.

After the adult class had gathered, her students had little interest in the lesson she had prepared. "We're all worried about Mrs. Knight," one of the high schoolers who had returned for the second session said. "Can we make something you can take to her? A giant get-well card or something?"

The others in the class murmured their agreement.

"That's a wonderful idea."

Sonia set out two of the largest sheets of drawing paper she had with her—eighteen inches by twenty-four. She added an assortment of colored pens, chalk, magic markers, and the like. She enjoyed watching which medium each student chose. The girl who had suggested the card turned out to have a fair hand for calligraphy, and she wrote "Get Well Soon" in the middle. The rest of the hour flew by as each person filled the paper with miniature sketches and personal notes and get-well wishes.

After her students left, Lydia Costillo called.

"I didn't expect to hear from you today." Sonia searched for a bag big enough to hold the get-well card.

"I stopped by Tony Cipoletti's gallery last night, and I saw a few of the stolen items. You know, Jonah's wood carvings and your angel pictures and one of Passo's paintings."

"That sounds about right." Anger rang in Sonia's voice. "Does he think nobody will notice?"

"That's why I'm calling. I think I should call the police or something. He could make it all disappear, you know?"

All too easily. But. . .Sonia didn't want the police involved, not yet. "Is his store open on Sundays?"

"Let me check." Sonia heard pages rustling. "No. He doesn't open again until Monday morning."

"I'll be there bright and early. Let's check it out together."

Chapter 14

Ty didn't think he had ever seen a prettier Sunday. In fact, the whole world seemed different. Max said his perception changed because Ty had become a different person—a "new creation." The phrase "born again" had always sounded like theological hyperbole until he had experienced it for himself. He may have been a Christian for only a day and a half, but he knew something fundamental had changed deep inside his spirit.

During the invitation at the end of the morning service, Ty almost trotted to the front. He couldn't wait to proclaim to the world what God had done in his heart. Max stood with him. The only sadness came from the absence of his family, who still kept Aunt Nel company at the hospital.

When the congregation formed a line to congratulate Ty, he caught sight of Sonia bounding down the stairs from the sound booth, a big smile illuminating her face. Genuine happiness beamed from her dark eyes as she joined the line. Full of emotion, those eyes, and this time they reflected the good news the two of them shared.

When Sonia reached Ty, she threw her arms around his neck and kissed his cheek. "I couldn't be happier."

"You had a lot to do with my decision." He hugged her back and released her. "I was listening, even if it didn't seem like it."

"If you were listening to anybody, it was the Holy Spirit. Praise the Lord!"

"Praise the Lord indeed." And the words felt natural. Whoever would have thought? "Wait for me?"

"Sure." She wiggled her fingers at him as she moved forward, greeting the pastor before exiting through the door. Ty followed her progress until the next person took the pastor's hand, and he returned his attention to the well-wishers.

◆

Ty was a Christian. Sonia hadn't stopped grinning ever since she heard the news on Friday night. When he'd asked, "Wait for me?" her heart answered for her. *Yes, I'll wait for you. Today, tomorrow—however long it takes.*

Josh found her to tell her the church was accepting bids on the new AV system. "Would you like to see the demonstration?"

"Of course. Although Barb is the best one to do that. She's the real expert."

"Barb will be there. She's on the committee. But we'd value your input as well."

Josh told her the meeting time, a late-afternoon appointment. With every week that passed, Sonia became more involved with the local community, more than she ever had in Denver. She could have a full life here, a satisfying life. She heard laughter and saw Ty leaving the sanctuary with Max and Pastor Perkins. They headed in her direction. A very satisfying life, indeed, if it included the special man God had for her.

If Ty was that man. If he straightened out the mess he had created. If he stayed out of jail. She shuddered.

"You cold?" Ty asked.

"No." No physical chill made her shudder, only a glimpse into a future she didn't want to contemplate. Hopefully tomorrow she and Lydia would uncover more answers. "Are we going to see Nel this afternoon?"

A slow smile warmed Ty's face. "I like the way you said 'we.'"

Heat flooded her cheeks.

"Take the girl out, before she faints dead away." Max's eyes twinkled. "She's dying of love."

If possible, her face flamed hotter.

"Nothing to be embarrassed about. Young love." Max put an arm around each of them and brought them close with a bear hug. "You know I'm just joshing you. Tell Nel we're all praying for her."

Ty didn't seem in the least embarrassed by Max's pronouncement. "I expect she'll have several visitors this afternoon. People kept asking for her when they came through the line."

"Then we'd better be going." Sonia hugged Max. "Thanks for everything. You're a true friend."

Ty's prediction proved true. Pastor Perkins arrived a few minutes after Ty and Sonia. As soon as he left, someone else arrived until Brian banned any further visitors when the cafeteria delivered Nel's supper.

"Perhaps I should leave." Sonia walked down the hall with Michelle to the snack machine. "I'm not family."

"No worries. You will be, if Ty has anything to say in the matter." Michelle giggled. "And now that he's a Christian, there's nothing standing in the way."

Sonia shook her head. Michelle didn't know the full story. "Then I'll stay." She stared at the selections. She would have made something to eat, but she had run out of sandwich fixings and hadn't made it to the store in time to pick up more. Peanut butter on cheese crackers gave her the illusion of protein. On a whim, she added peanut butter cups. The sugar rush would keep her going for a little while at least.

Back in the room, Nel had finished supper and closed her eyes. Brian smiled when Michelle and Sonia came in. "I was just saying that if Mum's X-rays come back okay tomorrow, she can go home."

"That's wonderful news."

Ty turned from his spot by the window. "I'll tell my boss I need a couple of days off, so I can stay home with her."

"You don't have to do that." Joe accepted the diet Dr Pepper Michelle gave him.

"I know I don't, but I want to."

"If I know Mum, she'll chase you out before the day is over." Joe grinned. "May you succeed where others have failed."

"I'll do my best."

◆

When Nel was released from the hospital late Monday morning, she insisted on going to a restaurant for real food. Ty operated on automatic. The time had come to tell all. Sonia wasn't there, but now that Nel's health had improved, he could carry the burden no longer. Must be that new-man business. He'd had to bite his tongue to keep from telling them over the weekend.

After the waitress brought their drinks and salads, Ty cleared his throat. "There's something I've been needing to tell you folks for a while."

The chatter around the table slowed. Joe put his hand to his heart. "If you want our permission to ask Sonia to marry you, you have it."

Laughter rippled around the circle, and Ty felt warmth creep into his cheeks. Only Aunt Nel gazed at him with steady blue eyes, signaling her readiness to hear whatever he had to say.

"It's not that. Besides, I believe it's traditional to ask her father's permission first." He chuckled briefly. "No, it's nothing so happy."

Michelle leaned forward. "What is it, Ty?" She looked at the others for support. "Are you leaving Ulysses?"

"I may have to. Look, I don't know how to say this except to come out with it. I arranged to have Joe's store robbed." He looked at his plate, unwilling to meet their eyes, but he couldn't avoid hearing the disbelieving gasps.

"You what?" Joe leaned back in his chair, away from Ty. "But that's not possible."

"Tell us about it, Ty." Nel's gentle voice cut through the stuttered reactions. "I suspect you need to unburden your heart as much as we need to hear your story."

One look into his aunt's calm blue eyes stiffened Ty's resolve. "It began when they discovered the fraud in Dad's company." He told it all. How his father blamed him for not discovering the fraud earlier. How he banished him to Colorado. How Ty wanted to return home a hero—a real Knight. He allowed himself a black laugh at that.

The family picked at their food and listened in silence, except for an occasional question for clarification. Ty's food grew cold as he continued his narrative. He didn't think he could stomach food in any case. Not while he explained his grand scheme to "discover" the artwork and take credit for it.

How he figured no real harm would be done since he planned on returning the merchandise.

"But then I came here and met all of you and Sonia and Max and. . .at last. . .came face-to-face with the Lord."

Joe maintained a neutral expression. Brian tilted his head to one side, as if weighing the evidence. Aunt Nel gave a slight nod of her head. "There's more."

"Here's the truly bad news. While I was waiting for the right moment for discovery, my associate sold the art. All of it."

"Was it the man you were talking to after the concert last week?" Joe asked. Ty didn't know he had observed the exchange.

Ty shifted, uncomfortable with pointing the finger at Kent for a theft he had initiated. But he wouldn't lie. "Yes, that was him."

"Where is it now? Do you know?" Michelle asked.

Ty sipped his now-cold coffee. "He wouldn't tell me. He, um, tried to split the profits with me and call it even, but I refused." He looked up. "I've looked into it. I think he might have gone to a dealer named Tony Cipoletti."

"Cipoletti. I've heard of him." Joe's face tightened in concentration. "In fact, I believe I met him at the Cherry Creek Arts Festival this summer."

Ty set down the coffee cup, unwilling to drink any more. "I'm not sure what to do next. Whether to go to the police and confess or go after Cipoletti and try to get the stuff back or what. I'll do whatever you think is best." He looked at each person, one at a time. "What I've done is terrible. I'll understand if you can't forgive me." He almost choked on the words. He let his gaze linger on Aunt Nel, sensing the others would follow her lead.

She didn't return his gaze, instead closing her eyes. He chastised himself. *You've gone and tired her out, and she's just recovering from pneumonia.*

But when she opened her eyes, they were clear, and her cheeks bloomed a healthy pink. "Stuff and nonsense, Ty. Of course we forgive you. How can we refuse to forgive you when Christ has already paid the price?" She looked at the gathered family. "I assume I speak for everyone here?"

"Of course." Michelle spoke first.

"I have to agree," Brian said.

"Cousin?" Ty waited for Joe's response. Of the gathered family, Joe had the most reason to resist.

When he spoke, though, his words surprised Ty. "Back when the store was first robbed, Sonia said maybe the thief needed the message of her painting more than any of us did. And I guess she was right. In a roundabout way, it brought you to the Lord." He smiled. "But I'm glad to know the full story." He started to speak, stopped, and then continued. "You're my cousin by your first birth and my brother by your second. Of course I forgive you."

Feeling lighter than he had for days—weeks—months—Ty signaled the waitress. "Could you box up this food for me?"

After they settled their bill a few minutes later, Joe asked Ty, "Do you mind if I ride with you?"

"Sure." Maybe Joe wanted to share what he had started to say at the table.

"Head for the highway." Joe buckled in. "We're going to Denver."

Ty found the northbound county road and headed out. "What about Aunt Nel?"

"I asked Judy to stay with her until we get back. She's a nurse. She'll probably take better care of Mum than either one of us could."

Ty adjusted the rearview mirror. "Why Denver? If you want to take me to the police. . ."

Joe shook his head. "We're not going to the police here. My priority is getting the art back. Not just for me, but for the artists. Not to mention shutting down a dishonest dealer. And Denver is the place to go for that."

"I can't argue with that." They reached the interstate and headed west.

◆

Sonia met Lydia at one of the several coffee shops dotting Larimer Street. Now that the time had arrived to check out Cipoletti's gallery, she found herself lingering over a cup of coffee that was big enough to float a small battleship. She took advantage of the time to describe the theft in greater detail—not Ty's part in it, but the rest. She owed her friend that much. "For now, I only want to verify that Cipoletti has the remaining pieces from Joe's store." She spread computer printouts in front of them. "These are from Joe's records. Go ahead and study them. I've pretty much committed them to memory."

Right after the robbery, long before she met Ty, Sonia had pored over the records. She needed to remind herself she wasn't the only victim. The affected artists had met once, to grieve their losses and debate what to do next. Since the police had no leads, they concluded they couldn't do much, except to pursue their next projects.

"I'm pretty sure I saw a couple of these." Lydia laid down the pages. "If we're going to do this. . ."

"We should get going." The weather had warmed during the past couple of days. Sonia still wore her red woolen coat, but no longer needed her hat or scarf. They could see Cipoletti's gallery—called simply CIPOLETTI'S FINE ARTS—a couple of blocks away.

They made their way through the stream of people scurrying about on business here in the center of the city. Sonia glanced up at the loft apartments, which many of the city's upwardly mobile population called home. They must have a fantastic view of the mountains from their aeries. Before she left town today, she'd treat herself to a drive down a westbound street to soak in the soaring Rockies before she returned to plains-bound Ulysses.

Ulysses might be bound by the plains, but she had found herself again during her stay in the small town. Today's venture meant one more step on the way. Spirit lifting, she picked up her pace and headed for the store with a simple yet elegant sign, a large *C* with an *F* on the left and an *A* on the right.

They paused to look at the display in the front window, in case Cipoletti had chanced such a public display. He hadn't. Peering inside, Sonia spotted a young woman sitting atop a high stool. No sign of Cipoletti—she relaxed a smidgen. "Let's do it."

Lydia pulled the door handle and held it open for Sonia.

The clerk, a young woman, perhaps a college student from the nearby Auraria campus, looked up, but when Sonia didn't signal her, she returned her attention to her textbook.

"Feels like coming home, doesn't it?" Lydia paused in front of a painting where a blue columbine exploded on the canvas.

"Cipoletti does have a knack for display." Sonia allowed herself a moment to study the brushwork that brought the flower to such vibrant life. But this wasn't her reason for coming, and she moved on to the next painting. They circled the showroom but found no sign of the missing pieces.

Sonia whispered, "Am I missing something? They can't all be gone."

The clerk may have sensed the customers' waning interest. She closed the book she was reading—a math workbook—and slid off the stool. "May I help you?"

"When I was here on Friday night, I saw this absolutely adorable wood carving of a couple singing a duet. But I don't see it here today." Lydia blinked as if expecting the piece to magically appear.

"Oh, I know the one you mean. I liked that one, too. It has sold, but we have others by the same artist. Would you like to see them?"

"Oh yes. My parents' twenty-fifth anniversary is coming up, and I'd love to get them something special." Lydia followed the clerk into a back room, with Sonia tagging along behind. As soon as they passed through the door, Sonia spotted several items from the stolen inventory.

"My boss isn't sure if he's ready to part with these pieces, but I'm sure we can reach an agreement if the price is right. I especially like this one." The clerk gestured to a carving of a bride and groom dancing.

While the clerk made her sales pitch, Sonia wandered the room. In all, she counted twelve of the missing pieces.

A door opened, and Tony Cipoletti came in

Too late, Sonia realized her danger.

"Well, if it isn't Sonia Oliveira. How kind of you to stop by."

Chapter 15

W e've been aware of Mr. Cipoletti's activities for some time, but we've lacked sufficient evidence to bring about a conviction." A petite Latina detective sat straight in her chair, tapping the file in front of her with the end of a pencil.

Ty and Joe had decided they needed to involve the Denver police to succeed in tracking down Cipoletti. They hadn't expected to learn the dealer was already under investigation. The receptionist at the central police station directed them to Detective Yolanda Torres as soon as they mentioned art theft. The detective frowned at the interruption, ready to dismiss them as a waste of time, until they had uttered the magic words: Tony Cipoletti.

"What do you know about Cipoletti?"

Joe looked at Ty and gestured, as if to say, "It's your story."

Ty sucked in his breath. "I, um, know someone who used Mr. Cipoletti to fence several pieces of art."

Detective Torres's perfectly penciled eyebrows rose a fraction of an inch. "Who is it?"

Ty looked at Joe, who said, "We're willing to tell you, of course, but it's in connection with a theft that took place in Ulysses. So who has jurisdiction over the robbery?"

Torres shook her head. "I need his name. If he brought stolen goods to someone in this city, that crime took place in *my* jurisdiction."

Although he hoped it wouldn't come to this, Ty had known he would have to reveal the truth. "His name is Kirby Kent." He paused a long beat. "I should also tell you that I hired Kent to commit the robbery."

Torres rocked back in her chair. "*You* were involved with the robbery?" Her eyes swung between Ty and Joe. "Insurance fraud?"

"Nothing like that." *Worse and worse, if they start suspecting Joe of any part in the robbery.* "I had a crazy plan that I was going to 'find' the stolen merchandise and return it to the family. Crazy, I know. By the time I realized I needed to come clean, Kent had sold the stuff without my knowledge."

"To Cipoletti."

"Yes."

Torres turned hard eyes on Ty. "And you are coming to me now because. . . ?"

"I recently became a Christian. I want to make this right, if I can."

Torres looked skeptical, and Joe took up the tale. "We want to recover the stolen items. Before they disappear again into private collections. We know one painting at least has already passed into private hands. Here." He extracted a sheaf of papers from a briefcase. "Here are the photos and descriptions of the stolen pieces. The one that's reappeared is the painting *Light Shining through Darkness*." He explained the discovery of the sale.

Torres went through the pages without speaking, taking her time with each one. When she finished, she picked up her phone, keeping her eyes on the two cousins. "I need a search warrant for Cipoletti Fine Arts." She listened. "Of course today." She made a note and hung up the phone. "We'll take it from here. Mr. Knight—Joe—I'll let you know if we find your inventory." She rose to her feet, and Ty and Joe stood with her. "I'm sure you gentlemen have other things to do with your day. Although, Mr. Knight? Mr. Ty Knight?"

Ty resisted the urge to squirm. "Yes, ma'am?"

"Don't make any plans to leave Colorado anytime soon."

"I wasn't planning on it."

She escorted them to the elevator. When they reached the first floor, Ty's mouth dried. Surrounded by institutional gray walls, metal detectors, and officers with guns strapped to their belts, he couldn't help but think of a possible future in prison. *God, give me courage to face my crimes.*

Joe checked his cell. "Michelle called. Marked urgent. I'll call as soon as we get outside." He grinned. "If they find the inventory today, we'll have all kinds of reasons to celebrate tonight."

Ty would find it hard to celebrate with the possibility of jail time hanging over his head. Maybe Joe didn't realize the fear gripping him.

They walked into sunshine and a temperature hovering around forty degrees, fairly temperate. Joe flipped open his cell. "Hi, sweetheart. You called?"

Joe stopped walking and raised his hand, signaling Ty should stop moving forward. "She's not?" He listened some more. "And she's not answering her phone either?" Another pause. "Yes, please pray."

Joe turned concerned blue eyes on his cousin. "Michelle found a note Sonia wrote on the phone pad."

Ty's blood stopped flowing, and he felt light-headed. "What did it say?"

"Three words: *Lydia, Cipoletti, Monday.* Lydia is one of the students who comes from Denver to Sonia's master class. Michelle thinks the two of them went to confront Cipoletti. She's not at the studio. And there's more." He put his hand on Ty's shoulder, a lifeline offering support. "She's not answering her phone either. Michelle has been trying to reach her for two hours."

◆

Cipoletti turned to the college student. "Kimberly, go ahead and take your lunch break. I'll look after the store. I might be gone when you come back."

Kimberly looked resigned to missing out on a sales commission, which suggested her innocence in Cipoletti's shenanigans, and left as requested.

"We'll just be leaving then." Sonia's voice sounded high and strained to her own ears. "I heard such wonderful things about your gallery, I had to check it out." She pivoted on her right foot.

"Not so fast." Cipoletti interposed his body between the two women and the exit and reached behind him. "You're coming with me."

"Really, that's not necessary."

Cipoletti held up an X-ACTO knife, the tool of choice for cutting mats for paintings—deadly sharp. "Don't make me use this."

"Do as he says, Sonia," Lydia pleaded.

Sonia lifted her chin. "At least let my friend go."

Cipoletti looked amused. "She's the one who led you to me. I saw her in my store the other day. I want both of you." Holding the knife in his right hand, he rummaged through the drawer with his left and extracted packing tape. His eyes glinted with pleasure as he flicked the blade open and swished it inches away from their wrists as he cut the tape before wrapping their hands together. For a final touch, he added strips across their mouths. "This way." He pointed toward the back door where Sonia saw a panel van with the FCA logo on the side.

Run, Sonia, run. Don't climb in like a helpless victim. She took a single step backward. The knife flashed, and Lydia cried out. He had nicked her forearm with the knife. "I wouldn't do that if I were you."

Swallowing, Sonia stopped moving. She couldn't climb into the van without the use of her hands. Cipoletti opened the door to the back of the van and half lifted, half pushed her in after Lydia. She fell onto the floor beside her friend. He climbed behind the wheel and started the engine.

Sonia prayed, keeping her eyes open to communicate encouragement to Lydia. Her friend looked downright terrified, and who could blame her? The nick on her arm bled freely and looked terrible, but it wasn't. . .fatal.

She couldn't quite believe he would harm them. Fencing stolen goods could almost be considered a victimless crime. Not violent, in any case. But the memory of the ease with which he flashed that knife around gave Sonia chills. She continued praying.

Where was he taking them? Sonia had read thrillers where the victim kept track of direction by counting left and right turns, but she couldn't do it. She guessed they had left the downtown area, and the continuing stops and starts told her they were stuck in city traffic. So, probably not the highway. He wasn't headed to some secluded mountain hideaway, but her imagination could conjure a dozen different locations in the city where she had no desire to go.

What options did they have? Maybe when they reached their destination she could kick her feet out and catch Cipoletti in a vulnerable spot.

The van stopped—it could have been fifteen minutes, although it felt more like an hour—and Sonia tucked her knees close to her body, ready to kick. But Cipoletti grabbed Lydia by the hair and held her close to his body, his knife at her neck, only the safety catch keeping it from digging into her skin. He gestured for Sonia to get out of the van, and she hung her legs over the edge, almost stumbling in the process. They were in a garage. He opened a door and took them through a laundry room into a kitchen. Sonia's imagination ran through a dozen potential weapons available in any kitchen, but Cipoletti prodded them forward into the living room. He closed the blinds and faced them.

"I am going to remove the tape from your mouths in a moment. Don't think about screaming. This is *not* a neighborhood watch area. If anyone hears you, they won't care. There is a chance you will get out of this alive." He leaned to within an inch of Lydia's face, and she flinched. His eyes flickered over Sonia, as if daring her to interfere.

"All you need to do is answer one simple question for me. Who else knows? Who have you told? The cops?"

I wish we had. Too late for regrets.

Lydia shook her head.

Ty knew about Cipoletti. But she hadn't told him her plans for the day. He had no reason to suspect anything was wrong. She couldn't, *wouldn't*, tell Cipoletti about Ty. She wouldn't put him in danger. Tears formed in her eyes while she fought the panic clogging her throat.

"There *is* someone. You will tell me who it is." He slid his thumb on the safety catch, and the knife slid forward.

◆

Ty and Joe left the police station, and Ty turned in the direction of the parking lot. Joe shook his head. "We'll get to the gallery faster on foot." He moved in the opposite direction and broke into a jog.

Ty wished he had on running shoes instead of loafers. "Should we tell someone?"

"Do you want to wait?" Joe sped up a bit.

Ty considered. "No."

"This way." Joe worked through the maze of streets and after about five minutes reached Larimer Street. "There it is."

FCA, in a circle. Cipoletti Fine Arts. Ty could see the sign from several blocks away. They worked their way around a few hearty souls enjoying a cup of cappuccino on an outside terrace when he spotted a familiar Toyota. "That's Sonia's car."

A parking ticket fluttered under the wiper blade. The parking meter, with a maximum time of two hours, had expired. That suggested they had stopped for coffee before heading to the gallery more than two hours ago. Not good, not good at all that they hadn't returned to feed more coins into the meter. "I've got a bad feeling about this."

Joe checked the gallery door, but it was locked. A young woman approached the door at the same time. "I'll let you in." She took out a key and unlocked it. Ty looked at Joe, and the two of them followed her inside.

The showroom was empty. The woman called, "Tony?" but received no answer. She reappeared in the showroom, her sales-persona smile on her face. "May I help you gentlemen?"

Ty looked at Joe. "We're looking for a friend of ours. Wavy dark hair, pretty, probably wearing a red woolen coat?" He could have continued cataloging her assets but decided that was enough.

"Sonia Oliveira? Yes, she was here when I left for lunch. I didn't know who she was until Mr. Cipoletti said her name. I was thrilled. I'm a big fan of—"

"Cipoletti saw her?"

"Yes." She smiled happily, as if imparting good news. "In fact, I think they might have gone to lunch together because she was still here when I left. He told me he might be gone when I got back. I thought he wanted to entertain the artist."

Ty drew quick, shallow breaths and imagined possibilities, none of them good.

"Do you know where they might have gone?" Joe asked.

"Maybe The Brown Palace? Mr. C likes to wine and dine his clients there sometimes." The woman giggled. "I can tell her you stopped by when they get back."

Joe circled the room and shook his head at Ty. "Do you have any other art for sale?"

The clerk looked uncertain. "Are you looking for anything in particular?"

"Do you have a Passo?" The postmodern painter. The worst painting in the bunch, as far as Ty was concerned, but unforgettable.

"You probably should speak with Mr. Cipoletti about that. Here, let me get you his business card."

Ty guessed they had the painting, but she had been told not to display it without Cipoletti's permission. Joe glanced at the card. "Can my friend have one, too?"

Ty accepted the card from the girl. Business, cell—home phone number. "We won't bother you any longer." Once outside the door, he broke into a run.

"Where are we headed?"

"Let's go get the car. We're going after Kent. He'll know where to find Cipoletti."

◆

"I can't take you to him. He'll kill me."

Ty held Kent at arm's length, wanting to unleash the anger writhing inside of him. "Better you than two innocent women. Where can we find him?"

Kent looked at Joe. He stood still, as unmovable as a suit of armor. Neither cousin flexed a muscle or made any threatening move. They didn't have to.

Kent wilted, a coward more afraid of the present threat than of possible future danger. "He has a home in Cherry Hills." Kent rattled off an address. "Let me go, will you? No harm done, right?"

Joe smiled, a slow, thin smile that had no humor in it. He bounced on his feet, and Ty could see the muscles rippling across his back. "You robbed my store, you sorry piece of work. You can be glad I'm a Christian and I know vengeance belongs to the Lord."

Kent turned frightened eyes on Ty. "What are you doing with him?"

"It's a long story. One that might teach you something, if you're willing to learn. But that's for another time." Ty grabbed a fistful of his shirt and shook it. "You're coming with us. If this information is false,"—he gestured with the address—"you will regret it."

"He lives there. I promise." Kent's voice squeaked. Ty tugged him in the direction of the car.

"You call the police. I'll drive." Joe slammed the door shut and started the engine before Ty had buckled his seat belt.

Ty reached Detective Torres's voice mail. He left a message. "She's off serving that warrant, I bet." He called 911, but couldn't get the dispatcher to catch his sense of urgency.

"What is the nature of your emergency?"

"I think my girlfriend's been kidnapped. Can you send officers to this address?" They wanted to send officers to interview *him* instead of acting now. Red tape.

"You called the police? I need to get outta here." Kent fiddled with the door handle.

Ty twisted in the seat. "The police are the least of your problems right now." He looked at Joe. "I have an idea. One that involves my one-time partner." He explained his plan.

"I can't do that. He'll kill me." Kent didn't relish the idea.

"I don't care. You see, it's our fault—yours and mine—that the most wonderful woman in the world is in danger. And I'm not going to let anything happen to her. You *will* help us."

"Recognize this place?" Joe steered the car into a cul-de-sac. "This is the address you gave us."

◆

Cipoletti looked at Sonia without blinking, as if gauging her willingness to cough up the information he wanted. "I should have expected you to show up when Mr. Jones called to tell me that he had met *the* Sonia. Quite excited about it, he was. You couldn't leave well enough alone, could you?"

Part of Sonia wanted him to remove the tape from her mouth, so she could let loose with the string of epithets she'd composed in her mind. She'd borrowed liberally from the New Testament: Brood of vipers. A blind man leading the blind. Whitewashed tombs. She especially liked that image. She wanted to vent her rage and her fear.

Her fear presented the most pressing reason to leave the tape in place. As soon as he took it off, he'd expect an answer to his question. An answer she didn't want to give, but she didn't know if she could hold out against pain—especially if he cut Lydia again.

"You're not thinking about Mr. Jones though, are you? You don't seem upset when I mention him. There's someone else." He tapped the capped end of the knife against his chin and then snapped his fingers. "I know! It must be that fool Kent's secret partner."

Panic flooded Sonia, and Cipoletti laughed. "That's it, isn't it? Don't look so worried, my dear. Kent will give me his name. You don't have to betray him."

The doorbell rang. "Company." He pushed the women into a bathroom and shoved a chair against the knob. "Don't try anything."

❖

Ty and Joe hung back behind the car while Kent rang the doorbell. Cipoletti spoke with him on the stoop before motioning for him to enter.

Ty dashed for the door at world-record speed, hitting it as the screen began to close. He burst through, Joe close behind. Ty crashed into Cipoletti, sending him to the floor. Ty knocked away whatever the man held in his hand before sitting astride him and pinning his arms to his sides. Joe grabbed his legs and handed Ty the rope he had stored in his trunk.

"What are you doing? You can't attack a man in his house—"

"Where is she?"

Sirens sounded in the distance.

Cipoletti glared at Kent, who trembled in a dejected puddle in the corner. Ty heard a thump, followed by a louder thump.

"They're here!"

"I got him." Joe moved up Cipoletti's body until he straddled his chest. "You go check."

Ty spared a glance at Kent and prayed he wouldn't do anything foolish. Then he hunted for the source of the thumping, harder to hear now as the sirens grew louder. He found the chair propped against a door. "Are you in there?"

Thump, thump.

He yanked the chair away and opened the door. He slashed through the tape that bound the women's wrists and uncovered Sonia's mouth. Her eyes filled with tears. "Ty, I knew you'd come."

He took Sonia in his arms and held her until the police arrived.

◆

"Chin up. It could be far worse." Ty held Sonia loosely in his arms, her head tucked under his chin, for a final few minutes before he had to pass through airport security to reach his departure gate.

Thanksgiving and Christmas had come and gone since the confrontation at Cipoletti's house. Today was Valentine's Day, but this wasn't the way either one of them wanted to spend the day.

"I know." Tears turned her eyes into black diamonds. She let go of a shaky laugh. "Not quite the home going you expected when you came to Colorado, is it?"

"No. It's better." He took her hand and walked down the magnificent concourse, past the sculpture of birds in flight. "But it wouldn't hurt if you said a few prayers that my father sees it that way."

She lifted his hand to her lips. "You know you have my prayers."

"He won't be pleased. He sent me out West to become a man, and instead he's getting back a convicted felon." In light of Ty's full confession and his help in bringing Cipoletti and Kent to justice, the judge had commuted Ty's sentence to two years of probation. He had even agreed to transfer oversight of Ty's probation to Virginia so that he could return home and attempt a reconciliation with his family.

"You're a *new* man. I'll pray that your father sees that." They returned the way they had come.

Ty looked at the board listing departure times. "I have to leave."

"I know." But they continued holding hands.

"Sonia, it's too soon but. . ."

"Shh." She put a finger to his lips.

"I'll be back for Joe and Michelle's wedding, after Easter."

"I'll be there."

Epilogue

April in Colorado was a chancy proposition, with everything from heavy snow to warm spring days equally possible, but God smiled on Michelle and Joe's wedding day. It dawned crystal clear, and the skies rang with the cries of ducks as they headed north for the summer. Sonia turned the radio to NPR and heard the strains of *Eine kleine Nachtmusik*. *Perfect.*

Sonia had remained in Ulysses for a few weeks past the official end of her six months as artist-in-residence. Joe had generously offered her the continued use of his studio, and Michelle welcomed her presence at the house until her wedding day. "After all, how convenient is it to have my maid of honor in the house to help with all the last-minute details?"

Michelle's choice of Sonia as her maid of honor surprised her. Even knowing the privilege would have gone to Michelle's long-time friend Carrie Romero—except Carrie had given birth to a baby girl in late March—didn't dim Sonia's pleasure.

Carrie and her family—husband, Steve; son, Viktor; and baby daughter, Lila Pauline—would of course be in attendance, and the couple would provide special music. Judy joined Sonia as a bridesmaid, Pepper served as a junior bridesmaid, and Poppy got to scatter rose petals. All the women had pastel yellow dresses with sprigs of purple. Not Sonia's favorite combination of colors, but they looked pretty as a group. Pretty as a picture. She giggled.

Thinking of pictures brought to mind her finished painting, *Freedom's Flight*, which had taken the place of *Light Shining through the Darkness* on Mr. Jones's wall. A true gentleman, he had agreed to the exchange and had even paid a premium for the new work. "Because you have grown as an artist, my dear. *Light Shining* was an amazing work of art, but the joy in *Flight* is stunning." *Light* now hung on the wall of Ulysses attorney Stanford Dixon's office, the man who had purchased it before the robbery. The prints of her watercolor paintings were also selling well.

Ulysses held so many happy memories and so many people she had come to love: all the Knights, of course, Josh, Max, Hugh Classen and his high school kids, Stanford Dixon, even Nel's arch nemesis, Esther.

But the one person she most associated with Ulysses had finally returned a week ago. Ty was both musician and groomsman in the wedding. They had spent every waking hour—more and more each day, as if they wanted to make up for two months' separation—together. E-mails and video chats helped pass the intervening months, but they couldn't compare to face-to-face time. Last night Ty had vowed not to call before the wedding. "Unless there's an emergency."

So far, none had arisen, which suited Sonia and Michelle just fine. They had both experienced enough excitement in the past year to last a lifetime or two.

Last night Michelle stayed with her parents in the local motel, and the house seemed strangely quiet without her. Both the women had packed their belongings, prepared to move out. Sonia had rented an apartment in Denver and would move back to the city, at least for now.

The clock chimed noon, and she walked through the house, savoring every memory. She touched one of her presents to the couple: the finished fairy-tale puzzle, which she had framed for two friends enjoying their own happily-ever-after. Anyone who lived in a castle would understand. She had given other, practical gifts at the several bridal showers she had attended.

Perhaps. . .God willing. . .Sonia would have her own happily-ever-after ending as well.

She closed the door and walked into the future.

◆

Ty picked up his violin and prepared for his solo. He glanced at his parents sitting on the groom's side of the sanctuary, still not believing they had come. Taking a deep breath, he nodded to the pianist and let the melody soar as a prayer. Joe had requested "The Lord's Prayer," in the musical setting composed by Albert Hay Malotte. God had taught Ty so much in such a short time. He rejoiced to return to the place where he had been reborn.

In a few minutes, once he finished his music and the pianist began the "Wedding March," Ty would join Joe and Brian at the front of the church and watch for the back door to open. All was as it should be. Joe hummed with anticipation for his bride. Brian's heart sang for his wife and daughters. But Ty would welcome the best of them all, his Sonia.

He finished the music and went out the side door, only to return behind Pastor Perkins, Joe, and Brian. Joe was resplendent in his black tux. The groomsmen wore matching tuxes, with the addition of yellow cummerbunds that matched the bridesmaids' dresses. Ty bet Sonia had suggested that detail. She loved a dash of color.

The doors opened, and Pepper came down the aisle, followed closely by her mother. Brian's face beamed, as if reliving his own wedding. She had eyes only for him. When she reached the front, she moved to the left of the pastor.

Next through the door appeared a vision in satin and lace, dark hair capped with golden lace, hands clasping a bouquet of lavender lilacs. Sonia kept her gaze straight forward until she reached the front and joined Judy.

Then she turned her eyes on Ty, luminous joy shining from her eyes. When Poppy joined them at the front, Ty hadn't even seen her procession.

At last Michelle entered, tall and slender and radiant in a sheath gown with a train.

The giving of the bride, the vows, the unity candle, the presentation of the bride and groom. . .the service that took so many months to prepare ended in a short fifteen minutes. Joe and Michelle appeared to float out of the church. Even though Brian was Joe's best man, they had agreed that Brian should escort his wife and Ty would walk with Sonia. He stepped forward, took her arm, and marched down the aisle with her, tall and proud, a man free at last of guilt and failure.

They joined the receiving line, and Ty spotted his parents. "You'll never believe who showed up at the castle last night."

Sonia turned to him, her eyes glittering from happiness. "Who?"

"Who is this angel?" Mom, dressed in a floral dress that floated around her, asked.

His father asked, "Where have you been keeping her hidden?"

Ty told himself to relax. "Sonia, I'd like you to meet my parents, Thomas and Terri Knight."

Sonia's laughter rang free and clear. "I am *so* glad to meet you." She looked at Ty then at his father. "Does this mean. . . ?"

"We have buried the hatchet." Ty's father clasped his hand and shook it. "He talked so much about what happened here. I know he came back a changed man. I had to come and check it out for myself."

"We're glad to have you." Sonia flung her arms around his father's shoulders.

Dad laughed. "Ty, this one's a keeper. That's for sure." He winked and went on to congratulate Joe and Michelle.

"I'm so happy for you." Sonia squeezed in the comment before greeting the next person in line.

When Michelle called for all single ladies to stand behind her, the bouquet landed at Sonia's feet. She scooped it up.

Dad watched the byplay. "I think you've made the right decision, son. Although if you ever want to come back to Knight Industries, you'll always be welcome."

"Thanks, Dad. That means more than you can know." Tears stung Ty's eyes. He prayed Dad would see his own need for a Savior. At the moment, he was as blind as Ty had been. He'd pray for God to open his eyes. After all, he knew that prayer worked.

Across the way, Sonia was holding baby Lila and giggling with Carrie. She looked so natural with the child; Ty's heart clenched, and he decided he wouldn't wait any longer. He made his way across the fellowship hall. "May

I have the pleasure of your company, Miss Oliveira?"

Sonia lifted laughing eyes to his, which turned serious when she saw the expression on his face. "It would be my pleasure. She's adorable, Carrie." Sonia handed the baby back to her mother and accepted Ty's arm.

"Let's go for a walk." He patted her arm and took her to the library. . .the place where they had had that fateful conversation so many months ago. . .the one place he could find privacy on this busy day. He shut the door behind them and then brushed the back of his hand against the smooth skin of her cheek. She closed her eyes and swayed toward him. He took advantage of her distraction and knelt in front of her, feeling in his pocket for the other ring, the one Joe *hadn't* given to him for safekeeping.

She sensed he had moved and opened her eyes, gasping when she saw him on his knees.

"Sonia. I know I'm not worthy of you. I never would have met you if I hadn't made such a royal mess of things—let's be honest—if I hadn't sinned in such a colossal way."

"God has a way of turning those things to our good." The words trembled on her lips.

"I'm learning the truth of that statement. I do know you are the very best thing that ever happened to me. I thank God every day for you." He stopped. Words faltered at times like this, but he had more than words—he had a song. He smiled. Lifting his voice on the wings of melody, he sang. "God gave me a song when He gave me you—will you be my wife?" He opened the jewelry box where a diamond and ruby ring sat.

"God gave me more than a song when He gave me you—He gave me my own knight." She smiled. "The answer is yes, today and always."

He slipped the ring on her finger and let her lift him to his feet. Gathering her into his arms, they kissed—a kiss that created its own kind of knight music.